STORIES BEYOND BELIEF

STEPHEN SUTTON

Author Reputation Press LLC
45 Dan Road Suite 36
Canton MA 02021
www.authorreputationpress.com
Hotline: 1(800) 220-7660
Fax: 1(855) 752-6001

Ordering Information:
Quantity Sales. Special discounts are available on quantity purchases by corporations, associations, and others. For details, contact the publisher at the address above.

Printed in the United States of America.

ISBN-13   Softcover   978-1-951727-38-3
             eBook   978-1-951727-39-0

Library of Congress Control Number: 2019918013

STORIES BEYOND BELIEF
PART ONE

Stephen Robert Sutton

Artwork by Stephen Sutton.
Thanks to Kari Cooper
Thanks to Anja and Ulf for their friendship and hospitality
Thanks to all my friends and colleagues at Hawksyard priory
Thanks to my friends in Lichfield and Manchester
Thanks to friends past and present including Geoffrey Kay and
Dorothea Goodwin
Thanks to my father Leonard James Sutton, my mother Rita Sutton
and my children Gemma, Jennifer, Michael and Daniel

ABOUT THE AUTHOR

Stephen Robert Sutton has been writing ever since he was a child, although he has dyslexia he never let it beat him. In fact it seemed to make him stronger and more determined to fight for what he wanted, which was to be an inspired author of fictitious books. Stephen has always had a vivid imagination, which he spent inventing characters and story lines about ghosts, witches, vampires and all kinds of strange creatures. He has a fear of mirrors which stemmed from watching Snow white and the seven dwarfs at an early age, seeing an animated face in an enchanted mirror. Stephen studied at Netherstowe comprehensive school the teachers there said he would never get anywhere and classed him as a dreamer. He classed himself as an ambitious dreamer with a set direction to go in, he was always drawing picture that helped to describe the characters in his drawings, this included cartoons in comic style formation. But it wasn't until Stephen went to University that he finally decided to write seriously and started the outline for cracked porcelain based on his own ward experience as a nurse, Ruth who was the main character in the story was a female version of himself, with a similar past. Since writing the series cracked porcelain Stephen has written many books under various names including Sarah Ruth Scott and Simon Robert Sinclair, his books include Blood trail across time, For the love of Charlotte, Understanding Jodie, The Harrington curse and many more.

Stephen hopes to do screen plays and see his stories portrayed on the big screen, is he still a dreamer or will this be a reality for the writer with dyslexia, who knows this could be a success story waiting to happen. Stephen does claim that cracked porcelain was written partly by a female ghost called Sarah who haunted him in Sweden, she inspired him to write the story. He also claims that For the love of Charlotte was written in a similar way, inspired by ghosts who related aspects of the story to him through spirit writing.

Sincerely a friend

ABOUT THE BOOK

Stories beyond belief comprises of a collection of stories designed to entertain you beginning with a legend about witches called the eight skulls of Teversham. This is followed by a vampire story with a difference as Siena travels through time to find a cure for her condition as a vampire, she faces both slayers and vampires who aim to prevent her doing this. The third story is the Harrington curse which will scare you away from mirrors for life, as a team of reporters and investigators seek answers to a curse bestowed on a family called the Harrisons. The fourth story is about a mental health nurse who is stalked by a youth who dresses like her only to cause major problems in her life. Our fifth story is understanding Jodie a young girl who seeks her own identity after being bullied at school becoming a goth and joining a gang only to get into trouble. The final story is a light hearted look at life as an angel as Faith is sent to earth to experience human life as a punishment for misdeeds in heaven.

CONTENTS

EIGHT SKULLS OF TEVERSHAM

S R SUTTON

INTRODUCTION

Throughout history legends are born, they develop and are passed down through the ages, the eight skulls of Teversham is no exception to this. The legend tells about a coven of dark witches who were renown for their magic and treachery, they would terrorise villages and its occupants even killing them. They claimed it was in revenge due to the witch hunting that was going on throughout Scotland and beyond the border into England. Eric Butterworth was a young man who had lost his family to such witches, eight witches had entered the village at night and stormed into Eric parents home killing all but him. Years later Eric became part of a witch hunt to find these witches and avenge his family, this was backed by the local Mayor who wanted to get rid of them for his own reason, he was after the secret of the resurrection which only the witches possessed. It should be noted that not all witches are bad, white witches act for the good of people and are known for their herbs and all kinds of natural remedies they were often targets for witch hunters who considered all witches were evil and had to die. This story shows both sides from the dark witches to the white witches and their battle for survival, in a violent age of terror and injustice.

PART ONE

HUNTED

I t was a cold dark night in October with a full moon in the sky; it was the sort of night where no one would venture out unless they were mad or had a cause to. For the village of Teversham was certainly cursed that night, as the villagers hid away in their houses, listening to sound of night birds such as owls, making the occasional sounds amidst the silence. Suddenly the silence was broken by terrible screams coming from the village as the Druids searched for innocent souls and virgins, looking for those they could sacrifice and in the chaos there stood the silhouettes of eight ugly women holding broomsticks all watching the village from a hill. They were eight witches who had stood outside the villagers homes chanting spells and cursing the ground that they walked on. The witches were known as Albelenda, Florina, Babeth, Nabara, Renilda, Rosalinda, Jeliana, and Passara. As they circled the family they swept their broomsticks across the floor making a ring in the dirt "Pity on you for you will die a certain death" Albelenda said speaking for the others "I am Albelenda and you must fear me and my friends, for we seek to avenge those who killed my family. Dread the darkness and fear the ones who will take your lives this very night"

Albelenda was the leader of the witches, she had long black scraggily matted hair a long nose and a wart resting on her chin. The other witches looked similar except for Passara who was shorter than the others and was badly scarred on the left side of her face. Babeth was slightly thinner than the others and Rosalinda was a little larger than the others. Each one of them were as wicked as each other but Nabara was exceptionally bad and hardly ever spoke, but she hated all non witches and wanted any excuse to use her magic and destroy people.

A female villager walked bravely towards the witches and tried whispering to them. Nabara grabbed her by the arm and pulled her toward her saying, "Speak to me if you know what's good for you" Nabara held her firmly spraying her saliva in the woman's face.

The woman wiped her face with her hand that was shaking with fear, as she stood looking into Nabara's wicked eyes.

"Speak!" Nabara yelled

The woman pointed to the last house of the village in the distance and spoke nervously "The family that you seek live there, but please don't harm the other villagers" She said pleading with Nabara.

Nabara raised her wand and pointed it in the woman's face, she had hatred in her eyes, then gave a wicked smile.

"I suppose you want rewarding for your information and betrayal of your friends?" Nabara asked

"No, just for me and my family to be safe" The woman pleaded.

With one swish of Nabara's wand the woman flew in the air and then landed in a heap on the ground.

"I really hate kindness" She said laughing

"That was mean even for you Nabara" Babeth said in disgust.

"Enough" Albelenda shouted "This village of Teversham is about to experience an awakening, at the hands of the witches who have lost so many due to the persecution and constant witch hunts that have taken place around the woods, the Mayor of Teversham town will know what its like to suffer".

"Albelenda are we going to kill all the family?" Florina asked

"Yes, all the Butterworth family must die, Father, Mother and children" She replied

"Yes, kill them all" Nabara insisted.

"When do we do this?" Renilda asked.

"When the moon is full, on this very night" Albelenda explained "We attack on my command, be ready to ride your brooms and approach from the sky" She instructed them all. They all went back into the forest and waited for the clouds to clear from in front of the moon, and then each one of them mounted their brooms and flew into the sky. They were silhouetted by the moon and descended onto the Butterworth's cottage sweeping around it and waving their wands causing explosions. The Butterworth snuggled together all but Fredrick (Eric) who was in the cellar sweeping the floor, one of the explosions knocked the grandfather clock over which landed on the cellar door. The witches entered the cottage and killed the family one by one, starting with the parents; Nabara killed the youngest child Rosa as she lay asleep in her bed. All Eric could hear was screaming and loud explosions; he stood nervously below and wet his trousers in the process. Everything went silent; Eric listened for any sounds that would indicate that the witches would enter the cellar and find him. Suddenly he heard movement the cellar door began to creek open, and the shape of a woman appeared at the door. He began to shake with fear as the figure got closer to him, and then he sighed with relief as the woman spoke.

"Eric, it's me Martha" Martha was his neighbour

Eric hugged Martha but did not speak, he was in shock, Martha turned to face her husband Basil and began to cry.

"My god, Basil what do we do?" She said trying to make herself understood.

"Let's take him to our home" He advised

"But how are we going to get him out of here?" she asked thinking about the devastation and all the family lying dead upstairs.

"Cover him in my cloak and lead him out of the front door" Basil suggested

Martha did as he instructed and helped Eric up the stairs into what was left of the cottage, there were gaping holes in the walls, scorch marks and the bodies of his family lying dead around the floor, Rosa was on the bed with scorched sheets over her dead body. Eric was almost at the door when he managed to look through a gap in the cloak and noticed his mothers body, her eyes were looking up at the ceiling.

"Mother" He shouted and broke away from Martha running to her side, Basil was close behind and caught hold of Eric's arm.

"Come lad, stay with us" He could see the sadness in Eric's eyes "Come on, you can't help them now".

Martha felt helpless and just wanted to hug him, she wanted to tell him everything would be alright, but in her heart she knew that wasn't true. If the witches knew he was alive they would hunt him down and kill him, he was destined to spend his whole life looking over his shoulder.

Eric remained with Martha and Basil Bakewell and from that fateful night when he was a mere eight years old, he grew up with their son John aged nine, Basil was a soldier who had fought for England. He taught Eric to defend himself, fighting with many weapons including the sword and long bow, he also showed him how to use his skills with a cross bow. Eric became skilful and cunning in fighting, he knew that some day he would have to face the witches who killed his family and avenge them. Eric had nightmares for years about that night, he relived the events although he didn't actually see them killed, He remembered the screams and saw they're dead bodies lying dead everywhere.

Eric celebrated his twenty first birthday in a banqueting hall in the town of Teversham, quite a few people attended including Martha and Basil, it was a fine feast, with various meat dishes, pies and other savoury delights. Eric was delighted by the feast and in meeting so many people, some he knew others were friends of Basil, some of them were soldiers. He was considered old enough to be a soldier, he showed great discipline and leadership skills, and he was proving to be quite skilful with the sword and cross bow, he also learned to ride a horse.

Meanwhile in another town close to Teversham the eight witches decided to terrorise the village, kidnapping children and murdering innocent people. Albelenda led the witches into the town at night and it was then that she was made aware of Eric's existence, she was furious to find that one member of the Butterworth family had survived and ordered the witches to find him. She expressed her feelings as the witches coven sat around the cauldron; she hated the family and would not rest until they were all dead.

A new Mayor had been elected in the town of Teversham and he was keen to find the witches who caused so much chaos in the town and surrounding village. Unusually so Teversham was the name of the town and the village, this confused the people from outside the area. The people all knew about the Butterworth family and how they were slaughtered by the witches, people were frightened to go out at night or venture into the woods. It is said that many a poor soul have been captured, tortured and murdered by witches, people have heard they're chants and awful cackles, the sound of wolves and owls that indicate the presence of night time ghouls and goblins, and the sound of the devils hoofs running across the ground in a frantic effort to capture lost souls. The bravest knight fear to enter the woods and forests of Teversham, knowing that danger lurks around every corner. Only the witches themselves would stay there and live with other creatures of their kind, surrounded by wickedness and growing up to be bad. Lurking in the darkness they go out at night, taking what they liked and worshiping their demon master the Devil, this is what is taught to children and they grow up living in fear of witches. But be aware that not all witches are bad and understand that their magic is not necessarily wicked, it can be used for good, white witches are known to be good witches, they remain pure and refined, or so legend tells us. The purification of their blood is an abomination to the black witch, they consider them to work outside the witches' coven and not worthy to be called witches. None other than freaks or mutants, who use the name to show humans that some witches are more human who have feelings for mankind.

Eric the twenty-year-old man grew up handsome with fair hair and a cheeky smile, He was strong and fearless just as Basil hoped he would be, a fighter with a reason to hunt the witches that killed his family. Eric worked hard mentally and physically, he was injured countless times with swords, fires, wooden sticks and various obstacles used in simulation battles. Finally he was ready to face the witches, but he would not be alone as Basil had mustered an army to help Eric in his quest. But the Mayor had other ideas, he was a fat stocky man with fair receding hair, which he combed over his forehead, he also had a fat Roman nose and beady eyes that could just be seen beneath the heavy wrinkles. Mayor William Mallet was a cunning man who managed to deceive the people in voting for him as he promised to make the town and village of Teversham safe. But he was a wealthy ambitious man who just wanted to be popular and richer than anybody around him. Mallet wanted to gain power by deception and got rid of anyone in his way, it's amazing how many people simply disappeared, no one asked questions for fear of vanishing themselves. The mayor stood waiting in a room for Basil and Eric to appear, he had arranged the meeting weeks before so that it would fall in line with his re election, if they could kill the witches he could be popular with the people and win votes.

A knock came at the door; this was followed by a pause, then another knock at the door, finally the Mayor answered.

"Come in" He shouted abruptly

Basil and Eric entered the room, marching proudly towards the Mayor

"Good day Mayor" Basil says addressing the mayor

"Good day gentlemen" the mayor grunted

"What do you want from us" Basil said bluntly.

"I need you to hunt down these witches and make this area safe again" He said with his eyes glancing from one to the other.

"That could be possible although that would come with a price" Basil said considering his finances and supporting his family.

"I can offer you fifty crowns a head" Mallet offered "Mean that literally and that's me being generous".

"I agree that's a good price" Basil said looking at Eric for approval, and then the Mayor.

"But I need evidence that you have killed these eight witches" Mallet insisted

"Proof" Basil said confused

"You want us to bring back all the bodies?" Eric asked

"No, just the skulls, eight to be exact" Mallet replied

"Eight skulls" Basil said

"Eight skulls to hang on poles around Teversham town" Mallet said sniggering

"The eight skulls of Teversham" Basil said wittily.

"It sounds good and it will keep the witches away from Teversham" Mallet said "I must agree with that" Basil replied

"Me too" Eric agreed.

The following morning Basil and Eric set off with a small army to hunt for the witches of Teversham, None of them were aware that the witches were seeking to find Eric at this time, Eric had learned to ride and was given a horse called Alestra, it took a while for Eric and Alestra to get along but after a while they were friends.

It took a few days travelling before they reached a cottage where Rosalinda lived, she was sat discussing Eric with Passara, and the soldiers listened to what they had to say in order to find out their plans.

"Passara, I think we ought to consider what Albelenda has asked of us" Rosalinda said sipping from a cup.

"What do you mean?" Passara asked

"Finding that young man and killing him" Rosalinda reminded her.

"Who do you mean, Eric?" Passara asked gazing into her cup.

"Yes, do you remember that night?" Rosalinda seemed concerned.

"I was against slaughtering that family, but they killed our relatives and friends" Passara said trying to justify their actions.

"But they didn't kill children, we would never harm children" Rosalinda said remorsefully.

"I agree but Albelenda was insistent and she wants to kill Eric" Passara said sipping from the cup.

"We have to obey her otherwise we could die ourselves" Rosalinda said fearfully

At that moment Basil ordered the attack on the witches, they rushed into the room taking them by surprise Rosalinda was cornered in the room and Passara managed to escape their clutches and ran out of the back door only to be greeted by John and two other soldiers.

"Are you going somewhere witch?" He asked her

Passara stopped and stared at him, she seemed powerless

"Let me go or you will be very sorry" She hissed at him

"I don't think so" He said holding his sword to her throat "Come with me" He insisted

Suddenly her eyes changed colour, they were yellow and her finger nails turned into claws, she began to growl like a dog and leapt at John. He fell to the ground and began wrestling with her, they rolled about for a while and then one of the soldiers plunged his sword into her side. She jumped off John and another soldier decapitated her with one mighty blow.

When John entered the cottage he noticed that they had already killed Rosalinda and her head was chopped from her body. Basil was holding her head up by the hair and looking around the room at all the other soldiers.

"Behold the head of a witch" He said proudly.

John held Passara's head up "And another" he said comparing it to Rosalinda's head "Two skulls and six to go"

They continued their journey with the two heads in sacks, Eric found the whole ordeal a little gruesome and vomited, he had never experienced this sort of thing before. He rode beside Basil and remained silent, reliving the events over and over again, trying to make sense of it. Basil watched him closely showing fatherly concern, he had grown fond of Eric as if he were one of his own, it was painful to watch him go through such mental torture just like the night his family died.

"Eric, are you alright" He asked

"Yes sir, I am" Eric replied

"You witnessed the killing of two wicked witches, who as you heard were after you" Basil explained.

"I know, but why behead them?" Eric asked concerned

"A witch can only be successfully killed by the severing of her head, for some reason it breaks their spell" Basil patted Eric on the back "You will see a lot worse ahead lad"

"I know, I will be alright" Eric said smiling.

PART TWO

JUSTICE

In a cave deep within the forest a group of witches sat by a fire discussing the deaths of Rosalinda and Passara, Albelenda lead the coven as usual she had this expression of distaste like she was eating something sour like lemons. She deliberately kicked the fire and made the other witches jump.

"Damn that young boy Eric, he survives to tell the tale, be fearful for they now come for each one of us" She said pointing her wand at each of them.

"They apparently want our heads" Florina said concerned.

"Our heads" Renilda said clutching her neck.

"Let them try and get me" Nabara said waving her wand sending a bolt of energy from it into the fire and causing an explosion.

"They don't scare me" Babeth said "I will turn every one of them into pond creatures"

"Jeliana you are the spells and potions witch, you can do this" Renilda said looking at Jeliana.

"I can do almost anything necessary, but it's Eric we really need" She said staring back at Renilda.

"We must watch our backs and signal each other if we suspect anyone or are in danger" Albelenda advised them all "We must also seek out Eric and kill him"

"What about the soldiers?" Renilda asked.

"Kill them all" Nabara said

"Kill them all?" Florina asked.

"You heard kill them all" Albelenda said "And whoever gets in our way"

Later the next night the soldiers reached the edge of the woods each one looked at each other hesitant to enter, Eric looked at Basil waiting for him to speak.

"Now then all of you, listen carefully to what I have to say" He looked at each one of them "I know you are afraid, but we have to move forward and hunt for these witches, we need to do this for our families, the Towns people and the Mayor" Basil was also trying to re assure himself that all would be well.

The sound of night life could be heard by them all, the rustle of branches and the snapping of trigs broke the silence, and something was lurking within. Suddenly they were met by a flock of flying bats fluttering around their heads, one of the men yelled as he held his face and fell off his horse. When one of the troops dismounted and ran to his aid he was also struck by something, blood gushed from the first soldiers head; the second soldiers face was burned by something.

Both the soldiers lay dead Basil ordered his men to enter the woods, and so they moved in one by one. Basil led them deeper into the woods, hoping to catch a glimpse of a witch, each sound made the soldiers jump, they expected to share the fate of the two soldiers they had left behind. Suddenly a flash of light occurred and another soldier fell to the ground from his horse, he jumped back onto his feet, "I am fine" he announced before his head split completely in two. The soldiers formed a circle and all peered into the darkness, Eric was the next to be thrown from his horse and lay on his back with his arms and legs spread out, something burrowing out the ground around him, his hand and feet were being held down with bind weed, this was followed by weed creeping around his neck and strangling him.

Basil leapt off his horse and began cutting at the weed, he was joined by John who was also cutting the weed.

Eventually they managed to free Eric, but another soldier had already be strangled by another weed, once Eric was free he sighted a witch flying past on a broomstick, and so he grabbed a crossbow and fired at her, she fell down beside a tree, it was Renilda who was lying with the arrow in her neck.

"Now" Basil said "Finish her, take off her head" He said throwing his sword in front of Eric.

Eric was hesitant, but he knew he had to do it, he raised his sword above his head and with all his strength cut Renilda's head from her body.

"That's my boy" Basil said proudly

"Five skulls left Eric" John said looking at Renilda's head

They continued on their journey, by now the heads in the sacks were spelling badly of decayed flesh, it was that bad they all took it in turns carrying the sack. They tried to sleep during the day as the witches were active at night, two of the guards stood watch at all times day and night, this allowed the others to sleep and when they were on the move they used a wagon to sleep in. They spotted a woman on the road, she seemed weary so they let her rest in the wagon, and she offered to reward them when they arrived at the next village. This could have been the offer of food, food for the horses or even money, She had a kind face and seemed genuine, but after a short distance she changed her appearance and the nice lady was non other than Jeliana one of the witches they sought. She kissed one of the soldiers in the wagon and his face became disfigured and he suffocated and died. She hid beneath him until one of the soldiers opened the back of the wagon in order to let him out; he was supposed to be the next soldier resting. She leapt out at him and cut his throat. Basil rode up to the wagon and slayed the witch, with one blow of his mighty sword she fell to the ground and then cut off her head adding it to the other heads.

The next journey took them over a stream and through a valley; they felt vulnerable travelling through such a wide open area, but certainly not as much as the nights spent in the woods at night. But the witches were cunning and used all kinds of tricks and magic in order to trap and kill some of the soldiers, they were truly evil woman with only the desire to kill others not like themselves. They came to another cottage which looked similar to Rosalinda's home, it was quiet and very tidy inside as if it had just been cleaned. Basil entered first cautiously entering through the main door at the front of the cottage, all seemed fine until the door locked itself separating Basil from his men. He continued to walk around the cottage until he arrived at the kitchen; suddenly knives began to fly out of a drawer and towards him. Basil dived on the ground and hid behind a cupboard for cover, after a while this stopped and he picked himself up, he found himself accompanied by a woman. She had long black hair and a long dark dress; she had a narrow face and a long nose.

"I am Babeth and who are you?" she asked

"I am Basil" he replied

"What kind of silly name is that?" She asked smiling and showing her dirty mouth and the gaps where there was once teeth.

"Why do you want Eric?" Basil asked

"So that we can kill him" She replied.

"He is outside" He said hoping to provide some time to think of a plan of escape.

"I know, once you are dead I will tend to Eric" she replied holding up her wand

"Wait" he said looking into her evil eyes "Can I advise you against doing that"

"Foolish man stop wasting my time" she began waving her wand

Suddenly a arrow shot through the air and buried itself in her chest, it went straight into her heart and she was pinned to a cupboard door.

The soldiers battered the back door down and entered the room; Eric was holding his crossbow and John went over to remove Babeth's body from the cupboard door.

"I will take her outside and remove her head from her body" John said standing behind Eric.

"There goes Babeth" Basil said with relief.

The knights continued on their quest over hills across streams and brooks, their numbers had depleted since they began, so many had died at the mercy of the witches and some were reluctant to travel on. But only three witches remained Albelenda, Florina and Nabara, they were the worst witches who were determined to get Eric. That very night a storm began sending thunder in the sky and lightning that seemed to light up the darkness, this was perfect weather for the witches who took advantage of it. In all the confusion the soldiers were confused by what appeared to be the weather conditions and what was the witches magic, the men thought they were hallucinating as they sighted naked women walking towards them, each attractive. Suddenly one of the soldiers yelled out in pain and other cries were heard all around them, they witnessed strange creatures moving about before their eyes. After the storm had passed, Basil looked around him, only to find a lot of the soldiers lying on the ground, some wounded and some dead. But as he checked everyone was accountable but one man, Eric who was missing, it was thought that the witches had got him at last. Basil gathered the men together and buried the dead, he stood next to John and hugged him.

"The witches have taken Eric" Basil said sadly

"I know" John said with a sigh

"We must find them" Basil continued

"We will Father" John said confidently

The witches had arrived back in their cave accompanied by Eric, He looked tired but despite this he was well, he was tied up and sat near a fire. Nabara stood over him waving her wand at him and snarling, Albelenda and Florina were sat at the entrance of the cave looking out at the countryside. Nabara was angry and continued to tease Eric with her wand, sending sparks in Eric's face causing him to turn his face away from her.

"You are going to die soon" She said sneering at him.

"Why are you doing this?" He asked

"Because you killed my family" She replied

"I did nothing, I was a boy" He said "You killed my family, all of you did"

"They all deserved to die, I hated all of them" She said kneeling down and looking into his eyes "Aww little blue eyes is sad, go ahead cry sad boy"

"I don't need to cry" He replied "The soldiers will be here to rescue me soon"

"That's what you think, we will kill them before they even get near here" She explained "We have magic and we have cunning, we can trick them into walking into a trap".

"You hate families don't you, why is that do you hate children?" He asked.

"We all have children; they are wonderful, except for one child who is a bit of a freak".

"You mean only one child?" Eric asked

"She looks different, sounds different and certainly acts different" Nabara said looking at Albelenda.

Albelenda looked back at her frowning

"Are you talking about my freaky daughter?"

"Yes the one that has no name" Nabara said "The one you keep locked in your cellar, who is only allowed out in the dark in case she shames you"

"Do not speak of her" Albelenda shouted "She is no daughter of mine"

"A freak she may be but she is yours" Florina said

"Yes yours Albelenda" Nabara said "She walks about in this cave like an animal"

"It was a few days before the soldiers got close to the cave, the witches had laid traps all around it, some of them were pits with spikes and snakes others were nets and other devices that would trap, harm or kill them. Nabara was constantly tormenting Eric and repeatedly telling him that she would kill him.

"Your death will be slow" She said "I will drain the blood from your body and make you drink it".

Eric was getting thirsty but he never trusted the witches, thinking that they would poison him, or even give him some potion that would make him ill or hallucinate.

While the witches were out looking for the soldiers Eric was a approached by a pretty young girl who looked about eighteen years old, she brought him a cup containing water and put it to his lips. She never spoke but just smiled and went back into the deepest part of the cave; she did this repeatedly and even brought food for him, assisting by holding the bread to his mouth and feeding him soup with a spoon.

She poured water over his wounds and bandaged them so neatly around his legs.

"Thank you" He said "Have you got a name?"

She shook her head and walked away, all he could see was her silhouette disappearing into the cave.

The witches returned usually discussing the activities of the soldiers

"Did you see those spikes going into that man, like meat hooks through meat" Nabara said laughing

"I enjoyed poking at that man in the net, I burned him to death and listened to him scream" Albelenda said also laughing.

"I saw the man in the pit trying to fight off snakes that didn't exist, so much for my magic making him think things were there" Florina said laughing with them.

"Girl" Albelenda shouted "I hope you have been looking after Eric"

The girl came forward from the darkness, her pale skin shone from the light emitted from the fire.

"God, your so ugly" Albelenda said spitefully "Go away freak you make me sick"

"She is awful Albelenda" Florina commented

"I really don't understand how she turned out like that, she's nothing like me" Albelenda said looking at her reflection in a bucket of water.

"What do you think Eric?" Nabara asked him

"I didn't really see her" Eric said trying to ignore her

"Freaky like you" Nabara continued "Or your family"

As she spoke to him she deliberately set fire to his trouser leg with her wand, watching him yell in agony, then poured water over him.

"This pain is nothing to what you're going to feel soon" she yelled

The soldiers were camped about a mile away, there were thirty left from the fifty that began from Teversham, and some were weak and most of them frightened by the witches' magic. Basil was concerned about Eric and wondered weather or not he was still alive, he felt confident that he was and that seemed to keep him going. Basil had a plan to divide the men into two parties he would lead one and John would lead the other, this would mean that they could search from two directions east and west. This meant that each group would have fifteen men and they could make a sweep of the woods by spreading out, the object would be to meet in the middle. Basil ordered them to break camp and begin their search immediately, his plan was to take the witches by surprise and rescue Eric.

Meanwhile the witches went out in search of Basil and his men, they were hoping that their traps continued to work and reduce the army in numbers. But this time the soldiers were aware of the dangers and were very cautious not to fall into any traps that the witches may have set them. Eric remained calm and hoped that they may stumble upon the cave to rescue him, he sat fidgeting and suddenly felt thirsty, he had hoped that the girl may come to him after all she did cleanse the wound on his leg and offer him a drink. Eventually she did appear but she was holding a large knife in her hand, she moved forward until she was right in front of him, then she walked behind him.

"If you are going to kill me do it now" He said anxiously

She remained silent and stood behind him for a while, she held the knife firmly in both hands pointing it towards his neck, and she was so close he could feel her breath on his neck. And then just as he thought she was going to cut his throat she cut the ropes that had bound his wrists, and then she gave him the knife to cut away the rope around his ankles.

"Thank you" Eric said "You are not a freak, not in my eyes"

"I must rescue my friends" He said walking towards the entrance of the cave

"Thank you for cleansing my leg I will come back for you," He promised

Once he was out of the cave Eric rushed into the forest forgetting that he had a bad leg, it was almost as if it had healed, he felt no pain or discomfort, in fact he felt quite well considering all the brutality that he had suffered. He managed to see the shining of the metal armour from the soldiers as they were walking through the woods, He wanted to shout but he didn't want to alert the witches and give away their position. So he crept closer to them, and then spoke to one of them, they turned around to face him; one of them pointed a sword at his throat.

"Abas it's me Eric" He said

"How do I know it's you?" he said "You could be a witch in disguise?"

"You have a pimple on your" he was interrupted by Abas

"It's fine no one else needs to know" He said with embarrassment.

"Sir" he shouted "Eric is here

Basil turned around and noticed Eric, he immediately ran towards him and embraced him "Son your safe, but how did you get away?"

"A young girl freed me" he said with relief

"Was she a prisoner?" he asked

"No a daughter of one of the witches" he explained "Nothing like them, she was very attractive, she is at the cave up there" Eric said pointing behind him.

"We shall meet the others and find this cave" Basil said

Meanwhile the witches returned to the cave and immediately noticed that Eric had gone, they examined the ropes and noticed that they had been cut.

"Girl, come here" Albelenda shouted

The girl came from the darkness and walked sheepishly towards them, she knew that she would be chastised for freeing Eric and stood before her mother to except her punishment.

"Why did you free this man, tell me" Albelenda said shaking the girl

"Put her in a boiling pot" Nabara shouted

"Let her go home Albelenda" Florina said looking at the girl.

"No" Nabara said "She should be severely punished"

"I say she seems sorry to me" Florina said "Besides she can be dealt with later"

"You're too soft Florina" Nabara said grabbing the girl

"I will deal with her and you will be sorry girl" Albelenda said pulling her away from Nabara.

Albelenda took the girl to the entrance of the cave and pointed into the tree's.

"Go now, get out of my sight freak" She demanded

"Your letting her go?" Nabara said angrily

"Yes" said Albelenda "She will return home and go straight to the cellar where she belongs"

Nabara was not at all pleased and went off in another direction, she was so furious she accidentally met up with some of the soldiers, but they didn't see her and continued on their journey led by John. Nabara decided to play a trick on them and cried out in a child's voice.

"Help me" she paused and then continued "Help me please".

One of the troops raced forward into the bushes shouting

"A child is in trouble"

And then there was silence everybody looked forward into the bushes, but all was quiet, and then the soldiers walked cautiously forward, stepping over trigs. Eventually they came to the place where the voice came from and noticed the soldier pinned to a tree, with his throat cut and his stomach sliced open with all his insides hanging out. Nabara had clearly done this and was planning to do something similar to all of them, she seemed to be worse than ever now, a real psychopath far worse than the other witches, using her power to kill and cause devastation. Nabara decided to wait until night time in order to continue her killings, she liked the thrill of hearing her victims, yell and scream in pain, or their bodies quaking in fear as she tormented or tortured them.

Florina managed to find John and his soldiers and attacked them, she flew into a group of them wildly waving her wand and coursing chaos, leaving bodies lying across the ground. John and the few remaining soldiers hid behind trees, finally one bowman managed to send an arrow into her side causing her to fall to the ground with a thud. John ran forward and raised his sword severing her head from her body.

"Two left" He said holding up her head.

Meanwhile Basil had found the cave with the help from Eric, suddenly they heard a scream.

"That's the girl" Eric said anxiously "She is in danger"

He raced on ahead of the others, Basil was concerned about Eric and raced after him, but Eric was younger and more active, reaching the entrance in no time. Suddenly he felt a heavy blow to the head and stumbled to the ground holding his head. Albelenda was on top of him holding a rock covered in his blood. Although he was dazed Eric tried to fight her off, she tried hitting him again but this time she stopped holding an arrow that was buried on her chest. Basil raced forward and began hitting her on the head with a rock until her skull split open. Basil had saved Eric's life and knelt down to help Eric to his feet, but Eric was too weak and fell back to the ground, at the moment Nabara swooped down and attacked Basil sending a fireball into his back and then hitting him across the head with a heavy club. Basil was less fortunate than Eric and died almost immediately. Before he died Basil whispered to Eric.

"Be brave and fight them to the end" Basil faded away before he finished his sentence. John arrived to see his father whispering to Eric, and then watched him die with Eric close to him. Nabara had gone deep into the cave hoping they would follow her, she had wanted to use Eric to trap the soldiers when he was held captive but her screams brought them there anyway. The soldiers did follow Nabara into the depths of the cave, it was getting darker inside as they entered a long tunnel, and suddenly a swarm of bats flew at them. After a short while they disappeared and a bright light came from the distance knocking down some of the soldiers. Some of the men were overwhelmed by the smell of rotting flesh, a nauseated feeling came over all of them, this became more intense as they got further down the tunnel. They could feel a mixture of something soft and slimy along with a hard substance, looking down they noticed it was human remains, victims of the witches, but mainly due to Nabara. Nabara began tormenting them by sending snakes in their pathway, she also transformed herself into a wolf and began hitting some of the soldiers with her claws, scratching their faces. The room began to light up as Nabara set some of the soldiers alight, blood curdling screams echoed in the cave as Nabara picked off some of the soldiers, one of them dropped into a large bath of acid. Eric tried to follow Nabara's trail hoping to trap her into a corner, but she was too fast and managed to kill quite a few of the men in no time at all, making eerie sounds and laughing wickedly. She placed her hand on one mans shoulder and bit a lump out of his neck severing the jugular causing him to bleed to death. Soldiers fired cross bows sending arrows into the air, they were not even aiming just desperate to hit the witch, but the arrows bounced off the cave walls, some landed in them. She appeared unstoppable as she mercilessly killed more soldiers; it was like a blood bath the walls were covered in their blood.

In a last desperate hope to capture her Eric whispered to John and the both ran in separate directions, John shot arrows towards the large bath making a noise. Nabara responded to the noise and rushed towards the bath of acid, and then both Eric and John shot arrows straight at Nabara, she was so overwhelmed that having so many arrows in her that she yelled and fell into the bath of acid. Watching the acid strip the flesh off her body gave Eric an idea, he decided to put all the heads into the acid, thus getting rid of the flesh and stop the odour caused by the rotting flesh. Eric and John looked around them, they were the only survivors, they found fresh sacks and put split the skulls in to three of them. John had noticed that Albelenda's skull had been damaged but never mentioned it to Eric, he was afraid it might affect the reward money.

PART THREE

FEAR OF THE WITCHES

T he sun rose the next morning and it was almost as if the witches never existed, Eric and John had the only evidence in three sacks, eight skulls ready to show the Mayor. One thing puzzled them was the Mayors obsession with the number eight, he had a fixation on it, everything he did included the number eight. No one could deter him from that number, not in any sense of the word, in the bible it would signifies resurrection and regeneration, that which is beyond. This may be the reason that the Mayor sought power, he also expected respect and gratitude from the people, and perhaps he expected to be resurrected or regenerated in some way. When Eric and John returned to the Mayor, he was delighted to see them, he greeted them with open arms as if they were his long lost son's, he patted them on the back and congratulated them for their efforts. He opened his desk drawer and produced bags full of coins, Eric and John put three sacks on the table and the Mayor examined each one in turn, he called John over to his side of the desk and asked for his opinion of the one skull with the crack on the head.

"This one is damaged" the Mayor said expecting an explanation

"Eric knows about that one" John said trying to avoid answering the Mayor

"The skull is damaged" He repeated directing his attention to Eric

"Basil hit her on the head with a rock, she is the leader of the witches, she is called Albelenda" Eric informed the Mayor.

"Albelenda" The Mayor repeated "I can almost feel her power" he said looking into the eye sockets "To think she sent fear into the hearts of so many, I almost envy her".

Eric looked at John expecting a reaction, but John just gazed at the skull, the Mayor didn't seem surprised that only the two of them survived, he was glad that they returned safely with his skulls. The Mayor ordered a feast for the return of the two men and in fact he struggled to remember their names, just the deed. He gave a speech without mentioning the two gallant men, for some reason he forgot they even existed, instead he announced that he had taken care of the witches and made the town of Teversham safe again for to walk the streets. He even told the town folk that he had arranged for the eight witches skulls to hang on poles around the border of the town in order to warn any witches not to try to attack anyone again. For a time this worked and everyone felt safe until strange events took place such as food poisoning, crops dying and people suffering from all manner of illness, in fact everything that went wrong was blamed on the witches skulls, they were said to be cursed. Even things such as the miscarriage of babies and sudden deaths were all due to these skulls. Everybody who lived from miles around had heard of the eight skulls of Teversham, people were afraid to visit the town and village for fear of dying from a disease or being cursed themselves. The skulls remained for about two years until the Mayor was advised quite strongly to get rid of the skulls for good.

Eric was still a little annoyed by the Mayor taking the credit for taking care of the witches, John didn't seem to mind as much, although to some degree he felt as if his father should have got some notoriety, like being honoured or a statue erected in his name, or perhaps a statue of him dressed in his uniform. We never even had the chance to mourn properly, each soldier was remembered but no one but Eric or John witnessed their bravery in battle against those wicked witches. The last night that the skulls were around the town they actually glowed red and then green from some light within, by this time even the Mayor agreed that it was a good idea to get rid of them.

The following day the Mayor sent for Eric, he never asked for John for some unknown reason, Eric was pleased to go and see the Mayor hoping for some recognition for assisting to kill the witches. The Mayor stood proudly in front of his desk, soon he began pacing up and down in front of the window, when Eric arrived at the Mayors office, and Mayor appeared to be nervous and sharp.

"Ah, young man" He began "About these eight skulls"

"Yes sir" Eric said respectfully

"I need you to get rid of them" The Mayor said mopping his brow with a handkerchief

"Of course sir" Eric said "And where would you like me to dispose of them?"

"Take them up to the mountains of the north and hide them in a cave" He instructed.

"That way their spirit cannot harm people, did you know the witches feared me, they think I am powerful, even more now, I have the ability to control their magic"

Eric looked at him and couldn't believe what he was hearing, it was as if the Mayor had gone insane, but he was talking about his association with the number eight and the resurrection process, he also touched on his belief in the regeneration process and his association with the occult. Eric was not able to follow his conversation and became distracted by a knock at the door, the mayor seemed reluctant to reply, maybe he didn't want to be interrupted or maybe he was so engrossed in his own chain of thought, that he genuinely didn't hear the door.

The door was knocked again, this time harder with more urgency, this time the Mayor seemed to wake up from his fanciful journey.

"Come in" he shouted

"You wanted me sir" John said standing next to Eric

"Yes, have you brought the skulls" he asked

"All eight of them" John said holding up three sacks

The Mayor took the three sacks and placed them on the table

"These skulls will forever be the eight skulls of Teversham, I have held these skulls and feel their power" The Mayor seemed to go into some sort of trance.

"Sir" Eric said trying to break him from it

"I want you to take the skulls now and bury them in the ground by a cave in the mountains" The Mayor dismissed Eric and John then went to his bed.

The next morning Eric set off with the eight skulls of Teversham, he knew that it would take him days to reach the Scottish mountains, but he had plenty of supplies to take with him. It took days of riding across a rugged terrain before Eric was even close to the mountain that he needed to dispose of the skulls. Eric spent nights thinking of Basil and how he died, he had buried him in the woods and left a heap of rocks there so that he could locate it in future. He felt cheated by his sudden departure as if things had been left unsaid and he had not had the chance to thank him for his help and guidance over the years. He also felt as if John was jealous of their relationship, although John never said anything, his actions seemed to say it all, and also by the way he would look at him when Basil was showing him how to protect himself. Eric appreciated the praise from Basil, Basil was the type to complement the efforts that people made, he admired talented people and those who made the effort to practice their skills and reach a good standard of performance. Eric really showed him how he had mastered the art of sword fighting and accuracy with the cross bow, Basil was certainly proud of him and showed it.

Eric also had time to reflect on the kindness that Albelenda's daughter had showed him, cleansing his wounds and offering him food and water. She never really spoke to him, but her action spoke volumes, she had warm hands and kind eyes, but mostly her beauty shone through like a beacon on the hills.

Unlike the witches who's wickedness made them ugly on the inside and outside, they were so bad they scared each other, Eric was relieved that they were dead and so were the towns folk of Teversham. After travelling for a week Eric finally reached the cave marked with the hoof of Satan on the outside rock, Eric felt frightened as he entered the cave; he felt a chill run down his spine. The place was very eerie with a sense of evil within, Eric looked down into an enormous pit and then stood and looked around the cave with his blue eyes that seemed to sparkle, and he felt the presence of someone behind him. This was not unusual as he had this feeling from leaving the village, he felt like shouting out, but he thought this might attract attention to himself. He opened the sacks and began to empty the contents onto the ground, one all the eight skulls were out of the sacks he arranged them neatly on the ground in a circle. He sat for a while and just stared at the skulls, almost expecting them to move, He felt tired and wanted to sleep, but he had a long journey to make back home and just wanted to bury the skulls and go home. He was about to get his spade out of his pack when suddenly the place began to shake and the sound of rumbling could be heard in the distance, at first Eric thought it was thunder and lightning, the type of conditions that you would expect from a storm. But this was much worse, Eric was experiencing the start of the witches magic at work in the cave, for when he looked back at the skulls they were all lit up, and a green luminous substance began to trickle through the mouth and nostrils, this was followed by a form of electricity or energy travelling from one skull to another. Eric tried to run away but he became fixed like a statue in one position, he felt as if he were in a vice being crushed at one point, at this time he thought that he could see Albelenda.

And then no sooner did he see her, Nabara appeared and began cursing him

"I will finally see you die now Eric" she shouted

"Die Eric and go with your soldiers to your death" Albelenda shouted

After seeing them shouting all eight witches appear and circle around him all chanting "Die" and repeat it several times. Eric became dizzy and felt himself being drawn to the pit, parts of his body became numb and the voices had become louder, He felt the earth moving beneath him and the rumbling continued, slowly he began to drift closer to the pit. Suddenly with one mighty push the witches send Eric into the pit, Eric falls down and lands in some kind of lake containing a thick mixture and a film of mist covers it. The rumbling stops and everything is still, the atmosphere becomes calm and the skulls sink into the earth as if nothing has happened.

PART FOUR

RESURRECTION

The Mayor had wondered why he had not heard from Eric for five years, surly he would have contacted him telling him that he had buried the skulls. He had once heard that the secrets of resurrection lay in those mountains in Scotland and regeneration was also possible but again the answers remained in the caves high up there, but the Mayor never ventured there. Eventually he sent for his soldiers and a small team of explorers to go to the mountains in search of Eric, he never mentioned what he really wanted, but hoped that they would discover the secrets and return to him with the information. He needed to know if it was possible and only then would he venture out into the cave and use whatever information that was relevant to either prolong or restore his life.

The explorers and accompanying soldiers left the town of Teversham, in order to begin the arduous journey to the mountains, John was sent with them to gather information about the cave. They are also hoping to find Eric alive and solve the mystery of his disappearance; this would explain why he was gone so long.

John was leading the explorers who were called Aalef, a small man with a long beard and wearing a hat looking like a Goblin, Malbert was a thin man who walked oddly as if he had some sort of deformity, Gaud was a strong hard faced character who never smiled, finally Balian was the wisest of the explorers, very conscientious and keen on working long hours to discover things. There were few soldiers with them on this trip, it was considered an advantage to use fewer due to the cost of hiring them and because they were travelling light on this trip. It was the Mayors idea to do this, he wanted as few people to know any secrets about the cave, he certainly didn't want the town's folk to have knowledge of resurrection or regeneration.

On the journey John was telling the explorers the story of how, he and his father had battled with the witches, and about the eight skulls of Teversham. He avoided telling them about Eric and his part in their deaths, until one of the explorers asked him.

"What of Eric" Balian asked him.

"Oh, he fought well and at one point, he was captured by them" John explained

"A brave man, was he? Gaud asked "Strong like me"

"Yes, strong like you Gaud"

Malbert was travelling slowly behind them, his horse appeared to be more like a donkey, but he seemed happy to do this.

"Come on Malbert" Gaud shouted back to him

"Yes keep up, we don't want you picked off by outlaws or witches" John shouted

"I am coming, but the scenery is breathtaking don't you think?" Balian said looking around him.

"The only breathtaking thing will be you if you don't catch up" Aalef shouted

Eventually Malbert caught up with them and joined in their conversation, they talked until their throats dried and then it was time to make camp for the night.

In order to boost moral the explorers organise songs around the camp fire, they considered it better than telling spooky stories or boring the soldiers with any more tales of their own journeys exploring places of interest. Gradually the explorers singing began to sound out of tune, and they decided to retire to their tents and sleep, they soon slept leave two soldiers to guard the camp.

Meanwhile south of their camp miles away from the explorers, a witch's coven assembled consisting of seven witches namely Mirabell, Flora, Darnetta, Bittora, Zabal, Grisel and Ricolda. Zabal was the daughter of Nabara and just as cruel. Darnetta was the leader daughter of Florina, she was just as scatty as Florina but as wicked as the rest of them. The daughters seemed to be more powerful than their mothers and demonstrated their abilities by frightening villagers across the glens of Scotland. Zabal stood in front of the other witches and began addressing her audience, by shouting and stamping her feet in rage, she pointed her wand at every one of them.

"I will have vengeance on whoever killed my mother, he will pay dearly for his actions, all of you must help me find him" She insisted

"But, how will we find him, we don't even know his name?" Darnetta asked

"Yes, who is he?" Ricolda asked

"Don't be so negative, of course we will find him" Zabal shouted swinging around "Are we not witches, do we not have the power to find him"

"I was just asking" Darnetta said disgruntled

"We search through the glen in every village until we find him" Mirabell said looking at Zabal.

"Yes, and then we kill all those responsible for her death and for all our Mothers" Zabal said shaking her wand

"It will be like a resurrection of the witches" Mirabell said confidently "We stand for our Mothers all seven of us, as the eighth daughter is missing at present".

"Dear Lamia, the devils daughter" Zabal said "She will be the most powerful of all"

"Where did Lamia go?" Bittora asked

"She disappeared when her mother died" Grisel explained "I suppose she was heart broken"

"She could have been captured by the man your talking about" Bittora said in response to Grisel's answer.

"She will return when she is ready to join us, no one will keep her for long, she was a freak remember" Zabal said brushing back her long black hair.

"Oh yes, her mother never called her by name" Grisel said "Just, the girl"

"Well, Lamia will return soon and complete our coven" Darnetta said confidently.

"We will be the most powerful witches ever" Zabal exclaimed "And then we will fight the world for supremacy"

The explorers were travelling towards the caves in the Scottish mountains, they had set camp in a forest near a mountain only a few days ride away from their destination. Gaud the biggest member of the team, made a camp fire and he was cooking meat over the flames, the smell of the food enticed all the explorers to join him. John and the soldiers were sat away from them having a discussion on the task ahead, finding Eric and taking him back to Mayor Mallet.

"I fear we will be taking Eric's body back to Mayor Mallet" John said

"If he were alive, then he would have returned by now"

The soldiers nodded in agreement, each one were loyal to John as they were to his father Basil. John seemed a little uneasy and tried not to make any eye contact with the Explorers, he was told by the Mayor not to trust them and watch every move they made. So being sociable only complicated matters further, he needed to keep his distance but at the same time observe the explorers from a safe point. He was also trying to find the significance of eight in relation to the Mayor and the eight skulls of Teversham, he was aware of the reference to the bible about resurrection but there was more to this, the Mayor thought so too in connection to Magic and ultimate power. The witches knew about it and kept it a secret within the coven; they were in control of this great power and confident that it would help them to conquer the non magical element of society.

Gauds manners were much to be desired as he tore the meat from a bone with his teeth like an animal. Balian was disgusted by this and wandered off to another part of the camp, he was more interested in finding answers to the disappearance of Eric and the eight skulls of Teversham, so was Malbert who joined him, they had a conversation between the two of them. While Aalef the Jewish member of the team went to sit by Gaud and offered him refreshments.

"We need answers Gaud" Aalef said rubbing his hands by the fire

"We are in the dark in more ways than one" Gaud replied

"What do you mean?" Aalef asked stroking his beard

"I don't trust that Mayor Mallet, he is sly and cunning like a fox" Gaud explained "He is definitely up to something".

"I agree" Aalef said looking around at the soldiers "Do you think they are part of it?"

"Yes, I think so" Gaud said also glancing at them.

"I will warn the others" Aalef said standing up

"Do that, they should be aware of it" Gaud agreed.

The morning began sunny and fresh, the men gathered their belongings and continued their journey through the valley, crossing streams and passing a large lake. But by the afternoon the weather changed and storm clouds followed them, like an evil sense of foreboding; it was as if someone or something was following them. The men felt as if they were being guided to the caves on the hillside. This occurred for two days, the supplies were running low and the horses were tired especially the ones pulling the wagon carrying most of the equipment they needed. It was also useful if they needed to bring back Eric's body, should they need to do so, the Mayor was insistent of them doing this in order to prove that he was dead and try to find out what happened by the condition of the body. John was convinced that Eric was alive and had got injured or something otherwise he would have rejoined his family in Teversham. He left home in order to bury the eight skulls of Teversham in the caves and has not been seen since this time, nothing seemed to make sense at this point.

The finally arrived at the foot of the mountain, two of the soldiers remained with the wagon while the rest travelled up to the cave. The storm finally began with the roar of thunder and flashes of lightening in the sky; they just reached the mouth of the cave when the rain came down heavily on the ground and surrounding trees. Three of the soldiers burnt torches and guided the explorers into a tunnel, they passed a large cavity where Eric had fallen, but they were unaware of this so they continued travelling down the tunnel into the depths of the cave. Cobwebs were all around them and the occasional spiders within the web, as they got deeper down bats were moving about startled by the men, they began to fly about. Soon they reached the bottom of the cavity and immediately noticed a solid block of what appeared to be ice, closer examination revealed the shape of a body inside it. Suddenly a flash of light occurred followed by a bang which was something powerful hitting the block, each of them were knocked to the ground and all looked up at the block as it began to melt like ice. The body was Eric, John identified him but stood his distance watching him slowly coming to life, first his chest rose and fell, and then breath came out of his mouth like smoke and his eyes began to open. It was truly amazing seeing him come to life after so long frozen in this substance, one of the explorers touched it.

"It's impossible" Aalef muttered "This stuff kept him alive" he called one of his colleagues over to him "Come Malbert; bring a vessel so that I can capture this stuff".

Malbert rushed over to him and gave him a vessel small enough to take a sample, he filled it and Malbert replaced it in to his bag. The rest of the party gasped as Eric tried to speak to them, John offered him a drink and he appeared to sip it at first and then took it from John and gulped it almost choking.

"It's almost like he was in a woman's womb, growing like a child" Aalef said astonished

"I marvel at the way he is, seeing his skin, he is so silky and his eyes are sparkling" Balian said in wonderment.

"It is like he has been resurrected or regenerated" Malbert said "I have never come across this before"

"This is some kind of magic at work" Gaud said looking at the others.

"We must not tell anyone of this" John said nervously "It is to be our secret".

"I disagree" Aalef said "So many people could benefit from our find"

"I agree with Aalef, this is worth more than gold" Malbert said excitedly.

"No, nobody should know before the Mayor is informed" John said insistently.

The explorers looked at each other and then at Eric, who was holding his head.

"God, what has happened to me" He said groaning

"What exactly did happen to you Eric?" John asked

"I was burying the skulls, and they seemed to come to life, all of them glowed and this green substance came from all the orifices" Eric explained "I was thrown across the cave by something powerful and fell down this pit".

"How on earth did you survive the fall?" Aalef asked

"And, how did you get covered in this substance?" Balian asked

"I don't know, but I am here and well" Eric said "Saved by god"

They started to make their journey out of the cave, when the ground suddenly shuck beneath them, most of the men lost their footing fell backwards and dropped down close to the edge. Balian tried to pull him back with the help of Malbert and Aalef, John appeared disappointed by the rescue, as he continued along the ridge. They soon reached the mouth of the cave, at this point they heard a groining noise followed by sheiks of laughter, this time Balian felt a blow to the head and fell into the pit. No one was able to save him from his fate, but all watched helplessly as his body fell hundreds of feet to the bottom, and then he landed onto rocks, needless to say he was dead. The rest of them left the cave and went back to the camp, the two soldiers were asleep, and John appeared angry with them and began shouting.

"Wake up, what are you doing sleeping?" John said kicking them

"I am sorry sir, but we have been awake all night" one of the soldiers said dreamily.

"Yes, we didn't sleep for fear of the witches last night" said the other soldier.

"Well, get the horses ready we are going back" John commanded

"Is that Eric?" one of them said

"Yes we found him in the cave" John said

Nobody asked anymore questions, but Gaud repaired the wagon wheel and soon afterwards became ill, it was thought it was his heart, later he died after the men had eaten supper. Malbert was found dead in his bed, it was early morning and the men were almost ready to travel, but the most mysterious death was the very next night Aalef supposedly drown near the lake. There were no witnesses and no reason why this would have happened, but it seemed strange that all the explorers who witnessed the so called resurrection died before they could talk about the experience. The soldiers were very nervous, frightened to eat or sleep in case they met the same fate, once they reached home they sighed with relief.

John and Eric went to see Mayor Mallet providing him with information about Eric's supposed resurrection, the Mayor appeared to be surprised and arranged for them to join him for a meal.

"So, Eric" He began "Did you bury the eight skulls of Teversham?"

"I tried to, but as I put the skulls on the ground, some sort of powerful witchcraft occurred, they came alive" Eric explained

"Really, that's amazing, so they were powerful" the Mayor said

"I was thrown down a pit by some kind of force" Eric continued "It was as if I were fighting all the witches at once"

"I knew it" The mayor clapped his hands together "Go on, continue your tale"

"I fell down the pit, but it was as if I were travelling in slow motion, I fell to the ground but I had a soft landing and then I blacked out" Eric said "I know nothing until John and his men woke me up"

"I have a sample of the substance he was preserved in" John said showing Mayor Mallet the container.

The Mayor snatched it from John and held it tightly to his chest, he seemed to act strangely as John continued to talk to him, it was if he were in a trance.

"All the explorers are dead" John announced

"So, how many people know about what we have discussed?" The Mayor asked.

"Only a few soldiers" John replied "They will remain quiet I will make certain of that"

"Make sure John" the Mayor said with a cunning look on his face.

"Eric, my friend" the Mayor said walking around the table towards his chair

Eric felt a little uneasy as the Mayor placed his hands on his shoulders and continued to speak to him.

"Eric, I need you to do a job for me" the Mayor gripped his neck at the back "I want you to find eight descendants of the witches, and kill them, I want you to bring back the skulls as before"

"Can I give it some thought?" Eric said

The Mayor tightened his grip and his breathing changed becoming more rapid

"I can't tell you how important this is, they are so powerful and I fear they will destroy all of us" He said his voice seemed to quiver as if he was afraid.

"I have no weapons powerful enough to fight them and how will I find them?"

The Mayor released his grip and walked over to a cupboard in the corner of the room; he took a key from his belt and opened the door. Inside was a sword and shield, he took them both out and placed them on the table, and then he pointed to the shield in the centre of it there was a cluster of jewels, he held it up to the light and ensured they shone.

"This shield is the way you will find them, the light will shine in the direction of a witch and they will turn green" He explained "The sword will also glow at the presence of a witch" he seemed pleased with himself "The weapons will also defend you against the witches magic".

"Are you sure of this?" Eric asked concerned

"Yes, I am sure, they fear the shield and the sword" The Mayor said confidently.

"Then I will do it" Eric agreed.

"Good I will reward you" the Mayor said rubbing his hands again.

"When do I go?" Eric asked

"In a few days" he replied feeling more at ease.

Eric left the room with the shield and sword and headed to the stables to join his horse Alestra, while John remained with the Mayor.

"I want you to send the soldiers who went to the cave, they can accompany Eric on this Journey" the Mayor said smirking "They will meet their fate there as for Eric" The Mayor paused "I have further plans for him"

"Is it true about the sword and shield protecting him?" John asked

"No, of course not, but he will think so" he replied "He just needs confidence enough to fight them, but the shield will find them".

"You mean find the witches?" John asked

"The witches will find Eric, the shield will lead them to him" the Mayor said looking out of the window "I will take their power from them and become a powerful wizard myself, immortal and powerful".

PART FIVE

CONDEMNATION

I t was a sunny morning and a pleasant ride for Eric and the soldiers, riding through the glens of Scotland with the hills and mountains forming a picturesque back drop and contrasting with the green valley and flowing stream.

"This is what I call a magnificent country" Eric said to his horse Alestra "We are indeed fortunate enough to be part of this land, enjoying its scenery".

One of the soldiers looked across at him and then at the other soldiers

"Are you well Eric?" he asked

"That I am Hedrick, I am merely sharing my experience with my trusty companion Alestra" Eric said patting his horse "She has been loyal to me even found her way home when I was stuck in that cave".

"Yes, that was unbelievable, such a distance" Hedrick agreed

"I was gone for a while wasn't I Hedrick?" Eric asked

"Yes you were and John was concerned about you" Hedrick explained "He spoke of you often and feared the worst"

"I really can't explain what happened, I was burying the skulls and I suddenly experienced something pushing me, the skulls were alive and a dark green slime was coming out of their mouth and eyes, the force was so great it threw me down a pit. I travelled down and down,

I seemed to go fast and then slowly until I landed in some kind of substance and that's all I remember" Eric said

"It must have been frightening" Hedrick said bowing his head "I remember you recovering and that ice that contained you"

"It was strange, I was scared but then I felt a sense of security as if I was being helped, rather than attacked". Eric explained

"Perhaps a guardian angel was watching over you that day" Hedrick commented

"Perhaps that was so, I have had the feeling that someone has been following me for some time, I speak of many years ago to the present" Eric said looking behind him.

"Is this how you feel now, do we have company?" Hedrick asked concerned

"I do feel a presence, but I can't say what" Eric said shivering.

Eric led the soldiers into the mountains, leaving the valley behind them, they had been riding days before the shield began to glow brightly, it was dusk and darkness was soon upon them, the moon was full and the sound of wolves howling disturbed the horses.

"Witches are present men, be on your guard" Eric said tapping his horse "There Alestra be brave"

No sooner had Eric said these words Ricolda suddenly appeared on her broom flying around their heads, she produced a tornado effect and caused all the soldiers to fall to the ground, the horses all reared up and almost trampled on the soldiers. Eric held his sword and shield tightly and awaited the imminent attack, as Ricolda began throwing fire balls in their direction, the shields proved useless as a defence as did Eric's so called enchanted shield. Ricolda was relentless in her attack upon the helpless soldiers, she dodged the arrows from their cross bows and swooped down like an Eagle after its prey. Soon she had slaughtered all but Eric, who stood alone even his sword was useless. He was thrown to the ground by the force of Ricolda's wand as the power from it blasted him pressing on his chest, she was teasing him and decided to cast a spell that brought about bind weed, which twisted and curled around his arms and legs.

"Not this again" He said as the weed began to loop around his neck and strangled him.

Eric thought he was going to die as the weed tightened up and he became breathless and the colour drained from his face, his whole body was going numb and he felt limp. Grisel had joined Ricolda and assisted in killing the soldiers, she was busy sending electric missiles into the bodies of the soldiers making sure that they were dead, Ricolda flew over to Grisel in order to tell her about Eric.

"Come and see what I have done to Eric" Ricolda said boasting.

"These soldiers are all dead" Grisel said firing a last electric charge at Hedrick.

But when they returned to Eric, he was gone and all the bindweed was cut, with some areas burnt.

"Impossible, he's gone" Ricolda said astonished

"But how did he escape?" Grisel asked

"Someone has helped him" Ricolda said looking around

"But who, all the soldiers are dead?"

Eric found himself lying on the ground, his eyes were blurred and all he could make out was tall trees silhouetted against a bright sky, he must have passed out. It was now morning, bushes surrounded him and when his eyes began to focus he saw Alestra just outside of the bushes. Eric was shocked and bewildered finding himself in this place, after having a near death experience with bind weed, a lucky escape or was he helped by someone. Eric was upset by the fact that the Mayor had lied to him about the sword and shield, they were not enchanted at all, and he began to feel vulnerable and alone. He remembered the things that Basil taught him about self defence and keeping his mind focused at all times. He also reflected on Basil's death at the hands of Nabara, the evil witch that tortured him and the witch responsible for killing Rosa his youngest sister.

Eric walked up to his horse and stroked her mane and began whispering to her.

"We have an impossible journey to make my friend and we could well die"

Eric put his sword away and secured his shield to his horse, before riding on the road again, further into the hills through trees and shrub land. He had been riding for a few hours when he suddenly stopped and looked around him, he could sense the presence of someone behind him as he had done many times before. But as usual no one was there; this led him to believe that he had got some kind of guardian angel watching over him. He had believed that he was going mad due to all the things he had experienced, hallucinating or experiencing a form of paranoia as we would say today. Eric decided to rest for a while, he secured his horse to a tree and settled down on the ground curled up in his warm blanket, as he began to fall asleep, the shield began to glow and Ricolda returned. This time she was alone, as she crept up to him and held the wand in front of her.

"You won't escape this time Eric, time to die" she said holding the wand up in an effort to destroy him with magic.

Suddenly an arrow shot towards her and penetrated her throat, she held it and fell crashing to the ground, dropping her wand beside her, and lying lifeless in a grassy area beside Eric. Eric slept through this and eventually awoke to see her lying face down with her eyes wide open. The arrow indicated that the person who had been following him could be a soldier or someone human as apposed to something spiritual. He decapitated Ricolda and put her head in a sack, constantly looking around him for his stalker or protector.

"Someone is with us Alestra I can feel the presence of someone" Eric said to his horse.

Eric was travelling along a dirt track when he noticed the shape of someone lying on the ground, so he dismounted his horse and walked towards the person cautiously in case it was a trap, he carried his sword holding it firmly in his right hand. As he got closer he noticed the curvy shape of a female, and her long black hair, she was wearing leather trousers and a type armour across her abdomen. As he turned her over, he noticed that she was battered and bruised with scratches on her cheeks, but she was breathing. He went back to Alestra to fetch a flask of water, and then returned to her, brushing her hair away from her face and dropping tiny amounts of water onto her lips. She began to move her mouth and Eric gave her a drink.

She opened her eyes and was startled, her body jumped, Eric was amazed at how beautiful she was, despite her wounds and the dirt on her face. He thought she looked familiar at first, she reminded him of someone, but then she appeared different as she looked into his eyes.

"Thank you" She said "I am Annabelle, but you can call me Anna"

"I am Fredrick, but most people call me Eric" He replied nervously

"I bet I am a mess" She said

"No, not really" He hesitated "What happened to you?"

"I was robbed and beaten by outlaws" she replied "But not raped" she swiftly added.

"I am glad, I mean that you were not raped" Eric felt awkward as he had little experience with women.

"Are you able to ride?" he asked

"I think so although I ache so much" she explained still gazing into his eyes

"Then you can ride on Alestra my horse" he offered

"Alestra what a beautiful name fro a beautiful horse" she commented

"The best" he agreed "Let me help you up" he said assisting her to mount the horse.

"Thank you Eric" she said smiling

"Where are you heading for Eric?" she asked

"I am seeking ancestors of witches who killed my family" he said grabbing the reins and walking beside Alestra

"Witches?" she asked

"Evil creatures, who torture, curse and kill people" he said

"They must be wicked" she said with empathy "Treating people like that"

"I escaped from the witches who killed my parents" he said sadly

"Lucky you, but unlucky them, I am sorry" she looked at him sympathetically.

"I was given a shield and sword, and they are supposed to be enchanted" he hesitated waiting for a response "But they don't work".

"Really" she said negatively

"The shield is supposed to detect witches by lighting up from the green emerald" he pointed to the shield "But nothing, see it is lit up now and no witches in sight"

"Perhaps you need to have faith in magic" she said lightly

"I have no time for magic, it is meaningless to me" he shrugged "Besides magic was supposed to have killed my family"

"It is said that you can only fight magic with magic" she quoted

"I wish I could believe that" he said dismissively.

"And may I ask what of your life?" Eric asked Annabella

"My life?" she seemed on the defensive

"I am from a humble family, nothing special, I fought to defend my cause and believed in self preservation, I get what I want with my own power of persuasion" Annabella seemed very coy in her responses toward Eric.

Eric admired her radiant smile that lit up her face and illuminated her pale complexion, and her eyes had the power of enchanting him, so much so that he felt magnetised to her.

After a few hours travelling they stopped and rested, Eric took the shield from his horse and threw it onto the ground, and then he helped Annabella to dismount.

"That's no way to treat a shield" she said with disgust

"It is useless, see how it still shines and no sign of witches" He said angrily

"I told you have faith" she said

"I might as well not have it, it's useless" he said disappointedly

"No, don't do that" she shouted

Eric looked shocked at her reaction and went back to Alestra for the sword

"Put the sword next to the shield and see what happens" she said

"Nothing will work" he insisted

"Do it" she said stamping her feet

Eric was reluctant at first, but eventually he did what she asked and placed the sword right next to the shield, the shield became brighter and before long an image appeared, it was the remaining witches, all but Lamia who was a silhouette in the background. They were all sat around a caldron, a witch's coven discussing non other than Eric, who was watching them in disbelief.

"We must split up and search for Eric in order to find him" Mirabell said

"He should be dead by now" Zabal said angrily

"He is being protected" Darnetta said huffing

"Who is protecting her?" Zabal asked spraying saliva as she spoke.

"Some kind of sorcery if you ask me" Bittora said

"Can't you feel the magic Zabal?" Grisel said looking at her "It is all around you William Mallet is behind this I swear".

"I feel it breath it, smell it" Bittora said "And so does Grisel"

"That's you Grisel, the smell" Zabal said nastily.

"Let's not argue amongst ourselves" Flora said "It's Eric that we are after"

"Yes, lets find Eric and end this nonsense" Mirabell insisted.

Eric looked at Annabella and kissed her on the cheek, showing his gratitude

"You are a genius, it worked" he said excitedly

Annabella stood shocked at his reaction

"Oh I am sorry" he said realising what he had done "I got lost in the moment, I didn't mean to, you know, kiss you" Eric was embarrassed

"Kiss me?" she repeated

"Yes sorry" he repeated

Annabella turned her head away and touched her lips, then smiled, while Eric was trying to change the subject, finding a way out of the situation.

"We should camp here Annabella" He finally said

"As you wish" she replied still surprised at his reaction

They rested in an enclosed area of the woods; Eric suggested that they stay close to each other in case they are attacked

"I trust you will protect me from your witches" she said

"Indeed I will" he replied

Eric had found a comfortable spot and laid a blanket down one under them and one on top, they lay beside one another looking up at the sky. Eric had his sword and shield beside him, Annabella had her eyes open and began to yawn, and she gave a cough placing her hand over her mouth.

"Isn't it beautiful" she said

"The sky?" he replied

"The moonlight sky" she said pointing, "I love the night its so enchanting"

"I always think of bad things at night" he said despondently

"The night is wonderful, peaceful and perhaps tranquil" she said sighing

"Goodnight Anna" he said finishing the conversation.

"Goodnight Eric" she replied disappointedly.

Eric stayed awake for a while wondering about Annabella as she didn't exactly divulge any real information about herself, perhaps she had run away from home or maybe she was from a group of travellers or gypsies. But then they had just met and no one give information to perfect strangers, for who can truly be trusted in a place like this. They slept for hours and in the course of the night Annabella had cuddled up to Eric as if he were a large warm friendly bear. She had her arm across his body and her leg across his; she was so close that he could feel her warm breath on his neck. However once she realised what she had done she moved away from him and gave him some distance, he was surprised by her actions, but remained silent. They still had miles to go in order to reach the mountains, the roughest part of the journey was ahead of them, and the weather was changing, becoming colder. Grisel was ahead of them setting up a trap for Eric, using her wits to arrange his demise. Eric was crossing a wooden bridge high up in the air, across two mountains in order to find out where they were and plan the next route. Grisel had loosened the ropes and weakened the bridge ready for him to cross, all he had to do was walk across it and when he reached the middle it would give way causing him to fall down into the valley onto the rocks below. Annabella had stayed with Alestra while Erica started to work his way across the bridge, Grisel watched as he stepped across carefully until he reached the middle. Suddenly Eric heard something snap and the bridge collapsed sending him down, he was falling, his body was spinning in the air, but then he stopped as if he was floating on air, he landed on a ledge and seemed motionless for a while. Annabella reached down and touched him, she grabbed his shirt and began pulling him up, he pushed his feet against a rock and sprang up onto solid ground. Grisel raced forward on her broom and tried to pull Eric backwards off the ledge, Annabella grabbed the sword and began poking her, eventually Grisel let go of Eric and Annabella stabbed her in the stomach, she fell onto the ground holding her stomach, the sword lit up and sliced Grisel in half, Eric took the sword from Annabella and chopped off Grisel's head.

They continued their journey, it was now getting very cold and it was harder to travel, through the snow, they had been a long way and the months had passed.

"Two witches are dead and six are left" Eric said calculating on his fingers.

"Well done to you Eric" she said sarcastically "Six more witches"

"Are you alright?" he asked

"Frankly, no" she said grumpily "I am tired and sick of this cold weather"

"We need to find shelter" he said concerned for Annabella and Alestra

But this time Bittora was searching for them, she was known as the wolf or the hunter, she could transform herself into wild beasts of any description. Eric went hunting for food for Annabella and himself, he took his cross bow and shield for protection. Annabella was asked to stay with Alestra and watch for witches coming in their direction. Eric crept through the woods when he caught sight of a deer; he aimed his cross bow, and steadied his arm until he was ready to fire. Bittora seized her opportunity and pounced on Eric in the form of a wolf, she began clawing at him and then bit his shoulder, Eric hit her in the face with the cross bow and stunned her, but she came back at him biting him in his side. Eric continued to fight and then passed out, he was losing blood and too weak to fight, Bittora had her chance to kill him at this time. Annabella was present at this time, she attacked the beast with Eric's sword, she swung the sword and chopped the beast to pieces and she lay in her own blood and as Bittora transformed she chopped her head clean off.

Annabella managed to get Eric to respond enough to put him on the horse and lead him to a cave, when they arrived she helped him into the cave and lay him down. Once he was comfortable she made a fire and collected water in a bucket, she used all the items that she had such as rags and blankets as well as food and water. She began to cleanse his wounds and had to stitch his open wounds with thread that soldiers kept in their bags; she used an ointment from her own bag and then made some soup, hoping that he would wake to eat it. She used herbs and potions to help heal his wounds and control his fever; it took days for Eric to respond to his treatment, Annabella had hardly slept caring for him.

"Please don't die on me Eric" She said mopping his brow "I can't live without you, you have become my life, you must know this" became tearful thinking that he would die. Eric was actually sick for months, he was reflecting back in his mind and dreamt about riding his first horse and then remembered his horse, Alestra,

He thought back to his family and his youngest sister Rosa remained his, he remembered taking out with him and playing with carved figures. He woke up long enough to eat and drink, Annabella held up a flask and gave him some water, at that point he thought of the girl with no name who helped him in the cave healing his wounds and giving him water like Annabella, but she was Albelenda's daughter Lamia meaning devil child. Annabella was so much like her in her ways, but she was so different in appearance, they were both beautiful but her features were different. It made Eric feel good being nursed by Annabella; she even sang to him sounding like an angel with her soft silky voice, it was just like a lullaby keeping him calm and relaxed.

As Eric began to improve he felt as if he were falling in love with her, he hardly knew her, but he was felt as if he had known her forever.

Annabella decided to discuss her childhood and spoke of the cruelty that she faced, the worst child abuse known to mankind.

"I was treated badly as a child; my mother abused me in indescribable ways, not just by beating me and kicking me down the stairs, but locking me in a cellar. She hated me and called me names and when I refused to do her bidding she would burn me with hot sticks. I was treated worse than an animal scavenging for scraps of food, her friends were the same and so I ran away from home when I was old enough and fended for myself, it was hard at first but I did it. All I wanted to be was loved and treated as a normal child, not follow in her madness" Annabella looked at Eric for his reaction.

Eric gazed in her eyes and acknowledged her with a nod and a smile

She smiled back "But I have spoken too much and tired you with my chat and you have a long way to go in order to search for the witches".

"My dear Annabella" Eric began to speak

"Anna" She interrupted him by correcting him; Annabella is too much to say

"Anna, I am so grateful to you" he said

Annabella lowered her head and tears began to flow down her cheeks,

"My word Anna why do you cry?" he asked

"No one has spoken to me as nicely as you do, you are so kind and gentle" she said sincerely

"I treat you as I do anyone I care about, I care and I show it" he said

Eric put his fingers under her chin and gently lift her head until her eyes looked into his, they gazed into each other's eyes.

"You are the most beautiful woman I have ever met" he said wiping away her tears with his fingers.

"Your lips are generous and your eyes are alive, sparkling by the light of the fire, your skin is so soft to the touch" Eric was aroused by the warmth she sent out to him.

"You are handsome and strong, the bravest man alive" she said in response to his words "I feel safe in your presence"

Eric kissed her on the left cheek, but Annabella wasn't going to let him get away with this a second time, as she kissed him tenderly on the lips, a lingering kiss which took his breath away. They embraced and Eric was able to feel her heart beating fast, she felt so warm and tender, her body smelt fresh like fragrant flowers. Eric was already half naked and so Annabella removed her top, revealing her shapely breasts; her nipples were hard and prominent. He watched her chest rising and her breathing became rapid as she became more excited. Her fondled her with gentle hands and they kissed once more, Annabella removed the rest of her garments and Eric did the same, they both went under the blanket and proceeded to make love, starting with a gentle rocking and synchronizing their rhythm. They became more vigorous and passionate rising to great heights, their body heat could have melted all the snow in Scotland, they made love for hours and then their bodies entwined as they hugged and relaxed together.

"I love you so much" Annabella said

"I love you too Anna" he replied

"I am so happy" Annabella said smiling "I don't want this time to end" she said kissing his chest

"Me too" Eric said kissing her on the forehead

"I can never live without you Eric" she admitted

"I feel the same Anna" he said.

Another day passed as they continued to make love and it was almost as if Eric had forgotten about the witches and Eric's sworn duty as a soldier to kill the witches, and take their skulls back to Mayor Mallet at Teversham. The Mayor must have been anxious waiting for his trophies and to boast about his efforts to kill the witches taking all the glory. But the Mayor also wanted answers to the figure of eight and the resurrection process, Eric knew in his heart that he needed to continue his quest.

"We must go" Eric said anxiously

"Must we, can't we stay forever, just you and me" she begged him "Why spoil our happiness for your stupid quest".

"Anna I must forfill my quest and then we can live in happiness, I promise" he explained.

"But we are happy now and what will it achieve killing witches?" she replied

"They are after me and I can't exactly hide from them, I must face them and only then can I live in happiness" Eric said trying to get up.

Eric gathered his strength and got dressed ready to face the witches, he was fully aware that he would meet another witch soon and he was not disappointed. He had just made his way out of the cave, joined by Annabella they prepared the horse and began walking down the snowy mountain. Flora was waiting for them a few yards ahead, above them, she pointed her wand towards the rocks above and blasted a rock causing an avalanche. The snow descended swiftly Eric was in front of Annabella, she noticed it falling and turned to Eric in order to warn him.

"Look out Eric" she shouted

But she was too late the snow was almost on top of him, just then a light shone and a strange canopy formed over them like a giant igloo or transparent ball. Eric touched it and it vanished along with the snow that had covered it. Disappointed that her trap had failed Flora made another attack on Eric this time trapping him in a block of ice, another flash occurred and the ice melted.

Eric recovered and rushed towards Flora who appeared to be dazed, but she waved her wand at him, Eric raised his shield, deflecting a fiery missile omitted from her wand, she fell from her broom into the snow. Eric raced forward and noticed that she was on fire, he raised his sword and cut off her head.

"The shield actually worked" Eric said delighted

"That's good" Annabella said impressed with his performance

"Only four witches left now" he calculated

Annabella appeared to be unhappy about the remaining witches, she was quiet for a while as they entered the forest, and they had both experienced so much together in a short space of time. The rest of the day was peaceful and they were able to enjoy each other's company, they walked together most of the way holding hands and kissing, having a discussion about the beautiful scenery around them. Scotland was so different to England, not merely for it's landscape, but the mysterious legends that made the place unique, with its lakes and hills, valleys and castles in the mountains and by the sea. It was a place where the Druids lived and practiced their religion, where the brave Scottish tribes fought for land and where witches hid from others who threatened their existence.

It was night time and the sound of wild life was present, owls and other night creatures came out, this also brought about the wrath of Darnetta, she made her presence known by swooping down upon Eric and Annabella, throwing fireballs in their direction, Eric held his shield in front of them and the fire bounced off both the shield and surrounding trees. She attacked a few times and then stayed in mid air sat on her broom and cursing Eric, spitting as she spoke.

"Foolish man do you think that you can escape my wrath, I will show you my fury and burn you to death" she threatened

She made another attack, but this time Annabella fired the crossbow hitting her leg, she spun to the ground hitting a tree as she fell, her eyes gazing at Annabella.

"I know you" she said but before she could say any more Annabella sent an arrow into her throat.

"Kill her" Annabella shouted

"I think you have done it already" he replied

"I mean cut off her head" she said eagerly

Eric grabbed his sword and cut off her head with one blow, Annabella sighed with relief "I thought she had cast a spell on you"

"She did try to control me" he admitted, "Did she recognise you?"

"No, why would she?" Annabella asked

"I thought she knew you" he said puzzled

"Well, she didn't okay" She said sharply

"Are you angry with me?" he asked

"Never, ever look a witch in the eyes" she advised him "She could have cast a spell on you and you would surly die, dark witches are very powerful"

They travelled towards the cave where Eric was once captured, Eric felt uneasy as he approached a nearby wood.

"I need to rest" Annabella said holding her head

"I agree, we need to rest" Eric said leading Alestra to a tree and securing the reigns.

They made camp and prepared food, but Annabella hardly ate, she appeared unwell and her thoughts seemed distant, she removed the blanket from the back of the horse and lay it down. They snuggle up close in the blanket and began to kiss, but Annabella turned her head away from him, she seemed sad and tearful.

"What's wrong?" he asked

"Sorry, it's nothing" she replied

She gazed up at the stars and soon drifted off to sleep, Eric stayed awake for a while concerned about Annabella, he tried to analyse her behaviour, by piecing together the day's events, but nothing was obvious. She was a mystery at times and not the type of person to discuss all her feelings, at least that's what he thought. He found it difficult being in a relationship and he was always told that women are such complex creatures, very hormonal as we say today.

Later that night the silence was disturbed by Mirabell as she searched for Eric swooping down searching for his camp, she was looking for the campfire that would indicate someone was in the area and that person could be Eric. She noticed both Annabella and Eric lying on the floor and sent a bolt of lightening from her wand down at them. It managed to strike Annabella who reacted by yelling, she was injured, Eric was trying to put out the fire that was caused by the lightening. While Annabella brushed away the scorch in her shirt, Eric ran to collect his sword and shield, Mirabell sent more lightening towards him but he managed to dodge them. He held his sword up ready for her next attack, suddenly the sword lit up and a bolt of lightening seemed to come from it and hit Mirabell knocking her to the ground, her broom landed by Annabella's feet. Eric raced forward with his sword and shield in hand Mirabell pointed her wand and sent a fireball at Eric, it deflected off the shield and he was close enough to cut her down with his sword. Eric cut off her head, he dropped his shield and sword and then ran towards Annabella, he knelt down and opened her shirt.

"I thought you were wounded?" He asked trying to find the burn.

"It was nothing" she replied

Eric watched his shield light up and an image appeared, it was Zabal sitting in a cave, Eric recognised the markings on the cave wall drawn by Lamia, Zabal was sat by a fire.

"I know that place" he said "That's the cave where the girl lived, what was her name, Lamia"

Eric knew that he was to face the most evil of witches and at a place she knew well, he was prepared to face her knowing he was at the end of his quest, with only two more witches to find. He knew the eighth witch would be the most powerful and challenging. They packed everything in order to return to the cave where he had been captured and tortured, it was only a short ride away.

When they arrived near the cave Eric looked at Annabella and offered her the reigns to the horse.

"Take care of Alestra I will find Zabal" he said "I don't want you to be in danger"

"I can handle danger, just because I am a woman" she said

"My love I know you have been through so much, but I don't want you to see Zabal" he explained

"But she will kill you" she said concerned "She will cast a spell on you"

"But I have my sword and shield" he replied

"But they won't protect you against her" she said

"Trust me, I will defeat her" he said kissing her on the lips.

Annabella whispered in his right ear, which puzzled him.

"They get inside your head" she said "the dark witches have that ability"

Eric walked away and never looked back, her words stayed with him and seemed to echoed on his mind as he entered the mouth of the cave, he could hear her voice repeatedly, *they get inside your head.*

Eric walked down the darkest part of the tunnel and suddenly came face to face with Annabella.

"I thought you were staying with Alestra?" he asked disappointed

"But I wanted to be with you" she said kissing him on the lips

"But you agreed to stay away and whispered in my ear, saying they get inside your head" he quoted "What did you mean?"

Annabella looked strangely at Eric and then smiled "Who is Annabella?" she said laughing and watching his lips turn blue.

Eric looked in horror as Annabella turned into Zabal "We do get inside your head" by the time Eric had recovered Zabal was a few yards away from him

"Curse you Eric for killing my mother, you will suffer for that" she said sending electric charges towards him. Some hit his shield, others hit the cave walls, but some hit him. Eventually he fell backwards and hit his head on the wall, and knocked himself out, Zabal flew towards him and took his shield throwing it down the pit.

"Now you will die" she said aiming her wand towards his head

"No, he won't die, you will not kill Eric" Annabella said

"Lamia, so you did survive" Zabal said "the freak child, what happened to your face?"

"I changed it so that Eric would not recognise me" she said

"So are you going to slap me or are you stronger than you look" Zabal mocked her

"I have the strength to defeat you Zabal" she replied confidently "I shall end your cruelty"

"Who are you?" Zabal asked

"You know who I am, you have said it, I am Lamia the devil child" Annabella said

"You are a freak traitor of witches, you have killed your own kind" Zabal said angrily

"There are good witches you know and we care for people, we live for the good of mankind" Annabella said checking that Eric was breathing "I was called Lamia by my mother Albelenda, but I changed my name to Annabella along with my life"

"You are a witch" Zabal shouted

"I am my own person and a white witch" she replied

Zabal sent a bolt of lightening at Annabella, she dodged it and returned a flash of lightening from Eric's sword, sending Zabal flying across the cave. Annabella was younger and faster and continued to move around the cave as fast as lightening, dodging every missile that Zabal hurled at her. Zabal transformed herself into a wolf and Annabella did the same, they fought wildly scratching and biting, and then Zabal became a snake. Annabella set fire to the snake and tossed it down the pit, she was just about to help Eric when Zabal appeared by his side holding a dagger to his throat, laughing as she press the blade against his flesh.

"Surrender Lamia or watch Eric die" Zabal threatened

"I surrender Zabal, please don't kill him" she pleaded

"Guess what Lamia, I still want to kill him" Zabal said making his neck bleed

"You right Zabal, how silly of me I have been" Annabella said "I thought I loved him, but guess what, I don't"

"What?" Zabal asked confused

"Kill him" she said watching the expression on Zabal's face.

Zabal released Eric from her clutches and he fell to the ground,

"We could be powerful together" Zabal said "Rule the world put an end to witch hunters"

"Yes, we could" Annabella said "If I let you live"

"What do you mean?" Zabal asked confused

Annabella produced a cross bow from behind her back and fired an arrow into her forehead, she looked shocked at Annabella and fell to the ground, Annabella picked up the sword and chopped off her head.

She knelt over Eric and shook him by the shoulder, she began to open his eyes, and she decided to sit beside him for a while. She felt sleepy and closed her eyes for a while, but as she drifted off Eric awoke.

"Annabelle, wake up" he shouted

"We need to clean these skulls and take them to Teversham" Annabelle said

"Wait, there is one more witch to find" Eric remembered.

"Then we must clean the skulls we have and then bathe in the lake, and then consider about the last witch" she suggested.

They travelled down to the lake and both stripped naked and swam in the lake for a while, afterwards they lay naked on the bank and made love. For a while they had forgotten about Eric's quest and lived for the moment, relaxed in each other's arms admiring the view. Eric noticed the shield was glowing and stood up quickly, looking around him; he became very anxious and searched for his sword.

"Anna, a witch is approaching, where is my sword"

Eric felt the cold steel of a blade touching his throat, it was his sword that Annabella had taken and held it to his neck, it shone under the sunlight.

"You know who I am, don't you Eric?" Annabella asked

"Oh god" he muttered "You can't be"

"I am Lamia, the girl who supposedly had no name" she said "I changed my name as I also changed my appearance, now I have to kill you"

"But you love me" he said confused "Don't you?"

"Yes" she said hesitating "But you would kill me, I am the eighth witch"

"I am so mixed up in my head" he said in despair

"We mess with your head" she said "I don't want to kill you"

"I am your stalker, the one who followed you and protected you, ever since you were with me in that cave years ago, I loved you then and ever since. I deliberately messed myself up and lay near the road, every time you thought a guardian angel was with you, that was me, I have saved your life countless times. I used magic each time, I broke your fall down that pit and preserved your body, I revived you, resurrected you and returned your horse to Teversham. I formed a type of canopy around you with my wand. This, was in order to protect you from the snowfall, do you remember that? It was all me and no one else, I stopped you falling from that bridge and nursed your wounds, I brought you back from the dead using herbs and potions which are in my bag, I did all this because I love you".

"I suppose that means something" he said

"God" she shouted, "I can't kill you" she said giving him the sword "You will have to kill me"

Eric cast the sword into the lake and held her firmly in his arms "My god Anna, so god help me I love you and I will never hurt you"

"So, what now?" she asked "I am the eighth witch"

"We find another skull" he said "So how did you change your face?"

"By Magic" she said "Pure and simple, I cast a spell on you when you turned me over on the ground, I wasn't really attacked and robbed, I played with your memories too".

"We could take one of the original skulls" Eric said "No one will know"

"Let me go and get one" She insisted, "I can control the magic"

Annabella returned to the cave and dug up one of the skulls, it was her mothers damaged skull, fractured by Basil hitting it with a rock, she put it in a brown sack and raced back to join Eric. They took time to travel back to Teversham as Annabella didn't feel well, she soon discovered that she was with child (Pregnant) and judging from their time together, she could have conceived just after Eric had recovered from the fever a few months ago. When they finally did return the Mayor was eager to see them, he was alerted as soon as they arrived, and ordered their presence. They entered his office wary of his devious ways, expecting him to ask a lot of questions, using subtle means of interrogation I order to get answers about the resurrection and solutions to the figure of eight.

"Sit down Eric and friend" He said "And who is she?" he asked rudely.

"This is Annabella" Eric replied "My friend, lover and companion"

"And what of the skulls?" he asked

"All present" Eric said offering him the sack containing eight skulls

"Perfect" the Mayor, said rubbing his hand together.

"What now?" Eric asked

"I want you to take these to the cave and bury them along with the others" The Mayor insisted

"But, don't you want to display them?" Eric asked

"No, the town folk would not approve, they don't want the witches magic here in Teversham, causing miscarriages and the pox amongst other things".

"I understand" Eric said glancing at Annabella.

"You have done well Eric and you shall be rewarded by myself"

Eric attempted to pick up the sack containing the skulls, but the Mayor clung hold of it. "I will get John to bring these to you when you are ready to depart".

Eric stood up and Annabella followed him to the door, the Mayor looked at her disapprovingly before she left.

John entered the room through another door and sat himself down, the Mayor was looking out of the window at Eric and Annabella crossing the street.

"I seem to know that woman from somewhere, who is she?" he asked

"She is his woman and she is with child" John said

"His child I presume?" the Mayor asked

"Yes, of his making" John replied

The Mayor laid the skulls across the table in a neat line, and checked each one in turn, and then he grabbed one of them and held it up.

"Eight skulls and how many did I ask for John?" he asked

"Eight" John said puzzled by his question

"Then why has he brought me seven?" the Mayor asked walking towards John

"Seven?" John asked nervously.

"He has brought back one of the original skulls" He said angrily

"How do you know" John asked puzzled

The Mayor shoved the skull in front of his face "Remember this one?" he pointed to the crack in the side of the skull near the eye socket "Cracked, this is Albelenda's skull"

"Yes, I remember us examining it" John remembered the day they looked at it.

"So, that leads me to wonder why Eric brought this one back" he paused "And where is the eighth descendant, the missing witch".

"Perhaps they didn't find the eighth witch" John suggested.

"Or perhaps he did" The Mayor said pondering returning back to the window

"But I need eight for completion"

"Wait, are you suggesting that Annabella is the eighth witch?" John said

"Can you think of any other answer?" The Mayor said disgruntled she has cast a spell on him, he is bewitched"

"Shall I send for them" John asked eagerly

"No, I have another plan" The Mayor said "I will follow them to the cave and then we will take care of them there"

"You mean kill Eric?" John said concerned "He is like my brother I can't do this"

"My dear John, we kill the witch and maybe the spell will be broken and Eric will be himself again" the Mayor smiled wickedly.

PART SIX

ALL FOR LOVE

Eric was in the stables with Annabella and his trusty horse Alestra, he was preparing for his next quest to bury the skulls in the cave of witches. One of Eric's friends gave Annabella a horse for the journey and supplies for the journey. John entered the stable and showed Eric the sack of skulls, Eric took them off him, John had a strange look in his eyes.

"Here are the skulls that you gave the Mayor" He said

"Thank you John" Eric said noticing the concern on his face

"Is something troubling you John?" Eric asked

"No not really" John said looking at Annabella

"I do worry about you John" Eric said "Watch out for the Mayor he is not to be trusted"

"I will watch for him" John said wanting to say something about Annabella.

"Safe journey" John said hugging Eric.

John left the stable and Eric walked over to his horse Alestra, he stroked her mane and spoke to her.

"My faithful Alestra, brave and loyal, we have been to many places together, shared adventures and experiences" he said

He checked Annabella was well and packed for the journey; he helped her saddle the horse and check supplies.

"We need to make sure that we have everything Anna" he said

"Including the skulls" She replied

Annabella and Eric set off on their quest to bury the skulls in the caves of Scotland and with it their past, pain and misery that darkened both their lives.

They had been riding for some considerable time before Annabella complained about feeling sick and tired, she looked pale and her mouth was dry with chapped lips. It was as if her body was fighting against the child within, perhaps it was part of her mother's evil inside her, and her goodness was trying to reject it, like an alien being. She began to projectile vomit, clearing her body of the badness within, as she thought as she stepped from the horse and continued being sick in the nearby bushes. After a while she remounted her horse took a drink from her flask and wiped her mouth, she nodded at Eric and smiled.

"Are you able to carry on Anna?" he asked

"Yes, I think so" she replied "What was the Mayors name?"

"William Mallet" he replied "Why do you ask?"

"He was known to us, an evil man, cunning and ruthless, please don't trust him" she said looking at Eric "He wants to be a powerful warlock"

"He is a witch?" Eric said "I thought he was involved in the occult somehow"

"He has limited abilities and wants to process the power of the witches and the secret of the resurrection" she said "And regeneration"

"So, that's why he wanted to kill the witches"

"Yes, He wanted the witches killed all of them including me" she explained

"So, that's his game, what about the significance of eight and his obsession for that number?" Eric asked

"According to the bible and other old documents eight represents the resurrection, but it is all about regeneration and rejuvenation an art which my family perfected. The potion is active in the cave, I used it to bring you back, it can be found in a green vessel, inside a wooden box. I restarted your heart with a bolt of lightening from my wand, and the fluid that you were preserved in kept you young".

"I feel as if you have told me everything, but I feel as if I still know nothing" he confessed

"If the time comes you will remember and you will act accordingly" she reassured him.

The next morning, the mayor ordered the soldiers to mount their horses ready to ride, they were given instructions to kill Annabella the witch and arrest Eric, the Mayors instructions were very explicit, to kill her in the same way as the other witches were killed by beheading her. It was his way of killing their magic and making himself seem powerful and popular with the people although he hated them.

Eric and Annabella entered the forest, they both dismounted in an area sheltered by trees with long branches and many leaves decorating each branch with various shades of green. It so secluded and so far away from the problems associated with Teversham.

"We are close now Anna" Eric reassured her "We just need to bury the skulls and then we are free to live are lives as we desire"

"Not exactly" Annabella said lowering her head

"What do you mean?" Eric asked

"The skull I picked up was damaged" she said

"But that belonged to your mother, she was hit on the head with a rock" he explained

"I know I saw her die" she paused then continued "She was evil and needed to die"

"Why would you give him that skull?" he asked

"So that he would follow us to the cave and then I could rid Teversham of him" she said clenching her fists in rage "He has to be destroyed along with his evil".

"Anna do you realise what you have done?" he said angrily.

"Yes, he will realise that he will never be immortal or powerful as he desires, William Mallet the great warlock" Annabella said with relief

"In that case we need to get to the cave quickly" Eric said anxiously

"I love you Eric" she said hugging him and kissing him on the lips

Eric looked at her puzzled "I love you too Anna" he said returning a kiss

At that moment Eric's eyes widened as he felt a gush of air pass his left side and Annabella gave a heavy sigh and fell to the ground, Eric knelt down and noticed an arrow buried in her chest. Moments later Annabella died, Eric held her and tears came from his eyes, he looked up at the trees and shouted.

"Why" he began rocking her in his arms pressing his head against hers.

Suddenly a group of soldiers appeared and ran towards Eric; John stood behind him and put his hand on Eric's shoulder.

"Stand aside Eric while I remove her head" John said raising his sword

"No" Eric shouted "Leave her alone, you have already killed her" he said guarding her body with his own.

"She has put a spell on you" John said

"No, we are in love and she is not wicked"

"Then if you won't let me finish this, you must die first" John said attempting to stab Eric with his sword

Eric had his sword at hand and blocked John's attack, John was knocked to the ground by Alestra's hoofs as she reared up and kicked him in the chest. John rolled over on the ground and quickly recovered, he got up and attacked Eric again, this time he managed to wound Eric, the soldiers stood watching the fight by John's orders. Eric was bleeding from his side but he continued to fight, John was getting weaker from his wounds and eventually Sercombe dropping his sword.

"Eric, why are we doing this, we are brothers, what would father say to us now?" John said gasping

"You killed Anna, why did you do this?" Eric shouted angrily

"The Mayor ordered me to, he said you were enchanted by her love" John explained "I am so sorry Eric"

Suddenly a arrow spun into the air and landed into John's body, John fell to the ground and Eric ran to him and knelt beside him.

"Forgive me Eric" John said taking his last breath and dying.

Before Eric could attack the Mayor, the soldiers held Eric and one of them struck him on the head with the handle of his sword. When he recovered he was in the cave lying next to Annabella, fortunately nobody had beheaded her, and she seemed so peaceful lying on a blanket.

Eric looked around trying to focus on everything around him; the mayor stood watching him with a smirk on his face, he walked over to Eric and pointed to Annabella.

"She is Lamia, the daughter of Albelenda, and when I return from the pit I will behead her and finish the power of the witches for good" he said

"You are mad" Eric said "You will never succeed"

"Who will stop me?" the Mayor said mockingly "You?"

"They get inside your head" Eric said pointing to his own head

The Mayor shrugged him off and turned to address his soldiers

"I want eight of you to come with me and two to remain with these two, any trouble and you have my permission to kill them" The Mayor said leading them down a tunnel leading to the foot of the pit.

Eric noticed the wooden box that Annabella spoke about, it was close to the soldiers, he knew he had to find a way to distract them. He waited for a while trying to think of a plan, at this time a storm had began outside and strange noises came from the pit, flashes of light from the lightening lit up the cave and the roar of thunder caused the soldiers to jump and quake with fear. The ground began to shake and all the skulls began to rise up, a green substance poured out of the skulls and the bodies of each witch attached themselves to the skulls. Their souls were alive once more and they attacked the two soldiers as they tried to escape out of the cave, the witches worked jointly and used their powers sending electric bolts into the soldiers bodies. The men burnt away bit by bit, their flesh disappeared from their bodies leaving skeletons soaking in the rain just outside the cave entrance. Eric lay waiting for his fate, he thought that he would be the next to die, but the witches left them and entered the pit, before long there was a loud bang and yelling, screams could be heard from men.

Eric rushed to the wooden box and found the potion that Annabella had mentioned, she had described everything perfectly and Eric even followed her instructions on how to revive her. He put the vessel to her lips and tilted her head back, and then he used the substance and poured it over her body. Massaging her body with the substance and took the wand out of the box and held it to her chest hoping to recharge her heart like a defibrillator, but it failed. He tried again this time, he aimed it at her chest from the cave entrance and a bolt of lightening shot out, it was so powerful it threw him across the cave into the wall.

Eric heard more noises and saw the Mayor coming out of the tunnel with a look of horror on his face, he seemed disturbed and held a sword in his hand belonging to Eric.

"Stand aside I want the witches head" he shouted

"Do you know the significance of the number eight?" Eric asked

"The power of the resurrection?" he replied

"I know of that power" Eric said holding his hands up

"Tell me" the Mayor insisted

"I can do better than that" Eric said standing to one side "I can show you"

"What do you mean" the Mayor asked

"Behold" he said moving enough for the Mayor to see Annabella standing there

"Lamia" he gasped

"Back from the dead, just like me" he said smiling

Annabella was gleaming and very much alive, she raised her arms and a light emerged around her, the Mayor stood with his mouth wide open, while Eric took the sword out of his hand.

"But she had an arrow in her heart" he said

"That crumbled and fell like dust on the ground, she has been resurrected" Eric said happily

The Mayor threw a knife at her and it bounced off her chest and onto the ground, he snarled and ran at her, but she pushed her back with a great force of energy.

"I have poured that liquid on myself so I am invincible" he said

"That substance is nothing but Olive oil, we used it the last time we were in this cave, in order to refresh our skin" Eric explained

At that moment the ground began to move as before and the witches returned

The Mayor looked around him and saw all the witches together, he looked at Annabella "Save me from these witches" he pleaded

Annabella picked up her wand and pointed it into the air, she spoke calmly and clearly the words from a spell.

"Tamara lemus kathara" the cave shook and the whole place echoed with the sound of thunder.

Eric landed in her arms and remained there until it was all over, the Mayor fell into the pit, yelling as he fell and landed onto rocks breaking almost every bone in his body. Most of his blood poured across the ground, and no one mourned his death, he would soon be forgotten in Teversham least of all for his greed and corruption.

"Is that the end?" Eric asked

"No, my love, this the beginning"

The town and village of Teversham lived in peace; the witches of Teversham were a memory and soon became a story passed down generations like other folk tales, of course like any story things were added on and changed to suit the age.

As for Annabella and Eric they travelled north further into Scotland, they settled down in a cottage and had a daughter they called Rosa after Eric's youngest sister and they lived happily ever after or did they?

PART SEVEN

ROSA

It was summers day in the lowlands of Scotland, a young girl was running the glen, jumping over a brook and bending down to pick some heather. She had long flowing blonde hair, with a pale face and a long dress, her eyes were blue and sparkled like diamonds. She ran again through the grass towards a wooded area, she stopped and gazing around at the birds in the trees, she raised her arms up and began to float reaching the branches where the birds were. She perched herself next to them and smiled.

"How lucky you" she said to them "You are free from harm"

Just then she heard voices below her, it was a group of men talking

"The witch trials have begun in North Berwick and thousands of witches have been tortured and executed" one man said

"I, that is true and a good many more will die" another said

"Then we must warn the villagers of the dangers" another said concerned

"Yes because innocent woman are being tried and hung" another said

Suddenly the birds on the branch took flight and startled her, lost her balance and fell from the tree, plunging into a bush right next to the men.

"What was that?" one man asked

"Check those bushes" another said

One man looked in the bushes and noticed the girl lying down and remaining perfectly still.

"It's a wee lassie" he said "And she must have fallen from the tree"

"Is she okay? Another asked

"She isn't moving" he said concerned

"Let me see Gordon" a man rushed forward

"Amish, I tell you she is not moving" Gordon replied brushing her hair from her face "But she is breathing"

The girl began to wake up and looked up at three men watching her, she seemed a little surprised at their presence, but showed no fear.

"Who are you?" Gordon asked "Are you hurt?"

"My name is Rosa" she said to the bearded man

At that moment she heard someone calling out

"Rosa" seconds later she heard the voice again only closer to her

"That's my father" she said excitedly

"Over here" Amish shouted

"I am here father" Rosa shouted

She rose to her feet just as if nothing had happened, and then to the men's surprise began to walk away. She turned looking back on the men, each had auburn hair and beards.

"Thank you for helping me"

Eric was waiting for her in the clearing, he noticed how dirty her dress was and began chastising her, she looked back into the woods and the three men appeared.

"Your daughter fell from a tree, but she is okay, no bones broken" Gordon said

"Thank you for helping her" Eric said

"She is bonny" Amish said smiling

"The apple of my eye" Eric replied "Gentlemen will you join us for refreshments"

"That would be good" Amish said "May I introduce my brother Gordon Scott and John McGuire a trusted friend"

They all travelled to the cottage, they entered the door and were greeted by Annabella who was waiting to see Rosa, she looked apprehensive at the men, she had not trusted anyone since her ordeal years before with the Mayor and his soldiers, remaining quite secluded in the cottage.

Eric introduced them as Rosa's rescuers and Annabella reluctantly let them into her home, she asked them to sit down at the table and prepared some soup and fresh bread, Eric offered them some ale, but they came equipped with containers pouring whiskey from them into a vessel.

"Have you travelled far?" Annabella asked

"From Edinburgh" Amish replied

"Close to Edinburgh" Gordon interrupted

"Close enough to here the news" John said in a deeper voice

"What news?" Eric asked

"Witch hunting around the lowlands" Gordon said

Annabella dropped a glass container which shattered across the stone floor, making a loud noise and startling the men.

"Gordon your sending fear into these good folk's hearts" Amish said

"But they need to know, for fear that they may be pursued" Gordon said in his defence "The witch trials are being held in North Berwick and innocent women are being hung or beheaded"

Annabella looked at Eric, she had the look of fear on her face, apprehension knowing what its like to be hunted spending her childhood in fear of witch hunters due to her family of black witches.

"We only tell you these things in order to warn you of the dangers and advise you to seek refuge in the highlands" Gordon explained.

The family took heed of their warning and headed further north to seek shelter, years passed by and they continued to hear rumours of witch hunters. They were never away from the threat of witch hunters and Annabella had to prevent Rosa from using magic, although at this point she had not yet perfected her powers. She eventually lived with Martha in Teversham in her twenties, Annabella considered that she was safer than being in Scotland, while she and Eric remained in Scotland for a while.

DOUBLE EXPOSURE

S R SUTTON

INTRODUCTION

Two journalists from a magazine called Criminal world investigate the case of a missing girl in a castle in Scotland following a ghosting weekend. During the investigation they soon discover that they are not ghost hunting but playing a murder mystery game with dangerous consequences. Bodies go missing without a trace and weapons are left as clues to each murder, along with a calling card suggesting who the killer might be.

MISSING IN SCOTLAND

O ne of the main premises for criminal world was based in central London close to Piccadilly Circus. It was inside a tall building on the fourth floor with a bronze plaque outside indicating exactly where to find it. On the fourth floor was a door with a design of the world decorated on the glass saying 'criminal world magazine' opposite

Samantha entered the office walking gracefully down the corridor with her head held high, she seemed a confident woman with so much inner strength. She had long brown hair, which shined beneath the artificial florescent lights. She looked about thirty having young radiant skin that was slightly tanned. She wore a tight dress black dress that complimented her slim figure, catching the eyes of any man passing. But although she seemed confident she had a rather sad expression as if she were carrying the world on her shoulders.

Samantha walked through another door and found herself in a waiting area. A young man sat at a desk looking at a computer screen. Samantha gave a gentle cough to draw his attention then repeated a cough, eventually he responded.

"Yes can I help". He paused as he gazed at her beautiful face.

"I am Samantha I am your new reporter" Samantha said confidently

"Oh right" The young man said still staring at Samantha

"Would you mind not staring and finding Fiona?" Samantha said feeling uneasy

"I will ring her now" He said smiling

He picked up the phone and tapped out the numbers, he appeared rather clumsy as his fingers seemed to randomly press buttons.

"Have you got any identification please?" He asked her

Samantha produced a driving license from her handbag will this do it has my photo "I'm afraid I'm not topless on it" she said sarcastically

"Yes fine thanks" He said sheepishly

He finally got through to Fiona and began to speak

"Is that Fiona, I have a Samantha King here for you, your new reporter" He paused then pointed to one of the seats opposite "Can you sit there please, she will be with you soon".

Samantha sat and crossed her legs, her dress rose up her leg slightly and she quickly pulled it down. The young man had noticed but pretended not to and proceeded to knock over a pot of pens.

Fiona walked in she was a slim blonde woman around thirty-five years old, very attractive, but appeared to be very serious. She shook Samantha by the hand and smiled "I am Fiona".

"Come with me she beckoned Samantha" then looked at the young man

"Hadrian you need a tissue you're clearly drooling" Fiona said passing him by

"I want to know what you're going to do with your erection?" Samantha asked in a low voice after she passed him.

Fiona chuckled at what Samantha had said

"Hadrian is really harmless, he is rather special you know" Fiona said smiling.

Hadrian had tried to ignore their remarks and looked back at the computer muttering, "You don't want to know the answer to that one".

Fiona took Samantha through the main work area where most of the staff was concentrating on their tasks, people were walking about and some were talking on the phone she could see them picking up the phone and saying 'criminal world can I help you' this happened so many times. Some heads turned and seemed curious to know who was passing they entered the editor's office; he was sat at an untidy desk searching for something.

He looked up as they entered the room "Oh you must be Samantha from Australia"

"Yes sir" She said politely

"Manners as well, I am Bill not sir, we are more informal here". Bill said still searching amongst his papers.

"Ok well welcome to criminal world London" Bill continued

Bill had short but thick hair and a handlebar moustache; he was quite tall with a large stomach due to alcohol consumption this was known as a beer belly.

"Bill what are you looking for?" Fiona asked

"My cigarettes" Bill replied

"But you don't smoke anymore" Fiona insisted

"I do since your mother came back home" Bill remarked

"But Dad you have to be patient with her" Fiona said sternly

"She's hard work since her breakdown" Bill said finding his cigarettes

"OK I will visit tonight" Fiona agreed

"I hope you enjoy working with us my daughter will show you to your office" Bill said putting a cigarette in his mouth

Fiona gave a cough and pointed to the no smoking sign on the door, Bill took it out of his mouth while she left the office, and then returned it to his mouth.

Fiona led Samantha out of the office to a room nearby their were two desks there inside a spacious office, near the one desk stood a large filing cabinet and a plant on the top in a very decorative pot. The leave hung down the sides of the cabinet in long green strands, pictures were on the walls of other countries and one photo stood out it was of Fiona standing under the New York office with the criminal world logo above the door. She was standing with other members of staff all smiling and seemingly happy together.

"Nice picture Fiona is that New York?" Samantha asked

"Yes I used to work there" Fiona said reluctant to talk about it

"Did you like it there?" Samantha asked

"I was there three years until I lost my boyfriend in a shooting" Fiona said sitting at her desk

"I'm sorry" Samantha realised she had touched a raw nerve

"I am too Paul didn't deserve to die like that" Fiona suddenly stopped talking and turned on her computer.

Samantha didn't pursue the conversation and proceeded to empty her box of office equipment. She made use of every available space and put everything neatly away. Everything she had matched and she even lined books up neatly on a shelf.

"So have you got anyone?" Fiona asked Samantha

"No the last creep cheated on me" Samantha said continuing to count and line up all her pens.

"Waited until I was on an assignment and pissed off" Samantha said bitterly

"What a bastard" Fiona said in surprise

"Too fucking right took some of my fucking stuff too" Samantha went on.

"Men, they are just a load of tossers". Fiona smiled

"Too fucking right" Samantha said watching a man knocking the door.

"Oh Dan you're here, back from sunny Spain I see". Fiona said looking at Samantha.

Daniel Harrison had worked in war zones as a reporter and was an ex army man, He was thirty-six, muscular with short hair and a roughed face. He seemed quite arrogant on first impressions and seemed to hide a more sensitive self.

"Ladies may I say sunny Spain was excellent and I achieved all I needed to in a few days, one major story in the bag". Harrison boasted

"Well that's good" Fiona gestured to Samantha behind his back tosser.

Samantha tried to keep a straight face and just nodded, Harrison was oblivious to they're gestures and continued to boast about his new story from Spain. The phone ringing interrupted him and he decided to leave the office.

Fiona picked up the receiver "Hello" She said "Yes she's fine, he has just left here ok bye" Fiona said putting down the receiver

"That was Dad he was looking for Dan and he said he hopes your settling in ok". Fiona said looking across to Samantha.

"Yes everything is fine, no problem". Samantha said reorganising her pencils

"Have you got OCD by any chance" Fiona said tutting.

"Obsessive compulsive disorder Sorry I do have it a little" Samantha admitted

"So have you had any interesting stories in Australia?" Fiona asked

"Yes a few murders, but mainly missing persons and kidnappings" Samantha said

"Good well you will be sent everywhere from here" Fiona explained

"I read about one you wrote called 'cracked porcelain' about two models Pamela and Ruth lesbian women being pursued by a psychopathic killer that was a good story".

"You liked that one poor women were both abused as children that's why I called it cracked porcelain it was mainly about Pamela and her being abuse as a child it happened to Ruth as well but Pamela was a child model protected by her disabled mother".

"And what about Jodie the Goth girl" Samantha asked

"Yes poor Jodie got accused of a brutal assault on a young girl, she's in jail right now, but personally I think she's innocent" Fiona said

"Wasn't she bullied at school?" Samantha asked

"Yes learned to defend herself and suffered for it" Fiona said

"Meaning?" Samantha was asking for more information

"Well when she took up self defence classes she only wanted to protect herself but she was drawn into fights and lost control". Fiona explained

"So you understand Jodie?" Samantha asked

"Yes I do, its all about understanding Jodie and others" Fiona replied

"My stories involved murders in the outback's of Australia and city crimes in places like Melbourne and Sidney" Samantha explained

Samantha followed up a few local stories around London before venturing further, she was eventually sent to Scotland on a missing person story. It was quite usual for a simple story to turn out to be major news; Samantha usually got assigned to such stories. She was asked to travel to a small place near North Berwick, close to Edinburgh and stay at this castle near the sea; she was to go with Stuart Elliot the photographer. The missing person was Susan Macgregor the niece of a wealthy landowner called Gordon Macgregor. Both Samantha and Elliot were to pose as distant relatives, who are up in Scotland on vacation visiting uncle Gordon who happens to be an old friend of the editor Bill.

Samantha and Elliot set out by car and travelled through on the motorways of England until they reached the Scottish boarder. Samantha made Elliot swear not to sing on route after hearing him singing Scottish songs at the start of their journey. Even their taste in music varied so much and Samantha was not a very tolerant person, threatening to insert the radio into his anatomy. Elliot put it down to her time of the month but Samantha put her attitude down to her recent separation and her ex boyfriend being an asshole.

Samantha and Elliot arrived in Edinburgh at 16.00 hours and caught the train to Berwick

While at the station the other guests arrived in couples are as individuals, an eccentric couple waited on a bench the man wore a plain shirt, braces and a dickey bow with shorts and his partner wore a pale pleated skirt and a white blouse and pumps. They both had straw hats and between them stood out from all the other guests. Beside them stood a slim woman with short blonde hair she edged towards the couple and started to speak to them.

"I take it your waiting for the minibus?" she said jovially

"Yes" the man said "Going to Macgregor's castle and the haunted weekend"

"My name is Sharon" the slim blonde woman said

"This is my wife Sylvia and I am Reginald or Reg" He said extending his arm to shake her hand.

"Have you done this before?" Sylvia asked

"Yes many times I go all over the country searching for ghosts". Sharon admitted

"Oh that's nice have you ever seen any?" Reg asked

"Oh yes many times its so exciting" Sharon replied excitedly

"We have been a few times but not seen much" Sylvia said disappointedly

Samantha and Elliot were in close enough to hear the conversation

Samantha whispered to Elliot "We are in for a fun packed weekend with them" she said sarcastically

They catch the minibus to Macgregor's castle travelling through miles of countryside over a bridge and through woodlands. The guests were discussing previous ventures on the way until they reached their destination seeing the castle on the side of a cliff overlooking the sea. It was like a picture postcard the whole scenery was beautiful and the castle was well kept. The castle was a typical fairytale building such as seen in a Disney movie with high towers and walls with narrow windows that would have been used for bowmen to shoot their arrows at their enemy

They were taken to the main entrance and led into a main hall and asked to sit down on the many chairs that were placed neatly in one big circle. It was then that Macgregor made his entrance from another room; he was wearing a kilt and the rest of the attire typical of a true Scotsman. He was a tall man with ginger hair and a long ginger beard he was quite portly and had rosy cheeks and a slightly bent nose.

He introduced himself and explained about the rules of the household

"You are free to roam the castle but you are not allowed to go into that room" he pointed to the room by the main staircase "That room is private and I want all your phones and any other devices and I will lock them in my safe until you leave". He looked at each of them "This is a special weekend of ghost hunting and so no contact with the outside world". He noticed Samantha and smiled "We dine at six o'clock or 18.00 hours, so we will meet in the main dining room". He pointed down the corridor "My servants will show you to your rooms and settle you all in, after which feel free to explore these rooms".

A few men who looked hard took Samantha and Elliot to their rooms and menacing one of them had a short beard and a rough voice. The other never spoke but just made grunting sounds each time the other man spoke. After settling in Elliot knocked on Samantha's door, she fastened her clean blouse and headed for the door.

"Oh it's you" Samantha said sounding disappointed

"I get the distinct impression you don't like me" Elliot said smiling

"Nothing personal I don't like men at the moment" Samantha replied

"Ok I believe you" Elliot said

"Look if we are going to have to work together don't get in my fucking face ok" Samantha said abruptly

"Ok that suits me" Elliot agreed holding his hands up. "Anyway Macgregor wants to see us in the study". Elliot said heading towards the stairs

They managed to find the study and knocked on the door after a few moments waiting for a answer they went in. The room was virtually empty with a few pictures and a desk but the most curious thing on the desk was a board game Mystery murder game and figures set out on the table in various rooms as if someone was playing the game.

Elliot noticed the game and began to touch the figures

"Please leave them alone!" Macgregor shouted

Elliot jumped and dropped the figures

"I'm sorry but no one knows who put this here or why and so its evidence" Macgregor seemed worried

"Interesting and intriguing" Samantha said bending to look at the figures

"I suspect that we are the figures and part of someone's game" Macgregor continued

"Why do you say that?" Elliot asked

"Because I found a card beside my bed with a picture of a man in purple on it" Macgregor said "And before my niece went missing a card of a woman in blue was by her bed.

Samantha noticed a portrait on the wall "I like your painting its you isn't it?"

"No its my identical twin brother John, he slept in the room that you are staying in lass" Macgregor said almost smiling.

"So who are we?" Samantha asked

"You're my cousin from London called Samantha and you lad are Stuart another cousin from London" Macgregor explained

"So we are on vacation?" Elliot asked

"Yes and don't tell a soul" Macgregor insisted

"Of course not" Samantha agreed.

"So lets go and eat" Macgregor said leading them into the corridor and then into the large dining room.

They met other people in the dining room who were introduced by Macgregor, the room maids and servants were walking about and Elliot made a point of observing them. On the way to the dining room each one was a suspect for kidnapping no one escaped his notice. Samantha had also suspected one or two people mainly male staff as she was going through an anti male phase in her life. Her previous relationship with Derek caused her so much heartache she was ready to castrate any man at this point.

Macgregor introduced his guests to Samantha and Elliot, firstly my friend Janet the friend from Inverness. She was a tall thin lady with short dark hair and a pale complexion. A vicar who was from Aberdeen, he was a short bolding man who seemed to look over his glasses like you would expect a teacher to do. He was quite portly with chubby cheeks like a hamster he kept looking over at Samantha across the large oblong table. Macgregor sat at the head of the table the entire cutlery shone and the glassware sparkled, the servants came into the room and served each guest with a hot soup dish.

Both Samantha and Elliot were amazed at the banquet and at the way things appeared to be organised. Macgregor obviously enjoyed entertaining his guests, he also made a point of making them feel comfortable in his presence.

"I am pleased and delighted to have you all here and hope your stay will be comfortable" Macgregor said addressing everyone "I do hope my niece Gillian will return safely with us, I would like you to meet her as she is the apple of my eye". Macgregor looked around the table at all his guests in turn. "You are in the castle of Macgregor home for generations of Macgregor's so don't be surprised to see a few ghosts occasionally". Macgregor seemed serious when he referred to the place as being haunted.

Samantha was more interested in the large ring that he was displaying on a finger on his right hand. The ring had a ruby inset in the centre of the ring, which shone like a red light. Macgregor noticed her looking at it and smiled at her in a strange manner as if he could read her mind.

"This ring has been passed down the family through generations" Macgregor was addressing Samantha who was two seats away. "Its as beautiful as you my wee lassie and it will never come off".

Samantha smiled and began to blush "Thank you" she said looking down at a bowl of soup in front of her, then at Elliot, he just smiled and picked up his soup spoon and began to scoop up his soup. Samantha had a very delicate manner, which indicated that she had been to functions like this before. She knew exactly how to behave and displayed such elegance like a lady of the manor. Elliot however was much more down to earth oblivious of the other guests behaved more like a caveman in some cases.

Samantha could here conversations around her discussing Gillian's disappearance and Janet was sitting next to her wearing a purple dress, she seemed very observant pointing out items in various rooms. She particularly curious about Samantha and examined her like person buying a vase or other interesting objects.

"So Samantha" Janet began

"Call me Sammy most people do" Samantha said smiling

"Ok Sammy where are you from?" Janet asked curiously

"I am from London" Samantha replied

"Yes but I can detect another accent there" Janet said in a probing manner

"Well I am originally from Australia" Samantha revealed.

"So you are related to Gordon" Janet said

"She's my cousin" Gordon quickly interrupted.

"I see and I am a friend of Gillian's, we were at school together" Janet said watching the servant put her main meal in front of her.

"Game pie my favourite," the vicar said smiling.

"I aim to please Charles" Macgregor said cheerfully.

Samantha felt nervous next to Janet but was not able to understand why; something told her that she was hiding something or not quite who she seemed to be. She was also still curious about the mystery murder game on the study table that apparently just appeared there. No one knew why it was there not even the servants, but it had been there since the disappearance of Gillian a few days ago.

Samantha and Elliot were sat in the study with all the other guests, listening to Macgregor telling ghost stories. He seemed quite intent as he related each detail his eyes seemed fixated on the portrait of him as if something was wrong. He then looked at his audience then focused on Samantha's large brown eyes. He explained about his ancestors who lived in the castle and who according to himself haunt the many rooms and corridors each night. He was so convincing it was almost as if he believed his own stories and was relaying real events. This was all part of the performance with sounds and visual activity provided by a clever man hidden in a control room, Macgregor's missing brother had created the whole show years before in order to entertain the public. Now Macgregor had his audience and he was like the master of ceremony, circus master and storyteller all in one.

"Well ladies and gentlemen if you look and listen we have the weather giving us the atmosphere for my ghoulish stories" He pointed to the window where a storm was taking place, thunder and lightning followed by heavy rain.

"I must tell you the story of Angus Macgregor" He began with a solemn look on his face. "Who's wife was gravely ill, she was suffering from a painful illness stricken with fever and as pale as snow" He looked back at Samantha and smiled "She was very beautiful and a true lady, but her illness aged her and her hair turned white.

Samantha felt uneasy as she listened to his story almost as if he was talking about her but then she knew deep inside she couldn't have been.

Macgregor continued his story "Angus watched his wife as she began fading away but was attracted to a maid who gave him pleasure. They he was having an affair carried away by his weak will and obsessed with one so young and fair. However on his wife's dying day she beckoned him to her side and whispered in his ear saying I know and repeating I know. He began to shiver and became enraged sending the maid off but she walked up the north tower and threw herself off plunging to her death. She returned from the dead to haunt him shouting and screaming at him, you are a wicked man you will die a horrible death. Sure enough he did as he fell down the main stairs near the entrance hearing her words over and over again, he was crippled and had pneumonia and true as her words were he died a horrible death".

Macgregor pointed in the direction of the north tower "Every night you can see a white figure falling from the tower and on the stairs a floating shape moves down the stairs as for Angus you can hear him in his bed gasping for breath and you may even see him somewhere within the castle".

"What a chilling tale" one of the guests said shivering

Samantha looked at her in disbelief then whispered to Elliot "They take it all in don't they". She said smirking

Macgregor looked at the large antique grandfather clock standing by the wall and continued with another tale.

Angus had a younger brother called John who was in the woods at night when it began to rain; he sheltered under a tree and was suddenly struck by lightning. He survived but became mentally impaired he was so bad that he killed his wife by stabbing her to death with a knife, she was found by a servant in the library. Sometimes you can hear her screams or see her walking covered in blood. He walks about too with his menacing eyes and hunched up body moaning as he moves around the corridors at night. You think your safe until he suddenly catches you and stabs you over and over again, you can tell when he is about to attack because before he does you hear the striking of the clock at the midnight hour".

At that moment the clock struck and everybody jumped including the sceptical Samantha, each person looked at the clock but it was only Eleven o'clock.

"But that's not all" Macgregor said continuing his story "John died after killing his wife by shooting himself and blowing his brains out, you can clearly hear the shot every night almost in every room" He paused then yelled "Bang!" at the top of his voice, he then roared with laughter as they all jumped again.

After Macgregor had successfully scared the guests especially Sharon he left them to tell their own ghostly tales. Sharon kept jumping at every sound and saying 'what was that' even when no one else heard anything. Sharon had already stated that she had heard voices and spoke to them saying 'If your there contact me in some way, make a noise or something'.

Meanwhile he called Samantha and Elliot to one side wanting to speak to them in private. "I need to discuss Gillian" He said in a solemn tone

"Gillian went missing during the last haunted weekend. Before she disappeared she claimed that she could hear voices, as you know we set up the atmosphere for the ghost hunting by elaborate sound and visual effects".

"So it could have been one of these sounds?" Samantha asked trying to make sense of it.

"No this was nothing like our pranks, it was voices of command telling her to do things" Macgregor explained

"So was she ever assessed mentally?" Samantha asked concerned

"No never" Macgregor replied

"You think she may schizophrenic?" Elliot asked

"Yes maybe" Samantha replied searching for a rational explanation for her behaviour.

"I suppose it is possible" Macgregor admitted

"My mother was schizophrenic" Elliot said reflecting back on his past

"I had a friend who was schizophrenic and she used to have audible hallucinations she tried to drown out the voices by putting headphones on and playing music, this worked for a while but nothing works perfectly". Samantha said concerned.

"What was Gillian wearing when she went missing? Elliot asked

"She was wearing patterned T-shirt and blue jeans". Macgregor said giving a loose description of her attire, he produced a photograph from the inside pocket of his coat and showing Samantha and Elliot.

"She's pretty" Samantha remarked

"And where was she when you last saw her?" Elliot asked

"In the library looking at books" Macgregor explained

"Can we go there?" Samantha asked eager to find out more information.

"Yes of course" Macgregor He made his excuses to the other guests and took Samantha and Elliot into the library.

After a careful search of the room Samantha and Elliot were satisfied that nothing was unusual in the room. Elliot examined every inch even the walls for any signs of another exit like a false panel or section leading to a secret passage. He felt as if he was being watched and did notice tiny object, which could have been a camera in the corner of the room.

"What's this Gordon?" He asked

"Oh that's part of our elaborate equipment that we use for the ghost hunting, we project images in the room to give the elusion of a ghost the sound equipment is concealed in a few false books". Macgregor explained

"Very clever" Elliot said

"So you make people believe that ghosts exist" Samantha said

"Yes its all part of the fun and thrill of the weekend" Macgregor said playing with his ginger beard with his fingers.

Samantha was attracted again by the ruby ring again as she saw it sparkle.

Samantha asked to see Gillian's bedroom, it looked just like the other rooms even to the point of having a fireplace and wall panels. In the middle of the room was a four-poster bed with red silk sheets like Samantha's bed. There was no sign of dirty footprints or blood and according to Macgregor there was no sign of a struggle. Elliot examined the wall panels and around the fireplace hoping to find for a secret entrance or doorway. Nothing seemed obvious and everywhere was spotlessly clean like all the other rooms, which eliminated a possible, escape root in the area. Samantha thought that Elliot had been watching too many movies and had an over active imagination.

Macgregor led them out of the room and locked the door behind them; Samantha and Elliot decided to have a walk outside around the immediate area, examining each window and doors for any clues.

"Something doesn't add up" Samantha said

"Like what?" Elliot said bewildered

"Come on Stuart didn't you think Janet was odd asking questions like a detective or something?" Samantha said looking at another window

"I think you have a lot of imagination" Elliot said heading for the conservatory door.

"Fuck you Stuart why can't you see it are you fucking blind" Samantha said angrily

"Sorry but you're the reporter, I am merely a photographer" Elliot explained

"Well I know there is something about all this that doesn't make any fucking sense and that Janet knows something". Samantha insisted.

"I can appreciate that Sammy but why get so upset?" Elliot said checking the conservatory door.

"Because no one fucking listens to me, I don't know why I waste my breath honestly" Samantha said walking back towards the main entrance.

"Perhaps if you didn't swear or get stressed it might help" Elliot said hoping to get through to her about her attitude.

"Well I am sorry but I can't help it, I feel so fucking stressed" Samantha was certainly acting very emotional like she was hormonal.

"Ok I get it, but we need to be rational and think about this clearly".

"Yes I know sorry let's go back inside".

Samantha and Elliot entered the main door and began walking up the stairs when they noticed everyone rushing about frantically.

"What's happened" Samantha asked

"It's the vicar he was found dead in the study with marks around his neck, it looks like he has had a rope around it" Janet explained

They all entered the study and noticed the vicar on the floor with a rope around his neck; next to his body were a mystery murder game card with a picture of man in purple on it. The police arrived soon afterwards and interviewed the guests and staff. Janet spent a lot of time with them before they left; she then spoke to Samantha and Elliot in the library.

"Ok who are you two, you go outside snooping why?" Janet asked abruptly

"So who the fuck are you?" Samantha asked

"I am a under cover police detective searching for Gillian" Janet explained

Elliot looked at Samantha and back at Janet, he seemed a little confused at her explanation.

"We are from criminal world I am a photographer and she is a reporter" Elliot explained

"Reporters your kidding right, so what have you discovered?" Janet asked

"That this is a creepy castle, probably haunted and nobody is who they seem". Samantha replied.

"Well that's a fact" Janet said looking around the library

"I can't help feeling that we are being watched all the time" Samantha said also looking around.

"I know I have had that feeling since day one" Elliot admitted.

"Fuck now I sound like that daft bitch Sharon who jumps at every sound and sees things moving in the darkness". Samantha said jokingly.

Meanwhile in a secret room a figure sat watching them on a television screen, the screen was one of many that showed various rooms in the house. The pictures changed revealing more rooms including the bedrooms one of the rooms had a girl on a bed with her hands and feet tied to the bedposts. The girl was quite still and appeared to be asleep after a while she changed positions. On the desk near the television screen was a mystery murder game card with a picture of a white lady on the front.

The person picked up the card and examined it, then placed it back on the table near a card with a picture of a red lady.

Samantha went to her room which was close to Elliot's room, Janet had left them and joined Macgregor in the study. Samantha went into her bathroom and began to have a shower hoping it might relax her so that she could sleep. She was washing herself when she thought that she heard a noise in the room. It was as if something heavy had been dropped on the floor making such a noise that it could have been easily heard above the sound of the gushing water in the shower. She switched off the shower wrapped a towel around her and went into the bedroom.

When she got there she noticed the tall lamp stand was on its side on the floor, it was heavy consisting of mainly brass and could only have been pushed over. Samantha decided to lock the door in case someone had entered the room and perhaps stolen something. After checking all her things she discovered nothing was missing.

Samantha turned main light off and put her side lamp on turning it to a dim light. She put on her eye mask and tried to settle down for the night. She began moving from side to side trying to get comfortable and eventually she fell asleep. She was unaware of being watched by an infrared camera the observer seemed fascinated by her as she lay sleeping. He then stood up and walked towards the door dressed in a black jump suit and brandishing a torch.

The panel opened leading into Samantha's room after a short pause the figure emerged into Samantha's room clenching the torch. The figure walked towards the bed where she was sleeping and placed a mystery murder game card of miss scarlet on the table, then reached out to touch her. The figure grabbed her shoulder and shook her; Samantha pulled off her mask and thrashed out at the figure. The torch fell on the bed and she used it to hit him on the forehead and he fell to the ground. She then shone the torch in his face and gasped in horror as she saw his face looking at her.

"For fuck sake Stuart, what the fuck are you doing" Samantha said hysterically

"Ouch I found a secret passage" Elliot said holding his head

"So you decided to come in my fucking room and scare me" Samantha went to hit him again and realised what she was doing "How fucking smart was that?"

"Found this card near the secret panel, I thought I saw a figure in the passage" Elliot pointed to the wall "I thought he came from here".

Samantha looked at her hand and noticed blood then looked at his head

"You're bleeding my god it's running down your face" Samantha said worried

She held out her hand touching his face "Here sit on the bed" she advised him

"I will get something to clean you up". Samantha said rushing to the bathroom

She returned with a damp flannel and a towel "Let me deal with it" she offered

She began dabbing the wound with the flannel and cleaning his face

"Ouch that bloody hurts" Elliot exclaimed

"Man up it's only a fucking scratch" Samantha said continuing to clean the wound.

"It still damn well hurts" Elliot shouted

"Shhhh for fuck sake shut up everyone will here you" Samantha said in a low voice

"I didn't mean to scare you Sammy, but I had to warn you" Elliot whispered

"Ok I understand, I had a visitor before who obviously meant me to have this card" Samantha said looking at the mystery murder game card of a woman in red "I guess that's me" She said concerned

"Yes the person could have killed you" Elliot said with equal concern

"The noise from the lamp stand falling must have made him rush off and he exited through the secret exit. I heard it crash to the floor when I was in the shower it landed by that wall". Samantha pointed towards the wall

"My god you were lucky Sammy" Elliot said

"We need to stick together Stuart for our own safety" Samantha said concerned

"Oh I would be safer with you" Elliot said holding his head

"I am sorry really" Samantha said smiling and sounding so sincere

"Ok what have you got in mind?" Elliot asked

"You sleep here with me but on the side of the bed near that wall" She pointed to the wall where the secret panel existed.

"Ok" Elliot agreed

"But don't get too close and no touching ok" Samantha insisted.

"Understood" Elliot said with a smile.

Elliot lay on the bed facing the wall while Samantha lay with her back to him smiling to herself as if she really wanted something to happen. But Samantha was so mixed up at this stage her emotions were surging like engines in a race waiting for the flag to indicate go.

Meanwhile Sharon and another guest were walking around the ground floor near the study unaware that the killer was watching them on his screen. He was holding a remote control and opening the passage doors close to where they were walking. "Hello" Sharon said, "let me know your there give me a sign" Suddenly a door opened and Sharon vanished into the study someone covered her mouth and plunged a dagger into her back. The other guest took no notice of her thinking that she was doing her usual over dramatics and annoying sounds. Then she entered the dining room and saw the outline of a figure that she thought was part of the ghostly pranks until she felt a heavy object hit her on the head. The figure hit her viciously several times until she lay limp beside one end of the table. Sharon was cut to pieces in the study with a large sharp knife and the killer's hands were covered with blood. Then a calling card dropped with a lady in pink on the front of it and the bloody knife was placed next to it.

During the night Samantha was moving about restlessly and Elliot was just turned on by her presence in the bed. Eventually she turned towards him he felt her warm breath on his chest and she moved her head on the pillow close to his face. Elliot had turned his head towards her but kept his eyes closed then she pressed her cheek against his. Breathing onto his face she was now cuddled up to him and could feel his body heat as she pressed her lips against his and began kissing him. She had lost control perhaps she was thinking about someone else as her fingers began to wonder around his back. He returned a lingering kiss and his hands wandered up and down her back and started fondling her buttocks. She removed her top and they both continued kissing for a while before becoming completely naked and enjoying each other's bodies. They had totally lost control by the time they were kissing each other's body and made love unaware that they were being watched by the infrared camera.

By morning Samantha and Elliot were embraced naked in a comfortable position, the sun was shining through a crack in the curtains with a beam of light drifting across the bed. Samantha was actually lying on top of Elliot with her head on his naked chest gradually her eyes opened and she began to focus on the hairs on his chest. She stayed perfectly still trying to understand what she had done and why, as nothing made sense at all. She had obviously lost control of her emotions and he being a man took advantage of her feminine weakness. Foolish moments that she would no doubt regret and have to explain the best way she knew how. The embarrassment and humiliation and now lying naked on top of a work colleague, what was she going to say to him when he awoke. She finally pulled herself away from him and looked beneath the bedclothes at her naked body then at him.

"I did dream all this right?" Samantha said to Elliot as he began to wake up

"God not unless I did too" Elliot said just as surprised

They were both acting like virgins encountering their first sexual relationship

"No I mean it was a mistake, a foolish mistake" Samantha said trying not to give him eye contact

"Yes a moment of weakness" Elliot said trying to reassure her

Samantha put her hands to her head "Fuck me this isn't happening"

She began staring into space her eyes were wide and her mouth open, Elliot tried to touch her in order to comfort her.

"Just don't" She pushed his hand away "Just don't touch me ok".

"We need answers Sammy" Elliot said trying to change the subject

"Answers, I am fucking freaking out and you want answers, you are unreal" Samantha said hysterically

"No you don't understand I mean about the abduction and the murder" Elliot said

"Oh that well go and get washed and dressed and then come back here ok" Samantha said hiding under the sheets.

"Ok" Elliot said pulling back the sheets on his side of the bed

Samantha turned her head away trying not to look at him, while he put on his clothes.

"And Stuart don't mention this to anyone" Samantha looked at him for a reassuring reply

"Honestly I wont mention a thing" Elliot sounded sincere as he unlocked the door and left the room.

An hour later a knock came at Samantha's door and Janet stood waiting, Samantha opened the door expecting Elliot to be there.

"Ok I am ready" Samantha paused and looked at Janet

"Sammy I need to speak to you" Janet breezed past Samantha

"Come in" Samantha said sarcastically

"Another guest has been murdered, a calling card left this time a man in purple" Janet said moving up to the bed

"When was this?" Samantha asked

"Last night and I think it was your colleague Stuart" Janet said looking around the bed.

"Impossible" Samantha said dismissing Janet's theory

"May I ask how you deduce that" Samantha had her arms folded in a defensive gesture.

"Oh come on Sammy you must admit he has been snooping all over this castle" Janet insisted

"You can't accuse him he's innocent" Samantha insisted

"How do you know?" Janet asked

"I just do" Samantha answered swiftly

"He slept here last night didn't he?" Janet smiled

"What makes you say that" Samantha said innocently

"Because his socks are on your bed and there are fair hairs on the pillow on this side need I go on?" Janet said picking up a sock with her fingers.

"Alright he did so what now you fucking accuse me" Samantha said upset about being discovered with Stuart.

"Nothing but tonight we can all explore this castle for clues" Janet insisted

At that moment a knock came at the door, Samantha opened it and Elliot stood fully dressed. He entered the room acting as if the night before had never happened, and then he noticed Janet standing by the bed.

"Good morning" Elliot said cheerfully

"There has been another murder" Samantha said before Janet could speak

"Oh was that with a calling card?" Elliot asked wondering why Janet was looking around the bed.

"Yes I suspected you but you were apparently occupied all night" Janet said looking at Samantha

"Oh yes I was all night" Elliot said looking at Janet and then Samantha

"So why don't we go for breakfast?" Samantha said wanting to leave the room in a hurry.

Janet swept her hands threw her dark hair and smiled at Samantha she knew that she had embarrassed her and gathered from Samantha's response that she regretted the night before and just wanted to put it behind her.

"Oh I was left a card too with a purple man on it" Elliot said

"So we have all had one now?" Janet said "But how is this person entering the rooms?" she continues

"Secret passages I found one last night" Elliot boasted

"How romantic you entered Sammy's room via a secret passage and that's why you have a bruise and gash on your forehead, she wasn't expecting you". Janet said teasing them.

"Lets leave it shall we" Samantha said dismissively

Janet wanted to catch the murderer she suspected everyone but considered this one to be a clever psychopath who knew the castle well. Also this killer might have an accomplice as the bodies seemed to be being moved from one place to another. Evident by fibres on the shoes and blood stains by the walls which also meant that there was secret doorways and corridors around the castle once used as an escape route for the occupants during invasions centuries ago.

That night Janet had discussed exposing the murderer to her police colleagues they needed to be discrete in order to capture the murderer. She had arranged to set a trap for him by hiding police in certain locations within the castle disguised as servants. The killer seemed to strike at night when other activities were going on and so it was considered the best time to set a trap. The killer was obsessed with board games and mystery murder was his favourite game. He had left the board game in the study on a table. Occasionally he moved the pieces around according to who was murdered and where. The weapons matched the murder weapons used each time making it obvious that the killer had planned his or her murders to detail.

"We are dealing with a violent psychopath who could be anywhere in this damn castle, just be careful".

The weather that night was stormy, thunder and lightening with heavy rain. Samantha and Elliot entered the secret passage from

Samantha's room both carrying torches fighting away cobwebs and feeling insects crawling on their body. They were both dressed in dark clothes as if they expected to be tumbling in the darkness finding answers to this mystery.

"Didn't you find Macgregor acting oddly?" Samantha asked

"Yes a little I suppose" Elliot replied

"And he wasn't wearing that special ring" Samantha said tripping over

"Are you alright" Elliot said concerned

"Ouch fuck I can't find the torch, it must be broke" Samantha said searching around with her hands.

Elliot shone his torch towards her "Here grab my hand lets stick together". Elliot said holding out his hand

"This changes nothing Stuart, I am still not happy with you" Samantha said grabbing his hand and standing up.

They continued down the passageway until they reached a door, Samantha had been clinging onto Elliot's arm and let go as he opened the door. They had reached the roof and were heading across a narrow pathway to another door.

"We are on the roof" Elliot shouted

"No shit" Samantha said sarcastically

"Well let's go or we will be here all fucking night" she continued

It was very slippery with the rain pounding on the roof and water drifting onto the path forming a river before them. Elliot slipped a few times but Samantha managed to keep her footing until they had almost reached the door. Suddenly she slipped and a few bricks crumbled away and disappeared off the roof. Samantha was slipping through the gap, she began to scream sliding almost to the edge of the roof clinging hold of bricks. Elliot caught her by her arms and tried pulling her up still slipping himself.

"Find a footing come on I am slipping" Elliot shouted

"I can't fucking move" Samantha said trying to grip hold of another brick

"Come on Sammy" Elliot shouted in desperation

"I am going to fall" Samantha shouted

Samantha suddenly felt a ledge with her feet and began to climb up, Elliot pulled her the rest of the way and they both fell back onto the tiles. Elliot found the torch and they continued across the roof holding on to each other.

"I think I am going to find a new career this job is fucking dangerous" Samantha said in anger

They entered the door and walked down some steps into another secret passageway.

"Right hold my hand Sammy" Elliot said

"Not likely" Samantha said still moody

"So we don't lose each other" Elliot replied

"Ok just for that reason" Samantha said grabbing his hand

After walking a short distance Samantha was actually grabbing Elliot by the arm, she was so close he could feel her breath on his neck and her heart beating.

He was reluctant to comment in case she started shouting and swearing at him.

He came across a panel with a catch on it, which released the door mechanism; he pulled the catch and the panel opened into a bedroom. Lying on the bed was Macgregor's niece she had auburn hair and was wearing a green dress, she was awake and looking up at the top of the four-poster bed.

Samantha and Elliot raced over to the bed Elliot was trying to untie her legs while Samantha untied her arms.

"You must be Gillian" Samantha commented

Gillian nodded and looked down at Elliot who was holding the rope that he had removed from her feet.

"Who did this?" Samantha asked

"Uncle Gordon" Gillian replied in a weak voice

"We need to go" Elliot said anxiously

"Can you walk?" Samantha asked Gillian

"Yes I think so" Gillian said swivelling round on the bed

"Let's find Gordon and the other guests" Samantha said eagerly

"No" Gillian said "Why don't we find out what's really happening and enter the secret passage, we may catch Uncle Gordon before he kills again.

"Good idea" Elliot said eager to catch the killer

"Well alright" Samantha agreed "I just want this whole fucking mess over with".

"Excuse Sammy she is very hormonal" Elliot explained

"Fuck you Stuart" Samantha said heading towards the panel

Elliot looked around for the catch on the panel, suddenly it opened and they began to enter the passageway. Elliot led the way until Gillian made the suggestion to follow a thin faded line on the wall which she claimed she made when she was being lead down there from the library.

Meanwhile another victim had been murdered with a heavy spanner the killer hit her several times on the head, in a vicious attack and showing no mercy as he caved her scull in. The woman's dress was covered in blood and she was being dragged like a sack of potatoes along another part of the passage and left in the library along with a calling card with a picture of a woman in white.

No sooner had the killer left the library than Samantha and Elliot entered. Seeing the body they had a quick look and then re entered the passage. While this was going on the killer stuck again this time attacking a man with a candlestick using the same force, as before determined to make sure he was dead. He hit him several times with blood spraying all around him as he obviously severed the archery in his neck. He struggled with this body leaving him in the conservatory and placing the weapon beside his body.

A hand reached forward to touch Samantha's head it was covered with blood grasping at her hair then got disturbed. Samantha and Elliot were alerted by the sound of a gun shot which at first sounded like one of Macgregor's elaborate sound effects then another shot was fired sounding different. They all followed the direction where they thought the sound was coming from Gillian seemed eager to get there first.

They arrived at the main control area in the cellar and were astonished to find six monitors displaying various views of the castle. Suddenly they noticed Janet and a few others walking along a secret passage and behind them a well-built man shaped like Macgregor. He managed to catch up with them and attack one of them without the others noticing.

"My god he's picking them off one at a time" Elliot said anxiously

"They must be close to here by now" Gillian said looking around

"Look at all this stuff" Samantha said pointing to the board game

"But this is not the control room Macgregor used that was near the study not here in the cellar" Elliot said confused "why have two rooms to do this?"

"Obviously he wanted us to know about the one but not this one" Samantha explained.

Gillian picked something up from under the table and stepped back watching both of them. At that moment Janet appeared with two men and stand beside them each one looking at Elliot.

"So it was you" Janet said "Using Sammy as your accomplish very smart or are you"

At that moment a man appeared "Well what do we have here?"

Janet looked at him and frowned "Gordon I have your killer" she said confidently.

"Is that so" He said coldly "Well have I got news for you"

"I have been following them and they have been at the scene of each one" Janet said

Gordon raised his arm revealing a revolver "Well guess what?"

"You're the killer but how?" Samantha asked

"I used this remote control to operate all the doors and entrances I also followed you all at all times, those catches don't work and never have done. I have been in control of this game all the time and sadly all of you have come to your end" Macgregor smirked evilly.

"But how did you do this all alone?" Elliot asked

"He didn't" came a voice from behind each turned to see Gillian with a gun

Elliot turned to see a spanner flying in the air towards Macgregor's head, he swerved to avoid it coming hitting his head. Despite his efforts caught him on the temple and he fell to the ground groaning and holding his head. As this happened Gillian responded by shooting at everyone wildly, after a few seconds she realised that she was out of ammunition. She then pulled a knife from a sheath and proceeded to lash out at anyone close catching one of the men at the same time Macgregor charged at them too. There was a confusion of arms and legs everywhere, people were bleeding and eventually both Macgregor and Gillian were lying on the floor in handcuffs. During the scuffle on the floor Gillian had attempted to grab Macgregor's gun but couldn't quite reach it. It was thought that Samantha may have hit her at this point preventing Janet from getting shot. At one point Gillian had tried to stab Samantha in the chest but fell forward narrowly missing her throat.

Two of the men who were police officers had been shot but not seriously wounded while Elliot managed to cut his hand. Samantha had thumped Gillian at one stage but may have been trying to attack Elliot as she was still annoyed with men due to breaking up with her boyfriend. Janet looked at the killers then at Samantha not knowing what to say.

"Thank you Sammy, sorry I accused you of all this" Janet said shamefully

"You're welcome and its ok" Samantha said smiling

Janet smiled back and then told the police officers to take the prisoners away.

She then took other policemen and searched the cellar for bodies, during her search she discovered Gordon Macgregor bound and gagged in a corner. He explained about his brother John who had gone missing years ago, during Gordon Macgregor's absence when he was in Greece John must have installed all his elaborate equipment including a separate generator to power everything. The idea of operating monitors to watch everyone was clever although using a remote control mechanism to operate panel doors to the secret passages suggests a planned operation and the murder game could only be the work of someone evil and a dangerous psychopath, a person with no continence but an intelligent man.

By the time the forensics arrived and everyone was questioned it was morning. Macgregor had switched off the generator and disconnected the other systems so that only the lights and boiler system and any other necessary electrical equipment operated in the castle. The door panels on each of the walls were taken off while the police searched all over the castle for other bodies. Skeletons were found in various places including a vault and it was thought that John had been killing people for years mostly with the aid of Gillian. The one puzzling thing was that she was tied up at times Elliot saw her on the monitor tied to a bed. It was never explained why unless it was to lead Samantha and Elliot into the room as a diversion while John carried on killing. The other puzzling thing was that John never had a motive for murder; he just enjoyed murder mysteries and games.

The following morning turned out to be sunny with clear skies with a no rain forecast for at least three days. This was a welcome sight after all the storms and additional artificial storms over the last few days. Samantha vowed and declared that she would never enter a castle again except for Edinburgh of course. Elliot actually enjoyed the experience and being shouted and sworn at by Samantha.

Gordon stood outside looking at his castle when his surviving guests came out, He spoke to each one in turn feeling guilty about his

Brother John's behaviour. But no one blamed Gordon and knew the full story of how John had gone missing and that John tied Gordon up then replaced him in order to get about the castle and middling with the guests.

"I am grateful to you Stuart, you have a Scottish name to be proud of" Macgregor said shaking him by the hand.

"Thank you Gordon" Elliot said smiling

"And my beautiful guest Sammy, god bless you" Macgregor said kissing and hugging her,

"Thank you" Samantha said rolling her eyes and fighting her way out of his ginger beard. She also noticed the ruby ring that she admired on his finger.

They started to walk towards the minibus when Samantha turned and walked back towards him "Just one thing Gordon who was the ghost image in my room last night?".

Macgregor looked puzzled and so she continued to describe what she saw

"It was a woman wearing a ballroom gown with a diamond clustered tiara"

"Heavens my dear I don't know all the sound and visual systems were turned off last night so there wouldn't be any we ghosties from me".

"You're sure?" Samantha asked

"Absolutely" Macgregor said seriously

With that Samantha looked up at her window and a woman waved down to her.

After the castle experience Samantha and Elliot decided to return to Edinburgh for the tattoo. The experience was worth it and just happened to be the one of the most spectacular experiences of their lives.

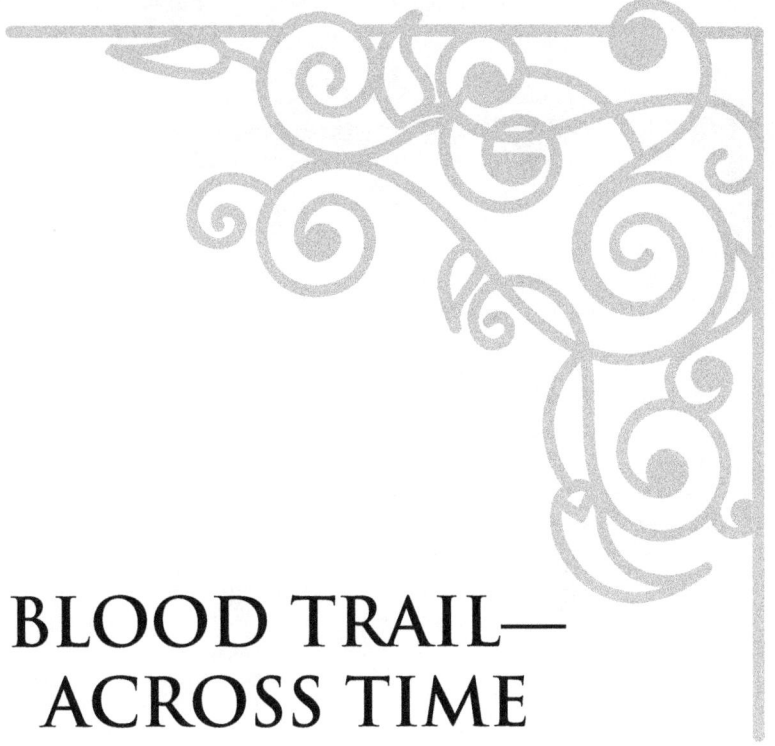

BLOOD TRAIL—
ACROSS TIME

S R SUTTON

INTRODUCTION

A woman called Siena enters the future through a picture or time portal and befriends a man Jack who later discovers he is in love with a vampire. However this is just the beginning of his problems as vampire slayers also enter the future and both are faced with more than they bargain for in this fast pace story of romance and intrigue. The story takes the readers through a journey through time meeting interesting characters and danger around every corner. Siena wants to be human again and asks god to help her reach her goal, a guardian angel called Faith appears with a mission to defeat the vampire that cursed her life, in order to be human again she persuades Jack and others to help her achieve this. But the vampires of the future are evil and treacherous, and their body armour protects them from daylight as they travel through time in order to harvest human beings for blood, is there hunger never satisfied as they abduct more and more humans and celebrate their grand feast.

THE BLOOD TRAIL BEGINS

It was a cold night, the moon was full and the trees blew wildly in the air, in the thick of the forest a woman ran frantically for her life. She had mud on her pale face and torn clothes, she had fear in her green eyes and constantly looked back holding back her hood in order to see her pursuers. She could hear them shouting holding flaming torches and clubs, the loud snapping of twigs suggested they were getting closer. Suddenly she caught her arm on a branch scratching the flesh on her wrist it began to bleed and she fell over another branch down a ditch. Her eyes started to blur as she desperately tried to get to her feet, she noticed a castle in the clearing and began to run towards it. She was followed by two of the men, who began to run behind her, she arrived at the main door, which was open and proceeded down a long corridor. She appeared to know where she was going and entered a room; blood began to trickle down her arm as she gazed at a portrait oil painting of a man. She noticed a strange thing about the painting as the man in the portrait began to look as if he was moving and the background appeared transparent. She put her hand on the picture and her hand seemed to blend into it, so she withdrew her hand in shock, the out of curiosity she placed her hand in a little further. At that moment she heard voices and noticing the blood dripping from her fingers put the rest of her body through the picture. She found herself rushing through some kind of wind tunnel with swirls of light travelling around her pushing her forward leading through another picture. She eventually reached the other end of her journey and landed onto the floor on top of a man.

After wrestling with him, she managed to break free and he stood to his feet and offered a hand to help her to her feet. She slapped his hand and managed to stand by herself looking very annoyed by his actions.

"Get off me and stay away from me" She shouted

"Hey calm down" He replied looking around him "I was only trying to help"

"How did you get on me like that?" She asked

"Well I was admiring that picture" He pointed to the picture "When you jumped out of it and you fell on top of me just to get things in perspective".

"Oh you mean that picture I feel really odd" She said holding her head

"What's wrong?" He said touching her on the arm

"Don't touch me" She said nervously "I warn you I bite"

"I am not going to harm you, I just want to help" He insisted

"So who are you and where the hell am I?" She asked

"I am Jack Clarke and this is an art gallery" Jack said "Don't you know where you are?" He said bewildered by her strange manner.

"I am Siena, I was being chased in a forest and ran into a castle, a weird thing happened, I seemed to enter a picture and landed here. Siena explained

"Wherever here is" She said looking round the room with her green eyes that seemed to sparkle in the light.

"Well you're here now" Jack replied "In the twenty first century"

"What?" Siena was shocked "I am in the future"

"Yes you look as if you have come from medieval times eleventh century maybe, come let's get some air" Jack said leading Siena to the exit

"Seventh century under the reign of King Charles" Siena replied

"The English civil war" Jack said with surprise

"There is a civil war in England?" Siena asked

"I take it hasn't happened yet" Jack thinking he had better not mention that the King was beheaded.

"So this is the future no wonder things seem strange" Siena said looking at the furniture and odd clothes being worn.

Suddenly Siena saw daylight and froze like a statue by the door

"I think I will stay inside for a while" Siena said hesitating and shaking like a leaf.

"Ok let's get a drink in the canteen" Jack suggested

"That sounds good to me" Siena said relieved

They walked towards the canteen passing art displays such as pictures, statues and other strange shaped objects. Siena was bewildered by the displays and appeared disorientated by her surroundings. The clothes that people were wearing also fascinated her; she continued to hold her head sitting at a table.

"So who was chasing you? Jack asked

"Chasing me" Siena thought for a moment "Oh a few strange men with clubs annoyed about something" Siena said not wanting to elaborate and avoiding eye contact.

"Oh that explains a lot" Jack said sarcastically "people can be so touchy"

"Look I have to get back" Siena said worried

"Back where" Jack asked

"Back home of course"

"But you're in danger there" Jack said concerned

"I am not safe here either, I can't explain it but believe me I am" Siena said trembling. "My master would be angry if I don't go back"

"Listen! You don't recognise objects and outside scares you so I can only conclude that you are from the past and that you entered some sort of time portal". Jack said, "I can't think of any other explanation".

"You're speaking nonsense I only know I have to return home" Siena insisted

"Well we need to get back to the picture" Jack explained. "There lies the answer to problems you have been facing".

"You have a master, so does that make you a slave?" Jack said confused

"Sort of we are all slaves and serve one master" Siena tried to explain

"Not me I am a free agent" jack insisted "No one rules me"

They finished their drinks and went back to the area where the picture was being displayed. No one was in the area and the gallery was about to close Siena saw the picture but it didn't seem the same, she went to touch it placing her hand on the canvas but nothing happened. She tried again and suddenly heard shouting from a distance as a guard approached them.

"It seems different somehow" Siena said gazing at it.

"In what way? Jack asked

"It is no longer alive" Siena said tapping it "Just a painting nothing more"

"Don't touch the paintings they are valuable" The guard said

"Sorry" Jack said "I was examining the texture"

"What do I do now?" Siena asked, "I am stuck here in the wrong time".

"I have an idea" Jack said leading her back to the exit.

It was dark outside but it was very busy with a lot of traffic, Jack hailed a taxi and gave the driver his address. When they entered the taxi Siena began to stare at him, she had not really realised how handsome he was with his blue eyes and fair hair, he was clean-shaven and had a prominent chin. He was looking back at her trying to see beyond a dirty face and frowning expression she had removed her hood revealing her long black hair and unusual fringe. She was suddenly startled by a car horn and jumped, then the sound of ambulance sirens, which raced past her window at great speed. She held on to Jacks arm and he could feel the tension in her fingers as they dug into him like a claw.

"Your quite safe Siena believe me" Jack said reassuringly

"I wish I could believe that" Siena said staring out into the streets fascinated by the neon lights, which lit up the area around them.

Jack could feel Siena's heart beating next to him as she drew ever closer to his side, he put his arm around her to reassure her and she began to relax.

They finally reached their destination the taxi stopped outside his apartment, Jack paid the fair and they walked out into the cold dark street. Jack escorted Siena to the apartment block and tried to enter discretely; unfortunately he was stopped by a friend.

Pier was a French friend who had spent a lot of time with Jack during his college days, he was dark skinned and smelt of garlic as Siena was introduced to him she ran into the building. Siena had also noticed a crucifix around his neck, Pier was a catholic and usually wore a rosary. But he had left France with a little Sinicism in mind, his exposure to the wider world made him think that the increased presence of evil was more than enough reason to doubt the existence of any god. The people that professed to be good and such as priests and nuns appeared to have a bad reputation, the exposure of child abuse or forms of fornication turned a lot of people against them. Jack said goodbye to Pier and walked over to a frightened Siena, He never spoke to her but led her into his apartment.

Siena looked around the room then began to yawn and lay on the settee, she soon drifted off to sleep. Jack found a blanket and placed it over her, he then took the phone off the receiver so that she would not be disturbed. He sat close by admiring her beautiful face; he couldn't help feeling that there was more to her than she admitted. He reflected back on his first encounter of her as she jumped out of the picture, from the time portal and falling onto him.

Once she had woken up Jack showed her how to operate the shower, he then left her to wash herself in private, and she couldn't believe the way the shower worked. Letting the water flow down upon her, he had pointed out the shower gel and shampoo and she seemed to be in the shower for a long time. When she came out she was wearing Jacks bathrobe, Jack had washed her clothes and sat watching television. But Siena noticed that he was watching a vampire movie called Van Helsing a vampire slayer. She seemed disturbed by the television alone but worse by the sight of someone killing vampires.

"Oh Siena was everything alright" Jack asked concerned

"Yes I feel a little better now" Siena said smiling "But what is this you are watching"

"Oh I love vampires, but let me turn it off, vampires as if they exist" Jack said turning off the television.

"If you say so" Siena said sitting on the settee "You love vampires seriously?"

"Yes but I know they are not real of course" Jack said confident that he was right.

"Really" Siena said looking into his eyes "Why do you say that?"

"Everybody knows it all began as a story about Dracula" Jack continued

"What if you saw one for yourself, face to face?"

"Well, then I would believe" Jack admitted

Jack dealt with Siena's wounded arm using a bowl of warm water antiseptic and a clean towel.

"This wound needs attention, you really need to go to hospital" Jack advised

"No not that, I will be ok" Siena replied "Really I just to rest"

"But you look pale, you must have lost a lot of blood, you may need a blood transfusion" Jack said concerned "You know they give you blood"

"I said I am alright, its nothing I have had worse" Siena said bluntly "Wait did you say they give you blood?"

"Then let me dress it" Jack said opening a dressing pack "My ex-girlfriend used to be a nurse" Jack explained. "You are definitely not from here are you?"

"I see well I am honestly alright so just dress it please" Siena insisted "And no I am not from here so stop talking about things I don't understand like blood transfusions."

Jack finished cleaning and dressing her arm and then put the remainder of the first aid kit away in the cupboard and returned to sit beside Siena.

"I looked up the seventeenth century on computer and found the castle you were referring to" Jack pointed to the monitor "There it is near the woods"

Meanwhile as they were having their discussion vampires were entering the time portal in search of Siena, they were sent by their master Vermont. He was determined to find Siena and return her to his family.

Siena kept yawning and nodding off to sleep with her legs elevated and her head on the arm of the chair, she looked so fresh and clean, with her hair shining and flowing down with her soft pale skin gleaming. Jack was admiring her as she slept; she had just come into his life and he considered himself very lucky to have her in his home. He was hoping that they would get together as a couple but he was not lucky with women and he had the feeling that she would suddenly disappear probably back through the time portal.

Siena awoke again and looked across at Jack her eyes were glazed and she seemed pale as if she was suffering from anaemia.

"Can I offer you food and a drink?" Jack said concerned

"Yes please" Siena said politely.

Jack went into the kitchen and returned with sandwiches cut and placed neatly on a plate went back out and returned with two mugs of tea with sugar and milk. She put two heaped spoonfuls of sugar in her mug and a tiny drop of milk, she stirred it slowly and took a sip from the mug. They had a brief conversation about Jacks job in a hospital kitchen just around the corner. Then Siena explained about the place she lived in, but seemed to be holding a lot of information back particularly about her family. Jack had not noticed, but Siena had no reflection in the mirror, that evening Pier visited Jack but Siena avoided him acting quite rudely. But Siena was trying to protect herself and avoid the crucifix that he wore around his neck, anything that would harm or destroy her, or even expose her as a vampire.

That night Jack offered to sleep on the settee while Siena slept on the bed, Siena reluctantly accepted. That night the moon was full and the sky was clear and full of stars Siena looked out through the window watching the wind blowing the trees. Siena opened the window and then crept towards the door and watched Jack sleeping, she then returned to the window and jumped out onto a tree and down to the street. She came to an alley where a woman was walking alone, suddenly she was joined by two men as they got closer one of them grabbed her the other man then spoke to her.

"Now just do as we say and you wont get hurt" He said in a deep gravely voice

She began to struggle and scream so one of the men slapped her knocking her to the ground. The other began to pull down his trousers while the other man held her; she continued to struggle as he attempted to remove her clothes.

Siena raced forward and knocked the man over with his trousers down his ankles, she had changed into a vampire and seemed to have incredible strength. She hit the other man and knocked him into a wall, he fell down the brickwork with his head bleeding.

"Go run away" Siena said but the woman didn't need telling she ran from the alley with great speed.

Siena walked back to the man who was conscious and pulling up his trousers, she grabbed him and held him tightly. Her eyes began stare at him, putting him into a trance.

"Let's make love" Siena said smiling

"Wow ok" He replied excitedly

Siena kissed his neck and then pierced his skin with her fangs and began sucking the blood from his body until he was drain of life and his limp body fell to the ground. She wiped her bloody mouth and then walked over to the unconscious man and did the same to him, sucked his blood and left him dead in the alley.

Siena had begun to feel better and wandered back to the apartment entering it via the window as she did earlier. She got undressed and settled into bed feeling that she could rest comfortably knowing that she had received her life sustenance, human blood.

The next morning Siena was fast asleep and Jack was in the shower, he had switched on the television and the news was on. The two bodies discovered in the alley were the main feature, but also Pier had been murdered in the same way.

The question was did Siena murder Pier because he too had two puncture marks in his neck, in the same way that Siena had killed the two men. The news report repeated throughout the day, Jack saw it later as he returned from work later that day. He avoided disturbing Siena knowing that she needed the rest.

He looked in on her sleeping soundly, lying across the bed with her head facing away from the window. He opened the curtains and Siena's back reacted to the sunlight by burning slightly.

"Please shut the curtains my body is sensitive to light, I have some kind of illness that reacts to light" Siena explained

"You never told me" Jack said concerned

Jack offered her a drink in a clear glass, a sort of strawberry cordial drink which she looked at and turned her head away.

"Please take that away from me" She shouted and began waving her hands in the air.

It reminded Siena of blood that she was once given in a goblet by Count Vermont as a form of ritual when she joined the family of vampire.

Siena sat beside Jack listening to him as he discussed the murders; she had tried to show no emotion as he went into graphic detail. She wanted to forget the experience and knew that she would venture out for yet another night, seeking out victims in order to obtain their blood and live another day.

Jack noticed that she seemed disturbed and sat closer to her, she glanced at him and smiled leaning on his arm and resting her head on his shoulder.

"You are very kind to me and a real gentleman" Siena said smiling

"I know how to respect women and as you have come from another time you are naturally bewildered by what you see and hear". Jack explained

"But you can teach me and show me your world" Siena said looking into his eyes

"Yes I can but so much has changed since your time, cars, planes and telephones" Jack said trying to imagine what she was thinking.

"Inventions and scary machines that are so noisy" Siena had not taken her eyes off Jack, she began to feel a tingle down her spine and the hair stood up at the back of her neck.

Jack drew ever closer to her, looking into her green eyes and feeling strange in her presence. It was like something he had never felt before and began to relax he began to drift off to sleep. At this point Siena began to kiss him on the lips and his neck, then she suddenly changed and her fangs appeared. She leapt off the settee and onto the floor, she had realised what she had done by hypnotising Jack and trying to bite his neck, fortunately she managed to stop herself in time.

Jack awoke from his trance and saw Siena sat on the floor; she had a suspicious look on her face and appeared nervous.

"What has just happened to me?" Jack asked her

"I think you fainted" Siena said in response "You were sat with me and made me jump when you suddenly woke up" Siena hoped that he was convinced by her explanation.

Jack seemed to accept her explanation and never mentioned the situation again. Siena was more aware of her actions after this time and the next time they were close was not due to her but Jack who made advances to her. Jack had been going out to work during the day and with Siena at night, Siena continued to sneak out and find her own blood bank choosing people who were in her eyes wicked or deviant souls. This was her justification for taking draining their blood and ending their life the only way a vampire knows feeding off humans and surviving leaving a blood trail.

Jack cuddled up to Siena and put his arm around her, Siena felt uneasy, as she was afraid of what she might do to him. Jack began to kiss her on the lips and she felt her heart begin to beat faster, her desire for him was become too great to resist and she kissed him back. A rush of passion overcome them both and they were soon in the throws of making love, items of clothing were removed they were both wild as they seemed to tear at each others clothes until they were naked. They headed for the bedroom and continued making love, neither relented as they went from the bedroom into the shower. Their naked flesh became entwined as the water from the shower trickled gently down their body and the steam from the water misted the glass cubical.

The months passed by and they lived the same way with Jack working at the hospital and coming home to a special lady and Siena at home cleaning the apartment and cooking delicious meals. Life seemed perfect for a while, but Siena continued to sleep part of the day and went out at night for her usual feast. Jack explained about Pier's death to Siena.

Pierre was walking past the forest when he heard a female voice coming from the trees, he followed the voice into the thick of the forest. When he stopped he was met by a woman who he couldn't see properly, she managed to hypnotise him before attacking him sinking her fangs into his neck and draining the blood from him. It must have been like being attacked by a savage animal.

But the vampire had to survive and the blood was keeping her alive, however what Siena failed to realise was that she was not alone, the time portal had invited others through and Tom the vampire slayer had followed her through the time portal along with others namely vampires.

Siena walked through the woods, she reached a stream and crossed an old wooden bridge that she recognised from her past. She looked down into the stream and saw her mother's face in the water as if she was really there.

"Mother help me, show me the way I am so lost, I have met a man called Jack and I want to live with him forever, I don't want to live alone as a vampire, living off other humans".

"My child I died here as you know, killed by slayers, you must choose your own course I miss you too", She said "You have to either stay here or return home to your own time, only you can choose what direction to take." With those words she faded away.

"Mother don't go please" Siena pleaded put her mother was gone.

INTO THE DARKNESS

Yet again it was a full moon Siena laid beside Jack she was feeling particularly weak and looked very pale, she looked at Jacks naked neck and suddenly her fangs appeared and her eyes became wild staring at her victims flesh. As she approached him slowly and breathed cold air on his neck, he suddenly awoke and turned his head towards her. Then looked in horror as she was still trying to bite his neck and suck his blood.

"Oh my god!" Jack shouted, "You're a vampire, you are actually a vampire, I have been sleeping with a vampire"

Jack pushed her away and she fell off the bed, she tried to get up but Jack pointed to her angrily and she stayed on the floor.

"I have been sleeping with a vampire, its all coming clear to me now, Pier had eaten garlic and he had a crucifix, so you avoided him, tell me did you kill him?"

"No I didn't" Siena said starting to change back to human form. "But then other vampires could have travelled through the picture as I did"

"You mean the time portal, so there are more like you?" Jack said worried

"And what about that vampire movie, you knew you were a vampire when we were watching it and said nothing" Jack began shaking his head "You were going to bite me and drain me of my blood".

"I know I'm sorry" Siena said with her head bowed "I wanted you to be like me and live forever".

"Well you might have warned me"

"It's not exactly what you bring into a conversation" Siena said upset "Oh by the way I am a vampire"

"Oh I see you're sorry that helps until I sleep again and you actually bite me". Jack said upset.

"For god sake I didn't plan to be a vampire, I didn't wake one morning and say I want to be a vampire or seek Count Vermont and say make me a vampire" Siena said angrily. "It's a curse not a pleasure"

"So how did it happen?" Jack asked

"I was walking in the woods one night when I heard the breaking of branches I ran further in to the wood and came out in a clearing. I began to run and was suddenly surrounded by bats that turned into vampires; two of them grabbed me and took me to the castle Vermont where I met the Count. He put me in some kind of trance and then bit my neck draining my blood, then he did a very odd thing he sent blood back into my body which brought me back from death making me a vampire. I then had to rely on him to keep me alive showing me how to take blood and survive in my present state" Siena explained.

"But it all began long before that night, for as a child my sister Catherine and I would go to bed and our father used to tell us stories about vampires, witches and werewolves. He was so knowledgeable about goblins and other creatures and told convincing tales of many things as if he had experienced them himself. We would sit in our candle lit bedroom watching the flickering of the light and observing the hot wax melting gently like tear drops down the candle. We imagined the creatures that my father mimicked so well, the sound of an owl hooting or the cry of a wolf. He told of vampire slayers like John Stokes, the best slayer of his time who would hunt down vampires and werewolves alike, killing them with stakes or silver bullets according to their kind. Pity the day that those devilish creatures ventured through the forest, when Stokes was around, leading his huntsmen searching in the darkness for their prey. Hunting witches was a common thing of our day any poor old hag was marked for trial and execution, tortured and kept awake in order to confess their sins and admit to their divination. Sorcery and magic would be committed though never truly proven and yet some poor wretch had to die, no one who was accused was ever set free. My father used to go out at night, while my mother stayed at home sitting by an open fire and resting in a rocking chair. I would pretend to be asleep and then as I got older I would venture out through the window and follow my father. It was at this time that I discovered his secret, for he was none other than the said John Stokes they spoke of assuming the name in order to strike fear into those he planned to slay. He spoke to his group and advised that they should stay close and not venture off alone, he warned of the dangers of trying to tackle the enemy alone. Strong are their powers and swift to take you off and kill you or worse make you one of their own, an undead creature or a person who is neither dead nor alive, living in perpetual darkness. Here you stand with just the light of the full moon to guide you, with the blood of man keeping you alive. Woe be you if you live this way amongst the demons and cursed for all time. When I was out following one night that's when I was grabbed but I had been seeing a man in the forest who I considered gentle and kind. His name was Matthew a farmer from a neighbouring village, a hard working young man so quiet and shy. He was waiting for me in the forest one night when he was taken by two female vampires called Emma and Lara they teased him because he was shy before feasting on his blood. Then another female vampire called Miranda made him her own by giving of her blood in his neck, he was a vampire and a slave to Count Vermont. When I became a vampire I journeyed with him in the woods, my father appeared and was shocked to see that I had changed; he disowned me and lifted his bow to kill me. Matthew noticed what was happening and jumped in front of me, he was killed by the missile that was shot from the bow and immediately disintegrated. I escaped on this occasion I ran and ran until I reached the castle and found the picture, or as you call it the time portal, I entered it and met you.

"That's quite a story" Jack said astonished

"You don't believe me?" Siena said sadly

"Yes I do but I must confess it's a lot to take in and we need to get help for you" Jack said concerned

"Who is going to help a blood sucking vampire?" Siena said

"Have you tried asking God?" Jack said confident that he had the answer to her dilemma.

"God? He helps good people not people like me" Siena became tearful

"Why don't you go to church and ask him, he is merciful and kind" Jack said trying to reason with her.

"If I enter the house of god I will die, I cannot even enter the doorway" Siena said becoming agitated

"Stop! My theory is this, if you are to be helped then you will be protected God will see the sincerity in your heart and help you". Jack felt that his explanation was enough to convince her to enter the church.

"Well what have I got to lose, I could risk being destroyed in church or by Tom the vampire slayer" Siena thought for a moment "Alright I will do it".

That evening Siena entered the graveyard and began walking up the pathway towards the church, suddenly she was startled by the voice of a woman.

"Are you going somewhere Siena?" Miranda's voice was heard clearly by Siena

Siena turned around and saw a blonde haired woman floating above her head, when she turned back two other women with darker hair stood in front of her. "We have been searching for you" Lara said with a hiss.

"Yes you have been hiding from us" Emma said floating in front of her.

"I stumbled into this picture and found myself here" Siena said trying to get past them "I never wanted to be here"

"My dear you must come with us to the master" Miranda said blocking her way.

"Yes the master is angry with you, you have disappointed him" Lara said also blocking her way.

"Come let's go" Miranda insisted

During the scuffle an arrow was fired into the air and hit the Miranda in the chest, she immediately disintegrated this was followed by another arrow that narrowly missed Emma. Siena ducked behind a gravestone and Lara flew away from Siena narrowly dodging arrows.

Siena entered the church aware that Tom the slayer was watching her from a distance, but she was hoping that he wouldn't follow her. He seemed surprised that she was entering a church and stopped by a tree waiting for her to reappear. But Siena walked towards the alter and tried to look at the cross in front of her, she gazed into the eyes of the statue of Mary holding Jesus in her arms. Tears filled her eyes and she fell to her knees, she then sobbed for a while then began speaking in a low voice.

"God please help me I know that I have done bad things and even caused deaths, I am cursed as a vampire and want to be human again" Siena paused and looked through the gaps in her fingers "I haven't disintegrated so I presume that you have heard my prayer and considering it".

At that moment she heard a voice coming from behind her

"Siena" came a soft female voice "Don't be afraid"

Siena turned to see an image appear it was an angel wearing a white dress and carrying a key, which was tied to a sash and hung down from her neck to her thigh.

"I am Faith, I am a guardian angel and have a message from God" Faith said sincerely.

"An angel but why are you here are you going to kill me?" Siena said concerned

"No I am here to help you, God is merciful and wants to help you, if you are prepared to help yourself, are you willing to do this and put your faith in god?" Faith asked.

"Yes of course, so what do I do?" Siena said eagerly

"Then you must perform a number of tasks to prove yourself worthy" Faith continued "You need to go back in time to where you became a vampire, you then need to collect a series of objects and take them to the castle Vermont the final object is worn by Count Vermont himself and this is a pendant to take this from him he must die and you will rid the land of evil". Faith said

"So about these other objects where do I find them?" Siena asked

"One will lead to another and each one will introduce you to someone who needs help and you will provide that help as part of your task". Faith explained.

"But what about me wont I need help in order to aid others?" Siena asked

"You must promise not to take blood from others and not kill anyone but the evil ones, you will be helped but you must have Faith in God". Faith said touching her wrist

"But I am a vampire I take blood because I would die without it" Siena said concerned.

"Look at your wrist Siena" Faith said pointing to a shining bracelet

"What's this" Siena asked

"This will prevent you from taking blood and keep you alive, never remove it this will protect you" Faith explained "Try to divert your mind from evil thoughts look only to good things and what is right".

"Thank you" then thought for a moment "Can Jack come with me?" Siena asked

"It has already been arranged my friend Harmony has visited him" Faith said "May God bless you and have a safe journey" With those words Faith vanished.

At that moment Tom the slayer entered the church and ran towards her, he knocked her to the ground and pulled a stake from his bag. Siena held her arm up in order to protect her and the glow from the bracelet shone into Toms eyes, he yelled out and dropped the stake and scrambled to find it.

At that moment Jack entered the church, he ran up to Tom and disarmed him.

"Siena I was visited by an angel called Harmony and she told me what I need to do in order to help you. She told me everything about you becoming human and what is required, I am coming with you, I want to help you"

"You have helped me Jack" Siena insisted

"I know but I don't want to lose you" Jack said holding her "I want to help you defeat the evil ones.

"Come with me because I feel the same, I want you close by my side" Siena said

"Tom we need your help in order to find Count Vermont, are you with us?" jack asked

"Tom help me become human again lets destroy the evil that has cursed our people" Siena said pleading with him

"I am with you what do we do?" Tom asked

"Go to the gallery and enter the time portal" Jack suggested

"Exactly we must return home Tom" Siena said.

"I am ready to face the evil of the dark world" Tom said positively

The three arrived at the gallery hoping to find the time portal; they searched for the picture that Jack would recognise, to his delight the portrait of a lady appeared. But it seemed just like the other paintings stunning and attractive, with nothing special to tell them that this was a time portal. It had no depth and looked nothing like the painting that Siena had came from and fell on Jack. Desperately they waited for the picture to change; meanwhile the security guards were ushering people out of the gallery. One guard approached them looking very official and determined to close the gallery on time.

"We are about to close" He said in a stern manner

"Can I ask you something about this painting?" Jack said diverting him away from the others.

"Yes of course it was imported from Germany, it was originally the property of Count Vermont said to have been a vampire" The security officer said pleased to provide Jack with the information "The painting is said to be enchanted and holds many secrets, obviously this is ridiculous just like the legend of vampires"

"Of course" Jack replied watching Siena and Tom vanish into the picture behind the guard.

Siena landed in the same room where she began her journey through time, she looked at the portrait watching Tom appear. It seemed a long time before Jack arrived, he fell to the ground and seemed dazed lying on the floor, both Siena and Tom helped him up.

"Welcome to Crompton castle" Siena said

"So this is it, the castle where you came from" Jack said holding his head

"Are you alright?" Tom asked

"Yes I had to lose the guard before following you, he took some losing believe me". Jack said looking back at the picture.

"I think we ought to go before anyone sees us" Tom said opening the door and stepping into the corridor.

They walked outside looking for the right direction to find the giant Fargo who would help them find Laura the witch.

Fargo was not difficult to find sitting on a rock, he was an eight-foot man with a brown beard, muscular body with long hair tied back in a pony tail. He had a fat broken nose and a scar on his chin; he appeared to have been involved in battle previously.

They approached Fargo confident that he would greet them with open arms and willingly help them. But the giant seemed hostile and defensive and resented Siena being there and wanting his help, he didn't trust her suspecting that she might lead them into a trap when they arrived at Castle Vermont if not before.

"You must be Fargo" Siena said offering to shake his hand

"I am" Said Fargo refusing to shake her hand "I have something for you"

"A red stone, perhaps a ruby" Siena said realising that he didn't trust her.

"Yes a ruby representing the blood of Vermont" Fargo said looking at the other two men. "It also represents the blood spilt on this land.

"Oh yes this is Jack and Tom they are helping us" Siena said

"We travel tomorrow you can stay in my cave behind those trees" Fargo said

"It is surrounded by garlic to ward away the vampires" Fargo looked at Siena and back at the trees covering the cave "But how will you enter the cave?"

"I have a protective bracelet which is helping me to survive at present" Siena explained, "Providing I do well I will be protected"

"Then its up to you to avoid evil and follow to path to goodness" Fargo said sincerely.

"Yes I must, I know this" Siena said

They entered the cave and Fargo found an area for them to sleep, the cave was well lit with burning torches every few yards. The walls were decorated with paintings of birds and wild animals; a book lay on a table near by written on the cover were the words 'best poems'. The floor seemed gritty and elements of sand were present indicating the presence of the coast, like a sandy beach.

"Are you hungry?" Fargo asked

"A little" Jack admitted

"Then lets feast my friends" Fargo said uncovering food on a table

Siena didn't eat much and became very pale and looking very tired

"I think I will just rest if you don't mind" Siena said walking towards the bedded area.

Fargo watched her leave the area and looked at the others in disbelief

"I don't trust her, she may be protected but she's still a vampire" Fargo said

"She is ok, I have been with her for a while and I was safe" Jack said looking at them both.

They spoke for a while then settled to bed, but during the night Siena was approached and the person concerned had a stake in his hand. He pressed it against her chest and attempted to hammer it into her chest with a wooden mallet. Suddenly Jack jumped in the way and got injured from the stake that pieced him in his side.

"Fargo stop it now!" Tom shouted, "Trust us she is of no danger to you"

"You maniac you nearly killed her" Jack said with his side bleeding

Siena hugged him then saw the blood "Help him Tom please"

Siena then turned to Fargo and spoke to him "Fargo let me tell you something, I have come here to defeat evil, to change my life and with the will of God become human again" Siena said angrily "Destroy me and you will continue to see people die.

"I will not try to harm you again, I promise" Fargo said ashamed of himself

"I want to be your friend and for us all to work together and destroy Vermont and his vampires" Siena said putting her hand out in friendship.

Fargo shuck her by the hand "I am sorry" He said sincerely.

"It's alright now lets help Jack" Siena said going back to Jack

"He is fine the stake just caught the skin" Tom explained

They all rested and the next morning Tom asked for weapons to protect themselves from Count Vermont's followers, Fargo showed them weapons crossbows with deadly arrows powerful enough to kill the enemy.

"Crossbows and other weapons" Fargo said

"A complete arsenal for us all" Tom said happily

"Well don't miss and hit me" Siena said jokingly

"I will watch out for you Siena after all you have to kill Count Vermont" Tom said discussed and disappointed with Fargo.

They went in search of Laura the white witch; Fargo knew exactly where to find her and seemed happy to lead the way.

LAURA THE WITCH

They saw the cave amongst the trees and bushes; they followed a small path towards it. Once inside they were taken by surprise as they saw all kinds of treasures collected from various places that Laura had visited. A picture of Laura was hung on the wall for all to see, that is the people she would normally invite to eat with her. Laura was a beautiful woman with gold blonde hair, pointed ears and glowing white teeth. She had a pale complexion and light blue eyes, to say she was a witch she was not the type that Jack had read about from books. He imagined an old hag stirring a caldron of dead bats and toads, possibly a broomstick and dolls that would simulate someone she despised with pins stuck in their bodies in order to harm them.

"This is no witches place" Jack said almost disappointed

"Not all witches are dark and sinister, some are good witches" Siena said

"I have never heard of a good witch" Jack said confused

"Perhaps we should go" Fargo said concerned

At that moment Laura appeared with her golden hair and a long pastel green coloured dress, she had blue eyes and her long hair was platted and styled, she had pointed ears and it looked as if she had a tiara on her head. She seemed to swoop down to them from above and was displeased at their presence.

"Who are you and why have you entered my home uninvited? Laura asked

"I am Siena I have been sent to you from the future a guardian angel Faith sent me to you" Siena explained.

"Then you are the one who is going to rid this world of evil?" Laura asked.

"Yes I guess I am" Siena said confidently "And you are Laura the witch that will help me".

"I have something for you" Laura looked in a treasure chest and produced a bracelet for her other wrist, which she put on her and kissed it.

"This will protect you from the vampires and from evil" Laura said "But never remove it until the evil has been destroyed".

"Are you not going to travel with us?" Siena asked

"No but I will be observing you and with you in spirit" Laura said

"So, which way do we go now?" Jack asked

"The home of Lily the child" Tom said

"Yes she is just over that hill my dear" Laura said pointing outside the cave.

"Thank you Laura" Siena said

"Please stay for tea, share my table" Laura said making a table appear.

On the table was an array of fine food and drinks, it was like a royal banquet fit for a King or Queen. A roast chicken stood freshly cooked in the centre of the table, garnished with sauce and surrounded by roast potatoes. This was accompanied by a selection of cooked vegetables and other savoury delights.

Help yourself to what you desire my friends and please leave nothing to spoil, for all is edible and will fill you for your journey. Siena noticed the goblets of berry juice and her mind drifted back to Vermont's blood ceremony, she visualised the other vampires drinking blood and killing some of their victims.

Everyone ate the food and drank the various juices that were on offer, nothing was wasted but a few heads began to droop as they were tired after their journey to Laura's cave. So they rested and Laura watched over them so that all could sleep through the night.

The next day each of them prepared for their long journey ahead, Laura was resting while they all washed and ate breakfast. Laura had a nice area for them to wash in private further inside the cave, but in safe proximity in case of trouble. By the time Laura awoke they were all ready to go, Tom was the first to get ready and stood waiting for the others.

"Good luck I hope you do well" Laura said smiling

Siena couldn't help admitting that she was disappointed that Laura would not be with them, if for nothing else she could have provided her with moral support and female companionship. But Laura had her own reasons not to join them and was reluctant to share them with Siena or her friends.

So Siena and her companions continued on their arduous journey travelling over the hillside in search of Lily. Lily was running around a garden beside an old cottage, she was a small nine year old girl with ginger wavy hair with pointed ears and blue eyes; she had a round face and wore a yellow patterned dress. She saw Siena and smiled sweetly standing still near a tree, she had a lovely smile, and her ginger hair was blowing about in the wind

"She too had pointed ears like a pixie" Jack commented "This is like a fairy tale"

"Hello she said sweetly I am Lily" She said politely "She said giggling at Jack's remark"

"I am Siena" Siena replied, "This is Jack, Tom and Fargo"

"I have something for you Siena" Lily said running into the house

"Pixie ears, really Jack" Siena remarked "That is so normal here"

Lily returned with a ring

"This belonged to my mother who was killed by vampires a while ago, you must put it on your finger" Lily explained "It will guide you to the castle Vermont"

"Thank you Lily are you joining us?" Siena asked

"No she cant it's too dangerous" Tom said

"I am coming, please Siena I won't be any trouble and I can help cook for you" Lily said.

"I want her with me" Siena insisted "She will be safe with us".

"Well you will have to protect her yourself" Tom said

"I don't mind get your things together Lily" Siena said "I will come in the house with you" Siena said holding her hand and leading her inside.

Inside the cottage the furniture was mostly made of wood and at back of the cottage was a small but quaint kitchen. Lily led Siena up the stairs she took her into a small room and packed a small rucksack with some of her clothes. Then she took a small cuddly bear and stuffed it in as deep as she could so that only the head was showing.

"I am ready" Lily said smiling and placing a small book in her bag

"Listen Lily it is going to be dangerous, I wouldn't like anything to happen to you, and don't you have any family?" Siena asked concerned

"No one at all I have had to live alone" Lily said "My book keeps me company"

"Very well let's go Lily" Siena said leading the way down the stairs and outside to join the others.

They walked across a bridge entering a forest, Siena was curious to know what was written in the book that fascinated Lily but she never asked.

They camped in the forest overnight Lily began to sing like a nightingale, her voice was soft and melodically they all listened to her intently as she sang of happy times. They all had supper and discussed their journey. Then Lily began to read her book out loud

"The poet writes his final line about things that couldn't be; he lives his life in solitude with things you cannot see. Hidden away in a fortress tower so high upon a hill, lost within his solitude with dreams he could not fulfil". Lily paused to observe her audience reaction then continued. "A trapped talent within a cell within his mind fresh thoughts do dwell, a man that is trapped within his mind, here the lost poet may dwell. Always thinking about the people you create, when your asleep fresh thoughts you motivate. Like a person within a person or fictitious people within a dream and nightmares make you awake and no one will here you scream".

"That's really intense" Jack said looking at the others "Deep and meaningful"

"Is that from your own mind?" Siena asked

"It came to me" Lily said turning the page "May I read on?"

"Of course" Fargo said smiling "Tell us more".

"So daylight is over and darkness will end the day, the candles burn so low and you must lose your way, and just as the hot sun melts the snow you must leave this life and go" she recited the poem then sang the final part. "The poet write his final line about things that could not be, the poet write his final line for me".

They all clapped and then all kissed and hugged her; everyone was impressed but thought it was just a poem and not a real event.

"I wonder how such a wonderful poem and song came to you" Siena said hugging her.

Soon after the discourse about the poetry they went to sleep, all but Tom who took the first watch sitting on the ground with his crossbow firmly in his hand

Meanwhile at Vermont's castle the vampires were preparing to do battle with anyone who was protecting Siena, each of the vampires were eager to avenge their own kind and blamed Siena for abandoning them. But they wanted Siena alive to face Count Vermont and humble herself to her master, to seek forgiveness and be his bride.

"You flock, you servants of evil" Vermont shouted "To you feel my anger, my pain, and my hunger, one of my children has betrayed me" He raised his arms

"Master we are with you" One male vampire said kneeling at his feet.

"Serpious fetch me my cloak" He said looking down on the limp creature disfigured by illness

"Yes master" Serpious groined

"Master let me go after Siena and bring her back" Another vampire said as she also sat beneath Vermont.

"My dear Alicia I know you want to avenge your sister Miranda but there is time and you are precious to me" He said putting his hand on her head. "I want Martha and Verity to capture the little girl Lily and then Siena is sure to come".

"I will send Stuart and Serpious to lead my army into attack after midnight and we will have two armies one to divert fire on my people and the other to take the girl. Siena will regret her actions, Lara you have done well to inform me of her plans to destroy me.

It was midnight and the moon was full, the forest was quiet until the first attack took place as a swarm of vampire bats flew over them, followed by flying vampires. It threw everyone into confusion as they watched the bats descend; this was followed by a second attack that was even more intense. Lily was suddenly lifted off the ground by one of the vampires; Tom took aim but was stopped by Fargo.

"Stop! You could hit Lily" Fargo shouted

"But they have taken her" Tom shouted back

"They won't harm her, they want me" Siena said "She is their bargaining tool".

"You promised to keep her safe" Fargo shouted "I might have known a vampire couldn't keep her word".

"Silence Fargo we all let Lily down after all we all said we would protect her" Tom said.

The group were confused after Lily had gone and they were determined to carry on and seek the lost poet in the fortress close by. Lily had dropped her book when she was captured, so at least they could find the lost poet easily.

Fargo had his reason for hating vampires as his wife and two children were killed by vampires, they died horrible deaths and their bodies left in the woods. Fargo threatened to avenge them by killing every vampire who walked the earth, or terrorised the land and satisfied their thirst for blood. Lily had left a clue behind, her book was lying on the ground for all to see.

"Of course that's it" Tom said

"What's wrong Tom?" Siena asked

"The lost poet, I know where he is" Tom said

"So do I" Fargo said pointing to a forest

"Through the forest and hidden away in a fortress tower high upon a hill" Tom said confidently.

"Here the lost poet may dwell" Siena finished his sentence.

"We need to go into the forest" Fargo said.

THE LOST POET

They noticed a fortress tower high upon a hill this is where the lost poet was said to dwell according to the poem. As they approached the tower they noticed a small door as they entered it they noticed stone steps that seemed to spiral to the top of the tower. They all went up the steps and arrived at another door, Tom pushed the door open and discovered a large room with a desk, a small table and a bed. On the table were candle sticks, a thick book and a coat hanging at the back of a chair. On the desk were other candlesticks, an open book a quill and ink well. The bed had a cover over it with an interesting pattern on it; in the centre was an embroidered crest.

Suddenly to their astonishment a figure appeared near the desk, it was a man dressed in old medieval clothes; he had long white hair and looked about sixty. He looked directly at Siena and spoke to her in a gentle voice.

"Who do you seek?" He asked

"We seek the lost poet" Siena replied

"Why do you seek him?" He said suspiciously

"He has something for me, I am on a quest to kill count Vermont" Siena said bravely.

"I am the lost poet, my name is John Gilbert Green and this is my home" Green said proudly.

"You live here in the tower?" Siena said looking round

"Yes this is my humble home and here is where I write my poems" Green pointed to his parchment on the desk "I need a quiet place to create my work"

"I just need a quill and I will be on my way, for we have a child to find captured by the Count". Siena said sadly

"I am sorry to here that I am but an image before you and my soul is also captured, I can only say follow your journey to your destination and you will find your child and me" Green said smiling "I sent a message to her it's in the book that you hold in your hand".

With those words he vanished and the quill was in front of her to take to Count Vermont's castle. The lost poet's voice could be still heard even after he had vanished, he was drawing the party to the castle in order to be found and set free. Siena led the partly out of the tower and back into the forest and towards another castle near by where King Robert lived, he was a King without a kingdom.

A KING WITHOUT A KINGDOM

The man sat on the king's throne he seemed sad and lost wearing a hat and no crown, he was of royal by blood but Count Vermont had invaded his kingdom with his vampires. The castle and the village was invaded and the people were either murdered with their bodies drained of blood, some fled to the caves or other places of safety, some were turned into vampires and increased Count Vermont's ever growing army.

Siena and her friend walked towards the castle, small green man appeared holding a long spear. He had long black hair and a fat nose; he had a thick belt around his large waist and spoke with a high voice.

"Who goes there? He said pointing his spear towards them.

"Its Siena and friends, we have come to see the King" Siena said positively.

"You're Siena, the vampire?" He asked

"Yes that's me" Siena said "But I am no longer known as a vampire".

"Siena I know all about you and Laura the witch" He said lowering his spear.

"You know Laura?" Siena asked "Your name means special inspirational empathetic natural beauty and with attributes to many to mention"

"And I am Bramble and yes she is known throughout the kingdom". Bramble said smiling at Siena in a creepy kind of way.

Bramble led them to the King who remained sat on the throne, He sat stroking his beard the party walked towards him and bowed.

"Tut tut, don't bow before me I am no king, see I have no kingdom" He swept his arms in each direction "See no one but us".

"But you are still a King" Siena said

"My kingdom was taken from me" The king stood up and shouted in temper "I am not a king and my kingdom has been scattered in the wind, I have been left to care for myself and the Count lives in luxury with my servants and subjects. So come and laugh at the man who once was a king, I am now but a grain of sand on the beach or desert". King Robert said bitterly.

"Then let us find Count Vermont and destroy his evil only then can we restore your throne and kingdom to what it was" Siena said.

"Yes your highness I am Tom the slayer and I have served you before as blacksmith, Fargo was one of your guards so we have served you and will serve you again I promise". Tom said encouragingly.

"So how did you find me?" The king asked

"Through an angel called Faith and a witch called Laura" Siena explained

"I once condemned Laura as I did the vampires" King Robert said shying.

"And yet you have statues of vampires all the way down the corridors of this castle" Tom said confused.

"What are you talking about I have no statues of vampires" King Robert said frowning.

At that moment the so called statues began to break away from the walls and flying towards the great hall, each detached themselves from the wall assisted by wicked green goblin Bramble who had obviously tricked and ambushed them. They all reached the hall and surrounded Siena and her friends.

"We have come for Siena, you must all surrender or die" One of the vampires said.

"Yes we want only Siena, kill the others" She hissed showing her fangs.

154

Bramble waved his spear about and tried to look menacing, but he just appeared silly in front of his vampire friends.

At that moment Laura appeared and immediately cast a spell on him leaving him in a giant bubble, He was kicking, yelling and trying to break free. As he was their mascot, his capture confused the vampires for a moment. They looked at each other for inspiration and then attacked everyone in sight. Laura stunned each one with her wand while Tom and Siena destroyed them with their crossbows, firing deadly arrows into their hearts. Each one dispersed into dust and disappeared the battle went on for half an hour until all the vampires were destroyed.

"Thank god that's over" Jack said sighing with relief.

"When are we going to be finally free from them vampires" Tom said lowering his crossbow.

"When we destroy Count Vermont" Siena said sweeping back her hair.

"We should rest here tonight" Tom advised.

"Siena are you alright?" Jack asked

"Yes apart from that strange little man" Siena looked at Bramble

"He is of no importance" Tom said

Bramble was removed from the bubble bound with rope and led to the Counts castle; King Robert made peace with Laura and promised that when his kingdom was restored she would become his personal adviser.

Siena and her friends continued their quest, mindful of their mission to free the villagers and kill the enemy, removing the evil from the land. On their journey Fargo was attacked by blood sucking bats while on watch it was his biggest dread and he was saved by Siena and Tom who managed to fight them off. Later on their journey Siena had a snake wrapped around her neck which Fargo destroyed and threw it into a bush. Jacks fear were heights, walking over bridges made him nervous looking down into rivers or rocky areas beneath him, they crossed many to reach the castle. As for Siena she was afraid of the full moon and although she wore the bracelets she was still affected by the desire for blood, she was looking forward to being human again.

"Siena I truly love you" Jack said sincerely

"I love you too" Siena replied kissing Jack on the lips.

"But I fear myself and my desires" Siena looked down

"I don't understand" Jack replied.

"My thirst for blood, sometimes it is hard to fight and being near you makes it worse" Siena sighed and stood to her feet. "Will this nightmare ever end".

"Be patient you are doing well" Jack advised her "Trust in god"

"Faith told me it would be difficult" Siena said looking into Jacks eyes.

"You will get there, reach your goal and we will be together" Jack explained holding her firmly by the arms.

Laura approached them with her long blonde hair flowing and her dress sparkling under the moonlight.

"It's a beautiful night" Laura said

"Yes it is but the moon is full" Siena said pointing upwards

"Be brave Siena and think of the future" Laura said smiling

"I wanted Jack and I to live forever" Siena said

"Who wants to live forever" Laura said looking up at the moon "Not me"

"Not me" Jack said looking into Siena's eyes "definitely not me", Jack then looked across at the moon.

"I desire only one thing, a happy kingdom" Laura said touching them both on the arm "And of course your happiness" Laura smiled and walked away.

THE EVIL OF COUNT VERMONT

After a long hazardous journey through a rough tureen with swamps, reptiles and other dangers, Siena and her friends reached Count Vermont's castle.

From the moment they arrived they could sensed the danger and smelt rotting flesh of human and animal carcasses. Dried blood stains could be clearly seen on the filthy walls and floors, along with dust and cobwebs. The corridors were dimly lit and Tom advised them to use lighted wooden faggots as torches as they moved closer to the hall way.

Eventually they arrived in a large open area with an enormous stairway leading to the upper level with rooms running off in all directions. Suddenly the count stood surrounded by his evil army of vampires they were all assembled ready to attack each of them eager to take the blood from the humans. Laura headed off to find Lily and whoever else they had captured; she went straight towards the dungeons undetected making herself in visible. She used her wand to disarm the guards causing them to collapse in a heap on the floor. Then took the keys from his belt and unlocked the large door to the dungeon, finding many people inside including Lily. However there was no sign of John Gilbert Green better known as the lost poet or his work, Lily said that she had searched for him in the dungeons but to no avail. This would suggest what Siena and Jack suspected that Green the lost poet was dead and what they experienced in the tower was a ghost.

The fighting was in progress when Laura returned; the vampires seemed to be everywhere until Laura cast a spell that drew them more together like a magnet. Count Vermont was fighting Siena, they were kicking and throwing objects at each other. Jack was trying to help but knocked to the ground with the Counts mighty powerful force, he lay holding his head dazed by the blow to the head and winded by a kick to the stomach. Laura drew the other vampire's right in order to finally destroy them. Tom and Fargo were the main vampire slayers although other people joined in finding wooden stakes from broken chairs and other furniture. At last they were winning the battle as the last few vampires turned to dust and vanished. Siena was suddenly cornered by the Count he was about to kill Siena with her own stake when Tom shot an arrow into his heart, he dropped the stake and Siena picked it up. She made sure that she actually killed the Count by plunging the stake into him; she forced it deeply then watched him slowly disintegrate. The vampire leader was finally dead, at that moment the lost poet returned he noticed Lily first then the others. Fargo suddenly raced towards Siena in a rage brandishing a stake.

"There is one vampire left" Fargo shouted.

Tom reacted by shooting an arrow over Fargo's shoulder and Laura shielded Siena with her body, the arrow deflected off the wall. Laura fell to the ground as she had been stabbed in the back and was bleeding, Bramble dropped a spear and with all the confusion he had escaped and headed for the woods. Laura passed away in the arms of Siena her last words were for King Robert.

"Siena help the king restore his kingdom and forgive Fargo because he fears you" She yelled in pain "Burn my body and scatter my ashes beside a rock by the stream" with those words the witch died.

The bell tolled at the church announcing the return of the surviving villagers and the death of Count Vermont and his vampires.

Jack explained to Fargo about Siena becoming human again at that moment Faith appeared.

"God is pleased with you Siena and you can remove the bracelets and return to the church with the items that you collected for you are human again".

After fulfilling Laura's wishes and seeing the Kingdom restored Siena and Jack said their goodbyes and returned through the time portal into the art gallery, the guard was still stood confused by the painting as if they had just left. Siena and Jack acted as if nothing had happened; they were amused at the guards reaction as they appeared.

"How did you do that?" He asked transfixed on the painting.

"Oh it's a special painting isn't it Siena?"

"Very special" Siena replied

Siena and Jack arrived at the church, they put all the items in the font and watched as a glowing light appeared and all items vanished. Siena watched the sunlight shine through the windows of the church and for the first time for a long while was no longer afraid of the daylight for she was indeed human again. The bracelet fell from her wrist and she embraced jack, kissing him tenderly on the lips.

THE
HARRINGTON CURSE

S R SUTTON

1

The Artist's Model

It was a midsummer day in a remote part of Scotland somewhere between Edinburgh and North Berwick near a small village called Aberlady, in a forest a man was walking on a dirt track dressed in a collarless shirt and a pair of brown corduroy trousers. He was carrying a shoulder bag and wore a hat with a brim that covered part of his face. He had a long nose and a small goatee beard, he was fairly young and probably in his late thirties although he looked older due to his appearance and harsh skin. But what was more noticeable was his large staring eyes that appeared menacing at first glance. He travelled along a dirt pathway carrying a shoulder bag and walked over a stone bridge across a stream, towards a group of rocks which were situated by a set of interestingly shaped trees. He then sat on a rock and produced a sketch pad and a set of pencils from his bag and began sketching the trees. He had been drawing for a while when a woman came walking towards him she crossed the bridge and walked up to him. She was wearing a hooded top and a pair of jeans; she removed her hood revealing a beautiful face with gorgeous large green eyes and a radiant smile.

"That's quite amazing," she said admiring his work.

"Why thank you my lady," he said respectfully.

She removed his hat and kissed him on the forehead. "My clever Ralph," she said smiling.

"Why Annabelle be careful that no one sees us together," he said concerned.

"To hell with anyone else, we are all that matters," she said laughing.

"Well you are the lady of the Manor and me a mere artist," Ralph said smiling.

"You mean John, he either abuses me or neglects me, and I don't know which is worse do you?" Annabelle said with a tone of anger in her voice.

"Annabelle my love, you deserve more than that," he said squeezing her hand.

"I have you and that's all I need, you are my true love," she said with sincerity.

"I will love you to my dying breath, you are my angel, my princess, I worship you," he replied.

With that he packed up his equipment and they walked over the bridge and towards his cottage in the woods. The cottage was surrounded by wild flowers and bushes, the cottage roof had red tiles and white walls with leaded windows and a slatted wooden door. They entered the cottage and inside was just as inviting with its wooden furniture and colourful walls and beamed ceilings. They entered the kitchen and Annabelle noticed the crockery in the sink, with dirty pans on the cooker.

"Ralph really, you might wash up occasionally," Annabelle looked at him disgusted.

"Well I am the only one here and I think why bother," he replied shrugging his shoulders.

"That's not the point, have some pride man," she said filling the sink with hot water and washing up liquid.

"Oh come on Annabelle leave it," Ralph said tutting.

But a stubborn Annabelle carried on washing up and ignored his pleas; instead he decided to make a drink for both of them. When they had finished they went into the studio, Annabelle was admiring his work, paintings, sculptures and wood carvings. He could bring anything he did to life with his artistic hands and mind; he was not just an artist but a creator who loved beautiful things. But his favourite subject was Annabelle who he sculptured and drew untiringly. Annabelle watched him preparing his art tools for the day, and then became distracted by an object in the corner of the room covered in a sheet. She looked at the shape for a while and then went to peep underneath grabbing the corner of the sheet with her hand.

"Stop!" came a loud hostile voice.

At that moment Annabelle withdrew her hand and fell backwards, she looked at her hand which was covered in blood. The sight of it caused her to pass out and she fell to the ground with a thud, almost hitting her head on a picture. When she awoke Ralph was cleaning her hand and searching for the wound which was on the thumb of her right hand.

"Annabelle are you alright?" Ralph asked concerned.

"Yes I think so, what happened to me?" she asked.

"You cut your thumb, it needs a plaster or something, let me go to the kitchen and fetch something," Ralph said heading for the kitchen.

As he left Annabelle noticed something moving under the sheet, it was something large and seemed to be very active. Suddenly a head appeared it was a snake, it appeared to have yellow eyes that were looking at her, she then noticed its fanged teeth which could have been what caught her thumb, she was petrified and froze with fear unable to speak. The snake slithered slowly towards her keeping its eyes trained on her and then opened its mouth to devour her.

As it struck out Ralph returned and it vanished as if it never existed, Annabelle passed out again and left Ralph bewildered by her actions. Again she awoke and looked at Ralph wondering if she had dreamt the entire events of the day.

"Annabelle I have dressed your thumb," he said looking at her with concern.

"Ralph what's going on?" Annabelle asked with an angry tone in her voice.

"I don't understand, I just didn't want you to see my surprise for you under that sheet," he said innocently.

"Oh really, a snake is that my surprise?" Annabelle asked.

"Snake?" Ralph said puzzled.

"Oh come on Ralph I know a snake when I see one" she said angrily.

"Mirrors?" Ralph replied.

"Mirrors?" she said puzzled.

"I have got you three mirrors which are under that sheet and I am presently carving the frames," Ralph explained.

Ralph offered her a glass of water and smiled; Annabelle had the drink and sat quietly for a while. She was convinced that Ralph was lying as the snake had appeared and almost killed her, but why did he lie to her, what was he keeping from her and was it necessary to deceive her like that.

Not long after Annabelle left still bewildered by the snake and just wanting to go back to the Stately Manor where her husband John was waiting for her. He seemed very suspicious as to her whereabouts and questioned her repeatedly he refused to give up until she admitted that she had been to Ralph's cottage. John knew that he was an artist and had many models posing for his work. But he suspected that his beautiful wife and Ralph had more going on that just art, so the next time she went there he followed her.

Annabelle met Ralph in the usual place in the woods and they went back to the cottage, Ralph had his hand bandaged up and blood was seeping out of the bandage.

"What have you done?" Annabelle asked concerned.

"Oh it's nothing I slipped with the chisel while carving the frame for those mirrors," Ralph explained.

"Are they finished now?" she asked.

"Yes do you want to see them?" he asked proudly.

"Of course," Annabelle was very excited.

Ralph uncovered them and revealed the most attractive mirrors with their wooden carved frames, three of them each looking similar and with one flaw in them a blood stain not just on one but all three frames and in the same place.

"I tried to hide those stains but they keep reappearing, I don't know why really."

"Is some of it my blood?" Annabelle asked curiously.

"Yes it is, it must be special," Ralph said jokingly.

"So I am special?" she asked.

"Yes," he admitted. "So will you now model for me?" he asked preparing his canvas.

"Yes do you want me to strip?" she asked.

"Yes please, this is for a sculpture of you, for my exhibition," Ralph prepared his paint brushes.

While Annabelle stripped naked and lay across the settee, Ralph studied her form admiring all her curves and posture. Her skin was as smooth as silk and as pale as snow, he stood watching her for a while, and then began to paint on the canvas. Annabelle relaxed but then thought about the last time they made love and began to blush, she was conscious of her body tingling with excitement and she naturally responded, her body welled up inside the more that she thought about Ralph. She tried not to think about him so that she could pose for him comfortably but her body was telling her different and she began to fidget. Ralph picked up on her vibes and he was also responding he dropped the brush on the floor and approached her; she wrapped her body around him and began kissing him passionately. She removed his shirt and kissed his chest then he removed the remainder of his clothes and made love to her. When they had finished, she lay beside him and looked into his eyes.

"I really love you Ralph," Annabelle said with tears in her eyes.

"I love you but what about John?" he asked.

"I hate him, he is cruel and hateful," Annabelle said.

"He will be angry when he finds out," Ralph said looking at the mirrors.

"So let's runaway together, tonight yes tonight," she said also looking at the mirrors.

"Are you sure that's what you want? Think of what you're giving up!" Ralph said concerned.

"I don't care as long as we are together and happy," Annabelle began to cry.

"Alright if that's what you want go and pack and we will go tonight," Ralph agreed.

A short while later Annabelle got dressed and left the cottage little knowing that John was outside; he watched Annabelle disappear into the woods and then entered the cottage.

"Have you forgotten something Annabelle?" Ralph shouted.

He had his back to John and didn't expect to be attacked, as John picked up a chisel from the table and plunged it into his back digging it deep and then twisting it. He pulled it out covered in blood and plunged it in again, he repeated this ten times until Ralph fell to the ground. He then found a pipe belonging to Ralph and lit the tobacco inside, then set fire to other items in the room. Before long the whole room was in flames then he left the cottage and ran out into the woods.

When the fire brigade arrived the studio was burnt to the ground but amazingly the three mirrors were intact the wood wasn't even singed or damaged in any way. No one could explain it. Eventually they went to the Harrington Manor and were displayed on the study wall. The servants witnessed a rough going on between Annabelle and

John over Ralph so everyone soon knew about the affair, but nothing else that had occurred.

The next day Annabelle had a black eye and a bruised right cheek, she remained silent and disappeared shortly after, her clothes were missing so the servants presumed that she had run away somewhere, one maid even thought that Annabelle was pregnant as she had morning sickness, perhaps she had ran away to have the child.

2

Emma's story

John was said to have died a short while after Annabelle went missing, he had cut himself off from the family and hidden the three mirrors away in the attic. Soon after, he was said to have thrown himself out of one of the top windows breaking his neck in the fall. No one could say for sure why he did this as he never discussed what was going on in his head, but the servants had their own tale to tell about how he kept speaking to the mirrors and became tormented by his wife's disappearance. John's suicide meant that according to his will his eldest sister Gladys's, being the next in line in the family would inherit the house, next in line was James and then Emma his eldest niece.

Gladys's moved into the house with Emma as she was her legal guardian, Emma's parents were killed in a car crash a few years before. Emma was already close to Gladys as she used to take her to play with another niece called Chloe in the Harrington household. John believed children should be seen and not heard and so he insisted they played in the nursery or in the garden, but the rest of the house was forbidden to them. But Annabelle used to allow them to join her in the study if John was out on business; they loved Annabelle but hated John. Annabelle wanted children but had a number of miscarriages due to the way John treated her, he wanted an heir to the estate and a figure head but hated children. Emma grew up believing that he was mad, although it was said that she in fact was mentally ill. She was said to be suffering from multiple personality syndrome or as it is known today as dissociate identity disorder, some even question whether or not this really exists in the field of psychiatry.

Gladys introduced herself and Emma to the servants and settled into the Manor, all was quiet for a few years until James came to visit with his wife Margaret. James was very eccentric and Margaret was just a puppet that James controlled, answering to his every whim like she had no mind of her own or at least that's the way she presented herself to the family. Gladys was a real lady just like Annabelle so gracious slim and elegant with an air of superiority which was different to Annabelle. Emma was a little more down to earth and definitely not a lady but could still be gracious when she wanted to. She was slim with long brown hair and big blue eyes, and in her twenties, her cousin Chloe was very much the same but with darker hair. Chloe had a child, a baby boy called Thomas she was also visiting Harrington Hall happy that she was free to roam the house.

James and Margaret were like vultures looking for things to take as they had not appeared since the death of John and knew certain things had a lot of value. Most relatives had come and gone as the will had been read and their were little left for anyone. Gladys even led them to the attic where many old things existed that were never considered nice or decent enough to exist around other parts of the house. This is where the three mirrors were propped against a beam gathering dust.

"I like them," James said admiring the mirrors.

"You may have one of them," Gladys insisted.

"Only one but they are a set," James said indignantly.

"We shall have one and Chloe can have the other," Gladys said sternly.

"But that's not fair," Margaret said looking at James.

"Of course it's fair, we can each keep one and that way they will stay in the family," Gladys looked at James then Margaret with a challenging expression on her face.

Neither questioned her but just picked up one of the mirrors and left the attic, Chloe picked up one of the others and Emma lifted the final mirror. It was fairly light considering the amount of wood round it. She was asked to take it to the study where the three mirrors once hung, Gladys then asked Albert the butler to hang it up above a decorative chair.

That night Emma heard a noise coming from the study, she opened the door slowly entering with caution; she was drawn to the mirror by the sound of a muffled voice and to her horror saw the head of a woman! The features were hidden by a dark mist and it appeared to be a severed head as it moved from left to right as if it was swinging like a pendulum. Emma was transfixed on the object then saw blood dripping down the mirror and onto the floor. She let out a scream which alerted the servants and eventually her aunt Gladys. As they entered Emma was trembling with fear and began crying at the sight that she had seen, she was eventually consoled by her aunt. But when she described the experience and pointed to the floor where the blood had landed, it had disappeared with no trace.

"Come dear you must have imagined it, there are no blood stains and the mirror is like any other mirror, you are tired and probably imagined that you saw something," Gladys said smiling.

"But it was there, a head and strange voice, blood everywhere!" Emma insisted.

"Well it's gone now isn't it," Gladys continued.

Emma went to bed thinking about her experience wondering whether or not she was imagining the image in the mirror or whether she was going mad like her dear Aunt Annabelle. The following morning she rang Chloe and asked her if she had experienced anything strange with her mirror. Chloe said no and so she rang James and received the same response. That night she returned to the study and examined the mirror for herself, she was looking for a mechanism that would cause the mirror to make sounds or visions that would explain what she saw. Eventually she found something near to where the blood stain was that Ralph had tried to remove and cover up. Suddenly she felt something sharp and fell back onto the floor, she began to feel faint and to her surprise saw a big hairy spider crawl out of the mirror and onto the floor. It crept along the floor with its six feet approaching her; she began pulling her body backwards feeling blood dripping from her finger. But she never looked as she didn't want to take her eyes off the spider she had travelled as far back as the door and pressed her spine against it, in a desperate effort to find some kind of object to knock the spider away she searched around with her hands. But nothing was close she quickly looked around then back at the spider, she noticed heavy books close by and suddenly ran for her life to a book shelf and grabbed some books when she turned to grab one the spider disappeared. Lolled into a false sense of security she put the book down only to find the spider crawling up her body from her feet to her stomach. She let out a scream and picked the book up, knocked it off her and dropped the heavy book on top of it with some force. Again a servant came into the room and she pointed to the book, her arm was shaking.

"Look under there, it's a spider, it's as big as a tarantula!" Emma said her voice was quivering.

Albert lifted up the book cautiously; Emma had her eyes hidden by her hands and slowly took them away. But there was nothing under the book the spider was nowhere to be seen, not a trace just like the blood and whatever else she had previously seen. Now she believed that she was going mad who would possibly believe her now! A mirror producing images that quite simply didn't exist. The next day Gladys advised that Emma stay away from the study and get plenty of rest. She rang Chloe with her tale but as expected was not believed; oddly enough James and Margaret visited acting very strangely. Margaret with her red tinted hair and bizarre dress sense like fashion gone wrong and James appearing as if he knew everything about everything in his arrogance.

"Of course you know she's insane," James said then went quiet as Emma appeared in the drawing room.

"As mad as Annabelle," Margaret chipped in.

"What was that?" Emma asked her.

"Oh nothing," Margaret said turning her head to look at James.

"I am not mad!" Emma shouted. "Tell them Aunt."

Gladys shook her head and looked at James and Margaret.

"She is just a little upset in a new home and it wasn't long ago that she lost her parents," Gladys said in her defence.

"Oh God Aunt don't tell them that, they want me locked up in some lunatic asylum, Emma the nut case, the fruit cake, well fuck you!" Emma said and raced out of the door slamming it in her rage.

Emma lay crying in her room when she heard a knock on the door; at first she didn't answer then a knock again this time louder.

"Who is it?" Emma shouted.

"Aunt Gladys" came the reply.

"Are you alone?" Emma asked not wishing to see anyone.

"Yes dear just me, the others have gone," Gladys reassured her.

Gladys sat on her bed and hugged her tightly; Emma got up and put her head on her shoulder.

"Oh Aunt sorry for swearing and losing my temper, but they got me so angry," Emma said sobbing. "Oh child don't blame their stupidity after all you have been hurt so much, now dry your eyes and let's get something to eat," Gladys said standing up.

They went downstairs and headed towards the dining room where the servants had prepared food, soup and sandwiches. The days went by without any mention of the mirror or so called hallucinations.

Emma seemed happy for a while until other events took place, this time others experienced things such as a servant and even Gladys.

Emma was looking in her mirror when it suddenly shattered, followed by the light bulb exploding. Emma was in darkness, she walked blindly across the room bare footed feeling glass under her feet. She felt around and kept walking until she hit the wall, then walked left holding the wall for support. Eventually she could feel the door but it was locked, so she yelled loudly.

"Help me, somebody I'm trapped in this room!" Emma shouted feeling scared and alone.

Then she felt something slimy crawl across her feet, it was moving slowly and then made a hissing noise like a snake.

"Oh my god!" she shouted.

Then the door handle moved and it opened slowly, a light appeared and the figure of a man was looking at her. Emma pulled the door open and rushed out seeing Albert standing there, a sigh of relief was heard by Emma.

"Jesus thank God" Emma said.

"Are you alright Madam?" Albert asked concerned.

"Oh marvellous. Honestly!" Emma said sarcastically.

"First my mirror breaks, then the bulb explodes, I have cut my feet and something crawled on me," Emma said annoyed.

"It's not just your room," Albert said trying to reassure her.

"What?" Emma said in disbelief.

"Every mirror in this house has shattered, all but one," Albert seemed upset.

"The one in the study," Emma guessed.

"Yes and other light bulbs," Albert said. "And the clocks all went backwards, others and I saw it too!"

"Backwards, you mean you actually saw them go backwards?"

"Yes. They all stopped at 10.30. Everyone single one!" Albert said.

"I have seen the image of the woman and heard her voice, I was also struggling in darkness for a while when the lights went out," Gladys said. "You are no longer alone."

"Thank god for that, I really thought I was going mad," Emma sighed with relief.

"If you're mad then I am mad too," Gladys said smiling. "The question is what do we do with the mirror?"

"Albert take it and burn it outside," Gladys instructed.

"Yes Madam," Albert said taking it off the wall.

The next day Albert took the mirror to the gardener to burn on a bonfire, but as it stood in the middle of the rubbish, it never even caught fire instead it shot out of the fire and hit the gardener who set on fire and burst into flames. He died of severe burns later in hospital and no one could explain how it happened. Not content with this Gladys had it buried in the garden deep in the ground it was missing for days, and then it reappeared in tact on the study wall where it had been before just as if it had never been taken down.

Gladys thought that someone had dug it up and put it back, she could never believe that it was a cursed mirror, some believed that Annabelle was dead and haunted the mirror. Then one day Gladys was at the top of the stairs she shouted Emma to come to her and when Emma came she saw a swarm of wasps around her, she screamed but Emma was too late she had fallen down the stairs and when Albert and the servants examined her she was dead with her head turned round. Her neck was broken and there were no sign of wasps, any stings or dead insects. Instead Emma stood at the top of the stairs staring down at her in shock.

The police arrived and took Emma to jail then on to a mental health ward, where she remained for a while until a decision could be made as to her sanity. No one could confirm her story about the mirror or any other incident that occurred in the house her only real friend and defender of truth was Gladys who was dead. Now she had to find help from another direction. She had been to university with Fiona from Criminal World magazine maybe she could help her.

3

Simply Mad

Emma appeared on the ward, she was very calm but weary, she seemed to be aware of her environment knowing that she was on a mental health unit. Ruth the mental health nurse made her presence known to her.

"Hello Chloe I am Ruth the nurse who will be looking after you," Ruth said in a soft soothing voice.

"Hello Ruth," Emma reluctantly replied.

"I need to ask you a few things if I may?" Ruth continued calmly.

"About my mental health condition, listening to mirrors, my hallucinations and paranoid episodes?" Emma looked into Ruth's large hazel eyes. "Look I know the jargon right, all this is in the family."

"Mental health?" Ruth prompted Emma to continue.

"Yes multiple personality or dissociative personality disorder," Emma said.

"Yes I had a friend with that. Go on," Ruth beckoned.

"Well I am not mad, but okay who gives a fuck!" Emma said admiring Ruth's shinny hair.

"Give a fuck," Ruth said smiling.

"I'm sorry it's not your fault, you're only doing your job," Emma said returning a smile.

"So let's start again Emma," Ruth said watching Emma fidgeting with her fingers.

"You have lovely long shinny hair Ruth," Chloe said looking at Ruth admiringly.

"Why thank you Emma, I was once a model but shush don't say anything!" Ruth said looking round.

"Is that why you have a lovely complexion and white teeth?" Emma asked.

"Yes I suppose so, but enough about me, tell me your story," Ruth prompted.

"Well I kept seeing a head in a mirror and an eerie voice, then I saw a snake come out of the mirror and a large hairy spider," Emma mimicked a spider movement with her fingers. "All the mirrors broke in the house and light bulbs blew up, I was so scared. I was in darkness and the door was locked, I felt something slither past my legs and feet. It sounds crazy but I felt like I was in a bog or quick sand being sucked down."

"It must have been terrifying for you," Ruth said with empathy.

"Simply mad," Emma said shrugging her shoulders.

"Simply mad?" Ruth said looking oddly at her.

"Simply mad, an unexplainable phenomenon that not only I experienced, but others like Gladys with her wasps, and she saw the head in the mirror, but then she's dead so what proof have I?" Emma said sadly.

"Did the staff witness anything?" Ruth asked.

"Albert did and the gardener was on fire due to trying to get rid of the mirror, it's like the mirror is alive, possessed or cursed it can't be destroyed, no matter what you try to do to it," Emma began to shake.

Ruth held her hands and felt her sweating palms, she could see the fear in her eyes and her anxiety, and she had seen it before with people experiencing phobias. The fear of spiders as in arachnophobia or agoraphobia fear of open spaces, claustrophobia fear of closed in spaces. What had actually induced her fear was uncertain in Ruth's eyes, but whatever it was it was real to Emma.

"Seriously do you think I am mad?" Emma asked Ruth.

"It is not for me to decide Emma, we have psychiatrists for that, you were brought here so that you would be far enough away from your home and would be able to think about things away from your district. I believe Chloe lives in Scotland have you spoken to her about this?" Samantha asked.

"Yes but she said that nothing has happened to her," Emma said.

"I don't quite understand, happened as in what?" Ruth said confused.

"The mirrors," Emma said puzzled.

"You mean there is more than one?" Ruth asked.

"Yes three identical mirrors the frames were carved by the same artist and only one belongs to me," Emma explained.

"So who has the other mirrors?" Ruth asked intrigued.

"Chloe has one and Uncle James has the other one but nothing has happened with them," Emma said quietly. " But my Uncle may be lying as he wanted me in here."

"Why do you think that?" Ruth asked concerned.

"Both he and my Aunt Margaret say I am insane and want all the inheritance," Emma explained. "They think I am simply mad."

"I see, what about Chloe?" Ruth asked. "Does she feel the same?"

"No I don't think so, we grew up together, then she moved to Scotland," Emma thought for a moment. "Can you contact her? She will be worried about me."

"Okay, let me do that for you now," Ruth stood up and walked out of the interview room to the office next door.

She tapped the number on the phone and waited, meanwhile Kathy walked in the office.

"Hi Ruth," she said.

"Hi Kathy how are you?" Ruth asked then responded to a voice on the phone.

"Hi is that Chloe?" Ruth asked.

"Yes," came a voice on the other end of the phone.

"This is staff nurse Ruth from the mental health unit I have Emma Harrington with me," Ruth said once she was certain that Chloe was listening, she then put her on speaker.

"How is she?" Chloe asked.

"A little low, but alright," Ruth deliberately restricted her information on the phone.

"Okay tell her that I am thinking about her and my mirror is active," Chloe said.

"What do you mean?" Ruth asked hoping that she would elaborate on what she meant.

"I too have seen a head, it was trying to communicate but the voice was slurred and murmuring simply mad," Chloe explained. "Quite scary really."

"I am sure it must have been," Ruth said looking at Kathy.

"I know you don't believe me, but it's the truth and I have been in darkness that was scary, the door was locked and I was alone," Chloe explained.

"Alright Chloe let me pass on your message," Ruth said terminating the conversation.

"Okay, send her my love, bye," Chloe said.

Ruth looked at Kathy for support as they were old friends and colleagues they could discuss patients at ease, they were able to share their thoughts and opinions.

"Now Ruth don't reinforce Emma's delusions and don't get too involved please," Kathy said concerned.

"Kathy I purposely let you listen to that conversation so that you would hear what I heard about the mirrors, there are three and there is something odd about them," Ruth explained all about Emma and her dilemma, then she told the full story about the family tragedy. Making sure Kathy knew the facts and could advise accordingly as the senior sister. Kathy was ten years older than Ruth who was in her early thirties and who had been through her fair share of trauma and tragedy in her life. Kathy had fair hair and was a little plump or as she termed it cuddly, unlike Ruth who was slim and beautiful. Ruth also had to come to terms with her own sexuality she once fell in love with a patient called Pamela who was tragically murdered by Ruth's psychopathic ex-boyfriend Malcolm. Kathy was heterosexual but understood Ruth at least most of the time, although some things that Ruth did appeared unorthodox at times. Kathy's life was more straight forward and unless she got involved with Ruth's affairs she lived an ordinary lifestyle.

Emma settled on the ward undisrupted until she experienced nightmares and became restless, some involved the mirrors or things associated with them. This included spiders, snakes being trapped or chased by Aztec Indians, she even dreamed of Annabelle and her violent husband.

Eventually she was visited by Fiona the reporter from the crime magazine Criminal World, Ruth recognised her and called her into the office.

"Emma said you would come," Ruth said acting a little distant.

"Yes she is a friend and once a fellow student at university with me," Fiona said removing her coat and adjusting her blonde hair.

"I wrote as accurate account as I could of you in my article 'Cracked Porcelain' I hope you believe that," Fiona said concerned by Ruth's response to her.

"Yes about the abuse Pamela and I experienced," Ruth agreed. "It was a good article."

"So how are you now?" Fiona asked.

"I am good though still wary about reporters, we also had bad press," Ruth said honestly.

"I agree not all reporters have a heart and some can be ruthless," Fiona admitted. "But Criminal World prides itself on good reporters who care for people's feelings."

"Well good for you, so do you want to see Emma?" Ruth asked not willing to divulge any more information due to patient confidentiality.

Instead Emma explained everything to Fiona from the mysterious fire to the death of John Harrington and the so called curse of the mirrors. Fiona wrote a lot of information down and promised to send someone to be with Chloe and try to protect her. Emma knew that she could rely on Fiona to help her and put an end to the curse once and for all.

"Emma we need to get you out of here and go back to the Manor, we also need to get Ruth to help us solve the mystery of the mirrors," Fiona explained.

"Will Ruth agree to this?" Emma asked eagerly.

"I can be very persuasive!" Fiona said confidently. "I have already sent Daniel Harrison one of our reporters to James and Margaret's home under cover, so just keep that quiet and maybe we can find out something there." Fiona winked at Emma in order to reassure her all was well.

Meanwhile in the home of James and Margaret Harrington all seemed quiet Daniel Harrison was working undercover as planned he had successfully set up cameras and other equipment in order to catch the couple out with their plot against the other members of the family in taking their inheritance. Attempting to take all the mirrors was the beginning of their devious plan.

As far as they knew Emma had suffered a breakdown and was on a mental health unit. But Emma had been telling the truth about the mirror and was planning to prove it somehow. She was convinced that the other mirrors were a clue to some kind of tragedy and that something was keeping the mirrors apart and at the same time something wanted the mirrors to unite. In the James Harrington household things began with the breaking of mirrors and Margaret getting trapped in a dark room similar to Emma's experience. They were being drawn to the mirror for some reason led to a face and a garbled voice, then sent away for no apparent reason.

James sat in the dining room talking to Margaret.

Daniel Harrison was close by working as a handyman; he was busy listening to James and Margaret's conversation.

"Look keep this quiet no one must know about this," James said in a low voice.

"But I did experience things such as the horrid face in the mirror and a weird voice, but it was garbled and incoherent just like Emma said," Margaret admitted.

"Exactly as Emma said, can't you see she imagined it?" James said trying to convince her.

"No James it was there as clear as I see you now," Margaret insisted.

"For god sake woman we need that inheritance, we need to prove that Emma is insane," James said sharply.

"What about Chloe?" Margaret asked

"Oh she will be easy, she can't cope with her baby, she is probably suffering from post natal depression, and don't you see it's in the bag, we have them all. All I ask you is keep a level head," James insisted.

"Fine maybe then we will be out of debt," Margaret said concerned.

"Yes the mirrors will see to that," James said confidently.

At that moment one of the butlers entered the room.

"Phone call sir, it's your niece Chloe," he said.

"Thank you Jarvis," James replied.

James stood up and followed him into the study; he picked up the receiver and dusted it off with his handkerchief then cleared his throat and began to speak.

"Hello Chloe how are you?" he said jovially.

"Uncle James have you heard from Emma?" Chloe asked concerned.

"No why?" James asks hesitantly.

"I heard that she was going back to the Manor," Chloe informed him.

"Really," James said in a surprised manner. "But I thought she was ill."

"Yes well one of them is a mental health nurse and the other is a reporter, they are staying with her," Chloe said awaiting his response.

"Well evidently they think she is normal, although I can't think why," James said with disappointment in his voice.

"Define normal Uncle, compos mentis or simply mad, those are lay man's terms a little non- descriptive don't you think?" Chloe was trying to expose her uncle by teasing him.

"So you haven't experienced anything with the mirror then?" Chloe prompted.

"Not at all, it's ridiculous," James insisted. "Why have you?"

"Yes I have seen the head, not clearly but it was there and I heard a voice it was horrible and muffled very scary," Chloe admitted.

"Well perhaps you should tell someone and let it know," James encouraged her in order to show that she was also insane.

"Oh I have someone called Samantha King, she is staying with me soon," Chloe explained.

"Oh where is she from?" James asked curiously.

"A crime magazine called Criminal World, she's a reporter like Fiona at Emma's home, it's because of these mirrors they have raised a lot of interest," Chloe said hoping he would take the bait.

"That's good tell her everything and don't hold back explain about the haunted figure and the blood coming down the mirror, the spiders and big snake!" James sounded very excited. "Listen Chloe I am being called I will phone you later bye for now."

James put the receiver down and hurried out of the study; he entered the drawing room and re-joined Margaret who was eager to hear the news.

"Well what did she say?" Margaret asked impatiently.

"She like Emma is walking right into our trap, it's only a matter of time and we will be rich," James said excitedly.

"Really, so have they kept Emma locked away?" Margaret asked.

"No. But they have reporters going there and they will prove that they are insane," James said confidently.

"They are both experiencing the same things, both Emma and Chloe," James continued.

"How very odd," Margaret said looking towards the mirror.

"So don't mention about your experiences," James advised. "I don't want you locked up."

"No of course not, but we need to get rid of the mirror," Margaret said. "It gives me the creeps!"

"Fine, we can take it to the antique shop and sell it," James said in agreement.

4

Criminal world

Criminal World is a magazine dedicated to investigating crime all over the world; the reporters and photographers gather details of crime from victims, police records and also the criminals themselves. The team take steps to ensure that the public are provided with detailed accounts of events with graphic pictures that questionably cannot be compared with any other crime magazine.

Fiona Ellington is one of the reporters who are strong-minded and a force to be reckoned, with as she immerses all her energy into finding a good story. Her life is Criminal World and anything else in life takes a back shelf including love and marriage. Although she did lose a boyfriend during her time in New York, he was shot in action.

Samantha King is a reporter who joined the team from the Australian office of Criminal World. She is courageous and determined to get what she wants despite upsetting a few people on the way. She can be outspoken using her beauty to her advantage. She is known to offend people with her bad language which she often says she's working on.

Stuart Elliot was a photographer who spent a few years as a wedding photographer and then ventured into the world photographing models. He then moved into the area of crime where he found himself actually photographing a murder as it happened!

Daniel Harrison another reporter that used to work in war zones had a history in the army and used it to help him on location in remote areas. He achieved many things in his younger life recognising an opportunity for a story at every moment. He was said to even sleep with a notepad in his bed.

Many other people worked for Criminal World of course and the main offices employed computer experts and retired scientists surprisingly enough. It was a thriving concern and the connections with other areas of expertise helped to make the magazine more accurate and credible. The World Wide Web or internet serves as a valuable asset for Criminal World in order to receive vital information for the magazine.

Samantha sat opposite Fiona sharpening pencils, organising her papers and measuring each pencil checking that each one fit into her neat box.

"Sammy what are you doing?" Fiona asked.

"Tidying up why?" Samantha replied.

"Because you're getting on my nerves must you do that?" Fiona asked aggravated by Samantha's habits.

"Sorry but I can't help it," she said continuing to measure the pencils and sharpen them even more.

"No wonder you have trouble with men," Fiona said laughing.

"Well men are just dick heads who think of one thing" Samantha said laughing.

"Oh Sammy that's a sweeping statement," Fiona said playing with her blonde hair.

"It's fucking true Fi you know it is," Samantha said taking the bobble out of her hair and looking for her brush.

"So what about Scotland, are you looking forward to that?" Fiona asked.

"Oh yes being in some creepy Manor like that fucking castle, yes of course I am!" Samantha said finding her brush and using it on her long brown hair.

"Ashley Manor will be nice and not at all creepy, besides you will be looking after Chloe," Fiona explained.

"Oh some nut job that talks to mirrors and spooks herself silly," Samantha said tying her hair up.

"Sammy she is nice and has a baby, you like children don't you?" Fiona said smiling.

"You know I don't. It's all about commitment and all that," Samantha replied knowing that Fiona was teasing her.

"You're going to Harrington Manor with that mental health nurse, I feel sorrier for you with the lesbian," Samantha was responding to Fiona tormenting her by making her own remarks.

"Oh how homophobic is that Sammy!" Fiona replied.

"I am not but from that article you wrote about her and Pamela, what was it called? 'Cracked porcelain' she deserved what she got for messing about with patients."

"I thought you liked it?" Fiona said disappointedly.

"Oh Fi I am only playing you up, Samantha said laughing. "I loved the article."

"Anyway pack for a week, I believe it is chilly in that part of Scotland," Fiona continued. "Have you read up on the mirrors?"

"Yes about the things they have supposedly seen and heard," Samantha said.

"Good we need someone with an open mind and you and Elliot will be just the right people," Fiona said confidently.

"Wait did you say, Elliot?" Samantha said frowning.

"Yes Elliot will be going too," Fiona said surprised by her reaction.

"You are fucking joking of course," Samantha said angrily.

"No we need him to get photos of the place and camera equipment as evidence of paranormal activity," Fiona explained.

"Rubbish you just want to freak me out even more, fucking with my head I call it," Samantha said clearly annoyed by the idea.

"Sammy you need to curb your language and deal with your issues with Stuart," Fiona said seriously.

Samantha went quiet which usually meant that she was sulking; she began reading a magazine which was another indication that she was upset by what Fiona had said. Fiona recognised that she had upset her.

"Sammy you're a good reporter and friend please do this for me," Fiona gave her the look that no one could resist as if she was pleading. "Please Sammy for me".

"Okay. Just for you, but if he upsets me can I have your permission to slap him?" Samantha asked.

"Yes that sounds reasonable," Fiona agreed.

"I will try not to swear," Samantha agreed.

At that moment Elliot walked in to the office, he was dancing and full of life as he approached them.

"Hello ladies so we are going to Scotland then Sammy?" He said pointing to a map on the wall.

"Yes I believe so," Samantha replied trying to contain herself.

"Just like the McGregor castle nice and creepy," Elliot was trying to annoy Samantha, and Fiona was watching her waiting for Samantha to react.

"Me and you again," Elliot continued. "Like old times."

"Elliot it was last year!" Fiona said.

"My word only a year, down them creepy corridors in a murder mystery with you my love," Elliot said laughing.

"That will do Stuart, leave her alone," Fiona jumped in.

"Like she left me alone, all over me like a rash," Elliot jumped quick as he noticed a book being hurled in the air towards his head.

"You fucking conceited bastard, don't speak about me like that," Samantha said angrily.

"Go Elliot please," Fiona said pointing to the door.

"Sorry Fi but you saw what happened," Samantha said.

"Look you can swap with me have Ruth and Emma," Fiona offered.

"The rampant lesbian no thanks I am safer with Elliot, I can handle him," Samantha said smiling.

"Ruth is a nice woman and so kind, she really is nice," Fiona said in Ruth's defence.

"Yes but it's the patient thing with Pamela, hey alarm bells and hello forbidden territory!"

Samantha said. "No offence but that's going too far, out of order."

"Sorry you feel so strongly," Fiona said disappointed.

"And Emma is definitely a fucking nutter believe me with the mirror thing, like you said we will be gathering evidence to show there is no such thing as a haunted mirror."

"Maybe, we will see," Fiona said.

"You don't seriously believe in this nonsense?" Samantha said.

"I like to keep an open mind," Fiona replied.

With that Elliot re-entered the office like a tornado.

"I'm just going to pack, anything you need Sammy, flick knife or a sledge hammer?" Elliot said laughing.

"Fuck off Elliot!" Samantha shouted.

"Isn't she wonderful, beautiful with a nice figure and a mouth like a sewer," Elliot said tormenting her.

"That's really funny Elliot, go fuck yourself!" Samantha said looking back into her magazine.

"She's at it again, moaning, swearing and giving me grief," Elliot went on.

"Look Elliot I am not apologising for anything so forget it." Samantha said not even giving him eye contact.

"Okay I can live with that I'll see you at two o'clock," Elliot actually left the room without another word.

Later they set off for the north east of Scotland near Edinburgh; Samantha remained quiet listening to Elliot's favourite classical music which eventually sent her to sleep. This was probably a plot by Elliot to keep her quiet while they travelled miles up north. When she finally woke up Elliot was admiring the scenery and driving around the smaller roads through the mountains and valleys of Scotland.

"I love the scenery, the heather and the hills," Elliot said noticing that she was awake.

"Really," Samantha replied.

"Oh here we go with the attitude," Elliot said.

"Tell me Elliot was it your idea to come together," Samantha said.

"No why?" Elliot said with surprise.

"So you don't want to fuck me?" Samantha said bluntly.

"Nothing further from my mind," Elliot said innocently.

"Like at the McGregor castle experience," Samantha said.

"Oh that again don't you ever forget?" Elliot said.

"You obviously do so was I that bad?" Samantha said prompting him.

"Look you came on to me, not the other way round," Elliot insisted.

"No I didn't how dare you, stop the car," Samantha insisted.

"What are you serious we are in the middle of nowhere," Elliot said.

"Stop the fucking car now!" Samantha said becoming rigid.

Elliot stopped the car and looked at her puzzled.

"Now get out," Samantha was frowning again.

Elliot got out of the car and slammed the door, Samantha got out the other side and they both stood for a while looking at each other.

"Right get this straight it was a mistake never to be repeated," Samantha shouted pointing her finger.

"But you came to my bed and made me feel as if I had done wrong," Elliot said in his defence.

"Only because I was scared and you took advantage of me," Samantha started pacing up and down.

"That's bloody rubbish and you know it," Elliot said.

"Anyway I don't want to talk about it," Samantha said turning her back on him.

"But you brought it up," Elliot pointed out.

"Just fuck off," Samantha said dismissing him.

"Look we have to work together, that means getting on," Elliot said trying to reason with her.

"Okay," Samantha took a deep breath. "But let's forget the incident," Samantha said walking towards the car.

They continued their journey to Ashley Manor saying very little to each other and then when they arrived Elliot offered to carry Samantha's bags. Samantha refused and struggled to the door almost falling over. As she reached the door the butler stopped her and carried them in looking disgusted at Elliot, Elliot was surprised at the butler's response as he struggled in with his own luggage. Once inside the staff took their luggage upstairs and one of them showed them into the drawing room where Chloe was waiting for them.

Samantha entered the room but there was a delay before Elliot finally entered the room.

Elliot clumsily entered the room, "Sorry I am late." He said sitting on a seat beside Samantha.

She merely gave him a look of disgust and began talking to Chloe.

"So tell me about the mirrors, from your point of view," Samantha said in a professional manner.

Elliot looked at Samantha and then at Chloe, "No pressure of course."

"Thank you Elliot," She said frowning at him.

"Can I ask are you two married?" she asked.

"No," Samantha said shocked. "Why do you ask?"

"Nothing, you act like it that's all," Chloe said smirking.

"Me with her I don't think so," Elliot said laughing.

"Look can we get on," Samantha said obviously irritated by Elliot's reaction.

Chloe explained about the mirror "At first everything seemed normal and then the trouble started," she paused to think for a moment. "I was in the study looking at the mirror when I felt around it hearing what Emma had said about cutting her finger, it was then that as I cut my own finger, that things started happening such as seeing the image of a head that seemed to sway from left to right, then a horrible voice that wasn't at all clear."

"Muffled you mean?" Elliot asked.

"Yes she didn't even sound English," Chloe explained. "Then I heard weird noises like wild monkeys and tropical birds like I was in a jungle!"

"Strange. How did you feel?" Samantha asked.

"Dizzy and weak, I began having feelings in my body," Chloe explained touching her body. "I saw a head swinging from the hair, it was cut off in a rough manner as the skin seemed to hang down in strands, the voice was definitely not audible and as I said seemed to be foreign."

"It sounds creepy," Samantha said shuddering.

"Do you want to see it?" Chloe invited.

"Yes of course," Elliot said excitedly.

"Come, follow me to the study," Chloe offered.

They entered the study after Chloe struggled with the door, the door was very stiff and the door itself seemed to be too big for the frame.

"The door seems to be sticking," Elliot observed.

"I got stuck in here, the light went out and I was in darkness I felt trapped away from my child and heard jungle sounds, then my feet seemed to sink as if they were in quick sand. I felt like I was dying I couldn't breathe, my heart was beating out of my chest as if I were having a panic attack!" Chloe said holding her chest and her eyes widening mimicking her actions.

Elliot walked up to the mirror and gazed into it, and then he had a cheeky look on his face as he spoke into it.

"Mirror mirror on the wall, who is the fairest of them all?" he paused. "Samantha he replied to himself in a deeper voice, "She is the fairest in the land.""

"Stop it Elliot you prick!" Samantha shouted.

"It's only a mirror," Elliot said mocking her. "Are you afraid?"

"I was traumatised as a child by Snow White and the enchanted mirror, my mother thought it was the wicked queen who turned into a witch, but it was the enchanted mirror." Samantha explained.

"It was just a Walt Disney cartoon nothing more," Elliot went on.

"Not to a child," Chloe said sharply.

"I was only joking," Elliot said innocently.

"Well don't it's really not funny," Chloe said in Samantha's defence. "Fears like phobia's can seem real you know."

"Okay, point taken I will just continue admiring the mirror," Elliot said looking around the frame.

"I suppose you both want to settle down and rest," Chloe asked.

"Yes I need a shower," Samantha said.

5

Mirrors

That evening Samantha and Elliot were shown their rooms, Samantha's room was opposite Elliot's and next to Chloe's room the nursery was a few rooms away. Samantha unpacked and went into the bathroom to have a shower. Elliot was in his room examining his new camera playing with the aperture and adjusting the lens. He focused on a picture on the wall, it was a portrait of a woman so beautiful and yet her eyes were sad. It was a portrait of Annabelle painted by Ralph Bedford the artist the more Elliot looked at the portrait the sadder he felt.

Samantha was enjoying her shower when she thought she could hear a voice, she stood still and listened, but all she could hear was the water coming from the shower. She continued to wash and again heard a female voice, this time she turned the shower tap off and listened. Again she heard nothing so she grabbed her bath robe and put it around her. She walked into the bedroom and looked around. "Hello," she said baffled.

"Is somebody here?" she shrugged her shoulders. "Can't be anyone," she said to herself.

She took her make up case and removed a mirror from her bag; she then lined her make up neatly across the dressing table. She noticed that a mirror was missing from the dressing table, observing the wood that supported it. Suddenly her mirror shattered in front of her and her make up flew into the air as if it was alive. She jumped and then stood up looking around her; she put on a pair of knickers and pink pyjamas. And Then returned to the dressing table to attempt to get some of the fragments of the mirror up from the table and off the floor. Suddenly the light went out and she was in darkness, she tried to move but felt splinters of glass under her bare feet. Cautiously she walked away from the dressing table feeling cuts to her feet "Ouch," she said walking with her hands in front of her.

"Elliot!" she shouted. "You better not be fucking pranking me."

She could feel something on her feet crawling around her, it felt warm and slimy, she stopped and listened. "What the fuck, okay keep calm," she told herself. "You're nearly at the door Sammy, come on it's not a snake they are silky!" Samantha reached the door and felt for the handle. "Why are all the doors either stiff or locked?" she asked herself.

She continued pulling the handle down and trying to open the door then she felt something touching her face and she screamed as the door opened and she ran into the corridor. She continued into Elliot's room, the door was open and she looked around.

"Elliot!" she shouted then heard a scream that seemed to be coming from downstairs.

She ran down the stairs leaving a trail of blood on the landing and stairs, she immediately headed for the study and found Chloe with her hands over her mouth and Elliot on the floor.

"Elliot!" Samantha shouted then knelt beside him.

"Oh God is he dead?" Chloe asked.

"No I don't think so Chloe he has just bumped his head," Samantha said examining him.

Elliot opened his eyes and focussed on Samantha, "An angel." he said holding his head.

"Fuck off Elliot," Samantha said checking a slight cut on his head.

"Is he hurt?" Chloe asked.

"Not as much as I would like him to be," Samantha said harshly.

"Well, that's a bit much," Chloe said shocked at her reaction.

"Sorry just my humour, besides I have had problems of my own," Samantha replied showing Chloe her feet. "Here help me up with him," Samantha said trying to get Elliot to his feet.

"Ouch! my head" Elliot complained.

"Get me a cold wet flannel please," Samantha asked.

"I will arrange it," Chloe said pulling the servants bell.

"So what happened?" Samantha asked. "I was examining the mirror and photographing it when I felt something hit me on the head, it came from behind me," Elliot explained.

"Well it wasn't me," Samantha said laughing. "I was too busy fighting off slimy creatures in my room!"

"Well I saw a head in the mirror and heard a voice," Elliot said. "Just as Chloe said earlier."

At that moment a servant entered the room, she looked surprised at seeing them.

"Can I help you madam?" she asked.

"Yes get me a cold compress," Chloe asked.

The servant looked puzzled at Chloe.

"A cold wet flannel, face cloth for the man's head, quickly," Chloe ordered.

"So how are you Elliot?" Samantha asked.

"Like you care," Elliot said grumpily.

"Oh that's not fair I am concerned you know," Samantha said sympathetically.

"How are your feet?" Elliot asked.

"Could be better, I need to soak them make sure all the glass is out," Samantha said checking her feet.

Two servants returned with a compress and Chloe applied it to Elliot's head then Chloe arranged for a bowl of water to bathe Samantha's feet. Some of the servants who lived at the Manor assisted them. They then retired to bed, Chloe checked on her baby before she settled down.

The next few days were uneventful then Samantha began to hear the voices again. She did not hesitate this time and dressed in her pink pyjamas she headed towards Elliot's room. He didn't seem surprised to see her and commented.

"The doors open by the way," Elliot said sarcastically.

"Elliot," Samantha began.

"Yes Sammy," he said sitting in a chair and reading a book.

"Can I stay here?" Samantha looked frightened. "Please!"

"In here with me?" he asked.

"Yes," Samantha nodded.

"Is this because you're frightened?" Elliot asked.

"Maybe or maybe not," Samantha said hesitantly.

"Oh for God sake Sammy make your mind up, why don't you give me a straight answer," Elliot said.

"Okay I'm alright," Samantha admitted

"Okay well there is room on the chair," Elliot teased.

"Err... I don't think so, I get the bed," Samantha demanded.

"No way it's my room," Elliot insisted.

"I'm joking we can share the bed if you behave!" she said smiling.

"I know how to control myself, you came onto me remember," Elliot said reminding her of the McGregor Castle experience.

"Not that again, forget all that lets have a truce," Samantha insisted. She put her hand out to shake his hand.

"Agreed," Elliot said shaking his hand.

They both got into the bed then Samantha started making noises demonstrating that she was clearly not happy; she kept looking at Elliot and continued making noises.

"Okay, what's wrong?" Elliot asked.

"Can I sleep next to the window?" She asked smiling at him.

"I suppose so," he agreed moving over.

There was a moments silence and then Samantha broken the silence with a random comment.

"I didn't enjoy the sex you know!" She said with her back to him.

"Sammy," he said grumpily.

"Sorry I won't mention it again," she said smiling to herself.

After a while Elliot could feel her fidgeting and shaking, she put her feet on his legs and yelled "Ouch!"

"You're shaking," he said feeling her cold feet on his bare legs.

"That's because I am fucking cold," she replied.

"Oh so you're not frightened?" he asked.

"No," she thought for a moment about what Elliot said about being indecisive. "Well a little maybe!"

"Sammy a straight answer please," Elliot said irritated by her reply.

"You feel warm at least your legs are," she said pressing her feet against his legs.

"What was that?" she said.

"What?" Elliot asked opening his eyes.

"The bed moved and I heard something," she said lifting her head.

She turned round and faced Elliot's back, then she clung to him tightly, "I heard birds not just birds but tropical birds, does that sound silly?" Samantha asked him.

"Elliot!" she continued. "Wake up!"

"What Sammy?" Elliot was getting irritated by her behaviour.

Samantha then put her arm around him holding his chest. " You are cuddly just like a hairy bear."

"Roar!" she said teasing him.

"For God sake Sammy what is wrong with you?" he asked.

"I enjoyed the sex really Elliot," she said kissing his neck.

"Oh good!" Elliot said sarcastically.

Elliot could feel her breathe on the back of his neck, and then her hand began rubbing his chest.

"Elliot," Samantha whispered.

"What Sammy?" Elliot replied also whispering.

"Hold me," she said eagerly.

Elliot held her hand that was drifting around his chest, he really wanted to stop her hand wandering as he was tired and avoiding what he considered was her advances.

"No turn around and hold me," she insisted.

He turned around, "If I hug you and keep you warm will you let me sleep?"

Elliot could see her brown eyes looking at him, they looked like Annabelle's eyes so sad but kind and yearning, she was wearing her pink pyjamas but the top few buttons were unfastened revealing her tanned skin. Her hair hung down the sides of her face and her soft cheeks seemed to glow from a nightlight outside.

"Hello," She whispered her thick lips moved with a moistness that covered both lips as she spoke, she moved closer to him her body pressed against him, then pressed her lips tenderly against his and kissed him tenderly. Elliot felt the warmth from her lips as she used her tongue to wet his mouth. Suddenly the woman that he found hard to bond with was showing him affection.

"Oh Elliot kiss me back," she said continuing to kiss him.

"Sam?" he said confused at her advances.

"Elliot," she said still whispering.

"Can't you call me Stuart?" He asked.

"Ohhhh Stuart," she whispered kissing his neck.

Elliot began to kiss her back and felt comfortable with her for once.

"Are you sure you want this Sammy?" he asked her.

"Yes you idiot I do," Samantha said pushing her hand down his shorts.

He copied her by pushing his hands down her pyjamas and stroked her buttocks, Samantha climbed on top of him unbuttoning her pyjama top and then revealing her breasts, her body tingling with excitement, she leaned over him thrusting her breasts in front of his face. Elliot cupped them in his hands and he began playing with her nipples between her fingers, she lifted her head back and gave a heavy sigh. Her skin was like velvet compared to his masculine rough hands. Samantha ran her fingers through the hair on his chest, her head moved forward again and her hair covered his face. She removed her pyjama trousers and they kissed again as she pulled down his shorts and then removed her knickers, they were getting a little more wild and hot as they made love for hours. Eventually they stopped and lay down together until they both drifted off to sleep.

The next morning, Samantha woke up first finding herself naked lying on top of Elliot.

"Fucking hell!" she said in shock.

"Morning Sammy," he said looking into her eyes.

"Elliot," she said.

"Sammy I said call me Stuart," Elliot insisted.

"Why?" she said confused.

"Because that's my name," he said puzzled.

"No, why did we do this?" she asked.

"Don't tell me you regret it again?" Elliot said still puzzled.

"No sorry Stuart I'm fine with it," she kissed him on the lips. "But you really don't understand women do you?" Samantha said.

"Why do you say that?" he asked.

"Oh God Stuart you think I didn't want you?" she said.

"You said that or at least you implied it," Elliot said.

"I didn't want commitment or complications," Samantha said concerned.

"I see," he thought for a moment. "No I don't," he was certainly confused.

"I want love yes, but as for something more complicated I mean more of a commitment; you know the trimmings, marriage and children," Samantha said smiling.

"Sammy no pressure. Whatever you want," Elliot agreed.

"You mean that?" she said in disbelief.

"Yes of course," Elliot said kissing her.

"Well I have never really been loved or understood; just because I am attractive it doesn't mean I am any more loved at least for the right reason." Samantha explained.

"So tell me Sammy what do you really want?" Elliot asked.

"To be noticed and loved not for my looks or my body, but for me," Samantha said. "After all love runs deeper you know."

"I don't know what to say," Elliot really didn't understand women especially Samantha.

"Just tell me how you truly feel, without complicating matters," Elliot said smiling.

At that moment they heard a scream, they looked at each other and then both leapt out of bed and got dressed into their pyjamas and rushed out of the door. They raced down the stairs and immediately headed for the study. They tried the door but it was locked and they could here a baby crying.

"Quick Stuart, kick the fucking door down!" Samantha shouted.

"Stand back," Elliot shouted as he stepped back and kicked at the door, with one great shove he both managed to push the door open and fell onto the floor. Chloe was holding the baby in her arms. "He's not breathing," she shouted.

Samantha took the baby off Chloe and rendered first aid, giving him mouth to mouth resuscitation, then chest compression with her fingers. Elliot held Chloe and tried to comfort her; she was trembling and trying to keep calm. Eventually Samantha got him breathing and had stabilised him, she then handed him back to Chloe.

"Thank you Sammy, you are marvellous," Chloe said holding her baby.

"Chloe what happened?" Elliot asked.

"Something came out of the mirror and landed on his face, it was like jelly but covered his face and was suffocating him," Chloe said in disbelief.

"Strange, very odd," Sammy said looking back at the mirror.

"Speaking about what happened, what is this with you two?" Chloe asked noticing how close they were. Samantha and Elliot looked at each other and smiled.

"Well we decided to get together," Samantha said smiling.

"I see," Chloe smiled

"What do you mean?" Samantha asked knowing what she meant.

"I knew it Sammy, I am happy for you," Chloe touched Samantha's arm with affection.

"Thanks Chloe," Samantha said happily.

"Children next?" Chloe said looking at her baby.

"Hey, let's not go too far!" Samantha said laughing.

"Let's get out of here that mirror gives me the creeps," Chloe said looking across the room.

"I know the feeling," Samantha said.

They all headed upstairs and Chloe watched Samantha and Elliot enter his room

"See you later lovers!" Chloe said teasing them.

While Samantha, Elliot and Chloe were experiencing problems at Ashley Manor James had been busy selling his inheritance or the third mirror. He had travelled to a distant shop in a remote village hoping to obtain a fair price, but was offered a minimal amount. Never the less he took the money, however when Margaret and himself returned from their journey on entering the study they received an awful shock. The mirror was back and in exactly the same place as before, James looked at it and appeared completely baffled.

"Margaret!" he shouted angrily, "Come quickly."

Margaret entered the room and was equally as shocked. "The mirror, but that's impossible we just sold it!" she said gasping. "Stay there I will ring them right now."

"Wait, leave it after all they robbed us anyway," James insisted.

"You mean by not giving us enough money?" Margaret asked.

"Exactly so we keep the mirror and the money," James said watching two of the servants pass the door. "I bet they took it as a joke".

"Not everyone is as crooked as you dear," Margaret said in a serious manner.

"Someone had to have brought it back, it can't have got here by itself," Margaret said puzzled.

"Well only us two knew about it and we didn't," James said feeling around the frame.

"What are you doing?" Margaret asked.

"Looking for wings," James replied. "Well it can't just appear here like magic."

"James!" She said annoyed by his remark.

"Well isn't it obvious I am searching for any clues that it's been tampered with in any way," James said continuing to search.

"It's only a worthless mirror," she replied.

James suddenly jumped and held his left hand, he was bleeding.

"God damn it that was sharp," James said in pain. "Don't just stand there get me something to stop the bleeding!"

"What do you need?" she said looking around.

"A damp towel or something like it, from the bathroom," James said panicking.

Margaret left the room and James started feeling dizzy, he started to see a spider come out of the mirror. It crawled along the floor and then a snake appeared just as menacing. James looked across the room and saw a shotgun on the wall; he picked it up and watched the snake moving across the room. He searched the cabinet below for cartridges;

they began spilling out on the floor. Desperately he tried picking them up, keeping an eye on the snake, and then the spider moved closer until it was close enough for James to see all its features, from its six legs to its eyes as it gazed at him ready to attack. It then seemed to pick up speed as it headed towards him moving onto a nearby table. James turned the shotgun around and using the butt he began hitting it and crushing its head and body, he could hear a strange high pitched screaming sound as he hit the spider several times. He also heard a crunching sound and saw slimy yellow matter coming from it. Then he noticed the snake charging at him with large fangs and a gaping great mouth, so he turned the shotgun around and shot it in the mouth. During this time the room seemed to be in a mist, this was beginning to clear, but to his horror his wife lay across the table with her head crushed and the butler lay on the floor with a hole in his head. James dropped the rifle and began yelling and then sat on the floor, Harrison and the servants stood watching him in disbelief. Blood was everywhere up the walls and on the floor, James had been hallucinating and murdered both Margaret and the butler. The police soon arrived and began questioning everyone no one was above suspicion although it was clear that James was mentally ill judging by his behaviour and the fact that he spoke about hearing voices and seeing spiders and snakes. Harrison kept quiet about the cameras and bugging devices as he wanted to continue with his surveillance of the house and mirrors.

Meanwhile at the Harrington household, Emma was experiencing more visions. This time she was subjected to bind weed which had wrapped itself around her hands and feet. She yelled out to Fiona and Ruth who ran into the room, but by this time it was wrapped around her neck and strangling her. But all they could see was Emma thrashing about on the bed and her face changing colour from red to white. Ruth grabbed hold of her and shouted.

"Emma what is it?" she said looking at her.

Just then she stopped and looked round, she noticed that the weed had gone and sighed with relief.

"Oh thank god, that bind weed had got me and I was being strangled!" she said in a serious tone.

"Well, it's gone now," Fiona said reassuringly.

"We had better stay close by from now on," Ruth advised.

"Good idea we need to bring beds in here," Fiona said. "Or at least the mattresses."

"I'm used to nightmares, but I guess you two are not," Ruth said seriously.

They arranged for mattresses to be brought into Emma's room that night and all slept in the same room.

The following day they were informed about James.

Emma relayed everything to Fiona and Ruth who were sat at the dining room table; Emma didn't appear shocked and continued having her breakfast. Harrison also informed Chloe and the others at Ashley Manor.

"Oh my God that's awful," Chloe said.

Samantha and Elliot were also at the dining room table; Chloe beckoned Samantha to the phone.

"Hi Dan how are you?" Samantha said putting the phone on loud speaker.

"Hi Sammy, I'm fine which is more than I can say for Margaret!" Harrison said concerned.

"Well the police are here at the moment, but I can say that James started hallucinating and killed Margaret and the butler," Harrison continued.

"What did he see?" Samantha asked.

"Spiders and snakes coming out of the mirror," Harrison explained.

"He smashed Margaret's skull in and shot the butler in the head, blew it apart!" Harrison explained in gory details.

"You don't have to be so graphic," Elliot said looking at his toes.

"Sorry but it was awful, I actually felt sorry for both of them," Harrison continued.

That evening Samantha and Elliot were lying in bed, Samantha was wearing her pink pyjamas while Elliot wore a t-shirt and shorts. They spoke for a while then Samantha began to get nervous again and lay on top of Elliot, wrapping her arms around him. Before long she was sat on top of him and removing her Pyjama top as she had done before, she then pounced on him like a tiger after her prey. Elliot was still sore from the previous time that she laid her claws on him, making scratches on his back. She made a roaring sound and began kissing his neck, then held her head back removing the rest of her clothes. Elliot removed his and Samantha began making love to Elliot wildly and passionately, he felt very subjective as Samantha took complete control. Elliot felt a little uneasy but allowed Samantha to have her fun, he did enjoy the experience but something was wrong. As she tilted her head back and gave her usual sigh, she brought her head forward and her head was replaced by Annabelle's decapitated head. The face was the one on the painting but her eyes were evil and yellow, there was also blood on her neck. Elliot yelled out and pushed her away, he then fell on the floor and began gasping for breath.

"For fuck sake Stuart!" Samantha shouted. "Jesus fucking Christ!"

Elliot was almost blue and still gasping for breath, he was hardly breathing when Samantha realised he was having an asthma attack. She rushed to the bedside table by Elliot and opened the drawer looking for his Ventolin inhaler; a few other items came out of the drawer too.

"Where the fuck is it? She continued frantically searching until she realised it was in his trouser pocket. She raced back to him and opened his mouth and pushed it in squeezing the top to release the spray. "Breathe for fuck sake!" she said spraying again.

Elliot started to breathe still staring at the ceiling.

"Come on Elliot speak to me," Samantha said anxiously.

Samantha felt helpless but continued to attempt to get a response, she continued yelling at him.

"Stuart come on please," she said repeatedly then slapped his face hard.

"Oh God Sammy," Elliot said.

Samantha smiled and said, "Thank God, are you ok?"

"Yes but why did you slap me?" Elliot asked holding his cheek.

"Two reasons, one you knocked me off the bed and the other, in order to make you respond, oh and I am still trying to think of a third reason!" she said smiling.

"I saw a severed head on your shoulders," he looked around at Annabelle's painting. "It was her!"

"Oh how horrid," Samantha said frowning.

"But her eyes were horrible and evil," Elliot said. "Unlike your lovely eyes."

"Oh my poor Stuart, in that case I am sorry," she said feeling guilty for slapping him.

"Yes well you can certainly slap!" Elliot said smiling.

"I had tough brothers who taught me to fight," she replied hugging him then, realised they were still naked. "Oh look at us," she said smiling back.

"Shall we try again," Samantha said kissing him on the lips.

"You bet lover girl!" Elliot replied eagerly.

The next morning Samantha and Elliot sat at the dining room table with Chloe and her baby sat opposite, Chloe was breast feeding the baby. Elliot seemed a little uncomfortable with this; although he had seen her do it many times it did rather put him off his porridge.

"Did you sleep well?" Chloe asked.

"Oh yes thank you," Samantha replied kicking Elliot under the table.

"Yes thank you." Elliot said and smiled at Samantha.

"Very comfortable and cosy," Samantha smiled back like a love struck teenager.

Chloe couldn't help noticing a scratch on Elliot's right cheek and a bruise on Samantha's forehead.

"Are you sure you two slept?" she asked suspecting activity in the bedroom.

"Oh yes I'm sure!" Elliot said unsure exactly what she was referring to.

Samantha realised straight away as she had looked in the mirror and seen her bruise, she also noticed the scratch on Elliot's cheek. She gave a smile to Chloe and began playing with her hair then tucked it behind her ears in order to eat her breakfast.

"Mm mm coffee delicious," she said sipping from the cup. "I love a nice cup of coffee."

Samantha seemed to be over emphasising her enjoyment for her drink and teasing Elliot by removing her shoe and playing with his leg with her foot. Then sending her bare foot up his leg which was easy from her position at the table, Elliot just smiled not knowing how to respond. He was about to drink when Samantha reached a vulnerable area making him jump.

"Oh Stuart did you miss your mouth?" she said laughing.

"Of course it's all in the beans," Chloe said also laughing.

"Obviously, go for the best I say choose the best and hit the right market, where it counts," Samantha continued teasing Elliot. "Isn't that right Stuart?"

"You sound like a bloody coffee commercial Sammy," Elliot said fidgeting.

They were interrupted by the phone ringing, Chloe walked over and picked up the receiver, and she remembered to put it on speaker.

"Hello Ashley Manor," she said politely.

"Is that Chloe?" Harrison asked eagerly.

"Yes what's wrong," Chloe said noticing his anxious tone.

"I have spoken to Fiona and Ruth they suggest we get these mirrors together and find out if there is some truth about a message," Harrison said eagerly awaiting her response.

"I don't know what does Emma say?" Chloe asked.

"She is in agreement but she said it's up to you" Harrison replied.

"I agree there is something in what you say, but I am concerned something may go wrong," Chloe said concerned.

"I say do it Chloe we need answers and who knows what we may find," Samantha said looking at Elliot for support.

"Well we can't just sit here wiggling our thumbs, let's see what happens, besides enough has happened what else can go wrong," Elliot said looking back at Samantha.

"Okay I'll head for Harrington Manor at around midday see you on route," Harrison said.

"See you on the road Dan," Elliot said. "Drive carefully."

"As usual Stuart," Harrison replied.

Chloe replaced the phone on the receiver and returned to the table, she was about to eat her toast when the phone rang again.

"Hello Ashley Manor," She said a little abruptly, putting the phone on speaker.

"Chloe this is Fiona are you all there?" Fiona asked.

"Yes all having breakfast," she said continuing to eat her toast.

"Oh sorry, but I need to know about the mirrors," Fiona said concerned.

"Daniel has just rang and mentioned it, we are all meeting at Harrington Manor where it all began," Chloe explained.

"Good see you here later," Fiona said. "How's your baby?"

"Sammy is holding him, she has got used to his vomiting and smelly nappies," Chloe said laughing.

"That's amazing for Sammy!" Fiona said laughing.

"I still don't want any," Samantha shouted to Fiona. "Not that he isn't a cute one."

"Watch this space Sammy," Fiona said. "See you all soon."

By midday Harrison was ready to depart; he put the mirror in the boot of his car with no resistance and started on his journey to Harrington Manor. He was driving at a fairly fast pace listening to the radio when he heard a loud scream which seemed to be coming from behind him possibly from the boot of the car. He ignored it and carried on driving thinking he may have still been tired from the night before, he then heard the sound of hissing and saw a snake in the passenger seat. He tried to slow down so that he could sort out the snake but instead he was taken by surprise as it attempted to bite him. Harrison swerved in the road a few times then slowed down, but landed in a ditch as he swerved a third time. His head hit the door and then he slumped forward. He must have been there for a time unconscious when Elliot pulled up in his car; he and Samantha rushed to Harrison's car.

"Dan are you alright?" Elliot shouted.

"Dan can you here us?" Samantha asked.

"Yes. I am," Harrison said holding his head. "Help me out of this thing."

Both Samantha and Elliot helped walk Harrison away from the car, and then they helped him sit down by a grass bank.

"The mirror." he shouted.

Samantha walked towards the car, suddenly it exploded and she was thrown in mid air and landed by a tree, she was motionless her body was limp and lifeless.

"Sammy!" Elliot shouted. "Oh no!"

He raced towards her not knowing what to expect as he lifted her head up and watched her eyes open.

"What the fuck!" Samantha exclaimed.

"God are you alright?" Elliot asked.

"Ouch my head," Samantha said holding the back of her head.

"God you flew about fifty feet in the air!" Elliot said knowing he was exaggerating.

"Get me up," Samantha insisted.

Elliot helped her back to Harrison who was still dazed, they sat for a while then Harrison remembered the mirror.

"I bet the mirrors gone now," he said disappointed.

Elliot walked towards the car, and then cautiously opened what was left of the boot.

To his surprise the mirror was in tact, so he tried to extract it from the boot. The others heard a great shout and a cry of pain as Elliot grabbed the painting.

"Elliot!" Samantha shouted.

"God damn it, I've burnt my hands," he shouted.

"Stuart you might have known that would be hot," Harrison shouted.

"Stuart you fool," Samantha said rushing to him.

Harrison found the strength to go to Elliot's car for a fire extinguisher and a bottle of water. He passed Samantha the water and bandages and then headed to his car with the fire extinguisher. He sprayed the mirror then wrapped a blanket around it, then picked it up and carried it to Elliot's car. Samantha and Elliot struggled to the car and sat in the back seat together. Harrison drove the car heading for the main road to Harrington Manor. They continued to hear banging and shouting now they had two mirrors. They were a mile away from Harrington Manor when a woman appeared at the roadside she was young and beautiful wearing a hooded coat.

"Can I help you?" Harrison asked.

"Yes could you take me to Harrington Manor?" she asked.

"Of course get in," Harrison offered.

Harrison glanced at her in disbelief then concentrated on the road, Elliot and Samantha remained quiet.

"Are you going to visit there?" Harrison asked.

"No I live there," she replied.

"I thought Emma lived there," Harrison said finding it strange that the others were quiet.

"Yes she does now and so do many others," the woman said.

"May I ask who you are," Harrison asked.

"I am the one you seek and the one you wish to free," the woman said mysteriously.

"I don't understand," Harrison asked suddenly feeling very cold.

"Put the mirrors together and you will find out," she said. "The answer is in the mirrors."

"I really don't get it. You want us to bring them together?" Harrison said.

"Stop, I will walk from here," she said.

Harrison opened the door and the woman walked into the woods then vanished.

"Jesus Dan!" Elliot shouted.

"What's wrong?" Elliot asked.

"That woman did you know who she was?" Elliot asked.

"A hitchhiker," Harrison said surprised at Elliot's behaviour.

"It was Annabelle!" Elliot said shaking.

"Are you sure?" Harrison said smirking.

"Oh yes it was her didn't you notice her neck was bloody and her voice a little strange?" Elliot said nervously.

"Yes but I didn't think it was Annabelle," he replied unperturbed.

"A ghost has been travelling with us, I don't believe it," Elliot said looking at Samantha who was asleep.

Two of the mirrors were placed in the library temporarily until they could be united with the other mirror in the study, but while they were sorting this out Samantha decided to enter the study looking for Fiona. Instead she saw Ruth sat at a table reading one of the many books out of the book cabinet.

"Where's Fiona?" she asked.

"I don't know," Ruth replied sensing hostility in Samantha's voice.

"No of course you don't," Samantha said sarcastically.

"What's that supposed to mean?" Ruth asked.

"Nothing, I mean you haven't tried to make a pass at her then?" Samantha said. "I mean she is pretty."

"Look just because she's pretty it doesn't mean I am going to fancy her!" Ruth said in her own defence.

"She's blonde like Pamela, but she's straight shame isn't it," Samantha said rudely.

"Look just because I am a lesbian it doesn't mean I like every beautiful woman," Ruth said angrily. At that moment the mirror began to glow and blood poured down it. But Samantha and Ruth were that busy arguing they hadn't noticed any activity.

"Why have you got to knock gay people? Ruth asked.

"It's you I don't like, my God you think you invented sex especially lesbianism."

"I stand up for my own kind, what's wrong with that? Ruth asked.

"No you flaunt it and throw it in people's faces, both you and Pamela did that on those fashion shows," Samantha said in disgust.

"Just because it was on television and radio, we were hounded by the press," Ruth explained.

"Fucking exhibitionism if you ask me," Samantha said.

"Not at all everyone was against us, we merely defended ourselves, against religion and political extremists," Ruth replied. "We had to challenge them".

"No you didn't, that's a lame excuse," Samantha said beginning to pace up and down.

"So you think the likes of priests are perfect, those who abuse young boys, they are so fucking untouchable, so righteous," Ruth was getting angry.

"How can you say that?" Samantha asked.

"Why don't you read the papers or magazines?" Ruth said pointing to a newspaper on the table.

"I do, they are inaccurate and lie to sell the paper," Samantha said folding her arms in defence.

"Like Criminal World, I mean you as a crime reporter?" Ruth was referring to all reporters not just Criminal World's staff.

"Just keep your lesbian ideas to yourself" Samantha said looking away from her.

"What are you afraid of?" Ruth asked.

"Nothing," Samantha replied swiftly.

"Yes you are that's why your against me, you're frightened of something, perhaps things that you don't know about," Ruth said realising that what Samantha was referring to ran deeper than she would care to admit.

"That's fucking rubbish," Samantha said refusing to give Ruth eye contact.

"I have touched a nerve haven't I Sammy," Ruth said trying to get her to look at her.

"No I am not gay or anything," Samantha said in disgust.

"You don't attack someone for no reason and you said you're not homophobic, so what is it?" Ruth said probing her.

"Fuck you!" Samantha said unable to answer properly.

"I will find out I am not being hated for nothing, you must have a reason, and so what is it," Ruth was determined to find out the truth.

"Okay you're right," she turned and looked at Ruth. "My sister committed suicide because she was a lesbian, her girlfriend and she had a fight and her friend left her. She said it was due to watching you and Pamela on television that convinced her that she was gay. She followed your story and when things went wrong she took her own life."

"I am sorry," Ruth said sincerely.

"No I am sorry, I blamed you but I can see now I was wrong," Samantha admitted.

At that moment the room shook and books started to fly in mid-air. They were both dodging the books and then noticed a snake slither out of the mirror. Ruth pushed Samantha to the floor as a series of poison darts flew in the air and pinned Ruth to the door. Samantha got up and managed to block a dart with a book as it was flying towards Ruth's head, then the snake travelled towards Samantha with its mouth wide open. At that moment Pamela appeared and grabbed the snake and threw it back into the mirror, but only Samantha saw Pamela who smiled at her before she vanished.

The mirrors were becoming more intense as the evil seemed to consume each mirror, it would appear that nothing could stop them. A cycle of murders had inevitably influenced the mirrors or the evil that caused the initial murder possessed all three mirrors. The force was undeniably strong and had the power to control, influence and possess the mind. Pamela appeared and captured John's spirit binding him securely with a rope; he struggled but was unable to break free.

He had little power when Pamela and Annabelle were involved, especially with all their personalities combined; John had become weak and helpless.

Annabelle assisted her in throwing him into a dark room and then the audience assembled in the study to witness the mirrors come to life.

By this time the others came in with the other mirrors, John appeared but was taken away by Pamela and Annabelle who bound him and put him in a dark place. Once the mirrors were up Annabelle's other personalities were freed and the host personality appeared to everyone. Each person sat down and watched as Annabelle appeared in the central mirror. She had strange eyes at first and blood on her neck.

"Thank you for freeing me from the darkness that dwells within these mirrors, my personalities have joined their host, the real me and I are one again. Please don't be alarmed by my head as I will explain it all to you keep watching these mirrors as I convey the story of how I became imprisoned in the mirrors," everyone looked at each other in disbelief, it was like watching a movie of Annabelle's past.

"Here lies the mystery of the mirrors which will astonish and shock you as I tell the tale. The story will unfold and you will be enlightened by your experience although no one will believe where you have heard the story from, I am Annabelle. Although I cannot offer you evidence of this experience I can provide you with reassurance that nothing else will happen to you on your journey of enlightenment".

"Thank God for that!" Elliot said then looked at the others. "Sorry," he said apologetically.

"It all began at here at Harrington Manor I was the Lady of the Manor and I lived with my husband John Harrington who was lord of the manor, we had no children as I had numerous miscarriages probably due to the way I was treated. John was a cruel and jealous man who beat me and locked me away in a dark room, sometimes I was missing for days. I shouted but nobody heard me, I banged at the door and tried turning the handle but it was no use. I could feel things crawling on me and screamed; eventually I was set free from my captivity. John used to humiliate me and mock me in front of the servants, I felt trapped even outside the dark room. John encouraged the maids to flirt with him and even had sex with some of them, usually when I was pregnant or sick of him raping me. I used to go for walks in the woods this was my freedom away from the Manor and his family who considered him perfect. It was during one of my walks in the woods that I met an artist by the name of Ralph Bedford, he was kind and courteous, a true gentleman who treated me nice. He was sat drawing pictures of the trees near a stone bridge, at first I was a little shy and perhaps nervous of him, but then I got used to him.

I used to wash my hands and face in the stream that ran under the bridge; Ralph was amused by this and used to gasp at my beauty. He eventually invited me into his cottage and offered me tea and cake just to be treated like this was so nice."

The silence was broke by Samantha who was sobbing to herself, comforted by Elliot.

Annabelle continued with her story her face kept changing in complexion and she was looking like she looked when she met Ralph. Ralph could not take his eyes off me; he told me that he was captivated by my beauty. It was then that he asked me to model for him; I was shy at first as I posed for a portrait and he painted me on canvas. He started with a head and shoulders painting using oils, then as I became more comfortable with him I undressed and posed naked. He was observing my beauty spending hours perfecting all the curves and crevices of my body, just like when he was drawing the trees. At this point we must have fallen in love and made love together for the first time, it was a wonderful experience unlike John; Ralph was gentle and treated me like a lady. Although his hands were rough from his work he was so strong, he treated me as if I were a fragile object or flower. After this day we met regularly and I was so in love, I felt my heart flutter and my whole body tingled in his presence, I believe he felt the same although he was a man of few words. He did announce that he loved me so many times and not just when we made love." Annabelle's voice began to change as she began to speak about the next events, she sounded upset as her voice quivered.

"It was a warm summer's day when I went for my usual walk in the woods, John and I had been arguing, he wanted to try for a baby, but his very presence began to repulse me and I left the house. I was unaware of him following me, he had evidently realised that I was having an affair and wanted to find my lover. I met Ralph in the usual place wearing a hooded top and jeans, Ralph was sat smoking his pipe on a rock by the bridge, drawing the stream and bridge that we liked so much, close by was a wishing well. He warned me to be careful as the well was deep and could be dangerous, I noticed he had brown leather bound book at his side. When I asked him what it was he became defensive as if he was keeping some sort of secret from me. We then went inside the cottage to his studio where I observed some souvenirs from South America and other exotic places. I noticed a sheet covering something large and asked about it, he explained it was some kind of gift for me. Out of curiosity I moved part of the sheet and something pricked my finger, I collapsed and when I awoke I saw a snake coming towards me. It was enormous with a large mouth that was trying to devour me. At that moment Ralph came into my room like a knight in shining armour, the snake simply disappeared and Ralph said that I was imagining things. The only thing under the sheet were the three mirrors that he had made as gifts for me; he had been carving the wooden frames."

Annabelle indicated the blood stains on each frame, "These blood stains belong to Ralph he told me that much, he had tried to clean if off, but he couldn't remove it. He did it on a chisel when carving one of the women's heads, apart from women's heads there were animals that he had seen in jungles and deserts everywhere. I felt better after a glass of water and Ralph's soothing words; I went home and returned the following day. I was followed again by John who by now knew about Ralph and myself. I posed for him naked as usual and this time Ralph and I made love in the studio, little knowing that John was watching from outside. After my visit I walked the usual way home and John entered the studio, he was so quiet Ralph was unaware of his presence. Ralph was relaxing smoking his pipe with his back to the door admiring his painting of me. He grabbed a chisel which was already blood stained from Ralph's accident and plunged it into his back right up to the handle, he then pulled it out and sent it back into his back then thrust the final blow into his neck. He had evidently hit an artery as the blood spurted out everywhere. He then took his pipe that was on the floor and emptied the contents on the floor. He took a match then lit a few flammable objects and started a fire. The studio was burnt to the ground, but amazingly the mirrors remained in tact not even a scorch on them, even the glass was in one piece!"

All Annabelle's audience sat with their mouths open unable to comment at this point, allowing Annabelle to continue her gruesome tale.

"It was then that John planned my disappearance, he had brought the mirrors to the manor and displayed them on the study wall and they were strategically placed as they are now. He had locked me away as usual but before doing told me about Ralph's death and how he knew about our affair. I was so upset that he had not only followed me, but also murdered Ralph in cold blood. I needed to tell someone about everything, but when John set me free he murdered me by stabbing me with that same chisel from the studio and not content with that he got an axe and cut off my head."

Fiona reacted as well as Samantha this time and even Elliot was forced to use his inhaler, each person reacted to the story in some way even Ruth who had witnessed many things.

"He had sent the servants away, saying how upset he was that Annabelle had been unfaithful and had gone missing, he said I had run away in shame. Once he had severed my head from my body he held it up from my hair and boasted to the mirrors. 'See the bitch that dares to fornicate and commit adultery, Ralph behold your lovers head!' With that he put my head in a brown sack and took it to Ralph's well and dropped it down followed by the chisel. As for my body that is buried by the rocks beside the stream you will also find the leather bound book in a hollow part of a tree in a plastic bag. As for John he called back the servants to clean the house, he had always liked Lucy one of the young maids. John committed suicide not by choice I might add, but when he was so remorseful and sad about my death, he was making love to the maid when my head appeared on her shoulders he was so shocked that he threw her to the floor and ran to the window. Lucy lay injured and he threw himself out of the window. That is the full story of my life at Harrington Manor I will now rest in peace knowing that you know the truth."

Annabelle faded away leaving everyone to think about what they had heard and seen, but nobody was able to convey anything to anyone. But at least Annabelle was at rest having told her tale; her spirit was at peace at last. As for the mirrors they suddenly set fire and despite all effort to save them, they disintegrated as they should have done originally in the studio fire. Amazingly nothing else was damaged not even the wall, only the mirrors that had kept the secret hidden inside them.

"Well follow that!" Harrison said completely baffled.

"So tragic," Fiona said, shaking her head in disbelief.

"The poor woman," Ruth said looking at Emma who simply nodded.

"I am really shocked," Samantha said wiping the tears from her eyes.

"What the hell are we going to tell the police about Annabelle's body?" Elliot said confused.

It was finally time for Harrison to leave and take his mirror to Harrington Manor.

6

On reflection

Now that the three mirrors were finally together it was thought that they would either consume the Manor or in one mighty wave, cause a massive explosion of energy, or it would endeavour to reveal the secret that has been locked away for so long. Whatever happens has a purpose and the meaning so clear to those seeking the truth. As it happened the truth was revealed and a mystery unravelled no matter how strange it happened.

"So what do we have as evidence that these mirrors even existed and what proof, if any that they were haunted or possessed in some way?" Fiona said leading the discussion.

"Well we all saw Annabelle's image as she relayed a story to us," Emma said confidently. "I also saw Pamela's ghost, now I have not met her before but I described her and Ruth said the description was accurate."

"Thank you Emma, but this would be classed as circumstantial to most people," Fiona said eventually chairing the meeting.

"The pricking of the finger on the corner of each mirror located by the old blood stains," Samantha said pointing to a photograph of the mirror. "I understand that a hole was discovered in this area containing a small cylinder resembling a bullet, inside was a substance that was analysed and found to be some sort of illegal substance that caused not only hallucinations but temporary paralysis."

"Safe to say that a number of people pricked their finger and became exposed to this drug, they then became subjected to all kinds of hallucinations and delusional ideation," Ruth added.

"No doubt the work of James and Margaret Harrington who not only tried to get their hands on the inheritance but also defrauded hotels and many people on the internet with their evil schemes using charity work as their front," Elliot said producing paperwork as evidence.

"I used cameras and bugging devices as further proof of their fraud, I did try to gather evidence of supernatural activity but the sounds were muffled and visibility limited," Harrison said disappointed.

"So what has happened to James Harrington?" Fiona asked.

"He was transferred to a mental health hospital on a secure unit, he was said to be delirious seeing a headless woman and then monkeys around his cell!" Harrison said smiling.

"James was said to have continued to tell his story about his wife being a spider when he killed her and the servant was a snake who he shot in the head and chest," Ruth said looking at Samantha for support.

"Yes Ruth is correct and clearly perceptive with her explanation," Samantha said smiling at Ruth.

"It would also seem that without steering away from the facts that people had a combination of hallucinations and imaginative ideas that were a little confusing. Annabelle herself had a mental illness known as multiple personality syndrome or dissociated personality syndrome which due to past trauma caused her to have an individual personality in each mirror, this needed to be brought back together in order for her to converse with us using the host personality or her real self. Arguably this is a real mental health condition and is very difficult to treat, usually it is done through therapies," Ruth paused looked around then continued. "Coupled with another personality questionably haunting the mirrors who is suggested to be evil may be down to John who evidently influenced James, although I would deem James as a sociopath who has no conscience and will probably spend the rest of his life in psychiatric care," Ruth finally took a breath.

Samantha began clapping encouraging the others to join in; Fiona was astonished by Samantha's sudden change in views and her opinion towards Ruth. Samantha even winked at Elliot which was clearly seen by Fiona who was sat beside her. She leaned and whispered to Elliot hoping Samantha wouldn't see her.

"What on earth did you do to Sammy, and did it involve drugs?" Fiona smiled.

Elliot shrugged his shoulders and he whispered back. "God knows but I hope it lasts!"

"I have something," Chloe shouted and came forward. "I have been to the cottage and discovered a diary tucked inside a tree," she produced a book approximately six inches long by five inches in wide; it had a brown leather cover.

"An entry on the fifth of July 1975 says that he was in the Amazon jungle when he discovered a cave, inside the cave was a series of paintings some seemed to relay a story of a tribe like the Aztecs who had discovered an odd shaped mirror with an image of a woman's head severed from a body, she was said to be some sort of sorceress and slain by warriors for putting a curse on their family," she looked at her audience who seemed to be in a trance. "Shall I go on?"

"Yes Fiona," said curious.

"This is freaky," Samantha said nervously.

"Go on Chloe," Elliot beckoned.

"Well, other entries are similar until I reached the part that mentioned Ralph being bitten by a poisonous snake, he was helped by a tribe of people who related to him how he was delirious and calling for help as he was attacked by wild monkeys and fell into a swamp."

Chloe passed the book to Harrison who examined it.

"I'm amazed at this even in my Army days I have never come across anything like this," he opened a page on a passage about the glass in the mirrors. "I have ordered the glass mirrors from here as the glass is made from minerals in the jungle and I am looking for wood from the trees in the forest," Harrison looked at his colleagues. "So that's what he was up to and he is suggesting the curse is from the jungle, a so called sorcereress."

"Well thank god the mirrors have been destroyed," Elliot said sighing with relief.

"So all those jungle sounds and experiences were from the Amazon jungle?" Samantha asked.

"Yes it appears so Sammy, but then we are dealing with facts and not fiction," Fiona reminded her.

"Of course but you know what we heard and saw it offers an explanation to me," Samantha said glancing at Elliot and back at Fiona.

Elliot smiled. "Yes no doubt about it Sammy is right, we did hear and see a lot."

"Stuart you know we deal in facts for crime reporting, conjecture or fiction has no bearing or credibility in selling our magazines," Fiona said sternly.

"Come on Fi, you know as well as me that sometimes what we see can't be explained even in the best surroundings where we visualise many things, I refer to ghostly places such as castles and haunted houses." Harrison said.

"Thanks for that Daniel" Samantha said, "You really know how to make a girl feel at home."

"Well we have little solid evidence judging by my camera and Stuart's photo's all seem very grainy and even inferred doesn't show much," Harrison said disappointedly. "In fact I have seen better on that television program Most Haunted!"

"Without the over dramatization you mean," Elliot said laughing.

7

A new start

Once everything was over Emma left the Manor and joined Chloe at Ashley Manor. They were happy together and soon forgot the events that took Place at Harrington Manor at least that was what they told each other. But they both had occasional nightmares of past events and could never forget Annabelle's severed head displayed in the mirror. Nobody ever looked at mirrors the same again without thinking that something was going to jump out at them, grabbing or clawing at them in a frenzied attack showing no mercy.

Elliot was driving home with Samantha; he was listening as usual to his classical music which Samantha loved so much.

"Oh come on Stuart this is funeral music," Samantha said rolling her eyes.

"You have no idea, this is quality music," Elliot said.

"Music to sleep through," Samantha said complaining.

"So have a sleep," he advised.

"I don't want to," she replied in an aggravated manner.

"Ok you win, put something on you like," he said keeping the peace.

Samantha looked through her bag and removed a compact disc from its case; she put it in the player. That's what you get by Paramore began to play.

"There we are real music," she said jigging around in her seat.

After they had been driving for a while Elliot was feeling tired, he swerved to miss what he thought was an animal on the road, which made Samantha think of Harrington Hall and Annabelle's tragedy.

"What the fuck was that?" she asked.

"I don't know I couldn't make it out," Elliot said continuing to drive.

"Stop!" Samantha said alarmed.

"Here we go," Elliot said.

"Stop the fucking car now!" Samantha said angrily.

Elliot stopped the car in a layby and got out not knowing what to expect from Samantha.

"I don't believe you Stuart Elliot," Samantha said pacing up and down.

"What do you mean?" Elliot said confused.

"You really don't care do you?" Samantha said flapping her arms about. "That poor creature could be injured and you just don't give a shit."

"What's this really about Sammy?" Elliot said knowing there was something else wrong with her.

"It's you, you're so insensitive at times, not a thought for others and God you annoy me," Samantha was getting tearful again.

"Oh come on that's not fair," Elliot said. "I have helped you and been close to you, now I am insensitive!"

"Yes," she paused. "No, I don't know!" She said confused.

"Indecisive Sammy again," Elliot said trying to get Samantha to say what she truly felt.

"I can't help it Elliot, I mean Stuart, I mean god knows what," she said putting her hands over her face. "I can see Annabelle every time I close my eyes and it's so sad, why couldn't she be happy with Ralph, its not fair, why Stuart?"

"I don't know but you're wearing the grass out beneath your feet" Elliot said trying to make her smile.

"Take us for instance enjoying each other having casual sex, no ties" She said ignoring what he said. "We're happy!"

"Well I am," he said still trying to get a reaction.

"So why couldn't she be happy?" Samantha continued. "What?" she said realising what he said.

"I said I am happy," Elliot waited a moment for her to react.

Inevitably she did react by slapping his face, and then thumping him repeatedly on the chest.

"Elliot!" She shouted in a fit of temper, "I love you."

She then held him and cried uncontrollably, she remained in his arms for a considerable time until they both returned to the car. The radio played 'Strange Magic' by ELO which seemed very appropriate for the occasion regarding the mirrors and how it had brought them together.

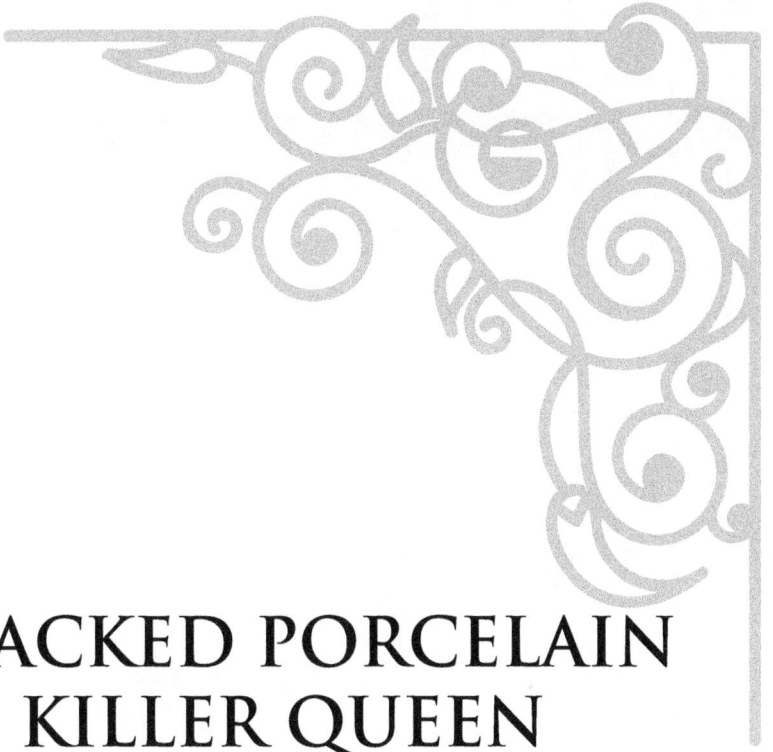

CRACKED PORCELAIN KILLER QUEEN

S R SUTTON

INTRODUCTION

Ruth is a psychiatric nurse who has faced dangers and lived through nightmares from her past. She had lived with a man named Malcolm, a once kind and loving boyfriend who was slowly revealed to be a murderous psychopath. Discovering her sexuality, Ruth left the man she thought she loved for a patient called Pamela, Malcolm, enraged and rejected, pursued both Pamela and Ruth. In a battle for their lives, the girls pushed Malcolm out of a window and he fell to his death, but not before he killed Pamela with a knife, thrusting it into her abdomen. The knife was supposed to kill Ruth, but Pamela jumped in the way to save her, it was Pamela's final act of love for Ruth. But what happened previously was nothing compared with her latest experience, when she was being pursued by yet another psychopath with evil intent.

A young man stands posing naked in front of a full length mirror, he has one of his favourite Queen songs on his C.D player called 'Bohemian rhapsody' and he is miming to the song and practicing dance moves almost like a ballerina. He is room appears tidy for a man, and displayed posters of Freddie Mercury everywhere. He was evidently a fan of Queen by the amount of songs he was playing and by the way he mimicked Freddie Mercury's moves, as he would have performed them on stage. But this young man appeared to perform in a more feminine way as if he had been observing a young woman's movements, he used his arms and legs like a mime artist and his body seemed to float on air. He was a slim youth in his mid twenties who was dancing to Queen he had short brown hair, large brown eyes with a rather unusually soft smooth complexion.

It was a summers evening in the early part of the week, the streets were quiet and only a few people were roaming about. Amongst these people was Ruth a slim woman with long dark flowing hair and large brown eyes. Ruth had a look of melancholy that some would mistake for sadness. Although she would have every reason to be sad judging by her tragic past living with a psychopath called Malcolm who murdered her mother and her girlfriend amongst others. Ruth is was mental health nurse who worked in the local hospital, on an acute mental health unit, dealing with all kind of conditions from bipolar, schizophrenia and clinical depression. Ruth had been deep in thought when she was suddenly distracted by a speeding car passing by playing loud music. She jumped and then returned to her thoughts, unaware that someone was following her. It was the young Queen fan who moved with a feminine walk using his hips to propel himself and wriggled his behind as he moved along. He had headphones on playing 'Queen' a song entitled 'You're my best friend'. Ruth entered a bar and joined a few friends, after a few seconds she walked the bar with one of her friends and ordered drinks. The youth stood at the bar, removed his headphones and stood close enough to hear their conversation, but remaining silent. Ruth was discussing relationships, making it known about her sexuality by her choice of words and from her tone of voice.

"Look Kathy, I don't care what people say at work; they all know that I am a lesbian, why should I hide it? The whole world knows after my appearance on TV and radio as well as the press" Ruth said

"Ruth, remember that was when you were in modelling now you're back in nursing and all that's behind you." Kathy said concerned.

"I might have stopped modelling but I haven't stopped being a lesbian, that's me and my sexuality" Ruth explained to her friend.

Kathy was a blonde woman with shorter hair and built slightly larger than Ruth, she was listening intently to Ruth along with the youth who by now had bought himself a drink. He kept glancing at

Ruth's beautiful face, watching her mannerisms then making similar movements as if he was deliberately copying her. But was this young man a stalker or had he got a more sinister thought in mind? He had sat down and made a point of staring at her, if Ruth had not been so busy maybe she would have noticed him watching her and felt uneasy. Ruth was too occupied and engrossed in her own thoughts and conversation to be bothered with anyone else. Ruth decided to dance with some friends on the dance floor, she was demonstrating how active she was and full of life. She was dancing for a while, with the young man watching her, but he was distracted by a woman passing comment about her in a very negative way. She was making reference to Ruth's sexuality and her past as a model on television, commenting on how she didn't like her. At that moment, the young man was distracted by the sound of a Queen song called 'It's a kind of magic.' It was the backing music for a magic act performed by an illusionist which lasted an hour. After a while the young man left the bar and headed down the street, but he continued to mimic Ruth's movements and when he arrived home he practiced them in a mirror to the Queen song 'I want to break free' played loudly. Talking with his mouth and hands as Ruth did, even giving a smile as if to express empathy and then looked away as if to get distracted. Usually she would then play with her hair and tighten her lips clutching a pen in her mouth, with a reluctance to continue speaking, allowing others to have their say. Ruth was very expressive with her eyes, mouth and the way she held her head she also used her hands in order to express herself, and so he had many things to copy but the young man seemed to master it all.

The next morning, Ruth picked Kathy up for work. She was sat in the car looking in front of her at a busy street. She was relieved that she was not in the crowd as she particularly hated crowds of people and the closeness of strangers. She felt intimidated and very vulnerable when people brushed passed her- especially men. The typical stereo type, fat men with horrible sweaty bodies and eyes that undressed women. Like the evil Malcolm's of this world, horrible perverts, who used women to provide them with their own sexual needs, no matter who they hurt. She felt secure in her car almost as comfortable as being in her wardrobe, that dark and solitary place that she was safe in, as long as she remained silent hidden away from her abusers.

Kathy made her jump as she suddenly opened the door and shouted Good morning. She was so bubbly and bright where Ruth took a long time to revive from her slumber and confessed to being grumpy in the mornings.

"Did I startle you sorry Ruth?" Kathy asked, sorting out her bags.

"It's okay Kathy, I was deep in thought" Ruth said smiling.

"You're worried I can tell. What's troubling you?" Kathy asked, concerned.

"The usual thoughts I suppose. And nightmares" Ruth replied.

"Come on Ruth, we discussed this, you must think positive and believe in yourself". Kathy insisted. "What happened was not your fault and you must move on for your own sake"

"I know your right I hear your voice in my thoughts and try to be positive" Ruth began to drive away.

"I read something that you wrote about some time ago saying, if you visit your saddest place you will find me there, amidst the broken wings and lost souls. Hold back your tears for your memories lie like peaceful doves in a tree, so peaceful, so white and pure. Remember those broken wings and lost souls, those forgotten dreams and ambitions that once captivated your heart, yet a glimmer of hope, flicker of light appears in the darkness taking you into the light, far from the dark and solitary place. New hopes, new dreams and a bright future await me, my positive thoughts and warm heart goes forth into the light." Kathy read the words from a sheet of paper.

"My words and you kept them" Ruth said holding back the tears.

"Yes to remind me that you can think positive, I will quote these words whenever you're negative" Kathy said firmly.

"Thank you Kathy" Ruth replied

"Don't mention it" Kathy said dismissively.

On the radio Queen was performing Radio Gaga, Ruth smiled remembering this tune from her training days, her first encounter with mental health being chased by an elderly male patient who was suffering from bipolar.

They arrived at the hospital and parked the car near a wall; Kathy was the first to step out of the car followed by Ruth who swept her hair back from her face with her hands. Kathy laughed as the wind blew it back into her face, smugly smiling because of her own short hair and the fact it was more manageable than Ruth's long hair. Ruth loved her long hair but it was less manageable in rough weather and awkward to tie up while on the ward. Close by the same young man who had watched Ruth in the bar continued to watch her and he was also amused by Ruth's actions, trying to mimic her while playing his favourite Queen music 'You're my best friend'. He watched them enter the building on the mental health unit; he seemed to wait for a while in the car park before entering into another building.

He had entered Accident and Emergency and wandered into the toilets, he sat in a cubical and proceeded to expose his arms, he was a thin man who looked effeminate and timid. He produced a small knife from his shoulder bag and held the blade against his wrist, with a deep breath he cut across his wrist once and then again until he began to bleed onto the floor. He sighed with relief and watched the blood trickle onto the floor. Shortly after a pool of blood surrounded his feet and drifted under the cubical door. He heard a door shut and two people were talking, young female voices he had entered the women's toilet. Suddenly one of them screamed having seen the blood, the other woman shouted out.

"Hello can you hear me, are you alright" She said

"She could be dead" The other person said expecting a woman to be in the cubical.

"Lets get help quickly" One woman said to the other

The receptionist quickly calmed them down and alerted security who ran into the toilet to deal with the situation followed by a nurse. One of the security guards pushed open the door and escorted the young man to an available cubical in casualty. The nurse dealt with his wounds after a doctor was satisfied they were superficial cuts, she asked him questions about how he was feeling and soon discovered that he was suffering from clinical depression.

"So what's your name?" The nurse asked.

"Colin" He replied

"I'm Kim" she replied washing his arm "So Colin why do this?"

"I wanted to end it all, nothing to live for" Colin said, wincing in pain.

"So how long have you felt this way?" Kim asked.

"For quite while now. Ever since my parents were killed in a car accident" Colin responded, avoiding eye contact.

"Sorry to hear that Colin, I will get some help for you, maybe you can discuss this with a psychiatric nurse" Kim said bandaging his arm

After a discussion with the psychiatric liaison nurse, Colin agreed to be admitted onto the mental health unit for assessment. Colin seemed pleased to be there and even more so when he saw Ruth walking down the corridor towards him.

"Hello Colin, my name is Ruth" She said smiling, "Come with me and we can talk about your stay".

Colin sat in a room with Ruth, spending most of the time watching her mannerisms. He was interested in her eye movements and the way she used her hands to express herself. She spoke with her hands and her fingers seemed to move about like a musical conductor, and seemed to touch her hair a lot. She seemed aggravated by her hair being tied back and seemed to fidget constantly as if she was uneasy being sat down.

"I like your eyes" Colin said staring at her large brown eyes.

"Thank you" Ruth swiftly replied, trying to steer the conversation back to the interview.

"You have long shiny hair and lovely teeth" He continued

"Can we just stay focused on the interview please Colin" Ruth said feeling very uncomfortable.

"I am sorry I didn't mean to embarrass you" He said looking away.

"Colin where are your parents?" Ruth asked

"They are dead, killed in a car crash" Colin said looking out of the window onto the ward.

"Colin that's not true is it?" Ruth said sternly "Why are you lying?"

"Yes they got crushed in the seats like melons" He insisted speaking coldly in a detached manner as if he didn't care for them.

"No they are alive and well, I spoke to them earlier" Ruth watched Colin's eye movements which told her that he had avoided the truth and he was being deceitful

"Why are you lying to me Colin?" She asked trying to get his attention "Are you upset with me because I stopped you talking about me?"

"No I just hate them" He looked back at her "I can't help saying things about you because you are beautiful" Colin admitted.

"I am flattered but I need to be professional and you are a patient" Ruth said trying to explain the rules about patient and staff involvements. She felt so uncomfortable because he just kept staring at her, and she thought that he was undressing her with his eyes. He spoke frankly to her expressing his thoughts and feelings, but Ruth could only relate such things to her past. He may have been complimenting her but his words only made her feel more uneasy. She was also so shocked at the cold way he referred to his parents as being dead, and without giving any response when she faced him with the truth about his parents being alive and well.

"I don't fancy you, it's not like that and I know that you are a lesbian" Colin said bluntly.

"Well, that's my personal business and my life Colin" Ruth said defensively "You have no right to judge me"

"I am sorry, really, but I am really not happy and I want to change my life. Even my parents" Colin said coldly "They disgust me, I want to be like you."

Ruth felt a shiver running down her spine as Colin related his feelings about his parents and his school life. He spoke about everyone having no eyes and of how he had nightmares of blinding everyone so that only he could see. He discussed many things, nothing positive. It was as though he could only see the bad in everyone, all but Ruth. He referred to a time that he was playing cricket and got into a fight, he was hit on the head with a cricket bat. The incident was recorded as accidental, although Colin insisted that it was a malicious attack and he was suffering from concussion. This was one of the many problems at school according to Colin, he claimed to have been bullied because of his feminine ways.

Ruth finished the interview feeling mentally drained, she was tired and even her speech was slurred when she was relaying the entire conversation to Kathy.

"Colin is clearly besotted with you," Kathy said smiling.

"Oh come on Kathy he's a patient. And besides, he's living in a fantasy world" Ruth said unconvinced by his explanations.

"Ruth I am joking he is psychotic and has a warped mind, he is unhappy and relates to you for some reason" Kathy appeared satisfied that Colin was just depressed and lonely.

"So I can relax then? Just not worry about another possible psychopath like Malcolm trying to ruin my life?" Ruth said with a sigh.

"He appears to have a psychosis but I wouldn't worry about your safety" Kathy reassured Ruth.

The following day Ruth was back on the ward going about her duties as a nurse, the usual activities took place such as handover from the night staff to day staff and reporting on each patient including

Colin. No problems were reported, no violence or suicides, nothing to really say of significance. After a quick handover the night staff went home while the day staff took over the care. But throughout Ruth's twelve hour shift Colin had been watching her every time she was in view either on the ward or in the office. He studied every movement from her walk, gestures and posture; he listened to her speaking and instructing the staff to carry out duties. He continued to do this every shift that she was on; she was oblivious to this and hardly ever came in contact with him until one day. Ruth was passing his room and overheard him talking to himself and looking in the mirror, behaving just like her, every movement was exactly like hers.

"Now listen to me. You know what to do so carry on all of you." Colin said.

A shiver shot down Ruth's spine upon hearing and eventually seeing him impersonating her. All she could think to do was wait anxiously for Kathy. When she arrived Ruth told her everything.

"Ruth are you sure about this, or is it about the other day when he appeared to fancy you?" Kathy said in disbelief.

"For fuck sake Kathy he is freaking me out" Ruth said angrily.

"Calm down Ruth, he is harmless, don't go by past experiences you're becoming paranoid" Kathy said trying to reassure Ruth that Colin's actions were normal for a patient at least.

"He is probably tormenting you or teasing you and your letting him get to you" Kathy explained "He's a healthy young man in his mid twenties, who has a crush on you".

"I wish he would just have a fucking crush on someone else." Ruth said looking out of the office window onto the ward.

"You ought to feel flattered, not insulted" Kathy said while watching him walking down the corridor.

"I just feel as if there is something else about him that we haven't seen yet" Ruth said watching him look at her from a distance.

"See that's what I mean. I really don't agree Ruth. It's your paranoia" Kathy dismissed Ruth's claim and started writing notes.

"And he keeps playing Queen songs that I used to love them until he started performing to them acting like me, 'We will rock you' was playing in his bedroom and he was performing like me, with every gesture…I hate Queen now."

After being treated for a month, Colin left the hospital on Fluoxetine (Prozac) He appeared more positive and able to cope with life a little better or so the experts were led to believe, Ruth reserved judgement and felt a little easier when he had finally left the hospital. She felt his eyes on her each time she was on duty and she couldn't relax at anytime at work, even her home life was affected when Cheryl was out visiting family Ruth simply couldn't be alone which was usually her way of unwinding. She went to a bar with friends more frequently; this was because she had a feeling something was going to happen at some point and craved company.

Everywhere she went she noticed every Queen song stood out more than usual, it was as if he knew where she was going and arranging for these songs to be played. Songs such as a 'Crazy little thing called love' which was quite apt at this time for Colin.

In the meantime Colin was in his apartment looking in the mirror, talking to his reflection. "Oh Ruth you don't know how alike we are. Don't worry I will protect you from harm my darling" Colin leant forward in the mirror "But I am Ruth I will protect me".

He had studied her make up from seeing her out at night in local bars, he applied it so perfectly applying each brush stroke and other appliance with ease. Then he stood up and walked just as he had observed, over to the drawers across the room. Out of the draw he pulled out a long dark wig and mutters to himself.

"Perfect" his voice was eerie as he played with it with his hands just like Ruth does.

He had photos of her from her modelling days all around the mirror; each photograph had been chosen showing her flowing hair and soft silky complexion. Unblemished looks that were specially designed to appear good by photographers, Ruth used to marvel at how they made her seem so flawless. Ruth considered herself like cracked porcelain she was modelling attractive on the outside yet scarred on the inside due to past abuse. This was one part of her life Colin was unaware of her abuse or most of her past, although he read about Malcolm in 'Criminal world' magazine. Malcolm the psychopathic killer who was once in a relationship with Ruth, the man that killed Pamela's mother and ruined her life by abusing her and leaving her with all those memories to deal with. Raping and killing her mother in front of her eyes, no one should ever experience that or being raped by another man present. Malcolm later killed Ruth's girl friend Pamela in a fight, where Pamela attempted to save Ruth's life.

Colin sat for hours in front of the mirror and continued speaking and mimicking Ruth, he was having a complete conversation with himself as Colin then as Ruth.

"Kathy who gives a fuck that I am a lesbian its my life and I will live it how I want, no one should be harmed for how they were born. Any fucker who does try to harm them, I will deal with them".

"But Ruth you will get in trouble" Colin responded

"Not me I will be discrete, I will pursue them in darkness and kill them quietly" He replied as Ruth producing a knife from a handbag "Cut and tear without a care, half a pound of two penny rice, half a pound of treacle this is the way I cut with a knife, I bleed you like treacle".

Colin prepared his outfit dressing like Ruth in a pair of dark jeans and a white blouse then put on a small black leather jacket. Then he walked towards the door and opened it placing the handbag neatly over his shoulder before leaving the apartment. With one hand on the door, Colin turns to the mirror by the door , smiling Ruth's smile and speaking in her voice "Dressed to kill" He remarks leaving the apartment and going on the hunt for victims that disliked Ruth. Colin walked for a while before seeing the woman in question, he waited for the opportune moment and when she was alone in a dark alley, he stopped her and spoke like Ruth.

"Do you know who I am?" He asked

"You're that gay Ruth" She replied "I would know you anywhere"

"Oh very good" He said sarcastically "So you don't like gays?"

"Wait are you trying to pick a fight, are you drunk?" She asked

"Fuck you bitch I am sober, but I don't like you" He continued

"Look I am not against gays each to their own as long as you don't bother me" She sounded nervous and began walking backwards against a wall.

"You fucking liar I know what you really think" He began fidgeting and pulled a knife from the handbag.

"I told you I don't want trouble, I just want to go home" She said in a quivering voice

Colin put the knife to her throat and forced the blade across her neck cutting her deeply and then stabbed her in the abdomen. She dropped to the ground landing at his feet; he could feel her body still moving for a while then nothing. After a short while he walked calmly away as if nothing had happened, he seemed to make it obvious that people saw him walking down the street deliberately bumping into people. He took his ear phones out of his handbag and proceeded to play the Queen song 'Killer queen' as he walked confidently down the street.

Colin went on to meeting other women armed with his sharp kitchen knife which he concealed in his bag wrapped in a thick cloth. He took one woman down a alley and questioned her about hating Ruth, she stood confused and certainly didn't expect to die.

"Why don't you like me" He said impersonating Ruth's voice

"I have nothing against you, just your sexuality" She replied

Colin got close to her and waited for his moment to strike, the woman began to edge away from him and said that she found the conversation boring and tried to get away. At that point he got close enough to slit her throat, making sure he severed the artery and watched her bleed to death before he casually walked away. Later he led one woman to his apartment and killed her in a similar manner; she spoke against Ruth in a pub one night overheard by Colin. He spent some time talking to her before killing her and dumping her body. He always played the Queen song 'Another one bites the dust' after killing each one at the end of the week he had killed several women.

The following week the murders appeared on the news and in the papers causing a lot of people to discuss the incident. Ruth was going to work it was Kathy's turn to pick Ruth up from her apartment. Ruth was late and looked particularly tired as she entered Kathy's car, she slumped into the seat wearing dark jeans and a white blouse with a spec of blood on the sleeve. Kathy didn't notice it as it was on the opposite side to where she was sitting in the passenger seat.

"Morning Ruth did you have a rough night?" Kathy asked looking at her tired eyes.

"Oh yes how did you know?" Ruth asked

"Well you look awful" Kathy said honestly

"Oh thanks Kathy that what a lady wants to hear in the morning" Ruth said feeling hurt.

"You a lady don't make me laugh" Kathy replied laughing

"Well shit to you Kathy dear" Ruth said almost smiling

"You see that's what I mean" Kathy continued "The gob on you"

"You wouldn't have me any different" Ruth said smiling.

"Well at least I got you smiling" Kathy said driving along to the hospital

When they arrived Kathy mentioned the murder and hoped that Ruth had seen the news too, but Ruth hardly ever switched the television on in the morning. She never even had the radio on that morning.

"I just caught a glimpse of the news this morning Ruth so I just heard it was a murder near you, down some alley". Kathy explained "But now they have found more bodies"

"I haven't heard anything" Ruth replied "A bit scary though".

As Ruth stepped out of the car Kathy noticed the blood on her sleeve, she couldn't take her eyes off it and made it obvious to Ruth that she had seen it.

"What have you done Ruth?" Kathy asked

"Oh shit I must have caught my arm on some broken glass" Ruth said hesitantly.

"So when did you do that?" Kathy asked concerned.

"I don't know" Ruth replied abruptly "I am okay"

They entered the hospital finding that everybody was discussing the murder; Ruth was surprised by the presence of police who were questioning people in the area. She was surprised as two officers approached her one of them grabbed her arm and noticed the blood, without hesitation he arrested her and they led her to a police car.

"What the fucks going on?" Ruth shouted

"Your under arrest" One of the officers said

"What on earth for?" Ruth yelled

"Just come quietly" Said the other policeman

"Read her the rights" one officer said

When they arrived at the police station Ruth was taken downstairs and locked in a police cell, she remained there while the police pieced together evidence enough to officially arrest her. Ruth sat thinking about previous events, she realised that the blood on her blouse was from her leg. She had scratched it badly in the night self harming from night terrors, but the police wouldn't believe this. She needed either Kathy or her girl friend Cheryl to be there in order to confirm her story, although even Kathy suspected that she was somehow involved in the murder.

After a while Ruth heard someone at the cell door and the sound of keys unlocking it. Two officers stood outside and eventually entered the room; they led Ruth out of the cell, up the stairs and into a small room with a table and four chairs. To her surprise Kathy was sat in one of the chairs, she gave a sigh of relief and greeted her warmly with a hug.

"Kathy what's happening?" Ruth said desperately.

"You are being questioned for that girls murder" Kathy replied "But don't worry I know your innocent".

The police officers sat opposite, the one introduced himself, he was a large fat man with odd teeth and bad breath.

"My name is detective George Mills and this is my colleague Gary" He said introducing his colleague who was a little smaller than him and had a kinder face.

"Gary switched on the tape while George quoted the date, time and details of the suspect and introduction to interview. George also had a package in his hand and seemed to be clutching it as if it was going to escape, he also had a smug look on his face as he proceeded to interview Ruth.

"Now we could make this as easy or as hard as you like Ruth" George began "I mean if you cooperate we can be finished and the job will be easy".

"Where were you last night?" George asked

"I was at home for a while and then I went for a walk to Sankey's bar" Ruth said calmly.

"Did anybody see you there?" Gary asked "it's a big place but nice"

"Yes it is nice and I was there with my friends Gloria and Sheena".

"What time did you leave?" George asked

"About 11pm I needed to get home in order to go to bed, as I was up early for work" Ruth said looking at George then Gary.

"We need you to go with a female officer and get changed out of those clothes, we need to examine them" George said

"What's going on am I being accused of murder? Ruth asked

"Ruth just cooperate please" Kathy pleaded

Ruth stood up and took some clothes from Kathy, she then left the room with a female officer. Soon after she returned dressed in some of her other clothes, she seemed less relaxed and less willing to cooperate.

Gary switched on the tape and the interview resumed Ruth tried not to give George eye contact as he resembled her father's friend and her abuser.

"So would you mind telling me where you got the blood on the blouse?" George asked

"It's from my leg I scratched them in the night" Ruth explained

"Oh, you mean when you were struggling with Janet?" George asked

"Janet?" Ruth asked puzzled.

"The woman you murdered" George said

"I didn't murder anyone" Ruth said shaking

"Oh you mean it was an accident" George continued

"No I mean I never met her or had anything to do with her" Ruth said looking at Kathy

"Well we have witnesses who say you had an argument with her months ago in non other than Sankey's bar" George sat back and again seemed to have a smug expression on his face.

"I remember an argument with a woman who insulted me, she was with a group of women who had been drinking" Ruth recollected.

Gary edged forward and looked into Ruth's large brown eyes, he was watching her expressions and eye movements as George was questioning her.

"I can understand you feeling angry and upset, possibly humiliated by what she said, maybe you had good cause to fight with her. But then it got out of hand and you killed her, no one would blame you for getting upset. What did she say to you?" Gary asked

"She was going on about my sexuality, saying that I was a lesbian who flaunted my sexuality on TV as a model with my friend Pamela" Ruth explained

"What a waste you're so beautiful, so I bet you were angry" Gary said trying to extract more information out of her.

"Thank you and yes I was fucking angry" Ruth replied

Kathy touch her hand and looked at her as if to say stay calm, but she felt her sweaty palm and her fingers were shaking.

"Is Kathy your girl friend Ruth?" George asked watching Kathy trying to comfort her.

"No, she's my friend my girl friend is Cheryl she is probably waiting for me outside this room" Ruth said glancing at George.

"Why can't you look at me when I am talking to you Ruth, is it guilt?" George baited her.

"No not at all I find you repulsive and fucking rude as shit" Ruth said almost spitting in his face.

At that moment she proceeded to vomit, Kathy grabbed a rubbish bin and tissues from the desk. Ruth continued to retch and brought up copious amounts of fluid that made Gary move away from the table.

"This is normal for Ruth" Kathy said rubbing her back

"I'm okay" Ruth said "Sorry Kathy"

At this point the officers decided to stop the interview for the present time they switched off the tape recorder and went out of the interview room. They continued to discuss the case walking down the corridor; Gary seemed unhappy and reluctant to continue interviewing Ruth.

"George something seems wrong about this case" Gary said walking into a nearby office "Ruth doesn't seem like the type of person who could kill someone"

"What a load of crap Gary, she is a typical psycho killer, a real bunny boiler" He insisted "You just fancy her, she looks at you with her big brown eyes and you are in her spell"

"Bull shit George, she has feeling you know and did you see how nervous she was?" He asked almost pleading her innocence "She doesn't seem strong and powerful enough to over power women"

"Nut jobs seem to gather up the strength to do anything mate" George continued in an arrogant manner "I reckon we will have her confessing when we go back"

George was given an envelope by one of the female officers, he looked at her as if she had two heads and then opened the envelope. Gary thanked her and watched as he pulled out half a dozen photographs and spread them across the table.

"Sick bitch, look what she has done to these women, now do you think she is innocent?" George said angrily "Let's get her to confess"

George marched back into the interview room followed by Gary, both of them seemed fuelled up for another interrogation of the accused

"Shall we continue?" George asked rubbing his hand together

"Why not go for it big boy" Ruth said "Do your worst you obviously think I am guilty."

"Are you okay Ruth" Gary asked "Only you seem frightened" he seemed genuinely concerned

"Oh, are you playing good cop bad cop, very cute" Ruth said with tears forming in her eyes "You are fucking pathetic, honestly, one who acts like a prick and the other complements me"

"We need to show you a tape from C.T footage see what you think" George said placing the envelope down on the table and putting a video into a player.

The video showed a figure walking down a street near the crime scene; the person was walking along with a hand bag over the left shoulder and touching her face with her left hand. It was dark and the street was dimly lit with a few street lamps, she stopped for a while looked around and then continued.

"This is you isn't it?" George asked

"No certainly not" Ruth replied "But it looks like me I must admit".

"It is you I am sure of it and so were witnesses who saw you out that night" George said

"I haven't got a handbag like that" Ruth said noticing the white handbag

"And if you look carefully that person is carrying it over her left shoulder, and using her left hand to do things". Kathy said pointing.

"So what does that mean?" George asked in a highly intellectual manner.

"George the person on the video is left handed, he is also a male" Gary pointed out to George who looked disappointment.

"It is not apparent from the outset but watch his walk and the general mannerisms" Kathy said as George reversed and reran the tape.

"Colin" Ruth said "It has to be Colin"

"Ruth that's ridiculous" Kathy said dismissively.

George presented Ruth with a series of photographs taken of the victims, he placed them strategically across the table "Do you recognise any of these?"

Each photograph made Ruth cringe, some of the bodies were cut to pieces and covered in blood, they were hardly recognisable, but Ruth did point out a few of them "I know this one and this one I argued with them in clubs and pubs"

At that moment a knock came at the door, almost immediately afterwards the police woman enters the room. She took George to one side and he seemed to get annoyed by what she said to him.

He walked back over to Ruth and leaned over the table, giving her the pleasure of his foul breath. Ruth waved her hand in front of her face and turned her head away. George seemed uneasy for a moment before speaking, loosening his tie and giving her a poor excuse for a smile.

"Well it seems your innocent and I must apologise" George obviously wasn't used to apologising and being humble, however he was presented with evidence of her innocence on a paper which her squeezed tightly in his hand.

"I would however appreciate your help with my enquiries as you seemed to know Colin Bailey" George said trying not to look at Ruth

"How does fuck off sound" Ruth said angrily "of all the cheek of this excuse for a man"

"Ruth we have to help" Kathy said abruptly "It's our duty"

"Why the hell should I help them with what they put me through" Ruth said frowning at George "He has been a real bully and you want me to help him?"

"Because you're the stronger person and we must stop being obstructive and help find Colin" Kathy paused for a moment "Wait a minute we never mentioned Colin's surname".

"Oh he rang asking what was happening to Ruth, when you mentioned Colin we realised who he was" George explained

"So you were right about Colin" Kathy said to Ruth "I am sorry for doubting you and I should have listened to you in view of past events".

Kathy also realised why Ruth vomited and walked over to George, she looked him up and down then stared into his eyes.

"Ruth is right you are a creep" Kathy winked at Ruth then sat her down and comforted her "its okay Ruth, I understand. But finding Colin will save lives"

They both explained about Colin and the way he behaved, discussing about him being obsessed with Ruth and copying her mannerisms. It was obvious by now that, Colin in his own mind wanted to become Ruth and modelled himself off like her, he even dressed like her. But what was worse he killed the people who were likely to harm her; Janet was only one of many victims discovered while Ruth was in the police cell. A total of nine bodies were discovered in various locations around Manchester and the greater Manchester area, Colin dressed as Ruth and went on a spree of murders trying to justify his actions by saying Ruth was defending herself. But who really knows what is in the mind of a killer, he was not sexually attracted to her, neither was he a homosexual or transsexual in the true sense of the word. Ruth could except any type of sexual preference and mixed with all genders, frequenting the gay village for fun. She was in a lesbian relationship with Cheryl but failed to understand Colin who dressed like her and killed people because they offended Ruth. What was worse Colin remained on the streets and could attack someone else at any time, only Ruth could stop him killing again or could she?

Colin used music to help motivate himself to go out and kill more women, his favourite being 'Another one bites the dust' and it always seemed to be songs by the pop group Queen. 'Another one bites the dust' and 'Don't stop me now' was his favourite songs, although 'We will rock you' was the one he played most with killer queen as his second choice. He was speeding in his car when he used to play 'don't stop me now' and by all accounts he was having such a good time as the killer queen. But he used these songs to fuel his anger and enhance his excitement prior and following his murder spree.

The police raided Colin's apartment and discovered all the photographs of Ruth and then found photographs of Colin dressed like Ruth, it was clearly evident that Colin was the murderer posing as Ruth. Much as Colin tried to simulate Ruth he still couldn't fully disguise himself as a female, it was sad but he really wanted to be Ruth for some reason. With this in mind he was still on the streets somewhere and even though Ruth felt safe, he was unpredictable.

Ruth was being watched by the police as she tried to lead a normal life, they knew that he would have to contact her at some stage, either at her apartment, at Emma's house were her step mother Diane once lived or at one of the bars that Ruth frequented. Ruth just had to be herself and wait for Colin to contact her, she was like bait on a hook sent into the water to catch a fish. She was moving about for weeks before something happened, then one night she entered a club with some friends, her girlfriend Cheryl joined her. She seemed relatively happy, joking with her friends as she walked through the door. After she had been there for a while she got up to dance, as usual joined by Cheryl, Kathy sat with her friends Sheena and Gloria. Ruth was unaware of the police presence as they were dressed in plain clothes, George was busy eyeing up the girls and commenting to his colleagues about how they looked in a chauvinistic manner. But no one was aware that Colin was present, standing in a dark corner, watching Ruth dance in her usual energetic way. He was wearing a long dark wig and a black dress, mimicking Ruth, he was quite relaxed until a Queen song started playing. 'I want to break free' encouraged everyone to start dancing, but Ruth left the dance floor upset.

"Ruth you used to like this song" Cheryl said confused

"I have gone off it" Ruth said walking back to her friends

"Is that because of Colin?" Cheryl asked

"Maybe" Ruth replied abruptly "Sorry I am just going to the toilet"

"I will come with you" Cheryl offered

"No, I want to be alone" Ruth insisted, looking at her friends and then walking away.

She entered the toilet and Colin appeared dressed like Ruth. She felt like she was looking into a mirror looking at her own reflection.

"I have missed you Ruth, have you been avoiding me" Colin said locking the toilet door.

"Colin, where have you been?" Ruth said nervously "I was arrested because of you"

"Oh you know here and there" Colin replied "And call me Ruth after all I am you now, I killed as Ruth and now I have become you. Tell me, do you like what you see?".

"I don't understand" Ruth replied "I am no killer, why do you portray me as such?"

"My dear, I was protecting you, I killed for you. I have solved your problems by killing your enemies" Colin said coldly

"But why dress like me, I don't understand?" Ruth asked

"I am you, don't you understand. I have been you for a long time, and quite frankly. Well, there is no room for both of us and so one of us must die" Colin produced the knife from his white handbag which was wrapped in a bloody rag.

"You know the police are aware that you murdered those women, how many did you kill, four or five?" Ruth asked glancing at the door then back at him.

"Well, nine or is it ten now" Colin said coldly "But that doesn't matter it's just a numbers game. You should be grateful your enemies are dead, it's just us now, but alas one too many.

"Do you intend to kill me?" Ruth asked "After all you did say one too many"

There was a silence while Colin looked into a mirror "Uncanny isn't it, how much alike we are I practiced being you for months and even on the ward when they gave me that electric shock treatment I suffered to be like you. Do you know what it feels like to have electricity surging through your body?"

Colin noticed her edging towards the door and jumped in her way, he held the knife to her throat and let the blade touch her flesh. He managed to puncture the skin holding the knife so tightly and blood trickled down her neck.

"One cut will end it all" He said grinning "Oh Ruth with so much beauty, so much love and compassion, a beacon of hope shining in the darkness, you are lighting the way for so many lost souls."

"But why be like me, what have I got that you want?" Ruth asked trying not to show her fear, but her body language betrayed her as she started to perspire and shake. Then she remembered in her training never show the patients that you are frightened.

"Don't make me angry or I will cut you like the others" Colin shouted "You who have beauty, love and not afraid to express yourself, you who are a lesbian but fights for your gender, you ask why be like you, when you are a living legend" He said holding out his hand and slicing open the palm of his right hand. "This is your blood not mine share it with me" He said wiping it across her face then onto her right shoulder. "This is yours I want you to have it, let our blood flow and become as one"

At that moment the door handle started to move, then came a male voice colin grabbed Ruth tightly around the waist with one hand and held the knife to her throat with his free hand.

"Ruth it's the police were coming in" The voice was that of the policeman George.

The next thing they heard was the door being rammed open by some heavy object, it took a few hard bangs before the door burst open and the police came rushing in.

"Stay back" Colin shouted "Or I will kill her"

George was the nearest to Colin "Come on lad it's all over, hand me the knife"

Colin hesitated "One of us has to die, there is only one Ruth"

George noticed Colin relaxing his grip and taking the knife away from Ruth's bloody neck, "That's it lad relax and let Ruth go"

Suddenly George rushed forward and Colin stabbed him in the shoulder, his large body fell with a thud to the ground. The other officers stood frozen to the spot watching George rolling about on the ground. Colin looked at Ruth and she stared at him for a moment trembling, he raised his knife pointing it at her.

"This is the end Ruth" His eyes widened "I did say one of us had to die"

At that moment he pointed the knife at himself and plunged it deeply into his stomach making sure it was enough to cause a fatal wound, he pulled out the knife and repeated his action. He fell to the ground and Ruth kicked the knife away from his hand. She knelt down beside him and bent her head down his mouth listening to his final words. Her eyes widened as she managed to catch his words and then take his final breath.

"There is only one Ruth and she is you besides who wants to live forever" Colin said before his death.

Kathy was standing close by with Cheryl and other friends each looking at Ruth, Kathy moved forward to comfort her, then Cheryl took over and led Ruth out of the nightclub. All the emergency crew were outside Ruth was helped into an ambulance with Cheryl while the others stood and watched them leave.

Amazingly Ruth did attend Colin's funeral, he was cremated and at the ceremony the family played a song that Colin always wanted for his funeral service called ironically 'Who wants to live forever' by Queen Ruth soon recovered and she was asked to get involved in the Manchester pride festival scheduled for the end of August, by that time she would probably feel better and able to cope with one of her worst fears, which is crowded places. The festival was a busy place and Ruth was used to the gay village as Cheryl and her frequented bars there. Ruth enjoyed dressing up and she would be in familiar company and amongst friends, she loved the parade and interacting with everyone there. Of course gay pride is world wide and both her sister and she were in the New York festival last year. But the biggest problem Ruth had to face was her frequent nightmares; if only she could master them then she could live a relatively normal life. Ruth put the radio on and the Queen song played as Ruth lay down and closed her eyes 'The show must go on' how very apt.

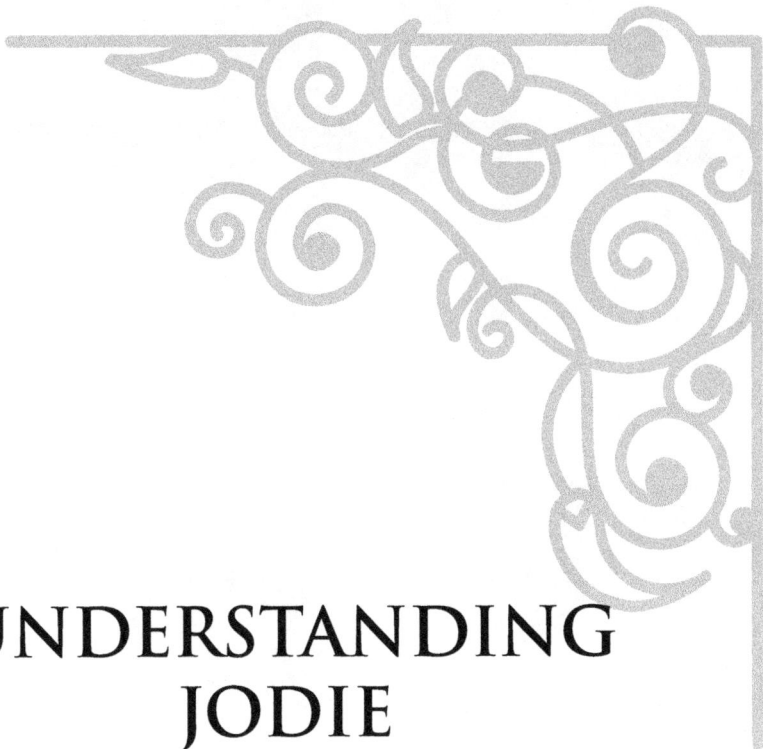

UNDERSTANDING JODIE

S R SUTTON

STATING THE FACTS

This story is fictitious but based on true life events, the aspects of bullying is sadly real and part of life today. During the course of this story the reader will notice that Jodie has a number of problems including dyslexia, this was classed as a disability in 2001 and has been dealt with in schools by providing various support for school children around the world. However problems remain and some children slip through the net undetected this is partly due to the child formulating strategies to deal with their disability. Schools also fail to understand other aspects of dyslexia such as poor concentration and short term memory deficit. The child also develops behavioural problems that stem from shear frustration, they get angry and upset, it is known that some smash or throw objects. Jodie tells her own story after being sentenced to jail for grievous bodily harm (G.B.H) she is very graphic and open about her sexuality, she is also out spoken and sometimes rude, despite this she has a heart of gold. Jodie discusses her sexuality; she was aware of her interest with other girls, as she tended to favour girls over boys and fancied one of her female teachers. Things were drummed into her about the woman's role and gender differences but Jodie was unable to comprehend why boys had to act masculine and girls feminine. She knew society wanted it that way, but why could boys express their feeling and cry. Today we have the solidarity movement for gender equality, which supports the freedom of men and woman to be free to act how they wish despite their so called gender. Jodie was bullied not just because she looked weak and feeble but because of being dyslexic and a lesbian. These are a prime target for bullies, both at school and in society at work or wherever they went in life. So many people are now campaigning for the rights of others and for their own rights in today's society to be free to do what they want with out ridicule and all kinds of abuse. People like Emma Watson famous for her role as Hermione Granger in J.K. Rowling's Harry Potter who has spoken for gender equality at various venues. Peoples rights to be who they want to be without ridicule and being bullied for their choice of what to play with as children such as boys playing with dolls or girls dressing like boys, role reversals in acting out family life such as the mother and father role.

INTRODUCTION

The is the story Jodie Brown, that is me and my so called misunderstood youth, I may seem like any other teenage girl going through puberty with her raging hormones racing about inside her bursting to escape. But along with the every day problems of growing up, I was also the target of school bullying, because not only did I appear weak, but I was so different. I had a problem with my education due to being dyslexic; I had a poor concentration span and short term memory deficit. If this was not enough to contend with I was and still am a lesbian or at least I presumed I was by the way I was attracted to girls, this made me an ideal target for bullies who also showed signs of being homophobic. I went through school in fear of being attacked each day and not knowing what punishment was to be bestowed on me, such as looking for the blue gold fish (or girls shoving my head down the toilet) school life was sheer hell. But then I recruited in self defences classes hoping that by doing this I could defend myself, unfortunately this rebounded and I was in trouble for fighting. So when I was a little older I joined a gang and assumed they would protect me, but my god, got into deeper trouble as I was accused of attempted murder after getting involved in a street brawl. I was imprisoned and the bullying started again, I was forced to face a worse experience in prison with some of the meanest women in society, so was this the end for me? Could I survive prison? Who knows I am still here in this hole and telling you the story.

I was taken through a series of locked doors the prison building is cold and uninviting a despicable place only fit for rats and degenerates, that's me out of the equation, my humble self living amongst thieves and murderers, god bless their bones. I was led into a room and told to sit at a table like I was about to partake in a meal, I was soon joined by a woman of large proportion and the screw that had escorted me from my cell, introduced me to her.

"This is Jodie, and Jodie this is Sally Guinness the Counsellor" She said looking daggers at me.

"Oh charmed I'm sure" I said letting out a little hostility.

The screw considered that I had been well behaved and needed a bit of special treatment, pampering a little; it was one of those goody, goody people who felt sorry for me no doubt. Like the spiritual presence of the local vicar, who considered I needed god on my side, giving me the holy shit. Well my god, anyone would think I had found god, not that he was lost or anything, but as the expression goes seeking his approval or repent and that crap. Well I was interrogated by the voluptuous lady with short hair and a robust figure, my god she took up two seats with her fat rump, one cheek on each seat and I was knocked out by her hair spray. This made a welcome change from some of the disgusting prisoners who had so much body odour it could knock out the entire Russian army, dirty sweaty bitches always rubbed against me. This counsellor Sally Guinness seemed okay, maybe a bit snooty, my gaydar was probably switched off as I couldn't detect any lesbian in her apart from her appearance. She was so butch with manly hands and a funny voice, I nearly shit myself when she first spoke and I must confess I would rather have been in my cell than being sociable with her. Her eyes sparked like diamonds and her chins drooped like a squeeze box quite funny to watch and so distracting, I had wondered whether or not she was a drinker the way her eyes glazed up. But I was mistaken as she looked at me like she was mother Teresa and I was a saint or a sinner waiting to be converted, my god I was never saintly.

"So, you are Jodie Brown?" She asked

"That's me" I replied abruptly

"I have been reading about you" She continued

"I bet that took a while judging by my past and that paperwork" I said making it obvious that I didn't want to be there.

"As you know I am Sally Guinness and I am your counsellor" She said gazing into my eyes.

"That's nice for you" I replied making it plain that I did not want to be interview.

"I am here to help you" She said trying to be nice.

"Do you want a medal?" I said folding my arms in a defensive manner

"No, but a little respect would be good" She said changing her expression from a smile to a frown.

She was clearly a Jekyll and Hyde type, changing her expression like the weather and revealing the persona of a monster whenever she was challenged, grumpy old tart.

"So tell me about yourself?" She continued "What makes Jodie tick?"

Oh, Christ she thinks I am a clock now I thought, I must say, I preferred being humiliated on arrival when they got me to strip naked and go into the shower supervised by a dirty bitch screw who got off on seeing me buff. I put on prison clothes and met other prisoners who looked me up and down like I had two heads.

"What can I say about myself that you have not already read?"

"Just pour your heart out, how did you come to be her?"

"But that must be in there" I said pointed to the paperwork

"You are not being very cooperative are you?" She said frowning again.

"Well, I was accused of causing injuries to a girl in another gang, she was in a rival gang and I was in a Goth gang, thus the image you see before you" I explained "But I am innocent" I quickly added.

"Naturally" She said sarcastically.

"I am really, but then, I don't expect you to believe me" I said knowing no one would believe me.

"Should I believe you Jodie?" She said looking at me oddly.

"Yes of course, but no one believes me or understands me" I said sulking.

"Understanding Jodie, is that what this is all about, no one understands Jodie?"

Suddenly I discovered that this woman was starting to understand me and willing to listen, maybe this was my turning point and I could find my way, my true identity could be revealed at last, instead of Jodie the dyslexic, lesbian Goth I might be someone else. Maybe she would fathom out what was wrong with me and my dysfunctional family who were work orientated, or discover why my schooling was so horrid, why I was bullied and fought back.

I took a deep breath and began to discuss my past from my school days onward, not excluding anything it was like I had verbal diarrhoea, it took quite a few sessions to really explain everything.

"It all began in my school days my parents were workaholics and my brothers and I were passed from pillow to post, going from one child minder to another. My older brother took me to school and escorted me home at night when I was in junior school; I hated my infant and junior school as they did not understand my way of learning. I am dyslexic and have dyspraxia which is a disability, I could not read or write properly and concentration was impossible. I used to get taken out of class into a special group people used to see me go out and mock me, she's going to the thick class one said.

"That must have been awful for you" She said

"Too right it was, I felt so upset and cried a lot" I admitted.

"Did the extra tuition help?" Sally asked

"A little but I really taught myself to read and write using comics" I explained

"How on earth did you do that?" Sally asked seeming genuinely interested.

"Looking at the bubbles that printed the conversation from each character, I fathomed out the words they may have used, it was easy" I said confidently.

"So you did amazingly well considering the barriers that you were up against" She said with surprise.

"Well, I mustn't boast" I said "But I was like the school joke and pupils made nasty remarks and played pranks on me, I suffered so much abuse in those days".

"No wonder you retaliated you had obviously had enough and needed to fight back and it must have made you tougher" Sally said with empathy.

"I was tougher and began to change in the senior school, I had nightmares and dreaded going to school, it made me suicidal and very depressed until I fought back" I had finally got some of what I felt off my chest but the real challenges had only just begun my story really started from high school onwards.

I did experience something really strange when a light entered the prison cell and a young woman dressed in white stood before me, she introduced herself as an angel called Faith and asked me to relate my past and say how I would change given the opportunity, I could only say that it was my past that caused my problems in the first place and discussed my life from my high school days.

I may have been tired and possibly in shock and so this may have been a visual hallucination, who knows for sure but it got me out of a terrible situation. It also made prison life bearable.

SCHOOL DAZE

I t was just another winter's morning, as a blanket of snow lay thick on the ground. I suppose that I would be regarded as a typical fifteen-year-old girl wearing my school uniform with pride and carrying my school bag on my back. I suppose you would consider me pretty with my tanned skin, perfect teeth and large hazel eyes. I am slim and conscious of my weight never eating at regular times with a highly active lifestyle that burns my metabolism like a girl on fire. I always put my hair into a pony tail, I suppose the colour is alright two tone brown, but no doubt when I am older I could be a blonde like my mother. I have started to have my periods, oh pardon me, my menstrual cycle or time of the month and believe me its painful and annoying. My god a woman's body is like so complex compared to a man's, they just get testosterone big deal, where's the pain in that, wankers.

My parents, well what can I say, we lived in a nice house, both my parents work so we looked after ourselves most of the time. My younger brother Gary needs watching though, he is so naughty at times. My older brother Tom who is sixteen took care of us both and walks Gary to school. I am old enough to make my own way to school, although the bullies are always there to ruin my day thinking that it is their god given right to beat up defenceless girls like me. I wonder what it will be today, stealing my clothes from the changing room, flicking a towel at my Derry air or ruining my artwork. Maybe their simple minds will conjure up a new way of making my life a misery, oh how delightful to experience their abuse, how fucking grateful am

I. How I wish they were beneath me so that I can piss on their head, I would so laugh at them for a change.

On my way to school I enjoy walking down the avenue; this was an avenue of trees, I would gaze up at the long thin branches imagining I am in some enchanted Forrest in a fantasy world. I could admire the snow on the trees and feel the breeze blowing gently on my face. It was blowing a spray of snow down like flour being sieved onto a table; I wish I had my paints right now so that I could paint this picture. Did I tell you that art is my favourite subject I spend so much time in that classroom, I feel that I can escape from life in my pictures. I can create my own fantasy and dictate who does what and be a heroine with admirers all around me, conquering my enemies with my sword and shield at hand. A proper Joan of Arc a French heroine or Boudica battling the Roman's as a leader of the Briton's yes surprisingly enough I know my history.

But my adventure ended as I left the avenue, I continued to walk to school my dreams were suddenly shattered by the impact of a snowball to my head, then another to my back taunting me and calling me names. The school bullies continued to throwing snowballs at me one after the other. Suddenly I let out a scream that must have sounded worse than any horror movie; it was that loud it must have penetrated the school building, it was almost blood curdling. Okay maybe not that bad but enough to fetch the teachers out and stop the bullies in their tracks. The booming sound of Mr Gilbert's voice was heard by everyone, he was my maths teacher. He was enough to scare anyone with his tall and broad physique, he was an ex boxer and one teacher that you would never answer back. He watched each of them go inside and gave them a look of disgust for bullying behaviour. I must say it's nice to have someone defend your honour even if it was the teacher

"Right Johnson, Dawson and Julie inside now"

He looked at me a girl that was wet and shivering with cold, suddenly his facial expression changed from annoyance to empathy as he spoke to me in a gentle voice.

"You had better go inside and get dry, Mrs Cooper will help you" He said pointing to the door "Hurry lass before you catch your death"

Bless the old bastard he really cared, I must have looked a sad bitch before his eyes, wet and pathetic looking, you know the type. The thought of being helped by Mrs Cooper, this was like music to my ears the teacher that I drooled over was going to dry my hair and help me to change. My god could life get any better I had the worlds most beautiful woman as my teacher. Mrs Cooper led me into a room in the gym and began drying my hair as luck would have it she was wearing a white blouse that had a few buttons open. I could clearly see part of her breasts wobbling as she was vigorously rubbing at my hair. I was in ecstasy the whole time until she turned me round to dry the back; even then her knees were rubbing against my buttocks. The whole experience was very brief but enough to affect me physically. How bad am I if ever my mind was read I would be in so much trouble, but it made up for the constant bullying I had experienced for years.

I rejoined the class and sat through geography, but instead of studying the contours of land I was back with Mrs Cooper studying the contours of her body. This clearly questioned my sexuality, if I fancied the female teacher like this then was I a raving lesbian or maybe I was bi sexual?. I never thought of it before I was evidently growing up and noticing the human form. Sex classes were no help discussing reproduction and nothing to do with gender types, comparing masculinity and femininity as a way of spotting the difference between male and female. There were no such thing as Homosexuals, gays, Lesbians, transgender or cross dressers, just boring old heterosexuals god bless them. Boys sniggered in sex lessons and girls giggled, some boys giggled but what the hell, usually the teachers that taught it were so old like dinosaurs, they must have had sex like in the last century and had cob webs forming around their genitals. One teacher was old with large drooping boobs, when she walked they banged on her knees and caused bruising. She was fat and clumsy like a bull dozer entering the classroom, bashing about hitting the furniture, deadly in a crowd and lethal in a china shop. Brilliant as an anchor in a storm though, god bless the old dear, I spent the entire lesson imagining her in a life raft with me at sea, thinking who ate all the pies.

Then there was geography who invented that one the best part of geography was the school bell for the end of period; I have never seen a class empty as quickly as Miss Hammonds. She had to be the world's most boring person she could cause the entire class to go to sleep in seconds with her droning voice and she doesn't stop for breath. I have actually seen her turn blue before she began to breathe normally; what's more if she did collapse with her weight she could crush you instantly into a great mush. I was to experience contours and graphs until they came out of my butt, this reminded me of the lesson, yes you got it a load of crap, who really wants to know about these things unless you're an explorer like Scott of the Antarctic or a mountain climber. Mrs Hammond the tranquilizer on legs, do you want a sleeping pill, no thanks Mrs Hammond will do. She lost her vocation completely the silly old bat; she should have a job in how to cure sleep deprivation. Class was over saved by the bell, each of us woke from our sleep like we had been in suspended animation, awoken after years of sleep to find we had been freed from the geography lesson.

It was now break time and I needed a serious bladder evacuation, I entered the toilets and as usual the female bullies were stood talking about boys and who would get a date first. I entered one of the cubicles and was suddenly drowned with water from the girls using plastic cups one after another. How I wished that they would find something original to do, the predictability of water being thrown over me I should carry an umbrella with me everywhere I go., perhaps one that you wear as a hat. Either that or wear a raincoat or some other form of protection, I had to dry out after the deluge, my god isn't school life fun. Only four years to go, I would sooner do time in some random prison, It can't be worse than this surely at least I thought that then, now I am not so sure.

Again I was thinking about that blonde twenty five year old teacher Mrs Cooper, I am going to date her definitely and she will take me back to her place and show me a good time. We would have Milkshake and chicken burgers with extra mayonnaise licking it off with her tongue. At that moment my fantasy ended with the banging of the door and a loud voice.

"Jodie Brown hurry up your late for English" the voice said

English, a lesson that I attend but never liked because of being dyslexic, it's so hard to understand and I always end up daydreaming. I can't concentrate and get into so much trouble with the teachers. I spent most of my school life in front of the headmaster listening to his lectures on if he lived his life again he would be a brain surgeon or dentist, honestly I would sooner be punished by having the Cain by Mrs boring Hammond. God bless the old dears bloomers, I bet she hasn't had a man since the turn of the century. Oh didn't I explain I was at school in the early eighties when corporal punishment was still in use at schools across the country. Teachers sometimes got off with hurting school children, the sad bastards, but I suppose they had to exercise discipline somehow. They must have trained in a concentration camp by the German secret service (S.S) one teacher even had a small moustache like Adolph Hitler, under his great big nose that he no doubt shared with Miss Midrange who had no nose, how did she smell I hear you say, terrible. The odd good teacher made up for the horrid ones, it made life bearable thinking that not all teachers were monsters sent to us to make our lives a misery.

As I sat in the English class, my god, I was given a book to read by another dyslexic William Shakespeare. Romeo and Juliet honestly why couldn't it be called Juliet and Juliet at least I could try to read it. Juliet flashes her tits over the balcony and Juliet two (meaning me) tries to climb up and grope her lesbian style. I would like to know what thee and thou is all about is it teenage slang for thou can't climb because I hast a gammy leg. Can't someone translate this crap into readable English, sorry mate you lost me on verse one, I read a line and wanted to top myself, you know commit suicide. I can't sit through an hour of this, I must think of a plan of escape. Perhaps the vomit routine might do it although my stomach is empty, perhaps a migraine, no I did that yesterday. Well here goes under the table fingers down the throat and result all over the desk and on one of the bitches that threw water over me, Hughie and here it is the girl's hair was a real mess. I laughed all the way to the toilet but the teacher soon got me outside and I was back in the cubical calling Alf and Bert or in your language being sick. Oh my god it was horrid but I soon recovered and sat thinking of Mrs Cooper once more. I must confess I did enjoy her classes even though she taught history I could imagine we were in the Napoleonic wars together or in Tudor times. I washed my face and looked at myself in the mirror wondering what I would look like at the age of thirty. Older and wiser with a different hair style and image without being terrified by the school bullies and hearing the school bell knowing it was for class or break time. I would love to walk down the corridors without fear of being bullied by other school kids; honestly you really don't know what it's like going to school and being terrorised. Dreading going and feeling physically sick each morning, I wonder how many people face being bullied and how they deal with it. I know some people have been known to top themselves (commit suicide) but I could never do that, I wonder is it braver to face them or run away and hide.

I used to play sports like tennis, basketball or hockey but I had problems in the shower or changing rooms because of other girls. They would steal my clothes or slap me, or push me against a cold locker. I have always been bullied and I have to say no one has ever been able to understand me. Understanding Jodie must be a contest and the winner gets to go to Disney for three weeks, well at least I understand me, I think. The thing is facing the humiliation of showering with these bitches they have to make remarks about your body, size of the breasts and such. Well nobody is perfect especially the ones who point out the obvious about the imperfections of my body, but I was growing and developing. One day I knew I would be a nice looking woman with a kind of curvy body, but still my body is the target of ridicule, but that's life I suppose and shit happens.

I am also cursed with a duff brain and a boring personality that's my lot in life, I have no real friends, parents that don't care and teachers I don't understand. But life goes droning on like Mrs Hammond may god bless the old trout. I suppose some people would say that I am being too hard on myself but if you are criticised too much you believe in your own mind that you are no good. If I were to describe my life at fifteen I would say crap, I can draw, paint and do incredible things with clay but it ends there. I am fairly attractive I suppose but no oil painting just boring Jodie Brown, who wants to change and be accepted for who I am and not what others want me to be. Or do I need a new image and a complete change in life, take up self defence classes and be wonder woman or super girl.

It was at this point that I considered that's enough, I have been the subject of ridicule bullied beyond belief and so I took up martial arts. My favourite was kickboxing, my instructor David Westwood said that I was champion material and he wanted me to go into contests. I have to say for a man he was nice and so kind, I built up mental and physical strength through him teaching me. He taught me how to control my emotions and channel it into my boxing, he demonstrated how to get rid of pent up frustration but then he never met Mrs Cooper. What a challenge that would be even for him if she joined his class he would have a permanent erection to deal with. God bless Mr George saveloy Sidwell so called because of his big sausage penis. If Mrs Cooper was in his class there would be no boxing only pole vaulting but then how rude am I, discussing the noble sport of gymnastics.

In cookery class we had a Mrs Totter with the most enormous arse ever, whenever she bent down to take something out of the oven we had a total eclipse of the sun or the moon shining. My god could she cook, she was a wonder with her pastry and roast chicken, she reminded me of a turkey with her fat arse waggling. Her chins dangled nicely down and her hair stuck up in the air, short red and sticky. I managed to bake cookies and cakes

Thinking about my family I must mention the formal dinners that my dear parents were so proud of, they used to invite their well to do friends to these functions. Some of them were so weird and had horrendous table manners, my god they were awful. People like Janet and Brian, Janet would slurp her soup and Brian chewed his food like a camel. His mouth went into the most amazing contortions and I swear I could see every item of food that he consumed over dinner in his mouth. Janet kept tooting like a Kangaroo with turrets, it was about as entertaining as watching an angry pussy spot burst. We were told to watch our manners and sit up at the table, bleeding hypocrites, why should we innocent creatures be subject to this torture every month. Its child cruelty of the highest order and not for the faint hearted, it needs a government health warning. Parent's guests are bad for your health, especially when they embarrass you with stupid remarks about how you look like this relative or that. Or pointing out your skin condition or the way you wear your hair it's simply oh my god how you can even comment you sad sacks. I think my parents must have chosen their friends from a circus full of freaks each one had their own strange ways and emulated facets of animals from a zoo.

And as for parties well all of them appeared in one room like they had been kidnapped and brought to the house, set to perform like seals or monkeys. My god all of them in one room, how can they be so cruel as to put us through that, their own children as a captivated audience. I thought even the Spanish inquisition wasn't as bad as this; it's so amazing what they put us children through. One couple were small in stature and I remember my parents lecturing us on being careful what we said. Tact and diplomacy were the key words in this case, don't mention snow white or reference to the seven dwarfs. But isn't it the case that, the more you try to avoid saying anything the more you slip up, such as 'would you like a drink?' a short or not so small drink. My father asked them if they wanted a short meaning a small drink, I nearly died and this was followed by similar references to their stature. None of these remarks were meant to offend them, but they inevitably did as they came at them like a verbal machine gun at full velocity. But despite the remarks they continued visiting my parents as if they loved to be insulted, my god I can imagine them saying I don't come here to be insulted and my father replying well where do you usually go? But my parents were really sociable and kind, they were popular with many people. I really don't blame them for the way I turned out; after all I was a rebellious teenager with raving hormones, who was out to avenge the world for my horrendous school days but I am sure that I am not the first or the last. Unleash the teenager into society and ravage the human race with uncontrollable hormones as puberty hits the ground running. Go for the jugular and spare no mercy as you vent your anger at the nearest victim, such as the parents, teachers or some other poor sod standing by.

I have already discussed my desire for women and the closer that I got to puberty the worse it got. I did concentrate in the classes on sexual development but again nothing mentioned about Lesbianism so that was balls. Oh but did the lecturer go on about periods like it was the only thing in life that mattered. Describing the time of the month (or the monthly cycle) as the breaking away of the uterus wall and a rush of blood flowing out, or something like that. Why didn't she say it would happen in English class at 10.00am when I was sat relaxed and not wearing a sanitary pad, what a soft bitch? I was so embarrassed and wanted the ground to open and swallow me up, I wonder how many women have had accidents like that, god I nearly bled to death right there and even the boys nearly fainted it was like a massacre. My god you would think I could have had some sort of warning, for instance a bell ringing from down below or buzzer.

Be warned you are about to bleed, sound effects and time to exit the classroom and go to the nearest toilet quickly; don't stop to chat on the way.

Apart from the near death experience I was shocked by how quick by breasts developed from tiny hills to mountains and not to mention the pubic hair, which grew like a thorn bush, both armpits were also blessed with the bush. Suddenly I was a woman its official the evidence was visible and even my body shape had altered into more curvy hips. Naturally this didn't happen overnight but over a few years I was now reaching sixteen and looking back at my early teens wondering how I survived. The bullying continued but the gangs were targeting new blood or students, I was left to the hard-core bullies who concentrated their energies on the strong survivors. I was now sixteen and experimenting with make up and listening to what my parents called annoying loud music, like they were never teenagers who must have annoyed their parents. As my mother often said "I really don't understand you Jodie" she was referring to the way I used to act, but being dyslexic takes its toll and you develop an attitude. It's all about survival and you learn to be hard, tough and with a carefree attitude that appears like you couldn't give a shit. When in reality you do care, you just learn to hide your true feelings in case you get hurt, it's something called fucking survival, not an uncommon attitude with teenagers without the added disability of dyslexia. Dyslexia is about not being able to concentrate properly and having a poor short term memory, but having a duff brain didn't stop me. Looking back at these times nobody ever told me that Albert Einstein or Winston

Churchill was dyslexic and that it wasn't all about intelligence, In fact I was clever after all judging by my academic achievements since my schooling. I was told that a dyslexic brain is different from other brains and the dominant aspect of our brains is in creativity. I was good at art and design and all that stuff, I apparently excelled at such things, I often doodled and created a small master piece that Michael Angelo would have been proud of.

The bullies reminded me of my embarrassing period in the English class by finding a sanitary towel and covering it with tomato sauce leaving it in my desk draw. Then making me know that it was there with subtle hints and innuendos very mature of them, god bless their nerdy brains for inventing an original idea. I remember standing naked looking at my new body in a full-length mirror at my front and then the back. I touched my breasts and rubbed my nipple until they went hard, it was like someone had given me a new toy to play with. Here is your new body Jodie have fun. I was also fascinated with my pussy, it was a new discovery and exciting to touch, I soon mastered the art of masturbation and enjoyed this immensely. I used to watch my fellow pupils in the shower and wonder what they would look like when they developed fully. I watched Television and movies and got turned on by the latest celebrities, women of course, my god they were gorgeous. I was entering a new world and loving it, all I desired was here before me and Mrs Cooper was at the top of my list. A sex goddess in my own classroom, my god I loved that lady and wanted her for my own. I was mature now that I had reached puberty so I could effectively be with her and we could have a thing going, my god dream on Jodie.

The puberty thing led its natural course to self-discovery as my friends and I loved an ice cool milk shake and sweet doughnut which we often shared. We were in a local cafe enjoying each other's company when the subject of sex, boys and girls came up. I had already indicated my desire for women and so my friend Rachel asked me about my interests in the female form, she was as subtle as a flying mallet asking me the question 'Are you gay, you know a lesbian".

"Well what do you think" I replied sharply

"Oh shit Jodie I didn't know" Rachel replied embarrassed on hearing the answer.

"My god Rachel you must have known" I said staring her right in the face.

"No honestly I didn't" Rachel said innocently.

"But all the things I said before, you must have picked up clues" I said trying to explain

"So how long have you known Jodie?" Rachel continued

"Since my body started changing I suppose" I said looking down and pointing to my breasts.

I already knew about my sexuality and gender orientation, I was a female but had no interest in males, the male form to me was revolting and about attractive as cow shit. I wanted to experience sex with men just to prove the point that they were as interesting as train spotting or fishing two of my pet hates. So I arranged to date a boy from school who I knew had a little experience with women in others words a male slag. John Green was anything but green he was said to be the hottest lover in school and I was the one to have sex with him convince him that I loved him and then dump him. I was called the black widow spider because a black widow spider makes love with the male then will destroy him or humiliate him. I was right of course the most boring experience of my life and not worth returning to in a hurry, I lay beneath him thinking about farming on a pig farm, don't ask me why. I don't rock to cock no way; I would rather have a donut with jam or cream, tasty and interesting sticking my tongue in the hole and licking the cream out. Of course I never really let on that I was gay just thrived on humiliating poor John, he became a right wanker of course, probably literally knowing him, perhaps I ruined his sex life.

My first female sexual experience was with a girl called Katie Barnes god bless her, we made out in the drama room. The front door was locked and we crept into the room via the stage from the main hallway. We had not intended to make love as we were just exploring looking for costumes to wear for a school go into detail; it's up to your imagination, I will never reveal the facts but my god I felt good.

After this event we regularly went to the same place and enjoyed each others company in the same way. I knew then that I never ever wanted to be straight and that my future would be with women not men. I had always desired women but had never dipped my cherry before and so hadn't experienced the wonders of same sex relationships. My future was equally as colourful but that another story and there is much more to tell about my rebellious life. I regret few things in my life and I must say we all make love differently that's what makes a colourful world. Despite any criticism I feel that you are what you are and fuck what others think, how can I help my feeling and what's in my head?.

My schooling continued with the usual problems I struggled through my classes due to dyslexia, no one helped of course. My parents despaired at my school reports and questioned me about my behaviour. I had an attitude but didn't care because I got no support and was expected to cope with subjects despite my disability; I was like happy one minute and like a volcano the next. My teachers concentrated on the bright pupils and fuck the rest, so I continued in my own sweet way saying fuck this or fuck that. My god no one understands Jodie or ever will, I am just crap under their shoes and people don't give a fuck about me. Jodie the nobody and Jodie the troublemaker forget my achievements in art or my amazing ideas. I was fed up of existing in a classroom full of time wasters and rebels and I wanted to fit in somewhere. I had wondered what it must be like being in a gang and not being picked on as an individual, I would be protected for once and not expected to defend myself. I would belong to a group of people and share their life style and learn new things from them.

Camp trips had to be the highlight of my schooling, whoever created the idea of camping I could kiss them. Each year pupils would be chosen for their academic achievements or good behaviour in class, guess which category I went under. Well it was the good behaviour of course; at least it was for the duration of the year when I might be chosen. We travelled on the coach and I sat next to my friend Rachel as usual, my dishy best mate. We had just set off when I heard the sound of someone vomiting, my god the smell was revolting, I could not enjoy my small bar of chocolate with someone having a hughy behind me. The moment was lost and I had let my chocolate melt through my fingers as I waited for her to stop being sick.

On the journey to the camp all I could think of was Rachel's body especially her legs, I thought to myself my god how can such a lovely body be wasted on a straight girl. I wish she was gay and then I could have my wicked way with her in our tent. At this moment I diverted my thoughts to the countryside at the roving hills and sparkling lake scenes so shapely just like Rachel, my god I am at it again with my perverse thoughts. Shit I hope the camp trip doesn't affect me, I must stay focused on something else or I am going to regret what I could potentially do. The fact that I am gay doesn't matter but to hit on my best friend my god that would be the cardinal sin, Rachel had a gorgeous figure and I was well aware of it, so I thought of chocolate instead.

We arrived on camp fairly late considering both the teachers and the driver professed to know the way. They had a navigation system and a map so how did they go wrong, oh don't tell me males created both of them and males were trying to understand them. Who is sexist my god it's a wonder we ever got there, the word dick head springs to mind. Never the less we made it in one piece, then came the putting up of the tents in the dark and the cussing and swearing that went on was worse than going down a mineshaft or entering a factory. It was all shit, fuck and bollocks and that was the clean stuff, my god I have never heard so much foreign language even in France. Once the tents were up (helped by a few torches of course) we were all told to assemble outside the tents while we were allocated our own tents, shining torches at each other in the darkness. Of course we got the usual lecture about behaving and sticking to the school rules, this meant no smoking, drinking, swearing, stealing and doing anything to upset the other pupils or teachers. Yeah like that's going to happen, like we will not obey any of their crappy rules, we are here to have fun in life, not join a convent.

Nobody mentioned sex I wonder why, is it because Mr Harvey fancied the knickers off Mrs Lewis from science, Old Harvey was one of the geography teachers who wanted to explore most female teachers contours and knock them off their equator. He was just a saucy bastard who had a permanent volcano in his trousers; you could tell when he had an erection when he walked sideways like a crab. Talk about tent pole he could jack up a car with that mother, I pity Mrs Lewis my god she was in for a challenge. Talk about the cave of wonders, he would need a good light to go potholing there.

It was actually day two when he got his wicked end away, How gullible does he think we are, my god he went into the Mrs Lewis's tent just after midnight, Rachel and myself stayed awake to hear her enter his tent and then we crept up and fastened the tent flaps with safety pins, then by five O'clock we heard her struggling to get out. I must say they must think we are deaf as they give it throttle in the sack, moaning and groaning do they think we are so daft that we think it's the wildlife. And what would their respective partners think of them acting this way on camp, do as I say not as I do, that's the rules here. The following nights he was flapping her tent flaps and this time he put his foot in a cow pat, god the smell followed him everywhere for days. Funnily enough Mrs Lewis didn't visit him for days afterwards, I wonder why.

On camp we got involved with competitive sports such as tennis, rounders and tug of war. Here came my big moment as I played rounders, me and my dyspraxia, no coordination or balance trying to catch a ball. I couldn't catch a cold even worse a ball, for me to be fielding was a complete wonder and disaster in one. I stood there watching the play and then low and behold my moment came, as the ball flew in the air and descended right above me. I cupped my hands and it was like slow motion as the ball landed right in the palm of my hands. Glory I had actually caught the fucking ball, my god, me actually catching the ball and everyone applauded me. I was living the moment right here right now like a famous cricketer or baseball champion, I actually caught it and I was experiencing my moment right there.

Well I have a new name for Mrs Lewis; I shall call her either Mrs Scabby knickers or sticky knickers which ever suits her most, god bless the trollop. She had certainly seen action in her merry little life as she made her way through the male teachers, I am truly grateful that she don't like woman as well. The anorexic nymphomaniac would have a field day with everyone.

The remainder of the camp trip was like carry on camping without the carry on crew. The showers were cubicles with holes in the walls with the male shower rooms next door, oh now where have I seen that before, yes in a scene from carry on camping with Sid James looking through the hole at naked women like Barbara Windsor. But I was prepared with towels and such to cover the holes or a good deodorant to sting the eyes. No purvey men were seeing my naked body or female bits sack that one, I have more pride than that and I will fight the perverts.

Mr Lawrence the religious teacher was with us on the camping trip, he joined us for spiritual guidance. To be perfectly frank I would have preferred a nun with a dirty habit or even the pope in drag. Mr Lawrence was a soft tit, who hated lesbians and thought that it was a sin for the same sex people cohabitate and have sexual intercourse together, I considered him to be lost up his own rectum and suggested that he read the beano instead of the bible. A child's comic would provide him with more insight than what he referred to as god's word, bless the dozy bullock. I was often criticized by Christians and Muslims alike who clearly did not understand anything about Lesbianism, what about reproduction they asked? "Fuck that, what about my own state of mind" I replied.

The only other things I remember from camp were the flatulence and the horrendous food leading up to this condition. Some of the pupils could strike up a band with the farting, it's a wonder that we didn't have explosions all over the camp when they sat by the camp fires to sing. We had burnt offerings almost every night which was said to be a barbecue, I am sure that the Australians didn't introduce this sort of barbecue to England. The songs were boring too what the hell is a ging gang goolie or whatever they were singing was it a testicle that hung funny.

So we went to bed and during the night we heard the sound of the wind howling through the trees and the odd bang. It sometimes sounded like whistling and explosions. My god we are under attack from Al Qaeda or some other terrorist air raid, maybe even the Russians. Rachel jumped into my bed and I must confess I was glad she did, speaking from a completely selfish point of view. I could feel her trembling body close to mine and I swear she had wet herself with fear, but I wasn't prepared to let her go as I was comforting her. She was convinced that we were under attack and were sure to die, imagine ending our lives here and not even experiencing full on snogging. It was at this point that we heard thunder followed by a heavy rain pour as the heavens really opened thrashing at the tent. Rachel and I sighed with relief and fell off to sleep in each other's arms, by the morning I had turned my back to Rachel and she had clung to my back. I could feel Rachel's breathe on the back and my god I felt horny, I had turned so not to get so turned on by her body. She suddenly woke up and climbed across me to look outside the tent.

"Come and look at this" she invited me to look outside.

"My god" I exclaimed as I looked around the camp only to notice that all the tents but ours had blown over.

It looked a complete mess with loads of tent poles and canvases everywhere, but where were the pupils and teachers?

We later discovered that they had all slept in an ex army billet that we would have used had we not gone camping. We had a good mountain tent and so we were comfortable, safe and dry, unlike our poor unfortunate friends. I have to confess to feeling exhilarated for more reasons than none, after all some of these were bullies from school. This is what I consider rough justice and as the religious teacher Mr Lawrence would say god moves in mysterious ways. I call it rough justice although some of the teachers and pupils were not so bad, it was one of those things.

Moving sweetly on in a fashion that I had become accustomed to I began to really get annoyed with the bullies. I was always getting in trouble with other girls or teachers although I earned respect when I dumped John. I was termed as lazy, thick and no good so much that I was beginning to believe it myself. But what everyone didn't believe was that I wanted to get on in school and be academic but my dyslexia was holding me back.

Mrs Cooper helped me but one day I was given the news that she had tragically died in a road traffic accident. I was in shock I couldn't eat, drink or sleep my world was turned upside down. I was devastated and that was a fact she was my salvation and strength and she had died so tragically, what was I to do?.

I headed for the toilets and threw my ring up, suddenly the bowl became huge and my head seemed small inside it. I held onto the sides and felt dizzy. At that moment I heard a voice outside taunting me challenging me to a fight, we were near the gymnasium and I thought this was it my chance to finish the bullying.

Donna welsh was built like a sumo wrestler big, mean and ugly with only one brain cell floating in her head. I could hear the bitch shouting abuse at me and banging at the cubicle door.

"Hey black widow come out here and get laid lesbian bitch" Donna shouted loudly in a mean menacing voice.

I opened the door and stared her in the eyes; her pig like eyes looked back at me with pure hate written across her expression.

We both walked into the gym and two other women each accompanied her holding a bat as a weapon.

"I hear you don't like me bitch" Donna said angrily

"I never said that" I replied confused

"Are you fucking calling me a liar" Donna continued

"No" I made it clear I wanted no trouble "I want no trouble"

"What's that noise, I hear a mouse squeaking" Donna looked back at her friends for support.

"Me too" said one of the gang

"Don't tread on the mouse girls" Donna said sarcastically

"I'm no mouse" I replied bravely or stupidly I suppose

"Sorry you squeaked girl, fuck she squeaked" Donna suddenly hit me in the stomach with her bat.

I fell to the ground holding my stomach one of the women went to hit me with her bat when Donna stopped her

"This bitch is mine" Donna said watching me trying to get up

"I said I don't want trouble" I told them again remembering the self control that my instructor George taught me.

Again Donna hit me this time in the ribs, this time I fell backwards but remained standing as she thumped me in the nose.

I felt the blood trickle down and onto the floor and knew by now I had to defend myself, despite what my instructor had said, I was in a corner with no way out. Donna rushed forward to attack again this time I swerved to one side and she hit the wall with the force of her body, I quickly turned and kicked her in the small of her back and she fell like a sack of potatoes. One of the other women raced to her defence and she was immediately knocked to the ground with a kick to the throat by yours truly. The other woman tried a pathetic punch, which didn't even connect, and I simply kicked her legs from under her and delivered a blow to her stomach so hard she yelled out in pain.

Donna tried to get up but I thumped her repeatedly on the face and drop kicked her in the chest and she rapidly returned to the ground, rolling round the floor holding her chest.

At that point the teacher came in clapping slowly

"Oh very good Jodie Brown, excellent for your school record" the teacher went on "So what do you do for an encore, break bones?"

I was so surprised at her attitude considering I was defending myself

"But miss I was ganged up on they were trying to beat me up" I said knowing that I was on to a loser.

"Looks like it Jodie, I think you beat them up" She said almost smiling

I really think she thought I was in the right but could not admit it, she must have wondered how so many of them had been injured by me.

At this point my parents were called into school and the facts were so twisted not even a judge would be able to fathom out the truth. My parents were certainly shocked at my behaviour but then they didn't quite understand my dyslexia or why they had me in the first place from what I could see both sat in the office not saying a word. Neither, mother or father gave me eye contact; I was just listening to the whole circus wondering why I bothered defending myself in the first place, I had been judged and sentenced right there at that moment.

The head of school gave a nice speech about self-control and how I apparently beat up three girls and used kickboxing to do this. The only one who actually believed me was George my instructor; he was not surprised at the story as I related it to him, according to George self defence can be a case of you defending yourself but the attackers injuring themselves through their own efforts to hurt you. But unfortunately that didn't help this situation and my school record; I had well and truly blotted my coffee book, or fucked up my school life.

"I have something to say" I announced proudly, this was my moment.

Everyone looked at me as if I had two heads, not one person actually cared what I thought, but I continued anyway.

"When I was seven and being bullied who helped me and as the years went on did I get help with dyslexia, no, I didn't and then I came to this poxy school and was I bullied again? yes I was and was I helped?, no I wasn't, so the day I fight back its all sympathy to the other poor girls but me I get punished. My god where's the justice in that?" After I given my elaborate speech for justice the room was silent I felt that I had given my all and that everyone would sympathize or even empathize, But no one did and nothing was ever offered to me, it was like I didn't exist. It was as if I had simply farted and not apologised for my actions, wasted gas from the ass a pointless exercise for me. Bullying was obviously acceptable in this society, schools actually sanctioned or so it seemed. What was the point of having self defence classes when I was in trouble for defending myself?".

However I did gain the respect of the school pupils after this day, I was conscious of the golden rule of not getting the other girls in trouble by telling the head teacher about their antics. Donna never approached me again and wanted me to join her gang, naturally I refused that treat and continued with my artwork without any further problems. I realised bullies just needed to know that they were not going to get away with hurting other pupils and that was good enough reason to punch the lights out of the bullies. The secret was to find the leader of a gang or ringleader and beat them up first, like skittles find the strongest and hit that and watch the others fall. Simple logic that even the dumbest person could work out, I was considered thick, but I proved that I was knowledgeable at times. I was instrument in helping the weak and stamping out bullying, but to be honest they used more subtle methods of hurting them as abuse has many evils.

There are many types of abuse and the pupils at high school know them all and use them to their advantage, it makes me wonder if we will ever fully stamp out bullying.

I hated being called out of class to the special lesson for dyslexia or other learning difficulties, it was quite obvious where we were going, when the special needs teacher blurted it out in class. My god, why didn't she just blow a trumpet, and announce my presence properly.

"Jodie, can you please come to your dyslexic class!" Honestly how discrete is that and my form teacher didn't help as she pointed me out so that all the other pupils would see me, like "Here she is" My god I wanted to die on the spot or hope the ground would open up and swallow me whole. My entire school days were embarrassing for one reason or another, poor Jodie the one no one understood or the dyslexic lesbian, labels on kids were common, no wonder bullies thrived in these places.

OH TO BE A GOTH

The next phase in my life happened by accident as I pointed out I never wanted to be in any gang, I never agreed to gangs or the problems that went along with them. Usually a gang hanging around a street corner meant trouble and could look menacing for others. Although I must confess I felt safer in a gang and found that I got into less trouble through defending myself, how weird is that getting in trouble for defending myself, so much for martial arts. Society is so strange and the balance doing good against being bad is totally off the scales. I was honestly on the brink of lunacy, my god was I fucked up and my screwed up family didn't help, banging on about being good following the code of conduct laid out by society. By being politically correct society enforced a type of bureaucratic control. How about that for a dyslexic numpty? Who I might add, was said to amount to nothing at school, one piss in the eye for you so called teachers. I term these people as dawks in dark clothes, or those who cause destruction of a good thing, and replace it with something absurd namely a school nerd. God I sound cynical giving it out about the clever bods of the school it makes me sound like I got the problem, bitter and twisted bastard.

But the best was yet to come when I was invited to a Halloween party what fun that was going to be me as a Goth like creature of the night, a type of vampire.

At first it was like experimenting with make up, mainly black, with a subtle application of face powder to give a pale effect to the skin which also covered up the present acne problem that most teens got. Then the eye liner and mascara with a hint of purple or blue on the eye lids and surrounding area. With black eye brows and black lip stick, I had already dyed my hair black and dressed in black with a black necklace and black nail varnish I was almost ready for the schools Halloween party which usually meant older brothers or sisters invited and gate crashers. I wore a black skirt and black tights with stylish boots to match and a black-laced blouse; looking back I was a dead ringer for Morticia from the Adams family. Such a scary sight to behold but fitting for a Halloween party, which was arranged by the school for a get together of students, teachers and parents and as I mentioned gate crashers. It was well organised I must admit but guess who's parents didn't attend? Yes surprise mine god bless them.

I reached the school hall and noticed quite a few people dressed for the occasion. It was most impressive inside like a horror movie film set such as Van Helsing with a long buffet like Harry Potter's Hogwarts School. It was a good turn out the hall was packed with witches, devils and vampires all feasting. But something was wrong not all the people fitted in seemingly slightly out of place, particularly one gentleman who stood out with his strange top hat and long black coat. He even acted oddly as he walk around with a blonde woman who seemed to frown at everyone.

He finally stood in front of me and eyed me up and down, then looked at his companion.

"Marsha my dear I think we have found a Goth" He said confidently

Marsha didn't seem impressed gazing at me and then brushing her blonde hair back with her hand. She was dressed very much like me but had some sort of flower in her hair and red ribbons in her costume. She was in her early twenties a very serious girl, who was probably afraid to smile in case she cracked her face; she disliked me from the start evident by the evil looks that she gave me. She stuck close to this man that she called snake, he was weird but nice if that makes sense.

"Well be polite and say hello" He insisted

"Hello" She said reluctantly

"My name is snake, and who might you be?" Snake asked

I looked at his rather long nose and narrow face, I remember thinking he was skinny enough to be a snake, long and thin.

"I am Jodie" I said hesitantly "Nice party" I said trying desperately to make conversation but failing miserably.

"But people call you black widow" He said looking at Donna across the hallway.

"I have been known as the black widow for certain reasons" I smiled at him because I knew what he was referring to.

"Poor Johnny got his tail cut off with you the spider who eats his lover after making love, I like it". Snake smiled cunningly.

I suppose Snake could come across creepy at first, but he had a lovable side to him. He had a dry sense of humour and loved the mystical side of life; he was very much into Gothic art and music.

As for Marsha she was very much in love with Snake and was so jealous of me, she detected an attraction between Snake and me, but I was merely fascinated by him, however he was obviously attracted to me sexually. I say this because his eyes wandered down to my breasts and his hands landed onto my bottom. Marsha refused to speak to me from this day forward; she also had a cruel streak in her and would often use it to push away possible admirers of Snake.

Snake was almost like a Messiah, people often followed him and would do anything he said; they latched on to his every word and believed that he possessed magical powers. His disciples were all around him most of the time I met them later when I visited their hang out as he called it.

It was an old disused church or at least the ruins which lay close to the city, it was a cold stone building with half the roof missing. When it rained the Goths would moved to the sheltered area near the old alter, Snake always led the way and became annoyed if anyone went in front of him. He was what people would term as a narcissist or one who had grandiose ideas, he was the main man and no one was higher. He would make displays of being important and often ran away with his own importance, he never really loved one person, but kept a female following close by his side, like the brides of Dracula. To describe Snake I would refer to Dickensian characters namely Fagin from Oliver Twist or Bill Sykes when he was angered. But still I would say he was a likeable chap despite his narcissism or his obvious personality disorder, he would wave his hands around majestically as if he was a king and conduct his flock accordingly.

I left the party with Snake, Marsha and a strange little man called shady he was so called this because he liked to walk in shaded areas and he was so quiet and maybe a cunning fellow. Once in the ruins I met Juicy Lucy a blonde bimbo who was always giggling and Mash a fat boy who loved mash potatoes. Clay was another member of the gang, a big hard man who never smiled. Fudge was a fat girl who was always eating, Drab was a girl who dressed more plainly and came out with boring things, these were the main gang members that I recall. The rest were not even mentionable and easily forgotten, all followed Snake and listened to his words of wisdom.

"My friend my people you are here to learn about the truth namely the reason for why we are together, I say this because you are like lost souls without your leader and it is I who keep you happy and fed. You have no life without me and I am the reason for your existence, but my children I will maintain your very souls and keep you warm. You will have your physical needs met and your psychological needs met, you will come to no harm while you are with me. I ask only for your loyalty, honesty and love". Snake spoke in such a poetic way and all his flock took in every word. He was almost like a messiah, some kind of holy man or saint, whatever comes to mind, oh yes, narcissist.

All I heard initially was Goth rock music, a strange sound which included 'I walk the line by Alien sex fiend, yumma yumma man by

Daniella Dax and were so happy by the dawn society. These were being played constantly and the odd smell of cat piss which indicated someone was on the wacky backy or cannabis. Snake approached me after attending the church a few nights

"If you're with us you need to prove it" He looked serious

"What do you mean" I asked not knowing what to expect

"Oh like an initiation into our gang" He replied looking at the others

"What do I do?" I said worried to death that he might get me to eat a live toad or sacrifice a lamb or expect me to have sex with him on the alter in front of all his flock. But he wanted me to do something strange for the first task by going into a catholic church and pissing on the floor in the confession box. That tasks were quite odd and I never fully understood why I did them was it an act of obedience or an initiation ceremony of some description. This cutting of my hand and sharing my blood with him I never fully understood it was something sacred to Snake, the first task was to go into a confession box and urinate in it, the second to steal fruit from a market stall, and then to cut my own hand while he cut his and share our blood.

My first task had to be the worst ever I entered a catholic church and the gang kept look out as I checked the door hoping it was locked and that I could be saved from the humiliation of this deed. Alas it was open and so I went in nervously and immediately dropped my knickers and urinated on the floor, it seemed to last for ages and although it was dark I swear I could see the shiny wet floor. I was soon out of there and actually saw urine coming out of the box that had to be evidence of my deed. A priest went in soon after with a catholic woman and came straight out in discussed. My second task was simple stealing fruit I took a pile of oranges off a fruit stall and ran swiftly, a man ran after me but he was too slow and I escaped unharmed. The third task was painful and bizarre as I cut my hand with a knife and Marsha was asked to cut hers, we were made to join hands and Snake captured our blood in the palm of his hand and licked it off like a vampire.

I was often curious about the plans made by Snake as he was clearly not singing from the same hymn sheet as me, he definitely had a slate missing off the roof and that concerned me greatly. I often wondered whether or not he was on medication for some sort of mental illness. Not being an expert I could not put my finger on what exactly was wrong with him. But I had joined the gang for a reason, for protection and that was my excuse for what it was worth. The weird eccentricities displayed by Snake added to an unsettled feeling that I had from the start, I suppose that I was curious to see whether or not he was truly insane or just bizarre. I might add that Goths don't always go in gangs or present in the way Snakes gang did, they were quite extreme and bizarre for Goths.

We often went for night walks especially on foggy nights; we were like silhouettes in the lamp lit streets immerging like figures from time. Imagine a Dickens movie like Oliver Twist or something like Sherlock Holmes, it was as if we had entered a time warp and were living in Victorian England. Goth was cool but I felt uneasy, as we seemed to up set a lot of people with our antics. For anyone who saw us I should imagine we looked quite menacing, wearing our black attire and acting strangely. I often got grief from my parents god bless them, they clearly did not understand why I dressed and acted the way I did, it was called being different finding my own identity that sort of crap. I played the Goth rock loud and wanted to hear the voices and deep bass sounds vibrating through my body, the weirdest sounds were the best. Their freaky friends thought I was odd how bizarre was that considering they were from the freak circus, no one could be that strange, they were the oddest people I could ever meet.

As Goths we were devoted to our music and life style I started living with Juicy Lucy for my sins and my god I was paying dearly for that, she was as freaky as they came and constantly chatting. She was one annoying bitch with her silly laugh and dozy ways it was only one step better than living with wanking Tom and tormenting Gary. What we lesbians have to put up with in our lives annoying people and dreaming about gorgeous women like pop and movie stars, I was melted by many performers, totally orgasmic.

Snake suddenly spun round his long coat flowed as it did so; he had a look of devilment in his eyes, which was never good.

"Let's have some fun" He announced "God the air is good"

He looked around him and smiled "It's a perfect evening for fun"

When he acts like this you can expect problems, he was bored and needed excitement, an ignition of explosive and dynamic fun. Everyone looked to him for inspiration after all he was the dark messiah and what he said happened, a plan became a reality or event.

Drab looked at the others with a vacant expression on his face

"Are you with us Drab?" Snake asked

"Just thinking" Drab replied

"Well don't fucking strain your head Drab" Marsha said teasing him

"Why do you keep picking on Drab?" I asked Marsha

"Keep your nose out widow" Marsha said poking me in the shoulder

I was so angry at her attitude towards me and constantly picking on Drab.

"Why what you gonna do if I don't Marsha?" I said challenging her

"Just keep on black Widow and you will see" Marsha said pointing at me

"Now girls lets be nice ok" Snake advised

"My god Marsha what have you got against me?" I asked her in order to bring our problems out in the open.

"I don't know I just don't like you" Marsha admitted

"But we all need to get on we are like family" Snake chipped in.

"So no bitchiness he went on".

"I agree" Drab said

"You would you freak because you fancy her, but she's gay brain ache"

Marsha ought to have been called Snake as she had so much venom she was sly and cunning, with that wicked look in her eye just like Donna at school. But when she verbally attacked one of her new found friends

"Hey dumb ass why don't you fuck off somewhere else, you sad miserable bastard"

That was the last straw I heard a remarks towards Drab and lost my temper, I charged at Marsha and pushed her. She stepped back at the same time and landed me a cunning blow to the face. I thought my nose was going to explode as her fist made contact with my chin, I fell back and Marsha saw her opportunity and jumped on top of me. Normally I would enjoy this but Marsha was one hateful lady and she had the advantage being such a crafty madam. Marsha was hitting my head on the pavement until I managed to knee her in the back, then I did what girls do best grab her hair and pushed her off me. I then returned a punch to the nose and a thump to the chest. We seemed to be rolling around the pavement for ages until Snake and a few others stopped us.

We both stood with blood on our faces staring at each other with hatred in our eyes. Snake was pacing up and down and so disappointed with us and the others just remained quiet. We were still being held while Snake suddenly slapped us both on the face in temper.

"This does not happen ever, you are both fucking idiots" He then noticed that he had blood from both off us on his fingers and sucked it off.

"Let's go back to the church" He insisted.

I had a nightmare that very same evening; I fell asleep and began dreaming of vampires. Snake appeared at the church and was making eyes at me; he put me in a trance and my god I was under his spell. It was horrid suddenly he had fangs and was sucking the blood from my neck. I went white and collapsed onto the church alter, where other vampires like Marsha also bit me and sucked my blood. I woke up in a cold sweat and staring into the darkness, hoping it was just a dream. It felt so real and Snake made a good vampire, his lust for blood made me think so and as for Martha well her wild behaviour was evident in my dream. I came to life as a vampire and walked through a graveyard; I travelled through mist and felt totally alone. Other vampires who floated around me in mid air, each one looked magnificent in their costumes suddenly joined me and their fangs were shining in the moonlight. A loud sound echoed in the darkness and we had vampire hunters pursuing all of us. I found it difficult to fly properly and felt something pierce my side, I fell to the ground and a ugly man held up a sharp steak to my chest. He drew back and then forced it into my chest and I awoke from the dream petrified.

Marsha and I continued to make verbal remarks to each other for months even years, but as time went on I saw less of my parents, they were relieved as I was a true Goth and proud of it. Of course this was not really so because a Goth would not do what we did and tended to dress the part but not be as outrageous as us. We were also part of a gang, where the other Goth's in society were quite placid and more sociable. We gave Goth's a bad name due to being aggressive and argumentative, but most of the gang blame the leader for their attitude towards society.

I remained with the Goth gang for two years, going to the church having parties and listening to the Goth music. I must say I did enjoy most of my time with them, until I reached the age of eighteen. In fact I even celebrated my eighteenth birthday with them in Gothic style. Snake remained the leader of the gang and Marsha remained by his side, he became stranger than ever. Marsha was always jealous of Snake and I, she hated the attention that he gave me although I am a lesbian; Marsha thought I was a bi sexual. Snake also attempted to kiss me and made a fuss of me, she even heard him discussing how fed up he was with her and her clinging ways. This made Marsha more determined to get rid of me out of the gang; she never liked me and was obviously planning this for some time. We had many verbal fights but tried to keep the peace for the sake of the gang. But even some of the gang members were finding other interests and were hardly ever together. People were starting to mistrust Snake and no longer think of him as some sort of messiah, he had lost his credibility since his strange behaviour.

Marsha left the gang for a while, but returned trying to rekindle her love for Snake, she thought she could carry on where she left off, but Snake still tried to come on to me and rejected her pursuits, this angered her and she continued to plan her revenge on me. Then on what I would consider the worst night of my life Marsha sat in the church beside Snake, she was looking a little sheepish with a guilty look on her face. It was as if she had done something wrong. Marsha managed to catch me alone and wanted to talk to me, she seemed sincere at first, as if she had regretted being my enemy.

"Jodie, I don't hate you but I admit I am jealous of you" She admitted

"Well, I am a lesbian you are safe" I explained "I only like Snake as a friend nothing else".

"Good because if you are lying I will kill you" She threatened

"I have no intentions of lying to you, but I am also not afraid of you and I would doubt whether or not you would kill me" I said making my stand

"As long as you know where you stand" She went on

"Oh I can look after myself and will do if necessary" I said smiling

"Friends then" Marsha said holding out her hand in friendship

I shuck her by the hand but never trusted her.

A few nights passed then one night when the moon was full, Snake was particularly agitated pacing up and down in the church. I noticed someone standing near him who I had not seen before; he was wearing a leather jacket and looked unshaven with a front tooth missing. I approach them hoping to find out what was happening but they were being very secretive. I asked Clay about him but all he could give me was his name 'Weed' and that he was into drugs. I must confess drugs certainly were not my scene and I was not about to try them. So the presence of Weed didn't please me, I was contemplating leaving them at this point but Clay gave me some cider and I foolishly stayed. I was relaxed drinking my cider god knows how much I had but I felt merry and I found that even Drab was interesting to talk to. My god I felt good at this point, but I remember saying to someone that I had a headache probably due to the cider. Someone passed me some tablets and I felt as if I was flying through clouds.

I think that it must have been Marsha looking back at the turn of events. Soon after this we went out and Snake was calmer although he seemed to be on a mission, he beckoned us on into the night under the light of the full moon. Snakes eyes were red and his pupils were dilated he was acting strange, out of character even for him. I think we were all high on something I remember being confused and my body didn't seen as if it belonged to me. Fudge seemed breathless clinging hold of her fat as she walked down the street. It was like looking at a dark marsh mellow and Juicy was dancing in the street.

Suddenly we met a rival gang across the street, they were rockers dressed in leather jackets and jeans. They began taunting us shouting abuse one of the Goths shouted back abuse but added a few choice words of his own. This cause tension between both gangs and we were soon in a fight. Fists were flying, kicking and brawling in the street. This is when Marsha seized her opportunity and began kicking one of the girls in the other gang behind me. She managed to get her on the ground and continued punching and kicking her. I tried to stop her but felt something hard hitting my head and I fell to the ground dazed. Marsha saw her chance and began kicking me; it was awful I lay next to the other girl who looked badly beaten. Suddenly I heard police sirens and before long both the gangs disbursed and both the girl and I were alone. I stood up and looked at her, I wanted to help her, but I was handcuffed and she was being helped by the police an ambulance came and took her away and guess who got blamed for her beating. Yes I did, although I was dazed and confused I could beat up a girl and do such amazing things. I could feel blood on my face and my ribs felt broken as I ducked my head down in order to get into the police car. I remember hearing the girls name mentioned Joanna, so I repeated it to myself so that I wouldn't forget it. I felt so bad about her although it wasn't my fault; I suppose I should have made more effort to save her. If my head wasn't so fucked up I could have helped her, but things were so insane and those tablets were no doubt ecstasy. So I am a druggy and maybe a murderer, in a Goth gang and god knows what else.

Following the tragic attack on the young girl Joanna who by some miracle survived, I was held in the local police station, I was sat in a cell looking at the horrid walls and iron door which I had previously seen on television in cop shows. I never thought for one moment that I would be in one, next comes the interrogation. The strong light in the face and asked to talk and reveal all, my god will I fuck. Although the heating is on it still seems freezing, colder than that church that I was in, oh to be a Goth. I still think of Mrs Cooper and being back at school those moments of being bullied and my glory day striking back. My god I defended myself that day, no fucker was going to bully me forever. You can only take so much then blow, give the bastards everything you've got, don't let them beat you.

PRISON DAZE

I always dreaded the thought of being in prison and felt one day something would cause me to enter a prison, but when it happened I was scared knowing I was to go to prison soon and at present remained in a police cell.

Oh here we go the doors being unlocked and footsteps; of course it takes an army to escort me to the interrogation room, my god sad bastards. They led me to a room with a great big mirror, probably two was so they could psycho analyse me and say what a poor child led into this situation, deprived of parental love and all that bollocks. My god I do love these places, sitting on a plastic chair with a wooden table and strangers in the room. A woman say beside me and introduced herself as my legal representative called Kathy, my god she was ugly, everybody has the right to be ugly but she abused the privilege. She had obviously fell out the ugly tree and hit every branch on the way down.

One of the officers sat staring at me like I was a freak, in the end I couldn't help myself I gave him a visual sign with my index finger basically saying screw you pal. It didn't go down to well I guess he wasn't getting any from his misses and took it out on me. It was a case of good cop bad cop the policewoman was nicer and I do love a woman in uniform, they are so superior and domineering. I must confess I am a submissive lesbian who likes to be told what to do sexually. So back to the interrogation with the policeman with a big nose postman pat with an attitude. He questioned me about my actions and reminded me of my school report, the one-day that I defended myself and I get this shit. He leaned forward almost in my face I could almost lick his nose, or tickle all the strands of hair growing out of it. My god he had more hairs sticking out of his nose than on his head, perhaps that's what happens to men, they go bold on the top and then every out of every orifice comes these hairs.

"So why join a gang?" He asked

Before I had chance to answer he was in with the next question

"Is it because you thrive on beating girls up?" He said with a smirk

"No I fucking well don't I was the one being bullied at school and who helped me then? No one so I had to defend myself or continued being bullied not like you arse holes would understand that" I said in anger.

"Wow temper Jodie" He said with his hands up

Even the female officer looked at him with discussed

She cleared her throat and began talking to me softly but with authority

"Jodie we realise its been difficult for you, but beating up a girl is no answer, "Why did you do that?"

"I guess I wanted to be noticed in the gang as they protected me"

"Explain Jodie" She said beckoning me on

"I completely lost it, I was lying so the gang didn't get into trouble I was actually protecting Marsha, knowing the bitch wouldn't defend me in any way". The rest of interview went reasonably well I just kept quiet shed a few crocodile tears and then waited for the outcome.

I was an hour in the interview room waiting for my parents to arrive, which was an agonising time when they came in and almost blanked me. I was clearly invisible as the police spoke to them in length about my behaviour. All I could do was sit there kicking my feet against the table with my boots on and thinking this is the first time that I have seen my parents in months. My father made an exhibition of himself saying how he had provided for the family and I was the only problem in his life, yes bull shit dad. Mother just broke down in tears and gave it the woe is me treatment. I suppose this is parenthood, not for me I am glad that I am a lesbian no kids and no hassle, apart from now of course.

The end result meant that I had to go to prison for a short time, on my fathers request he wanted me punished and was determined to let them do this. The judge said that I was to be made an example of to deter other gangs from doing the same harm to an individual. The jury sat looking at me as if I had two heads and came out of a circus, I dressed Goth so what get over it. I was going to explain that not all Goths are in gangs and fight but who would believe me, these chosen people the jury from all walks of life most of them didn't even want to be there. They didn't care about me just got their day off work and got paid for sending me down.

I still see my fathers face as he shouted send her down and punish her for what she's done and I suppose if the tables were turned I would have done the same thing. I understand that he was actually heart broken having to make that decision based on the evidence provided, I really don't blame him at all. I might even say the next years did me good because I became stronger and more determined to fight my disability called dyslexia.

I had explained a lot to Faith my long suffering guardian angel all about my life at school the Goth gang and how I truly felt about my life, it may have been a waste of time and for all I knew I could have imagined her presence. However

I continued to explain to Faith how things happened in my life and how I felt, little knowing the battle that was occurring in the spirit world between Faith and Fiona mainly. Fiona was said to be a demon that was the reason that I had suffered all these years and classed as a fallen angel. The fallen angels led by Satan were hoping to capture my soul apparently, and I was walking right into their hands, I suppose that I demonstrated this by my actions, but Faith was determined to win. Faith could see the good in me by the way I was with others, trying to help the weak ones in the gang just as I tried to help other pupils at school.

I was taken to a women's open prison for six months and my god was that rough, I was stripped which I have to confess was embarrassing and searched. I had to be showered in front of a female prison officer (a screw) and then examined by a doctor for my fitness, who was no doubt purvey bitch. I was then taken inside to meet other prisoners and officers, some were definitely butch lesbians and my gaydar was on checking them over. This is when I first met Fiona a female prisoner who was worse than Marsha; she was more mean and jealous than she was. In fact she was pure evil. She hated everybody at times, she wanted to harm everyone, but even she could be nice if she wanted something. Little did I know that she was a demon and at this point I was not informed by my guardian angel Faith.

I was assigned to a job in the prison on laundry as Chinese washerwoman calling me 'wha wen Wong' (what went wrong), a question I always ask myself. I visited all areas of the prison collecting washing from the beds and prisoners; I must say some bedding was disgusting. It was a case of blood, piss, other body fluids and shit, sometimes-sweaty towels and sheets. Often you could match the bedding with the prisoner just looking at each one and thinking my god I am in for a treat today. I did my time at that prison and knew about it blood sweat and years I called it, with no time off for good behaviour. Some young girls were less hard than me and got sucked into the meanest bunch of hard-core prisoners ever known; they were bait on the hook no danger.

I lay in my cell each night reflecting on my past I was a mere eighteen year old spending my time in prison bored out of my tiny head with my prison mate. I did wonder how that girl had been getting on that I allegedly beat up. I did feel bad that I was once being bullied and now I am classed as a bully it was not what I wanted. Now I was classed as a young offender and had a criminal record doing time in affect for Marsha. Fiona had fair hair and small nose with a small body and menacing green eyes just seemed to stare at me and make me feel uneasy, hiding in shadows and bullying the weak ones.

To be honest I wanted to punish myself for what had happened to that poor girl, after all who was to say that I didn't actually hit her I was barely conscious after being hit by Marsha. But I couldn't quite think of how I could do this effectively, and then I came up with a plan. If I could get someone else to do this I would be satisfied in my own mind that I was being punished and could sleep at night without having a conscience. T he way to do this was to approach the top dog and insult her, this would lead to her beating me up and therefore I was punished. This was possibly a strange way to get punished but effective if I wanted to be free from guilt. Fiona made me feel guilty by saying that I should punish myself for such crimes and suffer any punishment bestowed on myself. She even indicated that I should consider suicide taking myself out of this wicked world.

I planted the seed by making it known that I thought Doggie was a fat tart with nothing better to do with her time than shagging fresh new girls. It worked a treat telling the right people such as Fiona, the gossip reached her in seconds and she was after me. I headed for the shower and one of the women alerted doggie, I was in the shower when she arrived looking angry and mean.

"Well what's this then pretty girl?" Doggie began

"Oh, hi there" I shouted bravely

"What are you staring at, do you like what you see" Doggie said posing.

"No I don't like butch women" I said looking her up and down

"What did you say Lesbo?" Doggie asked

"You heard you're too butch for me, excess fat and all that" I was shaking with fear inside as I said this.

"Hey girls why don't we teach this gay bitch a lesson?" Doggie said addressing her friends

"Perhaps she prefers me" said one of her friends covered in tattoos

"I must admit you're dishy" I said admiring her tattoos

"Nah she wants it rough so lets give it her rough" Doggie said grabbing my hair and pulling her out of the shower, each girl began to slap me, but I wanted punishment not pleasure.

"Pass me that broom Debbie" Doggie said without taking her eyes off me.

She asked them to pin me down and I seriously thought she was going to insert the broom into my virginals. She held it tight and asked them to hold me still, then she stopped and laughed really loud, I was bracing myself for the worst and thought my worst nightmare was about to happen.

But she broke the stick on her knee and threw it away, and then in temper she started punching me hard in the stomach and face. Each blow was like being hit with a rock and I felt myself getting weaker and weaker until I collapsed. The floor was a mess with soapsuds and my blood, I crawled to the place where I had left my clothes and tried to focus but my eye was closing. The next thing I remember was my friend jasmine helping me back to my cell. My god my face was a mess and I could hardly walk I swear I had broken ribs.

Fiona was behind every attack dropping down the poison each time making it obvious that she was the real instigator of all the trouble. After this Doggie and every other bully targeted me I was like flavour of the month, every problem was caused by me and I was getting slapped, punched and a subject of laughter it was worse than school for a while.

Being bullied doing menial tasks treated like shit and taking it, I felt like a real wimp for a while, I shared a cell with Jasmine, she was a lovely girl a little younger than me with dark complexion mixed race, a little like the character in Aladdin. She helped me get through my worst moments in prison, she was guilty of theft and was in prison for a short term. I couldn't care less what happened to me at this point, I was pretty low. But I did go mad when my friend Jasmine got beat up she was so badly injured she ended up in the prison hospital. I was so angry I went after Doggie to teach her a lesson she would never forget.

I marched towards Doggies cell her friends Sue and Debbie were there guarding the door like 10 Downing street. One of them put her arm out to stop me and found herself on the floor in seconds holding her throat. So the other rushed forward and I drop kicked her in the stomach, and then punched her in the jaw. I remember shouting or screaming like a banshee as I entered Doggies cell, she knew I meant business as she was immediately on the defensive trying to attack me with a chair.

"Now bitch it's my turn" I shouted

"What the fuck" She said with surprise.

"You can hurt me but not my friends" I said running at her

I ploughed into her like a bull, firstly with a high kick to the chest and then without stopping I gave her one punch after another until she went down hard onto the ground. Debbie and Sue entered the cell but kept their distance from me as they tried picking Doggie up, I watched her chest rise so that I knew she was breathing then left the cell. Two prison wardens took me to the governor's office, but I was just given a warning and extra duties. Most of the time the wardens let you fight your own battles, as it was a tussle for power and survival of the fittest that's what prison is basically all about. Reform was just a buzzword branded about by the local goodie goodies that just wanted to be seen doing something for prisoners. No one fully understood peoples past lives and what made them commit crimes, the poverty and hardships of prisoners. Parents who were alcohols or drug addict what chance had any child got growing up in that kind of environment. Doggie was brought up with a schizophrenic mother and a violent drunken father; she just knew how to be a prostitute in order to survive. Pat was brought up to steal and it became a way of life to con people, she knew no other life. I was also amazed at the amount of dyslexic prisoners all went to school but slipped through the net struggling to survive in society. Either you form your own strategies to read and write or you just give in and blame society for your lack of education or in failing to acknowledge your disability.

Education was available in prison, but it was up to the individual to seek the courses and enrol, help was out their, if you made the effort to go and find out more. I was approached after the incident with Doggie and I took it, before long I was doing O 'levels in five subjects. Things were looking up after that day in the governor's office.

However later that day I was in the exercise yard, when Doggie approached me, she had a gang of women around her who formed around me in one big circle. A number of officers watched as Doggie moved forward towards me, no one else moved and the atmosphere was tense.

The prison wardens looked on but then appeared surprised as Doggie put out her hand in friendship. I was very surprised and put out my hand to shake hers; she held my hand firmly and smiled.

"Few people have dared challenge me, no one has ever beaten me" Doggie said humbly

I could only smile back and listen to her

"Your one fucking brave lady" Doggie looked into my eyes

"I was merely defending myself" I admitted.

"Well you can certainly fight" Doggie said admiringly

At that the crowd dispersed.

"How did you learn to fight like that?" Doggie asked

"I had a good teacher, he taught me to defend myself" I explained

"So why did you let me beat you up in the shower?" Doggie asked confused

"I needed to be punished because I fucked up being in a gang" I wanted to tell her everything and why not she was hardly going to meet Marsha.

So I told her all about the Goth gang and my circumstances and to my surprise she was so sympathetic and understanding of my situation. Her advice to me was to seek education fight dyslexia like I fought her and make peace with my parents. I swore never again to misjudge people and I would also help anyone who needed it no matter who they were. Doggie admired my artwork and made me promise not just to pursue education but also to seek a career. Jasmine came out of the prison hospital and joined me in my classes we became very good friends, but not lovers. I even remained friends after prison life.

As things turned out it seems that Joanna the girl I allegedly beat up explained to the police that I was innocent and that Marsha was the guilty one who assaulted her. So I was officially vindicated and guess who was coming to jail and doing time for her crime? It was one other than Marsha. Yes I was to be released and she was coming in and serving twelve months for that and a further time for drug dealing. I was to be released but had no idea where I was going for the next six months. My parents wanted me back but I was not prepared to go home just yet. I was given the opportunity to work in a holiday camp with good references and a clean record. That at least was a start and I could think about my future while cleaning out chalets and having fun at a major holiday camp.

I told Faith about Marsha and her reaction to seeing her again, the one that caused her so many problems in the past.

Marsha appeared in the prison and at that point I was being escorted out, we passed each other and I launched at her taking everyone by surprise. Two guards pulled me off her but not until I had punch her directly in the face. She was holding her face and blood was oozing through her fingers, she looked scared and was reluctant to retaliate, I was so angry at seeing her I decided to offer her a little verbal service.

"You fucking bitch, you nearly ruined my life" I said still being held

"Make her suffer girls, make her pay for what she has done".

Jodie left the prison free and innocent of the crimes that she had been convicted of throughout her past. Jasmine was released months later and immediately contacted Jodie and they continued in education together, both of us eventually got teaching degrees and never looked, well she never. Am I bitter, am I fuck, whoops sorry Faith, I just wanted to move on and do something different. I needed a further break from the parents and the holiday camp seemed like a good place to go away and rethink my life. I was now more educated and perhaps more mature; I was almost a sensible woman.

TIME OUT

I began working at the holiday camp it was nice to wake up and smell the sea. Up early with my equipment consisting of a mop, bucket and rags armed to the teeth to clean chalets.

"My word I was going to scrub them chalets until they gleamed I planned to be the best scrubber in the camp. By that I don't mean a tart there were enough of them about drooling after the entertainers enough to make me vomit. I was there to have some fun and seek out the odd woman or two my god some were odd too. Catering seemed to attract them as well as the entertainment department. Honestly if the entertainment held a contest for the dirtiest, scruffiest women I new a building full of them.

The funniest image was seeing teabags being dried on the washing line, as if there was a shortage, perhaps the foreign tea merchants lost their cargo at sea. My god I wondered what else was going to hang on the line, some things were asking to be pinched. It's funny what happens at these holiday camps plenty of fun for holidaymakers and staff. But no mixing together having relationships with the punters as they are called by the staff. But we did have chalet parties and anyone was invited and virtually anything goes, or so it seems. Faith often cringed when I explained things in my own way; it took a lot to understand Jodie and my unique ways.

I worked a season in this environment and people began to realise I could sing quite well. I was singing at the karaoke night and the entertainment manager arranged for me to have a personal spot in a show and my own stage show in another theatre. But I was not the type of person who liked fame or popularity; give me the bullying any time, my god not really. It was fun while it lasted and I will treasure the memories there, but I really wanted to go home and be educated. I wanted a career in art and design, or in fashion design demonstrating my artistic flair. I wrote in my diary it would be the last entry for a while as I was determined to get on with my life, without reflecting on my past. I did here that Snake had a break down and ended up in a mental health ward, he was probably encouraging the patients to join his gang of Goths, bless him.

I was pleased to see my own achievements; something positive I wondered was this what I would call the turning point in my life? At last some good in my pathetic existence. At teaching college I was assisted by Jasmine and the appropriate department (Diversity and equality) I supposed on reflection most of the school pupils were fine and apart from the bullies I did have my own peer group, one lesson to be learned is to always carry a spare supply of everything in order to save embarrassment like pads and pens, if you follow me.

I must say that I dreaded the moment when I had to see my parents again I took Jasmine with me as I didn't know how they would respond to me, after all my father wanted me to spend time in jail and pay my debts to society as he put it (Punishment). As I said 'I would love to have seen his face when he discovered that I was innocent'.

My god, may I say that I was getting more nervous as I got closer to the house; it was strange seeing the old curtains in the windows that I despised so much. I noticed someone peeping from behind the curtains and recognised it to be my father. Suddenly he rushed out the front door; he then stopped and stood in front of me. I looked into his eyes as he looked back at her then looked down in shame. They we both stood for a while neither of us saying anything, it was one of them moments that you dread to happen. Finally he gave a cough in order to clear his throat and spoke to me with tears in his eyes.

"I am so sorry Jodie, I feel as if I have let you down" He said his voice was quivering

"Dad I am sorry too, for putting you through absolute hell, but I am heaven blessed and given a second chance" I said sorrowfully.

"Jodie I never knew about your disability dyslexia dyspraxia and I feel so bad that I never supported you" He admitted

"It's okay dad you are here for me now and that's important" I replied

"I love you so much Jodie and so does your mother, we are proud of you" He said with tears in his eyes.

At that moment we embraced and the tears poured like a waterfall, the rest of the family, who had congregated around the door, observed us. Then my mother ran to me and hugged me she too had tears in her eyes, it was such a special moment in my life, I just hoped their freaky friend were not there too.

And my god the entire neighbourhood, may god bless the sad bastards who looked on at our reconciliation, a glorious moment never to be repeated. But I had turned my life around and persevered to do good for others, I had been proven innocent of committing actual bodily harm and I had simply followed the wrong pathway to evil or whatever.

I did eventually become an art teacher in the same high school that I attended as a pupil, years of teacher training and I looked out for the students who were struggling in education and those who were being bullied. No one was going to suffer, not on my watch, I knew all the signs and symptoms of both dyslexia and bullying and do you know everyone understands Jodie now.

CONFLICT OF FAITH

Introduction
Do you believe in angels?

During the course of human history man has believed not only in God, speaking of him in books such as the bible and the Quran as well as other religious documentation. But also spoke about spirit creatures that fly and take on many forms known as angels. In fact the angels were often described as wearing white robes and hallos, with large wings that help them fly though the air invisibly. The angels were gods creatures and given specific tasks by god to serve him and protect the earth and its inhabitants. But not all angels were considered good, as some rebelled against god and became fallen angels, Satan led these ones causing devastation and wars throughout the earth

"Now have come to pass the salvation and the power and the kingdom of our God and the authority of his Christ, because the accuser of our brothers has been hurled down, who accuses them day and night before our God! And they conquered him because of the blood of the Lamb and because of the word of their witnessing, and they did not love their souls even in the face of death. On this account be glad, YOU heavens and YOU who reside in them! Woe for the earth and for the sea, because the Devil has come down to YOU, having great anger, knowing he has a short period of time."

Taken from the book of revelation 12:7-12 new testament

Our story begins in Hollywood California in the 21st century, An angel called Faith has been sent to earth after failing to fulfil her duties as a guardian angel. She has to live on earth with human being as a human in order to learn their ways and understand mankind before being re established as a guardian angel. Unfortunately Satan is aware of this and sends a fallen angel called Dawn to stop her accomplishing her mission.

Faith shares a room with Rachel a human in a boarding school, who is unaware of whom she really is and involves her in parties and boys. When Faith is reluctant to conform to Rachel's worldly ways Rachel becomes confused and thinks she is someone holy like a nun who has been planted in her room as a spy for the teachers at school.

LIVING WITH FAITH

Amidst the clouds drifting in the sky Faith the guardian angel sat alone, her thoughts were her only company. Until another figure appeared to join her, she appeared older and put her arm on her shoulder.

"Bless you angel, we are with you Faith" She said comforting her

"Oh Hope I have failed you, I am no guardian angel" Faith replied

"But despite your failing Faith we will make you a model angel" Hope replied

"Oh but I let one woman die in a car crash, let a man commit suicide". Faith was interrupted by the presence of another angel.

"Faith honestly what are you playing at you have made a mess of your job on earth" She said

"Patience really Faith just needs guidance and understanding" Hope said concerned.

"And who is going to do that?" Patience asked

"You of course" Hope said smiling

"Me" Patience said alarmed.

"Yes the angels call out to you for support" Hope said excitedly.

"And what will we do about Faith?"

"She is to materialise on earth and live with mortals, you are going to be her guardian angel and will be only visible to her". Hope said excited by the thought of Patience helping Faith.

"So I will be visible to Faith and help her?" Patience said clarifying the situation.

"Yes that's right and Faith will learn to understand humans and their needs, that way she will be a better guardian angel".

"If that is the decision of our angels, so be it" Patience agreed.

"When do I go?" Faith asked.

"Well there is no time like the present" hope said sending Faith to earth with the wave of her hand.

Faith materializes on earth and clothed herself with items from a washing line; it took her a while to discover that she had lost her wings. She was told to go to a all girls boarding school and would be staying there for a while. She was sharing a room with Rachel another pupil who attends classes in her school.

Faith looked around the room in amazement, touching objects and gazing at posters as if she had never seen these things before.

"What an unusual room" She said smiling

Rachel was quite frankly astonished by her dress sense; she was not at all trendy for a teenager. She wore a white dress with long light brown hair and sparkling blue eyes, like a vision of an angel before me. I didn't believe in all that nonsense. Angels were something invented for a children's amusement, not for a teenager like me.

Faith continued to look around as if she had found a cave of wonders.

"It is wonderful" she continued

"It's a room with a few things in, what's your problem?" Rachel was feeling really intimidated by now.

"I didn't mean to offend you, sorry" faith said in a soft voice

Rachel watched her as the light shone onto her from the window, I must confess she thought she did seem angelic and I felt like such a bitch at this time. She was a vision of innocents and my imagination took over as I saw her as a nun.

"So have you travelled far?" Rachel asked her inquisitively

"Yes" she said looking up to the clouds through the window

"Care to elaborate?" Rachel asked trying to prize some sort answer out of her

"Oh Scotland near England" She finally replied

"Nice place Scotland" I replied, grateful for the great amount of information she gave her.

When she turned round Rachel was astonished she swore she could see wings on her back, but then I was tired and irritable due to the time of the month. Funny thing the mind it plays tricks with you, I looked again and she was normal. Perhaps I would see Lepricorns or Unicorns I could only imagine my day was going to get worse.

I showed her the bathroom and how to operate the shower; she immediately began removing her clothes. I left the bathroom quickly and gave her some privacy; she entered the shower and looked at her back where the wings used to be. She washed at her back and then looked down to her feet watching the water disappear down the plug hole. Her mind reflected back to a stream where she used to visit in the evening, joined by other spirit creatures all relaxing without a care.

Rachel was expecting Faith to come out of the bathroom after about twenty minutes, but an hour later she appeared with a towel around her.

"You ok, did you enjoy your shower?" Rachel asked politely

"It was wonderful" She replied

"That good hey?" Rachel had to admit she thought I had a head case with her

"I heard you talking in there" Rachel said hoping that she would confess to being a psychiatric patient who had escaped from a local hospital.

"No I was singing" Faith had the type of temperament that you couldn't argue with, so placid and innocent, unlike Rachel who was a bitch at times.

Faith seemed to fit in well and was willing to learn, Rachel had a feeling that she was different but couldn't exactly say how or why.

I was hoping for a clue to her previous life style but nothing seemed to emerge at this stage. She obviously had her reasons for keeping so secretive and whatever it was Rachel would no doubt find out about eventually.

Faith was sat feeling lonely and upset because although Patience was present she was thinking of her best friend who was a guardian angel called Harmony. She could talk to her and sort her problems out and not feel like a bad angel, Rachel was also nice but not an angel like Harmony. Suddenly a light shone in room and an angel appeared in front of her eyes "Harmony" Faith said in a low voice so she didn't disturb Rachel

"shhhh" Harmony tried to silence her

"What are you doing here?" Faith asked

"I sensed you were lonely and here I am" Harmony explained

"I'm lost Harmony, I failed as a guardian angel now look at me" Faith admitted

"Faith you made mistakes God knows that, you just need to learn as I did" Harmony said "You will get there and then we will be together again".

"Ok I understand" Faith said smiling

"Good I will be watching you Faith" Harmony said vanishing

Meanwhile Satan had his own ideas for Faith as he arranged for a demon called Dawn to attend the same school and try to entice Faith into bad ways and encourage her to join his evil home in hell. Faith had to prove herself loyal to god and pure in body and mind, Dawn who looked like Faith made every effort to entice her to evil. So once again the battle was on between good and evil, a problem that has gone on for centuries and will continue on for years to come.

Faith arrived in school equipped with her case and school bag, Hope had made all the arrangements for her such as her earth identity and general details for her own credibility. Faith was supposed to have an aunty in Scotland who cared for her after the death of her parents and she was sent to boarding school so that she could be well educated and interact with girls of her own age group. All seemed feasible and so she had no trouble with her registration, convincing the headmistress that she was genuine. But for the absence of her Scottish accent which she convinced her that her mother was English and a true lady.

She was introduced to Rachel and this is when thing began to happen, for living with Faith was not easy and to be honest she was enough to make a saint swear. She wasn't exactly bad as hard to teach and unquestionably hard to understand especially when she would talk to her imaginary friend Patience who Rachel later discovered to be her guardian angel.

Faith needed to learn so much about humans in the short time that she resided on earth. Many things that we take for granted she was experiencing for the first time for instance rain and thunderstorms. One day the weather was particularly bad and what did Faith do, she went outside in her nightgown and danced in the rain.

"What are you doing?" Rachel asked

"Isn't it wonderful?" she replied

"What?" Rachel asked shocked

"This water from the sky" she said excitedly

"Its rain" Rachel said bewildered by her actions

"Oh rain its amazing, rain" she continued

"Your crazy, come inside" Rachel said concerned

Lightning flashed followed by Thunder and she remained outside, suddenly a bolt of lightning headed towards her and before Rachel could speak knocked her to the ground. Rachel thought that she saw an angel before her at this point, but she was certain that this was a visual hallucination brought on by stress or something. Now Rachel can categorically say it was real and it was Faith's real image and not the image that she portrayed to us on earth. Faith lay on the grass for a while then got up as if nothing had happened.

"Are you alright that lightening hit you?" Rachel said concerned

"Yes just a bit stunned" She replied smiling

"But you could have been killed" Rachel held her arm and walked her inside

"Really I am ok" She insisted

"How lucky were you, you must have had your guardian angel with you" Rachel said jokingly

"I did" Faith replied convincingly.

Patience stood behind them shaking her head "Faith you are enough to try a saint".

We attended assembly together and were in the same classes, religious education was the main lesson that fascinated Faith as it involved what people believe, she sat in silence until a teacher picked her out asking her for her own opinion on god and angels.

"God is our creator and the angels support him in all his actions". Faith said confidently. "For each person there are angels in succession before and behind him they guard him by command of Allah or god, that's in the Quran chapter 13 and verse 11"

The teacher was impressed by her knowledge of various religions and knew the bible so well.

"God will command his angels concerning you in all your ways" Faith continued, "Angels protect mankind more that you will ever know".

The whole class sat in silence as Faith went into detail about creation; she was so convincing speaking about it as if she were there. Then the teacher asked her about Jesus and his final days on earth, she was so graphic about the crucifixion the girls wept and the boys sat motionless. After this they all applauded her for her fine performance, Faith had stood relating what she saw and was giving a eye witness account of events. She was no different from that time to now and found it difficult to understand why they applauded her for relating what she had seen.

"What a performance" Rachel said little knowing that she was actually there.

"Oh thank you" Faith said puzzled

At that moment Patience appeared to her and whispered in her ear

"They think your acting out a part in a play, don't act surprised" Patience said "We were both in Jerusalem with Jesus, but they don't know that".

Faith asked to be excused and went to the toilet to speak to Patience

"Patience!" she shouted

"Faith you have to understand that no one knows that you are an angel" Patience explained

"I know but I got carried away when they mentioned God and Jesus" Faith admitted

"I know but your identity must be concealed" Patience said anxiously

"I hate all this deceit its not like me, I wish I was back home" Faith said tearfully.

"Just be patient and try to learn from the humans" Patience advised her

"I suppose I will have to do this in order to be a guardian angel" Faith said in agreement

"You will get there believe me" Patience said confidently

The following day I decided to take Faith round the city, what a disaster that was, if she wasn't staring at people oddly she was asking questions about them loudly. I did wonder where she came from back then when she fell on the escalator trying to go the wrong way or in the elevator spreading her arms out saying 'I am flying'. She had trouble crossing roads and ordering food was a nightmare.

Faith was really wonderful despite being hard work, Rachel felt as if I had known her forever. She was polite, charming and very kind to others, the street people loved her, because she would randomly go to them and offer them food, drinks and advise even when they didn't want advice. She was not at all street wise, so I had to teach her what to do and how to deal with people.

"Do people really travel in these metal encasements?" Faith asked referring to the cars and buses.

"Of course, where have you been living?" Rachel said bewildered

"Oh just curious Rachel" Faith said smiling.

Rachel really didn't know whether she was serious or not, to ask questions about the things we take for granted. But looking back now I can understand, why would an angel know these things. I suppose unless they knew about humans and modern times on earth. We take for granted that angels just look after us, but they have other tasks to deal with in connection with the maintenance of the universe.

Faith went into a toilet in the city and began relating her experience in a cubical.

"Patience, I am bewildered by these humans; they have all kinds of aids to get them about, why don't they have wings like us?" She said unaware that somebody had entered the cubical next door.

"They would cause havoc with wings, they are bad enough with out them" Patience replied

"Well they go about in metal objects like fruit in a tin" Faith continued

"Eating drinking getting rid of their bodily waste in these things, what are they called toilets".

The woman next door could only here Faith talking and was intrigued by the course of conversation. The more Faith spoke the more the woman seemed shocked, she went to the sink and when the cubical opened she made a rapid exit. Faith just noticed her rush out and looked back at the cubicles, then at the door with a surprised look on her face.

"Did she hear me?" Faith asked

"Probably" Patience replied.

"Oh dear I do forget about these humans being everywhere" Faith said embarrassed

"I am afraid I do too" Patience admitted

Meanwhile in the deep cavities of the underworld amidst the fires of hell sat a girl who resembled Faith. She was dressed in a red dress and that was torn at the right hand side. She seemed sad and lonely just staring into a fire her eyes appeared glazed as if she had been crying. A man approached her also in red he seemed angry and upset.

"Come with me I have a job for you" He said in a rough voice

He led her to a room and told her to sit down; she obeyed and watched as he created an image on the wall.

"This woman is posing as a human on earth, she is an angel and she must be stopped, you are the one to do this". He looked at her with evil eyes

"Will I be set free if I do this?" She asked

"You mean from purgatory?"

"Yes because I am not that bad really" She said smiling

"You are damned" He replied

"But really I committed two hundred and fifty sins" She insisted

"Well do this job and I might consider it, oh and your name will be Dawn" He said looking at the image then at her.

"Dawn what kind of name is that?"

"Get used to it because it's yours" He shouted

"So what do I do to her?" Dawn asked

"You must cause her to sin and be finally cast out of heaven for good

Then we will have triumphed over god"

"Awesome a victory for us" Dawn said happily

"Then we can continue our conquest to take over the earth and rule it as we desire" He said laughing.

Dawn was transformed onto the earth and searched for Faith; it was not long before she spotted her in the school library. She watched as Faith approached the bookshelves and lifted her arms then snapped her fingers. Suddenly some of the books fell down on top of her she was buried by all the books. A teacher came to her rescue; other pupils who began to pick all the books up joined her helping her up.

"What happened?" the teacher asked

"I don't know the books suddenly dropped on my head" Faith said standing to her feet

"You were very lucky you never got hurt" The teacher replied

"Very lucky" Dawn said smiling

"Are you new? Faith asked

"Yes I am Dawn" she offered her hand to Faith

Faith shuck her by the hand and smiled "Thanks for your help"

"My pleasure" Dawn said and walked away with a cunning smile on her face.

Later that day Faith was sorting out her locker and suddenly all her belonging flew out onto the floor. Hiding round the corner was Dawn again with a wicked grin on her face.

Faith entered a church and walked up to the church alter where a statue of Jesus hanging from the cross-stood on display. She immediately thought back to the crucifixion as Jesus spoke his final words on earth before he died. Faith could feel his pain and agony as the nails had been driven through his hands and feet. Faith became tearful and knelt down praying to god, she was unaware that she was being watched. The school chaplain stood over her and placed his hand on her shoulder but to his surprise noticed a transition before his eyes. She was an angel he stood back in astonishment and could not take his eyes off her glowing body and glorious wings. Faith was unaware of her transformation and turned to look at the Chaplain.

"I was just praying" Faith said "Lord god help me to carry my burden this day"

"But of course why not" He said with a stammer

By this time she had transformed back to her human form, the Chaplain rubbed his eyes and made his apologies.

"I am sorry I must go someone needs me" He said and walked briskly out.

Faith was bewildered by his actions, but unaware that she had transformed into an angel when she was looking back at the crucifixion.

DAWN'S PLAN

Dawn was outside the class she noticed that Faith was not in class so transformed herself to look exactly like Faith. Her plan was to cause as much trouble for faith as possible, so she entered the class causing disruption. She sat down and the teacher looked at her waiting for an excuse for being late, even an apology would have done. But she said nothing just sat and stared back at the teacher.

"Nice of you to turn up, where have you been" the teacher said

"I had to go for a whiz, you know a wee" Dawn said in a matter of fact manner.

"Sorry I am late would have done" the teacher continued

"Well when you've got to go, you didn't expect me to piss on this seat did you?" Dawn said abruptly

"Get out of my class now you insolent girl" the teacher said crossly

Dawn threw her books at the front of the class narrowly missing the teacher and some of the pupils.

"Well to hell with you lot" Dawn said leaving the room

Dawn noticed Faith coming down the corridor and vanished, Faith headed into the classroom completely unaware of the trouble in class. She knocked on the door then entered the classroom in a pleasant manner. Everybody stared at her with mouths open and watched her head towards her desk.

"Sorry I am late Mrs Dainty" She said addressing the teacher

"What are you doing here?" Mrs Dainty said with disbelief

"I have come to class, I am sorry I was with Mrs Brown" Faith explained

"How many more lies are you going to tell me" Mrs Dainty said angrily

"I don't understand what have I done?" Faith said innocently

"You just don't care do you, get out of my class" Mrs Dainty said pointing to the door

Faith was very confused but left the classroom, she decided to go back to see Mrs Brown. When she arrived there she explained what had happened Mrs Brown was confused and asked her to sit down.

"You were with me so how did that happen?" Mrs Brown said looking at Faith

She could see that Faith was upset and confused by these events, she was low in mood, which was unlike Faith. Faith was a bubbly person by nature and would not act in the way she did in class.

Mrs Brown related these facts to Mrs Dainty, she pondered for a moment.

"I was shocked I must confess" Mrs Dainty admitted

"And what about the time factor, how could she be in two places at once?

Mrs Brown said trying to rationalise the situation

"I really don't know" Mrs Dainty said bewildered

Meanwhile Faith was back at her room with me, I tried to make sense of the situation. I tried to think of all possibilities but nothing made sense to me at this point.

Dawn tried similar techniques to get Faith into trouble in the dining hall by causing disruption with plates and other food utilities and in the hall by pinching a girl behind harshly. She made a ball vanish when someone was about to hit it with her racket and made a ball vanish when a boy tried to kick it. She did so many mean things as Faith; it flawed Faiths credibility as a sweet and innocent girl.

Faith attended the principles office with Mrs Brown at her side

The principle was a grey haired lady with a slightly hunched back and a stern look; she was quite plump and spoke with a deep voice from years of smoking.

"Faith I have been hearing very bad things about you and frankly I am shocked, You started off so well in your first year and now I hear you have been very disruptive is that true?" The principle said

"Why no I don't understand I am a victim in this place" Faith said confused

"Dear" The principle shook her head in disbelief "It's a good job Mrs Brown is here to defend you, she is like a guardian angel to you"

"Yes ma'am" Faith couldn't help smirking as she heard the words guardian angel knowing Patience was looking on

"Its no laughing matter girl you need to shape up and think seriously about your future" The principle gazed at Faith and noticed an innocence in her eyes and became confused "Now go and remember what I said"

As Faith left the office she did think that the principle was more like Patience, at that moment Patience appeared and began lecturing to her

"Faith what is going on?" Patience asked

"I really don't know Patience I cant explain it" Faith said bewildered

At that moment Dawn passed her and stopped in front of her

"My word did you get in trouble Faith?" Dawn asked

"You could say that" Faith said abruptly

Dawn noticed a faint light around Faith and moved away swiftly

"There is the answer a demon" Patience said looking at Dawn

"What?" Faith was surprised

"That girl is a demon, a fallen angel" Patience said looking back at Faith

"Are you sure?" Faith asked

"Yes why didn't I see it before she has been pretending to be you" Patience said alarmed "I should have guessed she can take on any form like we can, but with evil intent".

"She has been impersonating me?" Faith said realising what has been happening.

"Yes and so when things have happened it was her" Patience explained

Faith attended a fancy dress party arranged through school many people attended in fancy dress there was no theme people went according to their individual interests. Needless to say action heroes, Romans and angels, which made Faith feel at home.

At the party she met John, a tall handsome young man around her age group. John was a confident chap who was aware of his magnetic charm and seemed to draw girls to him. But when he saw Faith he became spellbound, he walked up to her and was astonished that she never noticed him straight away. She glanced at him smiled and continued talking to me, this displeased him so he stood between us.

"Hi I am John, you have probably heard about me?" He said confidently

"No I haven't sorry" Faith said in a dismissive manner

John was a little hurt and I actually felt sorry for him, He looked away checking whether or not someone was looking at him. He had never had such a negative response and knew it couldn't be his fault. So he bravely tried again with another approach, carefully choosing his words.

"So have you got a boyfriend?" He said directly

"That was as subtle as a flying mallet" I said laughing

"Are you referring to me?" Faith replied

"Yes I am" John continued

"No I haven't" Faith replied reluctantly

"So are you a lesbian?" John said boldly

At that moment Rachel lifted her hand and slapped his face, she couldn't help it he was being an idiot and needed to know it. He was so shocked at my response and so was Faith. At that point Faith walked away and went outside she was accompanied by her guardian angel that could only be seen by herself. At this point she knew nothing about Faith being an angel or she having a guardian angel.

"Patience these humans are so confusing" Faith said

"Why do you say that child" Patience said sympathetically

"The males ask females out on dates" Faith continued

"Yes that's how they start, then get to know each other, then they marry and reproduce". Patience explained

"But he asked if I was a lesbian, what is that?" Faith asked

"Oh well some women like women and some men like men" Patience was trying to choose her words carefully.

"You said like?" Faith asked confused

"Love, make love, be with and enjoy each other sexually" Patience said seriously

"Oh like in history" Faith realised what John had said to her "Goodness he thinks I love women, I must convince him otherwise".

John appeared at the door with Rachel, he was preparing to apologise when Faith suddenly copied Rachel's reaction from earlier, she slapped him across the face. Stunned he just held his face and looked at both Faith and Rachel, Patience just shuck her head and vanished. Clearly Faith had a lot to learn about human behaviour and the subject of dating.

Rachel took Faith under her wing and explained the idea of dating and about romance; She seemed quite excited about the thought of dating and of marriage. It was all-new to her and she wanted to know more, so I showed her a few movies about love and romance. She went through a very emotional time crying at all the sad scenes and excited about the outcomes. Rachel really couldn't believe she had never experienced even watching romance. I then introduced her to make up and wearing trendy clothes, this was in preparation for her dating boys. But she never told her this in case it caused her to not comply to her needs and work against teenage conformity.

RESCUED BY A DREAM

Faith was nervous meeting John especially after her history with him. What was she going to say and how would she respond to his kisses, after all she deterred him from being anywhere near her. She also embarrassed him in company by slapping him, yet he wanted to see her again. He met her that evening and presented her with a bouquet of flowers. They went to a restaurant and dined together sharing thoughts and conversing well.

"So how long have you known Rachel?"

"I met her at the start of term we are roommates" Faith explained dropping her spoon on the floor

John bent down to pick it up and Faith bend down too and they bumped heads, they both got up rubbing their heads.

"I like your perfume what's it called?" John asked

"Temptation" Faith replied

Patience was sat at the next table with a male angel ordering lunch

She heard the remark and tutted loudly, faith heard her and gave her a look as if to say go away.

"I like your dress" John said struggling to converse with Faith

"Rachel chose this for me" Faith said smiling

Dawn passed by with a boy she had met earlier and sat a few tables away

The waiter approached them and asked for their order at this point Faith had received their spaghetti and Dawn turned the spaghetti into worms Patience noticed and changed it back quickly. John noticed but thought he was seeing things, then a waiter fell and food headed towards Faith. Patience diverted the food towards Dawn and she was covered in soup and pasta. Dawn was confused by her tricks back firing and walked over to Faith with her dress covered with food.

"Very funny Faith I know you did this to me" Dawn said in temper

"Why Dawn why would I do that to you" Faith said surprised "When have you done anything to me?"

Dawn realised that Patience was close by and returned to her place, she dragged her male companion away with her out of the restaurant.

Rachel was close by in case anything went wrong she was worried about Faith at this time especially when Dawn started misbehaving. All went well until they decided to walk outside under the moonlight it was very romantic and Faith seized her opportunity to experience her first kiss.

Faith kissed him tenderly, her warm lips forming a seal around his wet warm and wonderful. Suddenly he became immersed by a powerful energy, which intoxicated him and caused him to fall to the ground. He was shaking and John almost had a convulsion. His body was cold and lifeless, Faith shuck him and shouted "John!"

He opened his eyes and he looked at her in amazement, he could see an angel before him. She was leaning over him, she was so bright almost aluminous glowing before him with her white wings behind her and her long white dress sparkling.

"Am I in heaven?" He asked

"No why do you ask?" Faith asked

"Because I can see an angel" John said bewildered

"You must have hit your head" Faith said trying to convince him he was dreaming.

"I swear to you" He said blinking he then saw Faith

"Faith what have you done?" Came a voice as Patience appeared

"See there's another one!" John shouted

"Wait you can see Patience?" Faith asked

"Yes of course" John replied

"Faith you've got to do something" Patience thought for a while "Kiss him again"

"What" Faith said shocked

"Kiss him again you could reverse what you have done" Patience said confidently

"Ok if you insist" Faith said leaning towards John

"No, that's what started this" John said putting his hand over his mouth

"Come on I can help you" Faith insisted

"Are you real angels or witches?" John said concerned

Both angels looked at each other then at him, I was looking on in amazement.

"We are angels" Faith said echoed by Patience

"I could be dreaming or even hallucinating of course" John said trying to rationalise the situation.

"We are angels" Faith insisted

"Oh ok as long as I know" John said sarcastically

"So what now Faith?" Patience asked

"I don't know" Faith replied

"He knows about us" Patience added,

"Oh please, I can forget" John hit his head with his hand "There forgotten, I won't say anything, please don't zap me"

John kept pinching himself to see if he was dreaming

"Why are you hurting yourself?" Faith asked

"I want to see if I am dreaming, oh god that hurts"

"Do you mind" Patience shouted "Enough with the god thing"

"Your serious, angels here with me" John said

"Yes angels" Faith said

"I need to go home" John insisted

"Ok I will give you a lift" Faith said

"No its ok I'm not flying" John said worried

"Its ok you wont be seen in flight" Faith said smiling

"No its ok I will walk" John insisted

John stood up but was too weak to walk, so Faith took him home

Faith did take him home, then appeared in our room. Rachel pretended to be asleep and she began to get ready for bed, she was muttering to herself as Rachel thought. In reality she was talking to Patience about the experience.

"What's going on?" Rachel asked her with my eyes half shut.

"Nothing" Faith said innocently

"How did your date go?" Rachel asked knowing something strange had happened.

"Oh well" Faith sat on the edge of my bed "we kissed"

"No way, what was it like?" Rachel asked

"Like heaven" Faith replied

"Did he like it" Rachel asked waiting for the bombshell

"He passed out" Faith said disappointed

"No way?" Rachel pretended to look shocked

"Yes way he folded right in front of me" Faith explained pretending to faint, mimicking his reaction "Ahhh" and fell flat on the bed

"How, why?" Rachel said pulling her up

"Just went no warning, bump hit the ground" Faith went down again

"Gee you must have given him one powerful kiss" Rachel said trying to keep a straight face, watching her actions

"I must have" Faith admitted

"Wow I wish I had that affect on men" Rachel said trying to make light of the situation

"No you don't its not good" Faith admitted

"Oh come on Faith you kiss him, he drops its terrific" Rachel said laughing

"Look there's something you should know" Faith said grabbing my arms

"What is it Faith, what's wrong?" Rachel said dreading this moment

"Faith don't you dare" Patience warned Faith

At that moment Faith grabbed Rachel by both cheeks and kissed her on the lips, then as predicted Rachel collapsed, she remembered feeling hot and dizzy, the room spun and she passed out. When she woke she saw two angels looking over me one was Faith and the other Patience, they were talking.

Faith was being chastised by Patience because of what she did to her; I was trying not to pay attention to them.

"Faith I don't believe you, why did you do this?" Patience asked

"I wanted her to know and to experience what happened to John" Faith explained

"She has an imagination that would do" Patience replied

"You kissed her she could think your coming onto her" Patience explained "That's a human expression for taking advantage"

"I never thought of that Patience" Faith said regretfully

"Sometimes I despair" Patience said angrily

At this point Rachel felt it necessary to intervene by being very dramatic and acting surprised

"Oh my god angels" Rachel said acting for my Oscar

"Its ok Rachel its me Faith" Faith said reassuringly

"And who is she?" Rachel said pointing to Patience

"You can see her?" Faith said surprised

"Yes" I admitted

"This is Patience" Faith said proudly

"Is she my guardian angel?" Rachel said bewildered

"No she is mine I need one right now" Faith admitted

"But I don't believe in angels" Rachel said dismissively

"You do now don't you?" Faith said moving her wings about

"I guess so" Rachel admitted with a smile.

Rachel was so relieved when the truth was out and they could talk freely. She just asked Faith never to kiss her again, she was heterosexual and wanted to make that clear I was only interested in males. Having said that Rachel understand why she kissed her and knew it was not for sexual reasons. Faith was also heterosexual but wanted to demonstrate her power and make me see her for who she really was, an angel. After this moment I could only see her as an angel and this made things much clearer to her.

"Can I ask you are all angels like you? Rachel asked

"What do you mean?" Faith asked

"I mean fair haired, gentle and kind" Rachel

"Are you joking Rachel, I am not perfect you know" Faith laughed

"Compared to me you are" Rachel said laughing back

"We are all gods creatures and strive for perfection and have free will, angels are divided into three triads the first are the closest to god called Seraphim's known as faithful angels. These speak to the angels on earth and inform them to protect the earth, the cherubim's are ready to defend mankind and the planet earth. These appear as half human and half beast, they are strange in form looking like a man from the front, a lion on the right and an ox on the left and an eagle from the back".

"Wow that's legendary and whoosh it went right over my head" Rachel said laughing

"The Ophanim's were giving positive energy to the people who needed help. The second triad organised the angels into positions of attack. The dominions carried sceptres and symbols of their authority. Harmony a friend and like me a member of the third triad are involved with life on earth acting as guardian angels under the archangels who are messengers of God". Faith was very graphic in her explanation

"So you are a guardian angel?" Rachel asked

"I was until I failed to help people and was asked to come down to earth to study human life" Faith said ashamedly

"I don't understand?" Rachel said confused

"I let someone die and made a few mistakes" Faith admitted

"So that's why I am here with you now" Faith said lowering her head in shame.

"My god but your perfect, how did that happen?" Rachel asked

"I was distracted for a moment, looking in a clothes shop at one point and saw a reflection in the window as the person got ran over" Faith admitted

"Bloody hell no way" Rachel said shocked

"Attracted by fashion such beautiful dresses" Faith confessed, "It didn't help the poor woman in the road".

Faith and Rachel went out for a walk in the park as they were walking along Faith said to Rachel "look at that man on the bench"

"The one in the shirt and trousers" Rachel said joking

"Funny, the man sat on his own yes" Faith replied "He's an angel"

"No way" Rachel said in disbelief

"Oh yes he is watching over people he will suddenly vanish and appear on a bus or helping someone in a disaster or crisis" Faith continued

"But he is no different to me" Rachel said bewildered

"Or me at present, but he is special" Faith said

"He has disappeared" Rachel said shocked

"Told you he was called away, someone may have prayed for help" Faith said smiling

"He is no where to e seen" Rachel looked all around the park

"Yee of little Faith, I told you he's an angel, they are everywhere on earth" Faith explained

SUNNY DELIGHT

It was a bright sunny day and I knew that this was going to be a good day; even Dawn was in a good mood and actually helping with the school fete. I must confess though I still didn't trust her, she could have been planning another trap for me. Not surprising I was right she had set a surprise for me in the gym, She appeared as me an untied ropes so they would fall when pulled. The equipment she had changed to react differently to the touch, wood became rubber. Then she acted badly in gym class to get a response from the teachers, but little did she know that Rachel could tell the difference between her perfect disguise and Faith. This was since I was kissed by Faith I could tell good from evil and saw the devil in Dawns eyes. I knew it wasn't Faith and suspected an evil element around me.

Dawn waited until some of the pupils grabbed the ropes then she made sure they all broke, she then ensured the girls climbed the wall bars which were made of wood. They all fell down when the wood was changed to rubber; even the wooden horse was rubber. Dawn chucked to herself and gave an evil glance over to Faith I had pre warned Faith about Dawn. I had overheard Dawn conversing with her master, she explained how she managed to transform as Faith. The whole idea of Dawn sabotaging Faiths existence on earth was beginning to become obvious and explained why Faith was getting in so much trouble.

Faith had to make a decision whether to stay on earth or rejoin her heavenly host. She was in love with John and found herself in a dilemma.

Dawn had transformed into Faith and arranged to meet John at the church. John thought that Faith had made a decision and arrived early. Dawn came through the door and headed for the churches alter towards John, she stood in front of John and looked into his eyes. He suddenly felt strange as if in a trance, something was wrong she didn't seem angelic.

"Kiss me" She said

"I did once and regretted it" John said reluctantly

"If you love me and want me to stay then kiss me" Dawn felt as if she was finally succeeding, if she destroyed John she could destroy Faith.

Dawn moved closer to him they held each other tightly and Dawn began to press her lips against his Dawn was expecting him to burn up. In stead Dawn fell to the ground holding her stomach and John changed into Faith. Faith stood over her and then became distracted by John running up towards her; I was close behind John hoping to stop Faith getting hurt.

During this time Dawn had recovered and fired a bolt of lightning at Faith, Faith drifted into the air and landed across the first row of the pews. John tried to punch out at Dawn but was struck by lightning along with myself we both landed badly on the floor. Patience appeared and delivered a flash of lightning towards Dawn and she fell backwards.

"Dawn stop it now" Faith insisted

"But I have to do this or I will be tormented forever" Dawn admitted

"Then let us help you please" Faith insisted

"Ok help me destroy you" Dawn said raising her arm for another attack.

Dawn used all her force to attack Faith throwing lightning bolts in her direction; Patience stepped in and deflected her attacks and knocked John back down to the ground. Patience lay injured from the many bolts directly at her and Faith was forced to send bolts back at Dawn. Dawn was getting weaker and began to fall down both Faith and Patience sent the final bolt of lightning. Dawn drifted into the air and disappeared with a bang.

Faith looked up to the heavens and spoke softly to her god

"Please heavenly father let me do your will" Faith said

With those words a light shone upon her and she did Gods will John, Patience and Rachel watched her glowing. She then turned to them and spoke to each of them in turn.

"John my love I wish I could share my life with you but my life belongs in heaven not earth" Faith said with tears in her eyes.

"I understand Faith" John replied, "Go to your world"

"And my dear friend Rachel I have loved your company and will never forget you, my spirit will always be with you".

"I will miss you too Faith God bless you" Rachel said sadly

With words Faith and Patience rose up and disappeared never to be seen again' only in my dreams. As for John and I we remained close and even married. We had two children a boy called John Junior and a daughter called Faith of course she was our real angel.

FAITH AND HARMONY

Faith and Patience arrived back in the spirit realm something seemed wrong, they were greeted back pleasantly but no one seemed happy.

Faith was reunited with her friend Harmony, Harmony was a confident guardian angel but had little faith in the human race since the crucifixion that she attended with Faith.

Harmony embraced Faith and kissed her on the cheek

"I have missed you" Harmony said excitedly

"Me too Harmony" Faith replied

"Did you really destroy Donna?" Harmony asked concerned

"Yes I had to she would have killed a few people" Faith explained "Both Patience and I did it"

"It has caused a lot of problems within the demonic realm" Harmony said concerned.

"Is that why things are so strange here?" Faith asked

"Yes they are concerned that it will have repercussions within the spirit world and on earth". Harmony said anxiously

"The archangel Gabriel wishes to see you"

At that moment Gabriel appeared a superior angel who shone like a glowing light before her, with fair hair and surrounded by other angels.

"Faith, my child you need to listen carefully to me, I speak to you about a pending danger on the earth. The demons are displeased with you as you have destroyed one of their sacred ones and wish to avenge her, you are being protected by us but in your duties as a guardian angel you must beware of this danger".

Faith looked at them and showed concern

"I am not afraid of them and will for fill my duties as guardian angel"

"Then god be with you and we will try to keep you safe".

With those words Gabriel disappeared leaving Faith and Harmony looking at each other bewildered.

"I have a seven year old boy to care for" Harmony explained

"Oh where are you going? Faith asked

"To Hollywood California" Harmony explained "He is not well and needs my help"

"I will miss you?"

"Don't be silly your coming along" Harmony explained

"You are caring for a sick three year old girl in the neighbourhood"

"Really?" Faith was so excited

"Yes there are six of us assigned to these two, Asha, Nathan, Lydia, Martha and us two" Harmony began to glow with excitement.

"Harmony your glowing" Faith said laughing

"Oh my word so I am" Harmony tried to calm down.

"I will prepare myself for the journey" Faith said beginning to glow herself.

"Alright see you soon ok" Harmony vanished

Later all the angels who were assigned to this mission assembled and stood before Gabriel, each one looked anxious.

"Fear not my sisters and brothers for you have been chosen by God through Jesus Christ to for fill this task and return safely to your family.

Bless all of you for doing this and be ever true to God spreading his message of love and peace throughout the earth. Now go on your way and do Gods work by protecting those children the way that you have been taught".

With those words the angels all flew together towards Hollywood and their destination. They were met by other angels and found the places that they were assigned to; they followed them to the homes in the area.

Faith arrived at a fine home in the Hollywood hills owned by celebrities her mission was to care for a eight year old child called Marie who was sick suffering from asthma and her mother had prayed for help. Faith, Nathan and Lydia all stayed at this home taking it in turns watching over her.

Meanwhile Harmony, Asha and Martha watched over a seven-year-old called Peter a few doors away, he was concerned about his mother being poorly and prayed for her recovery.

Faith also prayed for guidance on how to help Marie, she was aware that her mother Sharon had prayed for help, she also knew that anxiety and stress had triggered her daughters asthma attacks in the past. The one way to help Marie and her mother was educating them in stress management and to be calm at all times. Being invisible and watching them wouldn't help and so Faith had to find another method of helping them. She thought for a while before approaching Harmony for her advice, and then it came to her. Faith needed to materialise and be seen in order to help.

Faith and Harmony flew to the Hollywood hills and sat near a large white cross over looking the highway. It was misty as usual that morning and this always preceded the hot sunny weather typical of this part of California. Los Angeles had fine weather and many palm trees down the urban streets, which looked very decorative.

"What's wrong Faith? Harmony asked concerned

"It's the family I am guarding the girl I was assigned to has a human illness called asthma caused in her case by stress" Faith said worried

"And you want to help her?" Harmony said anticipating her response to the situation

"Yes but I don't know how to help her" Faith admitted

"You can materialise and become her nanny, that way you can teach her how to cope with her illness" Harmony explained

"Really I can do this?" Faith said excitedly

"Yes silly you are allowed if it is for the good of mankind and you don't reveal who you are" Harmony explained further

"It is done so many times angels do it all the time" Harmony looked at Faith realising she already knew the answer but needed reassurance from a friend. "Do it Faith for the child's sake".

"I will Harmony, thank you" Faith agreed

"Your such a good friend to me I don't know what I would do without you" Faith admitted

"You are such a numpty Faith, honestly but I love you anyway" Harmony said laughing

"What's a numpty?" Faith asked

"I picked the word up from humans funny word, I suppose it means silly or something" Harmony said laughing again and falling backwards hitting the cross with her head.

"Oh my word what's that? Harmony said rubbing her head

"A human symbol of the crucifixion" Faith said puzzled

"I know that but why is it here on the hill?" Harmony asked

"I don't know, but we were there at Calgary remember when Jesus was crucified" Faith said thinking back to Jerusalem.

"Yes how could they do that to him, sometimes I hate humans they are so cruel". Harmony said seriously

"But that's because of the evil in the world" Faith said

"You see good in the most wicked people, like these in Hollywood with loads of money, they put their careers before their children, selfish people" Harmony said crossly

"Misguided people they just need educating into thinking about others and reminding how to prioritise that's all". Faith said confidently

"They are rich because they think of their careers and not their children or families". Harmony insisted

"Well that's why we are here, the love of money is the root of all evil" Faith explained

"So we educated them to put their family first?" Harmony asked

"Yes that's right" Faith said

"Not so easy and people are not so interested in listening" Harmony said

"I know they are blind when it comes to family values" Faith admitted

"Still its our job to keep trying and one day people will realise the true meaning of Christmas" Harmony said standing up

"Back to work" Faith said adjusting her wings

"Back to do good" Harmony said looking down to the highway.

They returned to their respective families and resumed their roles as guardian angels, Patience did visit Faith and advised to do what Harmony suggested knowing that Faith would do this anyway being the type of personality she was wanting to do the right thing and being determined to succeed. Faith was popular amongst the spirit realm because of her determined attitude. Harmony was much more laid back but thorough; she was also meticulous and hard working. Both Faith and Harmony were good for each other because they could work as a team to achieve the same goal. They were known as the unseen helpers of many people mainly children Faith had come a long way since her problem period when she failed to fully understand her role. The earth bound period helped her to understand mankind and appreciate their need for help. Man is not able to guide himself even to direct his own steps as the bible points out. Man will always need God and his angels to guide him.

BELIEVE

Beneath the surface of the earth in the darkness lies the demons who were once classed as the fallen angels, a place where Dawn once dwelled before being sent to destroy Faith. Dawn was afraid of disobeying her master and died because of her conflict of faith. Faith tried to help her but she was not strong enough to save her soul from damnation. Her sister Sonia heard of her death and wanted to avenge her killers, she was more cunning than Donna and was not willing to be saved.

Sonia was sat amongst the fallen angels amidst the vilest demons and discussing plans to destroy mankind. Most of them were ugly creatures with pale faces and some had a red pigment in their skin. They spoke in groups eating and drinking biting their food with sharp needle teeth cursing each other. Then the leader appeared he was bigger and more obnoxious red skin and horns like a bull, with a long snake like tongue and piercing menacing eyes.

"What of this angel Faith" He said in deep voice that seemed to penetrate the body of living souls.

"Tell me lest I cut out your hearts and eat them"

"Oh master she is one of Gods guardian angels" one of the demons said

"I sent a demon to destroy her" He said angrily

Sonia stepped forward nervously he turned and looked at her frowning

"Dawn was sent and she was my sister" Sonia said

"She let me down and died for it" the master said

"I would not let you down master" Sonia said confidently

"I would destroy you if you did child" the master bellowed

"I know that and I do will destroy Faith believe me" Sonia said convincingly. "I want her dead".

"Go then and destroy her and all the other angels" The master insisted

"Yes master" Sonia said echoed by the others

"And don't return until you have her head in your hands

The demons left the pit of hell with Satan their master sitting on a throne waiting for their return. Each of the demons carried weapons to attack the angels taking them by surprise. Their plan was to also cause confusion and destruction over the earth making people think it was an act of God.

Back in Hollywood Sharon had turned down a major role in a movie because Claire was sick but she regretted it when it came to the Oscars, when the leading actress won the Oscar and announced that the part was written for her. But Claire was particularly poorly and Sharon had called out the paramedics, Claire became so breathless she had gone blue. It was at this point that Faith decided to step in and help her. Once she returned from the hospital Faith called upon Sharon's house dressed in suitable attire looking like any other teenage girl. Sharon had been crying and praying for Claire to get well and live a normal life. At that point Faith knocked the door and stood waiting trying to think of ideas on what to say creating her suitable references. The best of being an angel is that you cannot only transform into any from but you can also produce documentation at will. Sharon looked in the mirror before opening the door making sure their was no indication that she was crying. She opened the door and noticed faith stood looking at her as if she actually knew what Sharon was thinking.

"Hi I am Faith" Faith said smiling "I am a childcare assistant"

"Come in and meet the family" Sharon said

"Thank you" Faith said entering the house

"I'm afraid Claire is not well at present, she is suffering from asthma" Sharon explained

"Beastly disease asthma" Faith said with empathy

Sharon invited Faith upstairs to see Claire, the room was dark and you could clearly hear Claire wheezing. She sounded bad and very uncomfortable with her breathing; she was forced to mouth breath. When Claire opened her eyes she started to blink and focus on Faith, she immediately said "I like her".

Faith felt confident that she was going to like her; she could see the other angels in the room who both acknowledged her knowing that Sharon couldn't see them. Faith showed Sharon her documents they seemed to enchant her because she read them and accepted her immediately.

The following day Faith began to help Claire with her condition she held Claire's hands and spoke softly to her.

"Claire I want you to breath gently and relax" Faith explained

"Are you an angel?" Claire asked

"Yes but don't tell anybody" Faith said, "Do you believe in God?"

"I do believe" Claire said "But God made me sick".

"That was not God he wants you to be well, you can be cured just trust in God and believe that you are going to be well".

Faith spent a week teaching Claire to relax and eventually she managed to improve. Sharon was astonished by Claire's improved condition and was unable to understand why. Within a month she was completely cured and Faith had achieved what she set out to do.

"I can't believe how well she is" Sharon said joyfully

"It was stress that caused her illness so a change of her way of thinking and she will be well" Faith explained

"But I don't understand how does a child get stressed?" Sharon asked confused by what Faith had said

"Adults don't have the monopoly on stress, children can be under pressure too and often show it in physical ways such as asthma or skin conditions" Faith said trying to be diplomatic when she really meant because Sharon was working so hard to become popular as an actress.

"I suppose because I put pressure on her due to my own life style she responds to that". Sharon said in dismay

"Sometimes we don't realise what we are doing until we see the damage we are doing" Faith replied

"You are so wise for a teenager, anybody would think you were much older" Sharon said with surprise

"Maybe I am older than you think" Faith replied

Sharon touch her hand "You're a real angel" she said smiling

Faith just smiled realising it that Sharon didn't mean literally she was just pleased that she was able to help. Faith continued to monitor Claire and they spent time together going to the local park and visiting places of interest. Sometimes Harmony would materialise and join them but Harmony had problems with her own family.

David was seven his mother Sylvia was very ill suffering from cancer, she struggled to do things around the home and was a thriving star, then she found it too difficult to perform and was forced to stay at home. David tried to help and she had people helping her in the home, but the help was costly and even though her husband was a successful actor her illness and the cost of providing regular care drained their funds. Her husband was also having an affair with an actress and blaming it on her illness and him not being able to cope. In reality he was seeing her before Sylvia was even diagnosed and used the illness as an excuse to continue the affair. David became the man of the house he was strong mentally and prayed that his mother would become strong again. Harmony was sent to them for this reason; she was to support David at this time with the other angels.

David knelt down by his bed and leaned on the mattress, putting his hands together he began to speak in a low voice.

"God please help my mommy, she is dying and I can't help her, make me strong enough to help her".

David's mother heard this prayer and started to weep silently, she didn't believe in God but could understand her why her son turned to him for help. He was determined to make sure that she was well and would share his life for many years to come. His prayers of course were heard and the angels appeared soon after his prayers reached God, Harmony and the other angels were sent to him in order to observe initially, but angels do far more than this in some cases. Throughout history many stories have been recorded where angels have helped people, guiding and even healing the sick, rescuing people who are stranded and sometimes appearing as humans in order to help them physically.

Harmony appeared to them as a nurse and helped them for a few weeks; she wanted to do as much as she could within reason. She was aware that she was unable to control their destiny but just wanted them to be happy and live a comfortable life.

Harmony approached Faith about David they were in a park transformed as humans; they walked on a pathway and admired the view.

"Sometimes I think humans are so lucky" Faith said

"Why, they have sickness and some live in poverty" Harmony replied

"But they can walk on the earth, breath the air and fall in love" Faith said jumping onto a bench and walking along it.

"Oh Faith, are you on about love again, remember what happened with John" Harmony said helping Faith off the bench

"I know I really miss him" Faith admitted

"David's mom is very ill" Harmony said rapidly changing the subject

"What dying?" Faith said

"Yes a brain tumour, it's so sad" Harmony almost had tears in her eyes

"Oh Harmony what are you going to do?" Faith asked concerned

"I really don't know" Harmony said wiping the tears from her eyes

"Bless you Harmony, we must be able to help her, we are angels".

"Asha and Martha think I should help her" Harmony said

"Well Nathan and Lydia would agree, they helped me with Claire" Faith said reassuringly. "Seek Gods advice".

"But I feel so helpless and poor David will be all alone if she dies" Harmony said sadly

"Do as I did help her get well, cure her" Faith said

"But she has cancer, tumour in her brain" Harmony replied

"Remove it honestly Harmony we have done this before, its not like it's a new thing" Faith insisted

"But I haven't done this before and have we got the right to do this?" Harmony said as they passed an old man who was sat on a bench reading a paper. On the front of the paper it read 'Try it and believe in yourself and God'

At first Harmony thought it was a coincidence but then he spoke to them

"Faith can move mountains, you must believe in yourself to achieve this task, God be with you" The man said in a strong voice

Harmony turned to Faith then looked back at the man but he had completely vanished.

"God has answered you Harmony, do his will" Faith replied.

"I will it will be accomplished" Harmony said confidently.

When Harmony got back the house was empty she ran outside and spoke to the gardener.

"Where is Sylvia?" Harmony said desperately

"She was rushed to hospital very ill, I don't think she will make it".

Without thinking Harmony transformed before his eyes, he dropped his spade and stared. Realising what she had done she simply commented.

"What's up have you never seen an angel before?"

She disappeared and flew towards the hospital she sensed Asha and Martha in the waiting area with David.

"Where have you been?" He asked "My mom is dying"

"No David your mother is sleeping" Harmony said confidently

"She is dying and you can't help her" David said angrily

"Have faith and believe in God and his will" Harmony said

"What shall I do?" David asked

"Just pray and I will do the rest" Harmony said leaving the room

Martha materialised and sat with him while Asha joined Harmony. They walked towards a private room and found Sylvia lying in bed looking very pale and weak. Her vital signs were showing that her health had deteriorated and she was close to death. Harmony had to act fast if she was to save her, she appeared in a white doctors coat and began to examine her. Nurses were astonished with what happened next as they saw her on the cameras. Harmony began to touch her head and the whole room glowed suddenly a group of people dressed in white robes joined her and she began to recover. One of the nurses pressed the alarm and contacted security, but as they entered the room the angels vanished. Sylvia sat up in bed and smiled watching the angels vanish in all directions of the room, vanished without a trace.

During the time that Faith and Harmony were assigned to looking after Claire and David Sonia had been causing disasters across the west coast of America. All kinds of accidents occurred including plane crashes and fires in forest areas just south of Hollywood. Sonia was attempting to lure Faith into a trap in order to destroy her, by hurting humans she felt Faith would respond and help them. Each time she caused a disaster she made it worse hoping that it would be seen, but

Faith was preoccupied with her own problems and didn't even see the news until things calmed down.

Faith was still at Sharon's house when a fire occurred in the Hollywood hills the whole area was evacuated including Sharon and Sylvia's house the angels were alerted about Sonia and her demons. Faith, Harmony and other angels created a rainstorm to counteract the fire. Then Sonia attacked a plane targeting one of the engines, the pilot found it hard to control and it began to fall from the sky. Faith and Harmony flew towards it and levelled it off until the pilot was able to land it safely. Sonia then headed for the golden gate bridge in San Francisco, Faith and Harmony followed her and noticed her trying to force the vehicles off the bridge they managed to divert her and force her away from the area.

Sonia turned to face them with her demons; she had hatred in her eyes

"Faith I am here to get you for killing my sister Donna"

"She was your sister? I was trying to save her, I didn't kill her she killed herself" Faith shouted back

"Yes I have come for you" Sonia shouted back

"She tried to kill my friends, she killed herself" Faith shouted

"Your bound to say that I don't believe you" Sonia shouted in anger

"It's true she destroyed herself" Harmony shouted "So go back to Satan and stop causing trouble".

"You think that we are afraid of you and your God, how much power has he got and who on earth will follow him?" Sonia shouted almost spitting at them.

"Our God is loved by the world all his followers are loyal to him" Faith shouted

"Man loves himself not god, they are selfish and don't deserve to live" Sonia shouted being encouraged by others

"People of earth will be loyal to him even if you harm them or destroy their homes" Harmony shouted

"Let us see, we plan to spread disease and calamity everywhere" one of the demons shouted "See if your God saves them then and see if they remain loyal to God".

With those words they disappeared, Faith and Harmony remained to make sure the people on the bridge were safe. Police and ambulances were present; the emergency crew were running about checking for damages or injured people. Most of them were confused and dazed no one knew exactly what had happened or why.

When they got back the fire was out and people had returned to their own homes. Faith went back to Claire and Harmony returned to David, both families were well. Sharon was arranging the room ready for Christmas, Claire was starting to decorate the tree. Sylvia was so happy after being told that the tumour had disappeared without a trace.

"Moms cancer has gone" David announced, " God heard my prayers"

"Good then my work is done" Harmony said

Sylvia looked at her closely gazing into her eyes and looking at her fine hair and soft complexion. "Who are you?"

"Who am I?" Harmony said hoping she would not reply

"I was told that you were in the room when I was so ill and you cured me" Sylvia held her right arm up and pointed at Harmony

"I want to know who you are and why you helped me" Sylvia continued

"Mom!" David interrupted "She is an angel and she saved your life because I asked God for help"

"An angel that's not possible you can't be an angel" Sylvia seemed troubled

"Who do you think I am?" Harmony asked

"I don't know" Sylvia replied

At that moment Faith appeared beside Harmony "Mom she's the one that helped Claire" David said, "They are angels"

"Do you believe in angels Sylvia?" Faith asked

"I don't know I am confused how did you suddenly appear in my house next to Harmony?" Sylvia asked

At that moment they both transformed into angels Sylvia dropped to her knees and David ran to her "Mother!"

She then bowed her head "Forgive me I am stupid not to believe in you".

"Rise you don't need to bow to us, we are angels and serve God we are not Gods, no one worships us" Faith said

"No we do Gods will and help people, we are guardian angels". Harmony said helping Sylvia up

"Wow are those wings real?" David said pointing at Faith and Harmony's wings

"Yes and we can fly, but we are usually unseen by Humans". Harmony said amused

"But please don't tell anyone" Faith said

"It is important no one is supposed to know about us" Harmony said putting a finger to her lips.

The months went by and the guardian angels continued to help people around Hollywood and the rest of California. Did their efforts continue but so did the demons that were causing problems everywhere. News reports worldwide showed that disasters had increased and that people had become apathetic and disinterested in God. People had become so engrossed in enjoying life and making money that fewer people attended church or showed interest in religious activities.

Sonia and the other demons met back in the depths of hell and planned their next attack on mankind. Satan their lord and master sat listening to them.

"We have successfully caused problems on earth and steered people away from god, we now plan our biggest attack on mankind". Sonia boasted.

"You have done well child but I want more and I want to see man turn his back on god, then I will be happy".

"Master I can lead these fallen angels into battle and get results" one of the demons said dismissing Sonia's remarks

"Gubwink you are hardly one to lead the fallen angels with your scattered thinking you couldn't lead yourself out of this cave".

"How dare you insolent girl, have you destroyed Faith?" Gubwink said sneering "No you haven't because you're weak and feeble and all mouth".

"How dare you, you're a sleazy worm, a pigs swill and you have the breath of a dog". Sonia said but Satan interrupted her.

"Silence rabble!" He shouted "I want results not arguments you will go back to the surface and finish what you started, now all of you get out of my sight".

The demons vacated the bowels of hell and went to continue what they started to ruin the earth with corruption and disaster. Sonia was determined to find Faith again and this time she plans to destroy her.

THE FINAL BATTLE

Sonia and the other demons assembled from the east preparing for the spiritual battle, this was the final battle of good verses evil. So many fallen angels determined to ruin the earth and destroy the guardian angels that protect mankind. They bring with them disease and destruction in every land but who will survive their wrath, will man be loyal to God and his angels.

Sonia instructed a few angels to create a storm over Hollywood, sending gales and heavy rain across the hills and into valleys. Floods occurred and people were bewildered by this freak weather as they evacuated their homes. People began to panic as lightning struck a few helpless souls as they tried to shelter from the rain. A news reporter was struck when he was being filmed outside the Chinese theatre reporting on how Hollywood had increased its trade with a wide influx of tourists. It was a live recording seen by thousands of viewers shocked by the event, Sonia herself had actually caused his death, but she was invisible and undetectable. Faith had seen the incident on television and suddenly left the house and flew to Hollywood boulevard, she noticed Sonia as she was about to throw a bolt of lightning at another victim.

"Stop!" Faith commanded

"Oh its my sisters killer well what do you think of this?" Sonia asked

"Your Dawn's sister?" Faith asked

"Yes I told you before and you murdered her" Sonia said in temper

"I was defending friends and she attacked us" Faith replied

"Well now you are going to die" Sonia said throwing a bolt of lightening at her

Faith was quick to respond and jumped out of the way and the lightning hit a near by car which immediately caught fire, fortunately no one was in it. At that moment other demons had flown down and captured her.

"I knew you would do that Faith, your so predictable" Sonia said laughing "Take her to the cross on the Hollywood hills and crucify her"

The demons bound her and flew her to the hills; they found a white cross near the road and tied to it with wire. Then used barbed wire for a crown upon her head, she was helpless as they began scorning her and blaspheming.

"Let your god save you now, suffer like Christ suffered with no mercy" One of them said.

Faith hung bleeding from the head and where she was bound, helpless and alone she cried out "God save me hear my prayer oh Lord God"

In the sky thousands of demons flew in formation towards Hollywood some broke off and headed for Beverly Hills. They left death and destruction in their pathway as bodies and vehicles where spread everywhere. Reporters and cameras appeared trying to understand what had caused this mess, as the demons remained invisible to them.

It was at this time that Gabriel the angel and messenger from God appeared in front of the live cameras and announced his presence

"Behold I bring you a message from God you must have faith in him and believe that he will save you. You will be given instructions when the world goes into darkness you must light a lantern each and place it across the hills, valley's and on ships to demonstrate your love for God and show everyone you believe in the true God each country is doing this as an act of faith I will return to instruct you further" Gabriel disappeared

People looked at each other in disbelief, was the image real or not and what were these lanterns he spoke of. People gossiped all around uncertain of the message and thinking it was a Hollywood gimmick or prank. But then more devastation occurred as buildings were damaged including the Chinese theatre. People ran in each direction panicking and dodging fallen masonry some fell wounded on the ground and others trampled over them. Stampedes of people frightened and confused being filmed by the media; television news channels had recorded the message from Gabriel and continually broadcasted it.

One newsreader sat at his desk reading the news and speaking to his audience live as things were happening.

"Was it real or a hoax this angel appeared in front of a camera and claimed he was Gabriel a messenger from God" The newsreader paused to clear his throat "He said the world would be in darkness and gave instructions for us to light lanterns all over the earth as a act of faith".

The reporter sounded sceptical in his tone and seemed dismissive of the idea that demons or fallen angels could be responsible for the devastation around Hollywood. He was also amused that religious people were going round Hollywood with boards saying the 'end is near' and 'repent you sinners' the boards were old as if they had been used for years. This message had been conveyed on boards for years and people took no notice why should they do so now. The message depicting the end of the world began in the bible as prophecies but only a percentage of religious people or Christians followed it to convey it from door to door and not many people believed them. Such people were called god bods or religious nutters, those who spend all their time and effort to convert people to their religion. However now things seemed different and elements of their message were ringing true, so the question was is the world coming to an end?.

It wasn't until the fallen angels or demons actually appeared all over the world that people began to realise it was true. Dark angels with evil expressions appeared across the globe threatening mankind to follow them or die. Gradually the earth became darker as the demons formed a canopy like a mesh around the earth dark and gloomy. People were heading in churches, mosques and other places of worship in order to pray to their God.

The demons continued to create floods and other methods of destruction around the earth, in order to threaten mankind and make them worship demons as apposed to God. War had finally broken out on earth as the final battle for the survival of mankind had begun. It was now up to man to decide to follow their God or trust in the demons, people actually conversed from all denominations putting aside their differences of religious ideas and doctoring, finding common denominators and agreeing to follow the instructions of Gods messenger angels. This resulted in unity within the faiths to achieve their goal of demonstrating their faith and destroying the evil demons that had caused so much trouble.

As the darkness increased Harmony had collected a army of angels and rescued Faith from the cross, They tussled and battled the demons that were guarding Faith and successfully freed her from bondage. Faith was helped by Harmony to heal her wounds and gather up strength to fight off the demons.

The angel messengers returned to the earth in order to instructs mankind on how to serve God and survive destruction. The angels brought the lanterns and asked them to light each lantern and praying saying this light is for the only true God, then taking each one and forming a trail across the earth for the angels to follow. Once this is done they must seek shelter and wait until they hear a trumpet call before returning outside. This was the only guarantee for their safety by obeying God and doing his will.

People began to walk the earth and carry their lanterns, voices echoed in prayer as they obeyed the command of God and then with lighted lanterns they formed a long line for miles this was seen in the heavens as one line around the world. The angels formed an army and headed towards the light, everyone who obeyed God were sheltered and the battle commenced as the angels fought good against evil.

Sonia pursued faith as she followed the light watching over the people. Sonia kept throwing bolts of lightning at Faith, but none of it reached Faith the sky was full of demons and Gods angels were all close to the bright light. Suddenly the demons attacked and the battle for the earth took place, bolts of lightning struck all over the place and bodies dropped to the ground. Faith was continually under attack but fought back valiantly, Sonia was determined to kill her and continued to attack hoping to catch her off guard. Faith stumbled as she was still weak Sonia seized her chance and threw a bolt of lightning in her direction it shot through the air but was deflected by Harmony who flew in its pathway to save Faith, she fell to the ground in a heap. Faith saw it and threw a bolt back at Sonia this was followed by an attack from other angels and she exploded.

Faith shouted as she saw Harmony fall "No!"

Faith then flew towards Harmony with tears in her eyes "Harmony I love you my friend, my true friend don't die"

Faith held her hand and touched her face, I cant live without you you're my rock my foundation, don't leave me please".

Harmony began to fade her body was weak and her energy was draining away.

Faith looked up to the heavens her face was wet from crying, she lifted up her arms towards the sky. "Take me my Lord, God in the heavens I will sacrifice my life but spare my friend. Merciful God who loved the world so much you saved mankind so many times save my friend please I beg you".

Faith then bowed her head and suddenly the world was in silence all the fighting was over and the angels began to cleanse the earth. The bodies vanished and Faith was still lying over Harmony frightened to move away from her.

"Faith" came a voice "I hate to tell you, but your squashing me"

Faith slowly got up and noticed Harmony with her eyes wide open looking up at her.

"Harmony!" Faith shouted with delight "Harmony"

"That's my name don't wear it out" Harmony said smiling

Faith hugged her and kissed her on the cheek "Thank God your alive"

"Well yes I must say I am pleased too" Harmony said looking at her burnt clothing

"I prayed for you, I was scared" Faith said clinging to her

"Well if you keep crushing me I will stop breathing". Harmony said jokingly "Besides I did the same when you were crucified".

Peace was restored and mankind came out of their shelters and saw a new earth and God wiped away the tears from their eyes and death was no more the former things had passed away. Man was at peace and God had brought to ruin those ruining the world and the trumpets had sounded the bring the people out and they praised God saying glory to him on high for he has saved the world, peace and good will to mankind and Christmas was upon them once more.

Faith returned to the heavens with Harmony prepared for new instructions for the earth and the human race, a new world was present, and God bless all.

CHRISTMAS WITH FAITH

I f ever an angel was chosen to go on the Christmas tree it was Faith, as a guardian angel Faith shone like a beacon and glowed with her silk like flesh and shining hair. This Christmas was special for the family she was staying with they may be wealthy but they knew the value of Christmas and considered the poor in fact Claire went to the poorer areas of Los Angeles. They fed the poor and shared the Christmas message, Faith remembered the birth of Jesus and was present when the shepherds call at the manger. She was unseen by them but was delighted to be there and witness all the activities.

Faith and Harmony made the most of Christmas not only on earth but also in the spiritual world going from one place to another observing the warmth of mankind as they enjoy the food and entertainment of Christmas. Harmony returned to Sylvia's and spent Christmas with David she was their special angel.

Christmas morning was the best part of the day as Faith helped Claire to open her presents and then sang a few Christmas songs around the tree. Faith and Harmony flew over Hollywood and were amazed by the sight of coloured lights and decorated homes all was well in the world and the angels next plan was to visit the third world and help them.

S R S BOOKS

CRACKED PORCELAIN
OPERATION BRAINSTORM
FOR THE LOVE OF CHARLOTTE
NOTHING IS REAL
BLOOD TRAIL
EIGHT SKULLS OF TEVERSHAM
CONFLICT OF FAITH
UNDERSTANDING JODIE

CPSIA information can be obtained
at www.ICGtesting.com
Printed in the USA
BVHW031027210220
572990BV00001B/16

9 781951 727383